ENDOR~

In *Whispers in the Branches,* debut author Brandy Heineman pens a fast-paced, entertaining and ultimately touching story mixed with ghosts and genealogy and sprinkled with God. Her delicious prose sizzles and soars as she introduces grieving Abby Wells who uproots her life in Ohio to search for family secrets in Georgia. Abby encounters a haunted house, a feisty great aunt and a young, handsome caretaker in her new surroundings as she grapples with grief, the truth of her family's past and the unseen presence of something deep and spiritual.

*Elizabeth Musser, author of *The Swan House, The Sweetest Thing, The Secrets of the Cross* trilogy

As a lover of research and genealogy, this novel was a soul-treat. Abby Wells hears the siren call of buried family secrets. Add to that a ghost and a love triangle, and *Whispers in the Branches* is one suspenseful read. I was hooked and couldn't put it down. Heineman is a talented storyteller.

*Nicole Seitz, author of *Saving Cicadas* and *The Spirit of Sweetgrass* (www.nicoleseitz.com)

When Abby Wells returns to her family roots in Georgia, she has no idea that her passion for genealogy hunting will entangle her in past and present family ghosts. Fans of Southern mysteries and ghost stories will love this hauntingly redemptive tale of old and new loves, and what really matters at the edge of eternity. A beautiful, thought-provoking read.

*Yangsze Choo, author of *The Ghost Bride*

Whispers in the Branches is a lovely debut for Southern novelist Brandy Heineman, whose interesting characters and well-crafted prose create a story with heart and depth. As the tenacious young heroine explores the mysteries haunting her family tree, the past and the present come together with surprising answers and with lasting treasures.

*Meg Moseley, author of *A Stillness of Chimes*

WHISPERS IN THE BRANCHES

Brandy Heineman

Elk Lake Publishing
Whispers in the Branches
Copyright © 2015 by Brandy Heineman
Family Tree Artwork by Jenny Greenwood

Requests for information should be addressed to:
Elk Lake Publishing,
Atlanta, GA 30024
ISBN: 978-1-942513-12-4

Whispers in the Branches is a work of fiction. Real incidents, establishments, places, names, or people appearing herein are used fictitiously. All other situations, locales, and characters are products of the author's imagination, and any resemblance to actual events, places, or persons, living or dead, is entirely coincidental.

Cover and graphics design: Brandy Heineman and Anna O'Brien
Editing: Kathi Macias
Published in association with Jim Hart, agent, Hartline Literary Agency

To Jesus,
first fruits.

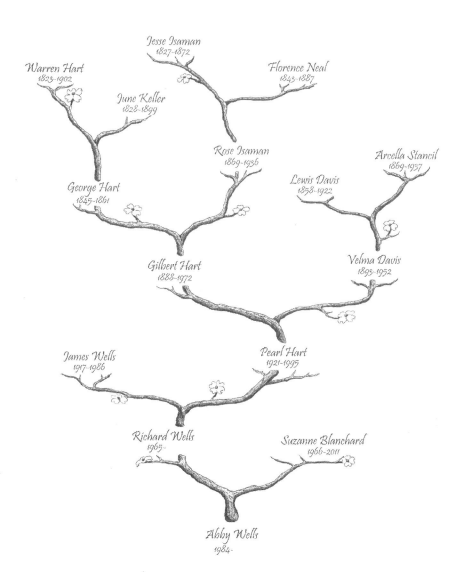

Jesse Isaman
1827-1872

Warren Hart
1823-1902

Florence Neal
1843-1887

June Keller
1828-1899

Rose Isaman
1869-1936

Arcella Stancil
1869-1937

Lewis Davis
1858-1922

George Hart
1845-1861

Gilbert Hart
1888-1972

Velma Davis
1893-1952

James Wells
1917-1986

Pearl Hart
1921-1995

Richard Wells
1965-

Suzanne Blanchard
1966-2011

Abby Wells
1984-

Surely every man walks about as a phantom;
Surely they make an uproar for nothing;
He amasses riches and does not know who will gather them.
-Psalm 39:6

To them I will give in My house and within My walls a memorial,
And a name better than that of sons and daughters; I will give them an
everlasting name which will not be cut off.
-Isaiah 56:5

"Behold, I stand at the door and knock; if anyone hears My voice
and opens the door, I will come in to him and will dine with him, and
he with Me."
-Revelation 3:20

CHAPTER 1

KENNESAW, GEORGIA
Wednesday, January 18, 2012

Keep your friends close and your beneficiaries closer. Ruby Watts clucked at herself. Poor words to live by. Even worse to die by.

That's why the letter showed up right when she needed it. Providential, maybe. A little excitement did the job of an egg-white facial—it didn't halt time, but for a short while, at least reversed its effects.

She glared at her nephew, Blake. His wide-mouthed snore shook the walls worse than the constant freight trains running through town. A graying five o'clock shadow gave his jaw and upper lip the appearance of a fine coating of dust. And he called himself a rock star. He probably awarded himself good-citizen points for enduring these boring afternoons. She didn't need a babysitter, no matter what that hotshot neurologist said. Humph.

No respect, these younger generations. All answers and attitude. Acting like they invented youth themselves, whispering "old and funny" and "she ain't right" like she couldn't hear. Like they wouldn't have their time. A few of them could take lessons in youth, if she was of a mind to offer.

She turned the volume on the TV as loud as it would go. Let them young'uns believe what they wanted. The same folks who shouted when they spoke to her usually added extra details if she pretended not to hear.

Dramatic music blared, and Ruby squinted at the screen without reaching for her glasses. These days a terrible lot didn't need seein'. She rested her eyes and found the backs of her eyelids lifeless as ever. That doctor practically had her on house arrest. How long since she had so much as a coffee date?

Not that her friends were much better off. They buzzed along without purpose, 'til Death picked 'em off like flies in a bug lamp. They flew right on in, and who could blame them? She nearly did it herself. "I'm ready when the Good Lord brings me home," she used to crow at church luncheons. He sure called her bluff, amen and amen.

But no, she escaped the bug zapper. Too bad for Blake. He would've had himself a nice payday. She'd put off fixing her will long enough. Might as well accept it.

That was another thing about old age. Outlivin' everybody. Buryin' the ones who ought to have buried her.

She pulled out the letter from the pages of the worn black Bible on the TV tray beside her armchair, though by now she had it near about memorized.

Dear Mrs. Watts,

We've never met, but I'm sure you know my father, Richard Wells . . . .

"Oh, we met." The paper fluttered in her hand. "You don't remember, but I do."

The girl—woman, as she had to be close to thirty—asked easy questions that Ruby could answer in the space of a two-page letter, but the request charmed her. Ruby wanted to like her. The letter contained room to hope that its writer wouldn't call a person "funny" on account of bein' old.

Must be she took after her mother.

"Are you deaf or what?" The TV volume done its work and roused Blake from his nap. That man's grievin' looked a whole lot like everybody else's lazy.

"Oh, you're awake. Be a dear and run to the store for me. There's a list on the counter." The sight of that lump of a man digging around in her pocketbook never failed to appall, but twenty dollars was the going rate for a gallon of milk and a half-hour's peace. "You best bring me my change this time."

He rubbed the corners of his eyes. "I brung it to you last time. You always forget."

The ledger hidden behind a box of antique china on the top shelf of her closet said different. It only had four blank pages left. At this rate she'd live long enough to need a new one, though it'd be in a safety deposit box if she had a prayer of ever collecting.

Besides that, there wasn't a blessed thing wrong with her memory.

Once the screen door slammed behind him, Ruby muted the TV. Good riddance. She could ignore a ruckus by retreating into her own mind, but she needed quiet to write.

She ambled into the kitchen. The drawer of the island stowed a tablet and a collection of pens. She dug three different spirals into the paper before she found one with ink in it. Purple. Good enough. She shuffled back to her armchair and tapped her pen to the page.

A ghost of an idea had come to her.

AKRON, OHIO
Friday, February 10

The fluorescent lights of Greg Grunewald's office shone harsher at six in the morning than at eight. He was positive.

Sure. Blame the lights.

He checked the clock. Six-twenty, to be exact. Even his early birds wouldn't be in for another forty minutes. The rows of empty cubicles between his office and the break room would fill up in the next two hours. All but one.

He poured a mug of yesterday's coffee from the carafe and gulped half of it down like a shot. Bitter and cold. Still tasted better than the whiskey residue in his mouth. He swirled the remainder and headed back to the privacy of his office.

The first time, he thought Chuck would see him on the security footage, but if his boss noticed, he didn't care. Greg's department pulled down good numbers, and hitting targets bought him latitude. He could get away with certain infractions. The thought bothered him.

Another night at his desk. His back ached, and the cottony dregs of the bender lingered in his head. He didn't have time to drive home, shower, and be back to the office by eight.

He couldn't keep doing this.

He drained the mug and set it down hard on the desk, bumping his mouse and waking the screen in the process. Abby's half-finished reference letter waited in draft mode. The screen brightness he used for daylight work also seemed abrasive by early morning standards.

His stomach lurched. It wasn't the lights or the whiskey. This was her fault. Her fault he had to stay late working on the letter. Her fault the words needed greasing before they hit the page. He read what he'd written before passing out on the desk.

To Whom It May Concern:

I understand that Abby Wells has applied for a position within your firm. I hired Abby almost ten months ago and am greatly saddened to see her go. I have been consistently pleased with her performance.

That was where he broke out the flask.

She is persistent and determined, a hard worker who meets her tasks with enthusiasm and diligence. She even took her work home on occasion. When she comes to work for you, tell her not to do that so she can't say you didn't warn her.

I mean she is a genuine pleasure, in and out of the office.

And now that she's gone, I'm amazed at how much I relied on her. Like I cut off my own arm. I don't know how I'll replace her. Probably won't. My loss, your gain.

What a train wreck. His finger hovered over the backspace key, but he kept reading.

But it's over. If I could change it, I would. I can't. She doesn't care. I used to like this job. She ruined it. She ruins everything she touches. I'm sorry I ever

He closed the file without saving. Whatever he'd been sorry for, he must've sweated out while he slept.

Speaking of sweat. The onsite gym had a locker room where he could shower, but he already took the dress shirt from the suit he kept hanging on the back of his office door. When he wore the spare, it was almost a relief to make the decision not to replace it. He wouldn't need another. Now he did, and for what? One more day as a spoke on the corporate wheel.

Tonight, then. No more contemplating. He'd mail his note to Sarah and fix the problem.

Except he promised Abby a referral letter. The very last thing she needed from him. Until he got it right, his other plan had to wait.

Best get down to business, then.

He punched out at five.

"Taking a half-day, Grunewald?" Chuck slapped him on the back. "I don't remember when I've seen you leave before me."

"Ah. It's Friday. Thought I'd check out early." Greg swallowed hard. Words that would be repeated and analyzed for double meaning on Monday. "I billed the State today for the Vital Records project. That one is all buttoned up."

"Fair enough, man. Enjoy your weekend." The smile waned. "I mean that. I don't need my top guy burning out. Especially in the middle of first quarter."

Their busiest season. Greg nodded. "Yes, sir."

"You've got a personnel budget. Use it."

"I will."

Satisfied, Chuck turned away. "See you Monday."

Greg echoed the hollow sentiment. It would've been good to shake Chuck's hand. Respectful. Memorable.

He dropped the envelope addressed to Abby into a shared outgoing mail bin. She would hear the news before she received the reference letter. Not that it made a difference either way.

He took the elevator to the basement-level parking deck, got in his Accord, opened up the radio. A girl from accounting gave him a strange look. He ignored her and peeled out of the garage. An outburst, not a strategy. Crashing was unreliable, and he didn't want to hurt his car. Irrational but true.

Traffic proved too heavy for any more automotive theatrics. He weaved for a while, but quit about halfway home. He wasn't in a hurry.

As always, the worst part of his commute was the trickle of cars into his apartment complex. He parked. Walked to his mailbox. Dropped the note in the slot like any normal letter. He didn't overthink it. Went up to his apartment. Paid his bills online. Cleaned out the fridge, took out the trash. The usual stuff.

The flask wasn't empty, but he needed to be sober. It would be easier for Sarah that way.

He retrieved the gun from his nightstand. Where he did it wouldn't matter to anyone besides him, but the bedroom had too many connotations. Another irrational decision. That made two.

Never mind. The kitchen was best. No carpet.

He sat at the table. He expected nerves chewing at his gut, but the hollow inside told him to get on with it. He lifted the gun. Put it in his mouth.

The door buzzer rang, chased by a jaunty "shave and a haircut" knock. Sarah. She was waiting outside his apartment. Why? Didn't matter. She was there.

Now the adrenaline flooded. He laid the gun on the table and answered the door.

CHAPTER 2

KENNESAW

Abby dropped her bags on the guest bed in her great aunt's house and stared at them. "What am I doing here? This was a first-class colossal mistake."

Too late to change it now. The adventure of setting out from her apartment in Cuyahoga Falls wore off somewhere in Tennessee. The road and the hours drew long lines ahead to unfamiliar places and people, and her curiosity if not her engine sputtered on the way. The ten-hour drive marked the longest stretch of time she'd spent awake and alone in months. She dreaded the return trip already.

"Freshen up and get some rest," Aunt Ruby had urged her. "We'll have plenty of time to chat tomorrow." Good advice, if only it were ordinary fatigue plaguing her. Sleep wouldn't quell the exhaustion. Soap and water couldn't rinse it away.

Her stomach growled. Nerves had blunted her hunger for a short while. When Aunt Ruby tried to offer a plate of fried chicken, like a dummy, she refused it.

Underneath the cinnamon-scented air freshener, the room retained a closed-up smell. The carpet bore evidence of a hasty vacuuming, but little else suggested much preparation for her visit. Someone, probably a man, had tucked the comforter under the mattress with the sheets. Abby tugged the blanket loose.

The boxy headboard housed a built-in shelf lined with books. Abby ran a finger along the row of slim paperbacks. *Of Mice and Men. The Legend of Sleepy Hollow. Alice's Adventures in Wonderland.* Odd. Except for a poetry anthology and a King James Bible, a strong reader could take in any of the titles in a single sitting.

And why not? Solving the puzzle, she scanned the shelf again with appreciation. No one wanted houseguests around long enough to read *War and Peace.*

Never mind. So eager to start the hunt that all she saw were clues. She couldn't afford diversions, not over a weekend visit. She unzipped her bag. Unpack first, then sleep. The rabbit hole could wait until morning.

A highboy dresser and a vanity partly blocked the narrow closet in the corner. She peeked inside and found it stacked full of Christmas boxes. No space, no hangers.

The top drawer of the highboy brimmed with a draftman's work supplies—old calculators, a slide rule and drafting paper, and nubby pencils with a weird red sheen rotted into their rubber erasers. A heart-shaped china trinket pot, nestled in the bottom of the drawer, caught her eye. She lifted the lid, saw ten or twelve bobby pins inside, replaced it. Its delicate flower pattern and crackle glaze stood out among the workman's oddments.

Every drawer contained assorted hodgepodge. Black plastic film containers with gray lids and commemorative plates and orphaned telephone cords and empty picture frames. Light bulbs. Batteries. Decals. No different from the drawers she'd cleaned out at Mom's house, until—

A gun. In the bottom drawer lay a long, narrow-nosed handgun, nicked and oily, with a dull patina of years worn into the wooden handgrip. *Never found one of those at Mom's.* She lifted it out. It had the heft of iron and wood. Her pulse quickened. Was it real? An actual, working, firing weapon?

She put the gun back and eased the drawer closed as if defusing a bomb. It was real enough. She turned toward the vanity. Her clothes wouldn't fit into the smaller drawers, but if she found a space large enough for her button-down shirt and Dockers, she'd take it. Instead of clutter, the drawer was empty except for another slender book, this one with block type labeling a flimsy cardstock binding.

"'Bell Aircraft Employee Handbook, Marietta, Georgia,'" she read. "Huh."

Abby picked it up and thumbed the pages, breathing the decaying tang of years. The manual's crisp edges suggested it hadn't gotten much use, but someone cracked it at least once to stash a yellowed business-sized envelope in its pages. She read the addressee's name, touched it with the pads of her fingertips.

W. C. SOSEBEE

27 ROCKY STREET

KENNESAW, GEORGIA

Her eyes flicked to the pre-printed return address. The Selective Service System.

She sat down on the bed and laid the employee handbook aside. The envelope had been rudely torn. Shaky hands, clumsy with impatience or fear? Maybe. She only needed to slide her thumb between the flaps to reveal the folded message still inside. It yielded to her fingertips and she balanced it loosely, half-afraid the oils from her skin would leave evidence of her snooping.

"'Order to report for induction,'" she breathed. The letter instructed W. C. Sosebee to report for duty at 7:30 in the morning on December 31, 1942. "We might finally have a hero in the family, Mom," she whispered, then frowned. "Or at least, I might." This, if it was anything, was on her father's side.

The quiet groaning of floorboards whispered admonitions. She replaced the book and tossed clothes over it, slipping the draft orders into the side pocket of her bag as the knock and muffled rasp came at the door. "Are you asleep, dear?"

"No. Come in." The door swung wide, and Aunt Ruby stood with her hands on her hips in a leopard-print robe trimmed with pink faux-fur, her hair tucked under a baby blue nightcap.

"Gracious, child. Ain't you tired after that long drive?"

"I'm not disturbing you, am I? I wanted to get unpacked before bed." Blood heated her cheeks, but if Aunt Ruby noticed, she let it go.

"Oh, you can't bother me. I'm up and down all night. You'll see when you get old. I heard you moving around, and I wanted to see if you're sure you ain't hungry."

Abby's stomach growled at the suggestion. "I don't want to be rude."

Aunt Ruby chuckled. "When a Southern woman offers you a home-cooked meal, you're only rude if you refuse. That goes for seconds and thirds too, by the way. Besides, no one can resist my fried chicken. Let's warm you up a plate and see what I can recollect about Richard."

Abby fought an impulse to take a step backwards. "That's okay. My mother gave me his vitals. I'm more interested in my grandparents and the generations before them. She didn't know any of them, of course."

Aunt Ruby eyeballed her. "Of course. Like as not to dwell on sour subjects. Oh, for heaven's sake, where'd that come from? I don't mean to talk ill of him right to your face. I haven't spoken to him in years myself."

She played with her watch. Her father was a sour subject? "I'll take you up on that chicken."

They made their way to the kitchen, and Aunt Ruby grubbed through the contents of her refrigerator. "That Blake ate up the whole bird. I'll tell you, Abby, your uncle is fifty-four-going-on-fifteen. Oh well, let's see what else I got."

"Is he close with my father?" The words were no more than out before Abby longed to reel them back, but Aunt Ruby hummed some faintly familiar show tune as she shuffled bowls from shelf to shelf. Oblivious? No. If she heard wooden drawers tracing their smooth, worn grooves from the next room, she couldn't have missed the question.

A pass. Abby took it and kept silent.

"Looks like he left us some crowder peas and cornbread. At least we can eat that without a mess." Behind her glasses, her eyes glittered. "We'll keep our fingers clean for poking through the pictures Will brought down from the attic."

Yes, clean hands. She could do better than greasy fingerprints for leaving her mark in history, couldn't she? Of course. The security logs back at the office, for instance. Old humiliation pegged her even as she smiled at her aunt. "Sounds great."

"You sit down." Her aunt pointed to the dining room off the kitchen. "I'll fix our plates."

Fancy portraits in cardboard sleeves littered Aunt Ruby's round glass table. Abby picked a browned cabinet card off the top. It featured a woman with delicate, pinched features. One corner threatened to tear away, and the image bore gouges and blemishes. She checked the back for a name and found it blank.

"Arcella Stancil Davis." Aunt Ruby set the steaming bowls on the table. "My mother's mother. My uncle toted that picture off to war with him. That's how it got dinged up, Mama said."

"What a great detail. I'll make sure to record that."

Aunt Ruby narrowed her eyes. "For after I croak?"

Abby set the photo down. "So her name and the fact that she was loved will never be lost to time."

Apparently satisfied, Aunt Ruby took her place at the table and chunked up cornbread with her spoon. "I met you once before. When you were a baby."

"Huh." Abby gave the peas an idle stir. "I can't believe Mom could afford to travel back then."

"Neither could I."

"We struggled until I was eleven or twelve. Mom always warned me, never go into debt."

"Is that right?" Aunt Ruby leaned forward, but Abby didn't feel like elaborating.

"You don't have any pictures from that visit, by chance, do you?"

"No. We didn't take any, I'm sad to say. How is your mother these days?"

Abby dropped her eyes to one of the old-timey portraits. "She passed away in November. Stomach cancer."

"Oh, dear. I'm sorry to hear that. Bless your heart."

"It's okay." Her fingers gripped the end of the spoon, but her leaden arm wouldn't lift it to her mouth, so instead she repeated the lie. "I'm fine."

"I liked her a whole bunch, your mother. And she'll always be alive in your memories." Exhausting platitudes, though maybe Aunt Ruby understood, because she didn't push any further. "Eat up that cornbread, dear, and tell me, what is it you'd like to know?"

When her eyes burned and her sides ached, Abby retired for the night. Was it too soon for laughter? Would Mom understand? Assuming she found some acreage in the sky to call her own, would she even care? More questions, unanswered and unanswerable.

She shuffled through duplicate photos Aunt Ruby let her keep, mollifying her residual guilt over the draft letter. No one would miss it.

W. C. Sosebee would probably turn out to be her late uncle's third cousin's brother-in-law, no one to Abby. She tucked the pictures in the stolen envelope, buried it at the bottom of her weekender, and climbed into bed without changing her clothes. Anticipation for morning glimmered at the edge of her consciousness. It'd been a while since she'd felt that way.

The pleasant ether of half-sleep took over until a sharp click startled her awake. Her eyes widened against the darkness; her ears pressed into the deep silence of night. The house settling, maybe? Or the wind knocking a branch against the window? The memory of the noise faded until she doubted she heard it at all. The room's resident shadows watched, stoic and unmoved.

Resisting the urge to check that the gun still lay among the jumble of clutter in the highboy, Abby forced her eyes shut. How did a firearm, with all its latent danger cold and dormant, end up in a forgotten corner of the house?

CHAPTER 3

Saturday, February 11

The girl didn't finish her cheese grits. Maybe they weren't kin after all.

Ruby scraped the half-eaten blob into the trash and rinsed their breakfast dishes. Her attempts to rekindle last night's conversation fizzled out at first. Abby was a quiet sort, like her mother. What else did she learn to be, growing up Suzanne's child? Impulsive? Stupid in love?

Hard to tell. She didn't have a job, nor a boyfriend—bit of a barb in her voice on that subject, Ruby noticed—and didn't volunteer much beyond her appreciation for the coffee. If she asked about Richard again, she'd get an earful. She didn't ask. The cache from the attic lit up her face like Christmas though.

Ruby dried her hands. Her *face*. Mercy.

She worked a crossword while Abby camped cross-legged on the living room floor, hunched over the thick pages of the heirloom Bible's family record section. Flouncy illustrated tree branches recorded generations of births, marriages, and deaths, reaching toward the gated heavens without quite touching. Now and then Ruby looked up to see Abby copying dates and names onto a blank chart. They went a good long while hardly speaking at all.

She might've dozed off for a bit when Abby clicked her pen. "It's funny. I'm so used to leaving half my tree blank that this actually looks weird to me." She paused and studied the page. "Amazing, but weird."

Ruby climbed out of her chair. "Let's see." Abby passed her handiwork off. Sure enough, all sixteen of Abby's great-great grandparents filled the eight-and-a-half-by-eleven sheet of paper, each with birth and death dates neatly transcribed. In five generations of direct-line ancestors, only one stubborn blank interfered with the chart's satisfying symmetry—the one for Richard Wells' eventual death. She nodded and held the sheet out.

"Then you're done with that?" Ruby didn't wait for a response. She scooped up the crumbly Hart Bible and nestled it back inside its archival box. "The family history always mattered to Daddy. Your granny took it up from him. Never could fire up much interest, myself." Ruby dipped her head toward two small but bulging boxes at the front of the room. "Over by the TV there's more papers from your granddaddy's side."

"I can't believe Uncle Blake or one of the others didn't want all this."

"He's the one who dumped it off here." Ruby pursed her lips. "He only cared about the valuables. John and me put the good stuff under lock and key."

"Wow. I don't care what else there is—these are the valuables to me." She held up Pearl and Jim's marriage certificate in one hand and a stray photo in the other, by way of example, Ruby supposed. "Thank goodness you kept them."

"Oh, I keep everything. I do wish it didn't take up so much room." She gestured at the boxes. Her hips ached for her chair. "But I seen most of it before and lived the rest. Once was enough."

"Enough for you. But what about them?"

Ruby sat. Sweet relief. She put on her glasses and peered at Abby. "I don't follow."

"It's like you said last night. They're only alive as long as someone remembers them." She waved the certificate. "We owe it to them, don't we?"

"Child, I didn't mean—" Ruby interrupted herself. "Don't you believe in heaven?"

The girl hesitated. "Not especially. Hell either, although I guess if one exists, the other probably does too. Day and night. Summer and winter. That much makes sense. But I can see light and dark or changing seasons. I can't see heaven. I can't touch it. Why should I assume it's real?"

"You can't touch a memory either," Ruby countered.

Abby let out a wavering sigh. "But it can touch you."

If Ruby lost the afterlife debate, then she supposed the awkward silence that followed made a fitting prize. "I hope you're wrong. Otherwise I want all those Sunday mornings I spent in church back." The joke fell flat.

Abby picked up her binder and poised her pen over a fresh sheet of paper. "Enough of that. I want stories. Scandals, secret weddings, jailbirds. Any family legends along those lines?"

She extended her jaw and popped her lower denture plate a couple times. "I'm sure if I think on it . . . "

Abby licked her lips. "War heroes, maybe? Mom's side came from Pennsylvania oil money. Way back, I mean. The stories say they used their privilege to get out of serving, and it must be true because we've never found a single veteran."

"Ain't that too bad." Heat crept up Ruby's neck. Her face would be broken out in red splotches in a minute. "No privilege to speak of on the Hart side. We were tenant farmers 'til my great-granddaddy came with the railroad. War heroes. Humph. The Bible says 'blessed are the peacemakers.' Or if you don't hold with that, then how about: heroes know how not to make wars in the first place."

"I'm sorry. I didn't mean to upset you. What if I get us both a glass of water?"

"Oh, don't mind me." Ruby pumped the lever of her recliner and gave the footrest a sturdy kick. "Do you take lemon in your sweet tea?"

Abby stared at her like she spoke Japanese. It was a simple question, for heaven's sake. "Yes. Absolutely."

In spite of her shuffling stride, Ruby left the room in the biggest huff she could manage. She had half a mind to send that girl packing. What did she think, showing up here and nosing around?

Tea sloshed over the rim of the glass. Ruby wiped it up and tried to slow her breathing. Abby didn't know. No use blaming her. Better dig deep for the gracious Southern lady Mama tried to raise, because the red-haired hothead she'd borne didn't need any blood pressure spikes at this stage of the game.

She fanned herself with a paper plate from the top of the bread box, then finished fixing their tea. When she returned to the living room, Abby was back to frowning down at her notes. "See if that's sweet enough. If not, there's a sugar bowl in the kitchen."

"Thanks." She sipped it. Ruby thought for a second she was gonna spit it right back out before she set the glass aside. "It's good."

"Careful you don't spill on the carpet." Ruby sank into her chair again and downed a quarter of her glass in one long swallow. "Hmm. Not bad for instant. Ain't as good as my sun tea, but it's too cold yet for that."

Abby's face remained blank. Probably didn't know about sun tea, either.

"While you were up, I double-checked my work. I think I made a mistake." Abby traced a finger over the page. "I wrote down that George Hart died January 19, 1861, but his son Gilbert—"

"My daddy."

"—wasn't born until 1888. Can I look in that Bible again?"

"Oh, it'll hold 'til we're finished with refreshments. And speaking of, are you hungry?" She reached down beside her armchair and withdrew her pocketbook. "I'm hungry."

The girl didn't budge. "I'm all right for now."

Ruby snapped open her wallet and frowned at the contents. That Blake sure got bold, or else her memory was sliding after all. "Past noon already. Why don't you grab us some lunch? My treat."

"Aunt Ruby, I don't want to take your money. I have plenty of cash."

"I want a chocolate milkshake." She ignored Abby's protest and waved twenty dollars at her. "Medium. Don't tell my doctor, and get whatever you want for yourself."

No mistaking that resigned slump as she rose, nor the long look she threw at the untapped boxes. "No, no. I'll pay for yours. It's the least I can do."

No sense arguing, Ruby figured. "Let me write this down for you first."

"One chocolate milkshake. Got it." Abby stood over her, crowding a bit. "I don't need directions. I can get to the highway."

Ruby struggled to make the pen obey as she wrote out the address, resenting her own feeble, childish strokes. A whole life of practice came to scribble-scrabble. "Stop here on your way back. You got one of them fancy navigators, don't you?" Abby nodded. "Good. I'll send my caretaker out at one o'clock to unlock it."

She held out the paper until Abby took it. "Where is this?"

"Right close. The other side of Main. That's where me and your granny grew up. I lived there 'til I married John in '68."

"Ooh, historic places. I definitely won't miss that. I don't want to be any trouble though. A picture from the outside will be good enough."

"Ain't no trouble." Not for her, at least. Will might disagree.

"But your milkshake will melt."

"I like it soupy." She rubbed her age-spotted hands. "Besides, how often do you get to see a real haunted house?"

That did the trick. She left in a big ol' hurry then. Ruby listened for Abby's car pulling away, then checked out the front window to make sure.

All clear. Ruby plain forgot about George Hart, and that was better than he deserved. Besides, all these questions gave her a yen to do her own little investigation. As far as she could recollect, she had written exactly one letter to Suzanne, not counting a combined wedding card and baby gift. If Abby brought that letter with her, Ruby meant to find it.

The binder and papers scattered across her living room would be a sensible place to start. Ruby crouched down stiffly, going gentle on the knees. Janice from her church group got both of hers replaced five years ago, and Ruby looked into it, but the doctor claimed her knees didn't need replacing. He put it so nice, too. "They'll carry you to the finish line," he said.

She shuffled the papers around. The girl must not be too organized. Dividers with no labels written on their tabs, pockets and notes without any sense to them, piles of blank charts and photocopies, and hurried transcriptions on wide-ruled notebook paper written in a hand distantly related to the careful penmanship she'd used to contact Ruby. No sign of the letter.

Well. Nobody reached the grand age of eighty-eight by quittin' easy. On to the guest room.

Poor Suzanne. Ruby hated to hear the news, though they never did straighten out their differences. Three versions of her face flickered like slides projected on a screen. First scared, then grateful, and betrayed forever afterwards. Did Ruby imagine a heaviness trailing her? Probably, but no sense taking chances. "Don't come hauntin' here," she called out. "Wasn't none of it my fault."

Never mind. That letter brought Abby here. The gist of it lingered like a musty odor, but the specifics faded with the rest of the relics strewn across her living room. So help her, she refused to believe that girl came all this way to fill in blanks on her little charts. No, she wanted something. Same as everybody else. Everyone had strings. The letter would tell her where to pull.

The door stood open a crack. Ruby gave it a push and stepped inside. The hinges creaked; the floor boards groaned; the vents sighed. Her house carried on day and night. Always talking, never anything to say.

Other than the dirty clothes stacked on an olive green tote in the corner, her niece left the room tidy, made the bed, and minded not to leave her belongings strewn around. Might as well forget the mess in the living room. She had chased her out, after all.

Forgiveness didn't buy privacy, though. Age had a way of putting the severity of sins in perspective, and there wasn't much wrong with keeping an eye on the rooms of her own home. Besides, she'd written the letter. Didn't that make it hers?

She shuffled the clothes around, careful not to disturb too much. Peeking out of a side pocket, she saw it—her own handwriting on the face of the envelope, familiar as a reflection and twice as revealing. Deep grooves, big loops. A testament to her force of will and lingering claims to girlish vanity, though well into middle age by then.

Holding it in her hands though, she hesitated. The past never quite disappeared, did it? Folks usually thought time moved forward, starting on the left and riding a right-pointing arrow into the future. Ruby didn't believe that. The future twisted uncertain, a shapeless dream, but the past—the past was set. It cast evidence behind it, photos and letters and bones, piling up in hidden places, waiting for the chance to spill out. An avalanche. A burial. The past consumed the future, always.

Old shame oozed fresh as her eyes traced over prattle she remembered writing now that she saw it again. Writing and wrangling her pride over who owed who an apology, but Abby would never guess it by this, a letter full of empty chatter cushioning the one line meant to imply what Ruby still couldn't quite bring herself to say.

No one's heard a thing from Richard in some time.

There it was. Blessed are the peacemakers. Hadn't she as good as admitted she was wrong?

Tucking the letter away through a tad of reluctance to loosen her grip, Ruby dug deeper to see what else she might find.

The Selective Service envelope lurked at the bottom of the bag, and once again, the past threatened escape. "You little snoop," she whispered. "War heroes, my eye."

She reached for the draft letter, then hesitated. Why bother stealing it back? Ruby sure didn't want it. Didn't even want to touch the paper with those words printed on it. Let the girl nose around all she wanted, but she'd never hear Christie's story. Not from Ruby.

From the living room there came a respectful nudge at the front door, the sigh of foam weather stripping, and the light-footed tread of one who tried not to show his longing to be elsewhere.

Caught, or about to be. Ruby left the rustled clothing. She stole into the bathroom, flushed the toilet, and washed her hands before emerging.

"William, you're late." She blunted the rebuke with a smile, but he ducked his head.

"I am? If so, then I'm sorry, but it's only now one o'clock, Mrs. Watts."

"That's right." Her hands dripped; in her haste she'd forgotten to dry them. "And I told Abby you'd show her the old house."

Will's smooth brow crinkled, but it didn't hurt his looks none and Ruby wouldn't be swayed anyhow. She might be old and funny, but she still had a stubborn streak wide as the Four-Lane and at least as long.

"Go on. Ain't nothin' here that won't wait 'til you get back."

CHAPTER 4

Abby parked on the street and picked at the last crunchy French fry bits, then brushed the salt from her fingers on a stiff paper napkin as she gazed at the house. Haunted. Hmm.

It certainly looked the part, with its foggy mottled windows and weather-beaten porch steps leading up to a crooked front door. Beside it, a black tin mailbox with newspaper hooks hung from a short chain. The peeling paint barely contained the splintered wood siding, and kudzu climbed one side of the house, not quite disguising the bent flashings at its peak. Malevolent ivy. Was that from a book? She couldn't remember.

"What do you think, Mom?" Suzanne Blanchard-Wells' great talent for interpreting clues had always made their mysteries a team effort. Without her perspective, Abby strained to see past the creepy, bygone charm the house exuded.

Don't look at how it is. Imagine how it was. A snippet of an old conversation returned, and she scrunched up her face. The memory of Mom's voice had become somehow . . . soft.

How it was. Under the decay was a modest home. Like Aunt Ruby said, no privilege. She tried to follow that thread to Mom's wisdom, but only her own observations flitted through her head. No whispers from beyond, no matter how much she wanted to hear them. The house bore the hallmarks of time's steady destruction—always a sure bet, haunted or not.

Abby watched for another car to pull up in front of or behind her beat-up Mustang. When the clock on the dashboard read ten after one, she reached for her cell phone to call Aunt Ruby. The tapping on her window startled her and she dropped her phone.

"Hello." She collected herself, appraising the lanky stranger before getting out of the car. When Aunt Ruby promised to send her caretaker, Abby had imagined a middle-aged handyman in coveralls, perhaps hiking a tool belt up around a sagging paunch.

This young guy dashed her expectations. His rangy height stopped half-a-head shy of a low-hanging cloud, and his sandy hair and light brown eyes gleamed with the brightness of afternoon. He belonged on a college campus somewhere. His sudden presence crackled with energy, a sharp contrast to the house, which stood as gray and silent as a tomb.

"You must be Miss Abby. I'm Will Laughlin."

"You blew in from nowhere, didn't you?"

"Sorry to keep you waiting." He checked his bare wrist with a grin. "I went to see Mrs. Watts a while ago and she told me I was fixin' to be late."

Walleggo. Ficsindabee. His words ran together in strange rhythms, like exotic bird calls. She wouldn't have expected a city-dweller, even in a small city like Kennesaw, to sound like such a bumpkin.

"Nice to meet you, Will. And please call me Abby."

"Short for Abigail?"

"Short for nothing." It was her usual answer for the common question, but it came out clipped and abrupt next to his easy speech. Nonplussed, he winked at her.

"'Nothing?' That don't suit you at all. I'll call you Abbs, how's that?" His dimples widened his narrow face. Was he being friendly or making fun of her? Hard to tell. He studied her face a breath too long. She blushed and looked away. Didn't matter. No way she planned to answer to that awful nickname. Even if he was sort of cute.

She glanced at the house, hoping to herd Will toward the point of their meeting, but he missed the cue.

"Did she tell you what-all you wanted to know about your dad?"

"I'm sure she would have. I didn't ask."

Will scrunched up his brow. "Oh. Why'd you come here, then?"

"I wanted to learn about my family in general, more than any one particular individual." She took two steps toward the house, but stopped when he didn't follow. "This is my one chance to visit the ancestral home. Aunt Ruby claims it has quite a history."

If he knew what she meant, he hid it well. He looked over his shoulder at the decrepit front porch, but still made no move to grant her entrance. "I don't guess I'll ever understand how old junk gets more interesting than when it was new. People, on the other hand, get all kinds of interesting the longer they stay on this earth."

Abby crossed her arms. "It was my aunt's idea to show it to me."

At last he took the hint. He dug the key ring out of his pocket, looking appropriately chastised. "I hope you're not disappointed. It's rough." He didn't make any hurry up the porch steps. Trepidation? Maybe he always moved that slow. She debated whether to ask him point-blank for his take on the supposed ghost, once the sharpness of her last words faded.

"The key likes to stick," he said, though he pushed open the crooked door without apparent difficulty.

The inside was no better or worse than the façade. As Will led her into the house, a false sense of nostalgia washed up around her like drops of dye curling inky black tendrils through crystalline waters. They stepped into a bare dining room and kitchen with low ceilings marred with water stains. The faded orange counter tops clashed with the dark wood cabinets. Beside an aging refrigerator was a doorway, and beyond it, a narrow hallway that led to the rest of the house.

"Rough, wow. You weren't kidding."

"It's been empty for years. To my knowledge all the appliances still work though." He brushed away a cobweb descending from the ceiling to the top of the fridge. "Built to last. Of course, they'll wear out eventually. Probably as soon as they're plugged in again."

Abby nodded. An odd little fact for him to know, caretaker or not. How did he expect her to respond?

The relative newness of the door left of the entryway struck her as out of place. "What's in here?" She pushed it open without waiting for Will.

"Used to be a formal sitting room, but they re-done it into a bedroom when they started renting it out. The last tenant was before Mr. Watts passed. A widow they knew from church." He paused for a reaction, or perhaps, for a memory. Abby listened, waiting for him to go on. "She was ninety-three and died in her sleep. She got what most people wish for."

He left it implied that the tenant widow had passed in the room where they stood. Assuming souls existed outside of imagination and longing, perhaps hers got stuck here.

Abby frowned. An elderly woman passing away didn't make much of a story, but then again, Aunt Ruby hadn't told her a ghost story. She only said the place was haunted. Surely there must be a reason.

She circled the small room. The gouged and scuffed hardwood floors groaned under their weight, and someone had done a poor job of taking down the wallpaper. She traced the jagged outlines with her finger. Here was a patch of green, there white and yellow, but not enough remained to reveal any pattern. Pausing before the window, she cringed at the collection of bug corpses littering the sill. She pretended to inspect the glass and casually spied on Will's faint outline behind her.

"It isn't bad," she lied. "It has a certain charm."

"You don't have to be polite. It's seen better years, and a lot of 'em." He stepped out of the doorway and led her through the kitchen toward the back of the house. "The living room and staircase are behind the kitchen. The house went up a long time before indoor plumbing, so the bathroom was converted from the pantry closet."

"The toilet is where the food used to be? That's so wrong."

"Better than the other way around." His eyes wouldn't leave her face. He made her nervous. Was he checking her out? Perfect. No better way to forget the old love than with a new one. And only seven hundred miles from home, too.

The living room featured banal beige-colored walls and more water stains. A hole in the ceiling exposed wires and pink insulation where the overhead light fixture was supposed to be. She stared up into it for a long moment, imagining the house as a living creature. Here the nature of every broken heart gaped at her, embarrassingly candid and unbearably true: a hole where the light belonged.

Will followed her fixed gaze. "I didn't know about that. It's a fire hazard."

She took a reluctant step toward the staircase and peered up into the dark. "How's the upstairs?"

"Dusty." Will laughed a little and gestured around. "There ain't much to see but more of the same."

"No ghosts?" She joked, testing him. Did his answering laugh hold a note of reservation? Not really. Maybe.

"Not a one." He paused. "It's crowded up there, though. They've always used it for storage. You can look around in the front bedroom, but I don't have the key to the back room."

"That's okay," Abby said. "I believe you."

He unlocked the back door and stepped out onto a small concrete patio, shielding his eyes against the sun. "The Baptist church's lot begins on the other side of that little side street. There's a sign that says 'No Trespassing,' but they'll forgive you."

Abby smirked. "I'm sure." She circled around the side of the house toward the car, and Will walked with her. The distant whine of an approaching train perked her interest. "I didn't know freight trains still ran through town."

"I'm surprised you didn't hear one last night. The railroad is the Kennesaw's heritage. The locomotive museum is right there off Main Street, across from the depot. You can't miss it. You should visit there."

She shook her head. "Not enough time for sightseeing. I need to head home tomorrow morning."

"That's too bad," Will said, although to Abby's ear, his voice held some relief. "I hope you got to see all what you wanted."

Decision time. She'd arrived at Aunt Ruby's with so little in mind. Quiz the older generation and put names on the empty branches of her family tree. She would walk away with that much fulfilled—and turn her back on the most intriguing question yet.

"Mostly." She pretended to examine her nails for a moment. "I'm curious though. Why hasn't my aunt sold this place?"

Her question caught him off-guard. "I don't know, Abbs. It's been in her family a long time. I reckon that's why."

"Do you know any special reason she couldn't rent it out?"

Will hesitated as if he didn't want to answer. "I suppose not. It's up to code. The City's especially strict in the historic districts."

"It seems . . . livable. And she could probably use the money. Why leave it vacant?"

He gestured at the house, in all its ramshackle glory. "Ain't hard to guess, is it? Who'd want to stay here?"

Simple. Someone with questions for a ghost. How would he like that? She squelched the quick response. Enough trouble for one day. "Need a ride back to my aunt's place?"

"No thanks. I should see about that light fixture, as long as I'm here.

Enjoy the rest of your time."

She thanked him and got into the car. Only then she remembered she'd meant to take a photo. Her eyes darted back in his direction.

Will still watched her from the front yard. When their eyes met, she could have waved, opened the car door, and called out, but she broke eye contact and the moment vanished. That cinched it. No picture. Aunt Ruby's milkshake was soupy enough. Whatever he was hiding, he didn't do well at keeping it off his face. In spite of his vague answers, Will looked like he had more to say.

CHAPTER 5

CUYAHOGA FALLS, OHIO
Sunday, February 12

After the spring weather in Georgia, gray Ohio resembled Kansas after Oz. The dirty snowdrifts around the apartment complex remained as before she left. Suspended in time. No rising temperatures to banish them, no fresh dusting of snow to disguise them. Abby parked the Mustang in her usual spot outside apartment building B. As she retrieved her bag from the backseat, the bite of frozen air, made harsher by comparison, nestled into her clothes and wound down her airways. "There are trees budding in Georgia," she informed a disinterested sky. Her breath puffed and faded.

As always, she gulped in a deep breath as she approached the elevator, but an Out of Order sign hung over the call button, saving her from the old cigarette stink of the ride and costing her the effort of trudging up two flights of stairs. She looked up into the stairwell and sighed, a last monumental effort between her and the apartment.

When at last she stood outside door B342, Abby crossed her fingers. "Please, please let Sarah be out with Sam." She might have added a few more pleases, but the banging of pots from inside canceled her wish before she even finished making it. The social mask had to stay in place a while longer. She trudged inside.

"You're back. Right on cue." Sarah cleared her throat and pasted on a showy smile. "Welcome to 'Mixing up a Miracle.' I'm your host, Sarah

Grunewald."

"Let me put my stuff down." Resigned, Abby hauled her bag and laptop case to her bedroom. She dumped them on the floor and returned to the tiny galley kitchen that Sarah forever tried to restyle as a "culinary arts center."

"Okay, sorry. What's tonight's miracle?"

"Tahini Tilapia. A quick, easy, better-for-you way to bread fried fish. It's going to be amazing. It's my audition entry for that new cooking show that's taping in May. Here, taste this." She tore the seal off a round container and handed Abby a spoon.

She scooped a tiny dab from the center and licked it clean. "Hm. It's almost like peanut butter. Needs salt."

"No. No extra salt. The point is to be in control of what goes into your food." She snagged a beer out of the fridge and removed the cap with a practiced twist.

Abby rolled her eyes. "I don't see you growing your own barley and hops in the window sill."

"Not this year," Sarah replied, then took a long drink.

Abby hid a smirk as she set the spoon in the sink. "Won't this be gooey for breading?"

"You say gooey, I say innovative. Extra points on the creativity component of the judging, plus the catchy recipe title. The real beauty of it is the simplicity though. Two steps. Coat the fish in the tahini and deep fry them. Gourmet cooking made easy." She emptied the tahini into a pie plate. "Your turn. How was your trip? Tell me about your dad. Is he a jerk? What did he say when you told him about your mom?"

"I didn't go for him. I went to meet my aunt."

Sarah raised her eyebrows. She practiced in the mirror for her auditions, trying to lift the left one and refusing to believe her perfect genetics would deny her. Greg couldn't do it either. "I thought you wanted to know about your family."

"Yes." Abby pulled back her shoulders. Sarah could poke fun if she wanted. "It was enlightening. I've got five generations going back, with photos for most of them, and I even visited a haunted house."

"Cool." Sarah twisted a dial and the gas igniter clicked as she dumped a bottle of olive oil into a stock pot. "My cousin saw a ghost once. Of course, he used to do a lot of drugs. That probably had something to do with it."

"Well, my great-aunt thinks it's real. I went to check out the house—"

And got checked out herself in the process. Will's long stares had pierced her. Was she still bleeding?

Sarah tapped her manicured nails to the counter. "And?"

Abby snapped back to the here and now. "And I didn't see the ghost, but I was only there for ten minutes in broad daylight. I didn't expect much."

Sarah tried to dredge a fillet through the tahini, but the thick paste wouldn't coat the fish. "Hmm. I might need to thin this out with some milk. Or maybe I can spread it on the fish with a knife. All right, so how come she thinks the house is haunted? Did somebody get murdered there?"

"I don't think so. She didn't mention a murder."

"And you didn't ask? You're slipping."

"I tried." The glint of Aunt Ruby's eyes had belied her. Abby recognized the look because she knew it in herself. "She kept changing the subject."

"Sounds to me like somebody's off her meds." Sarah glanced up. "Her, I mean. Not you."

Abby pinched her own stiff shoulders. She had filled her prescription only to placate Greg and no longer saw the point in taking it, but Sarah didn't need to know. "She seemed sharp . . . " Abby began, but Sarah, satisfied that her words hadn't done any damage, returned her attention to the fish.

"It's good that you got to meet her, of course." Sarah dropped the tahini-covered fillets into the oil and the subject with them. "Bingo. This one's a winner. I can feel it."

Abby rolled her eyes. "Good luck."

Sarah wiggled her fingers like a cartoon magician. "No luck involved. Pure genius."

"Good luck with your genius, then. I'm going to call Aunt Ruby and let her know I got back in one piece."

"Tell her I said 'Boo.'"

Abby retreated to her room. Sanctuary. She had no intention of calling her aunt or anyone else, no desire to think beyond the luxury of her own bed.

She bunched her pillow. Sprawled out. Laid her arm over her eyes to block out the light.

A real haunted house. Who'd want to stay here? Don't you believe in heaven? Bless your heart.

Abby sat up. No good. Too awake. Too many conversations stuck on repeat.

Might as well fire up her laptop. While it booted, she retrieved the yellowed envelope containing the photographs and W. C. Sosebee's draft orders. She laid them out across the bed and touched his name. "Who are you?"

She hadn't braved the topics of heroes or wars again. She and Mom became experts at searching online records for signs of their ancestors. It would take no more than a sprinkle of keystrokes to identify the man and find out why his draft orders were hidden in a drawer of Aunt Ruby's home. It might be tough to get meaningful results from initials, but Kennesaw was a small town. How many Sosebees could there be?

"One way to find out. Google, tell me what you know." The first page gathered Sosebees from all walks except historical ones. She added "Kennesaw, Georgia" to her search terms and skimmed the assortment of résumés and directory lists that appeared. None looked relevant to the man named on the draft orders.

Trying a different approach, she typed in the address. Maybe she could contact the current residents and ask them if they knew about Sosebee. The half-formed plan dissolved as she skimmed the oddly bankrupt results. She tried mapping the address, again with no luck.

"Huh. No such place. Weird. So much for that." She tucked the envelope with its seventy-year-old contents into a bulging pocket in her research binder and wedged it into its normal place on the bookshelf.

She didn't bother entertaining guilt for giving up so soon. Without Mom, the thrill of the chase wouldn't rise up to meet her. There'd be no one to share in the discovery if she made one. True, a quick hit on Google didn't exactly meet the "reasonably exhaustive search" criterion demanded by the Genealogical Standard of Proof, but then, what did it matter? The Georgia trip was reasonably exhausting to say the least, and it hadn't netted her even one imagined moment of the closeness their shared hobby had brought them.

A heavy burnt odor choked out her musings. Abby opened the door of her bedroom to acrid smoke filling the common area of the apartment.

"Sarah, what's happening?" Abby covered her nose with the neckline of her tee shirt.

"What do you think is happening? I burned the fish. And cut that out. You look like a fourth-grader."

Abby lowered her makeshift mask. The smell of Sarah's concoction assaulted her again. "Were you going to pull the fire alarm or let me go down in flames?"

Sarah hefted a box fan into the window. "No actual fire." She scrunched up her face. "But I had to throw the whole bit out. The tahini wouldn't stick to the fish when I tried to fry them, and I couldn't get all the floating pieces out of the oil before it reached the smoke point."

"Did you write down the temperature and cooking time for your contest entry?" Abby said with a mostly straight face.

"Shut up. You're not helping."

"I vote we order Chinese."

"Fine. I'll even buy if you'll promise never to bring this up again."

Biting her tongue didn't quite take the edge off Abby's laugh. "I don't know if I can make that deal."

Sarah waved her hand in defeat. "It doesn't matter. I'm going to blog about it." She retrieved the menu magneted to the fridge and gave it a brief perusal. "Beef and broccoli, family-style?"

"Gross."

"Were you this difficult before you left?" Sarah handed Abby the menu. "Here."

She skimmed the choices and picked one she'd not tried. "General Tso's chicken and a spring roll."

"Adventurous. I love it." She perched on the arm of the couch and faced Abby, all business. "But first, I have a minor issue to float out there and see what you think, okay? Don't freak out."

"Nice warm up. I'm fifty-percent freaked out already."

"No, for real. Sam and I have been thinking about getting a place together."

"Oh, yes. Minor." The sarcasm filter had evaporated from her lips, and her words struck her own ears as whiny. Abby expected a reminder not to leave towels in the dryer, or to hang her purse in the closet rather than on the doorknob. She coughed. "You're moving?"

"No, not right away. But you know it's getting hard to resist these interest rates."

Abby didn't know. "Definitely. But what if you win the contest? You'll have to move again right away."

Sarah rolled her eyes. "That would be a wonderful problem to have, but I can't put my life on hold for a maybe."

"You can't move out." She tried to smile. "Who's going to push me out of the plane?"

"We don't have to live together to go skydiving. And don't think you're getting out of that. My next birthday. It's happening."

Who knew that the pieces of her heart could splinter even smaller? Before long it would be like ground glass, too broken to break any more. "Right. How long have you and Sam been 'thinking'?"

"We were making plans before . . . you know, your mom. And then it went down with you and Greg. It wasn't a good time to bring it up." The subtext gonged beneath Sarah's well-modulated words. Abby had already received months of patience and pity without ever suspecting. "Like I said, don't freak out. There's no deadline. Sam knows you're out of work. We can wait until you catch a break."

"Sure." Abby barely heard her. A wisp of an idea came, as airy as the remaining smoke and perhaps as apt to blow away. "Thanks. For the heads-up, I mean."

With apparent relief, Sarah grabbed her phone to order their food, and Abby slipped away to her bedroom.

She'd make that call to Georgia after all.

CHAPTER 6

That Abby sure stirred up memories. Like seeing a ghost. Mercy.

One box of photos never quite made it back up to the attic after she went home to Ohio. It rested next to Ruby's armchair, hidden against the wall and protected from traffic around the room, the waning sunlight peeking through the blinds, and Will's diligent, good-intentioned help.

These unsupervised afternoons kept getting rarer. Ruby knew better than to wait for the next one. She held the phone with one hand and pawed through the box with the other. These photos stayed hid during Abby's visit. They'd taken such a few back then, when it'd been "shortage" this and "war effort" that. No one wanted to be the sort who fussed too much about rationing, or a wastrel caught spending money on whimsies instead of defense bonds. Plenty of time for photos after they won the war. They'd said so and she'd believed them.

The one of Pearl in her nurse's getup got lost somewhere along the way, but Ruby laid out the five remaining photographs representing 1942 like tiles on her lap, where she could look at them all together and baptize herself in that strange year. The attack on Pearl Harbor cut deep but stirred deeper, and far from the European battlefields or the South Pacific theater, even the dwellers of Georgia farmland mobilized in whatever ways they knew how.

Here Mama showed off her spinning wheel, pleased as punch over it though she'd never admit to the sin of pride. Here Daddy climbed a steel ladder up the side of a boxcar, indulging her for a pose. The image called to mind his quick laugh and had always been her favorite of him.

How she'd like to pick one more fight with her sister instead of talking to photos, this one a fancy portrait Ruby took herself. Pearl posed before a bedsheet draped over the door jamb, her face tilted to play up a superficial resemblance to Claudette Colbert. That same picture appeared in the newspaper a few years later, when she got engaged to Jim and had to crow it from the treetops. Ruby stuck her tongue out at the image and turned it face down.

That left the two she wanted, and she was in both of them. Not that Ruby much cared to study her own face—she knew what she looked like, then and now, and she'd as soon not dwell on the difference—but she'd been photographed twice in 1942, neither time alone.

Mama had taken the first one, which she always remembered because it was out of focus. Ruby could almost hear her own shrieking laugh coming out of that wide-open mouth, and her arms remembered clutching the low branch of their tree while a shadowy beanpole of a man boosted her from below. No one besides her ever knew it, but since the day when he was eight and she was five and he'd rescued her out of that pine, he'd been afraid of heights.

The other, a clearer shot, was their wedding photo.

Even in a national crisis, they'd found little pockets of happiness. Hadn't she been keen enough to make sacrifices for the boys on the front lines? She despised knitting but still sent endless piles of warm socks to soldiers. She saved as much scrap metal and cooking grease as anyone, and the taffeta wedding gown she loved stayed right there on the dummy in the window at Florence's Department Store while she made do with a borrowed dress. All this she offered, and still more was demanded. Even her friends whose beaus or husbands fell to the war's deep-bellied hunger hadn't lost in the same way she had.

She'd hated that year and still did, but she'd trade ten of these ugly wrinkled ones to live it over again. One year to shape all those that followed, with the first hint coming on January 23, 1942, Ruby's eighteenth birthday, the day they declared Marietta the site for the new Bell Bomber plant.

"Your call may be monitored for quality assurance." The recording played for the umpteenth time. Ruby hummed through the small silence of the line connecting. "Good afternoon, this is Yanira. How may I help y—"

She hung up and hit redial. A rotary phone would be better for this type of task. It tested determination to keep tickling the same phone number all afternoon. The redial button made it too easy, and paradoxically bred impatience. "Thank you for calling LifeCare Insurance Company, where our customers are our family. Your call is important to us. All our representatives are assisting other callers. Please stay on the line."

A robotic voice doing the job that made Ruby indispensable, or so she'd once thought. Mr. Rutherford filled her head with notions about her talent with the switchboard, and it didn't take long before Ruby worked her way up to special intelligence cablegram receiver—in her mind, at least. More than doing her bit, she would practically help run the war. And of course, on the off chance that Christie did ship out, she'd be first to know if disaster struck him. Not that it would. If she played her cards right, she might even have some pull over where he got sent. If he got sent. Which he wouldn't.

What a child, dreaming up such foolishness.

"Thank you for holding. Your call may be monitored for quality assurance." Kneading her forehead, she waited. "Good afternoon, this is Richard. What can I do for you today?"

Finally. She stacked up the five photographs and placed them in the box at her feet. "Richard? I want to buy me some life insurance."

His fake chuckle, the one he used to win friends and get his own way, came through the line. "You came to the right place. I'll need to ask you a few simple questions . . . ."

"Oh, it ain't for me. It's for my niece. Actually my grandniece, if you wanna get picky."

A pause. She threw him off his script. "I see. We have several products which may meet your needs. Let me get your name . . . ."

"It's Ruby Watts. Capital R, u, b-as-in—"

"I've got it." The fake chuckle again. "I actually have an Aunt Ruby myself."

"How 'bout that. And here I thought I was special."

"Our customers are our family," he said. "But *Miss* Ruby, I'm afraid I can't write a policy for a person who has already passed away."

"You're thinkin' of my other niece. This one's name is Abby. Abby Wells. Now I know you'll need her to sign off on it, so let me find you her phone number . . . ."

Oh, she could almost smell the toothpaste-scented bullets he'd be spittin' if not for his tape-recording babysitter. "What are you expecting might happen to Abby?"

"One never knows. I want a policy for fifteen thousand. Does that sound right? I don't have her Social, but I reckon you might. Richard."

"Tell you what. I'll check my files, and you can look up that phone number. Please hold." The line clicked over to playing elevator music, a Big Band tune Ruby recognized. She hummed along for three minutes, and then the line went dead.

She set the phone back on its base. A few more digs might have been fun, but the call served its purpose. The winners write the history books, but you didn't have to win the whole war. Not if you could take the historian.

Ruby picked up the Big Band tune again, humming off-key while she sorted through a pile of statements and bills. She couldn't sink much into this little project, but no use in getting carried away before she talked to Will. He was the linchpin.

In a while, he would let himself in with the key under the ceramic frog on the porch and make like she needed to know he was fixin' to cut the grass or weed the flowerbeds or do the edging around the driveway. "Didn't want to startle you," he would say, and then he'd slip into the kitchen to count her pills. Most times, he wouldn't be satisfied with the number and would fix her a bologna sandwich—mustard and lettuce, but no cheese or mayonnaise, not with her high cholesterol—and leave her medicines in a clear plastic dosing cup to the side. He wouldn't say a word so neither would she. Nicer to keep it their secret.

I know it's not much.

It's perfect. Thank you.

Then he'd ask to use the restroom and straighten up in there. Kept it scrubbed up and pearly, and once a week he'd run a load of towels. The first time or two embarrassed her, but bending over that washer to reach down inside turned out to be one of the little nits of old age. It hurt every joint from her fingertips to her tailbone. If he wanted to help, why not let him?

44

After his circuit through the house he'd give a cheerful word or two and mention if she'd run out of any staples. "I'm adding dish soap to the list on the counter," he'd say, or else, "You're low on bread." In the space of ten minutes, he'd nudge her household back on course, then head outside to do whatever yard work he could find.

Except today, she'd break the routine. Popular wisdom claimed a great shock would age you in seconds, but no. No, Ruby always found the catastrophes anchored her in time. It was day-to-day repetition that etched lines in her face.

And there came the key in grudging agreement with the lock, old married lovers. She'd been allowed to know that tranquility, finally. She and John shared a good thirty-seven years, and if the frostbite of jealousy nipped while her friends threw golden anniversary parties throughout the Nineties, still Ruby couldn't complain. Not now, with all of them on the wrong side of the grass.

"Afternoon, Mrs. Watts." Will slipped inside, looking like his normal self except for maybe a touch of sunburn on his face. "I'm about to do the hedges. Didn't want the trimmer to wake you, in case you were nappin'."

"William, sit a minute, dear." She gestured at the plushy blue couch. "We have a piece of business to discuss."

He sank down in the cushions. "Ma'am? Did I do something wrong?"

"Course not, bless your heart. No, but tell me about the old house. How's it look over there?"

"Fair to middlin'. The seals on the windows are all broke and the kudzu's overgrown again, but the water stains haven't got any worse." He spoke to the carpet. "The patch job Audrey and me did on the roof must be holding out."

She nodded and fished for the word Abby used. "Then you'd say it's *livable* inside?"

"With some doin'. You gonna rent it out again?"

"I am. And another thing. What'd you think of my grandniece? The new one, I mean."

He rubbed his forehead. "Sure was a shock to meet her. That's a strong gene. Don't know when I ever saw family favor each other so much, except twins."

Ruby nodded. "She's exactly like my sister was at that age. But that's not what I meant."

His gaze veered off to the right toward the window, betraying him. Not sure what to say, probably wishing he was out there gardening instead of stuck in here answering questions. She knew she was being unfair, but she waited 'til he once again looked her in the eye. "I promise I didn't mean to make her mad. When I asked about her dad, I was going off what you told me."

Interesting. Abby didn't mention any of that. "Oh, stop. You wouldn't swat a bee that stung you, much less stir up trouble with a pretty girl like her." The sunburn deepened.

"I don't guess it matters now that she's gone on home." That light remark inched as close to lying as she'd ever suspect of him, pretending he hadn't figured it out, but she could see understanding all pinched around his eyes. Ruby took off her glasses but she could still make him out, twisting his hands. Ready for it, dreading it. Oh well.

"Funny you say that. Turns out she's looking to move down. No sense in letting the place go to seed, right?"

Cruel, cruel. His Adam's apple bobbed. "No, ma'am," he said. "No sense at all."

CHAPTER 7

CUYAHOGA FALLS

Abby rehearsed The Talk in her head for two days beforehand, and still it spiraled out of her control in less than a minute. She should have known better than to try to plan a conversation with Sarah. The best she could expect was to launch out and let her steer.

She gritted her teeth. "It's already arranged. No point arguing."

"Oh, I am definitely arguing. Look, I didn't mean to hurt your feelings. If I'd realized you planned on being roommates for the rest of our lives—"

"No, I get it. You're ready to move on, and I'm in the way. I move out, problem solved."

"All the way to Georgia? Such an overreaction. Honestly. Would it help if I apologized? I'm sorry I made you feel like a third wheel."

"More like a roadblock."

"Whatever. The point is that I didn't mean it. I gave you a heads-up, not an eviction notice."

"It'll be an adventure."

"No. An adventure is trying something new, snapping a few pictures, and bragging about it on Facebook. This is lunacy."

"Sarah." Abby twisted her watch. "I'll be near family—"

"Family? You don't even know them."

"And Aunt Ruby's giving me an outstanding price for my rent. Unbelievably cheap."

"Which probably means it's infested with cockroaches. And what about me? I can't afford this place on my own."

Oops. "I didn't think of that," Abby admitted. "I'll pay the fee so you can get a single. And I'll help you move before I go. I'm sorry, Sarah. I fell in love with the house. There's so much history there. And the ghost—I can't walk away from that. I have to know."

"Know what?" she demanded, arms crossed.

"If it's real."

"Abby." Sarah squeezed her eyes shut and then opened them wide. "I feel like we've known each other long enough for me to tell you that's completely stupid."

Abby studied her shoes and didn't respond right away. Sarah was right, of course. Uprooting her life to become a ghost-hunter? Certifiably nuts.

"Maybe. Probably. I don't know. I need my life to be different. Right now it's the same as it's always been, but with holes."

Sarah held a poker face for several seconds before putting her fingers to her temples, as if to stave off a headache. "This is about your mother. Look, you don't have to go through this alone. I'm sorry my timing was bad. We can—"

"No. It's about filling the holes. Staying alive." She dropped her gaze. "I need a couple more reasons."

"Blah. Fine. Stay alive, then. But you should at least tell my brother you're leaving."

"Why? What do I owe him? He's the last person I need to explain myself to."

"Whatever. He didn't have to give you a reference, you know. And speaking of which, what will you do for money?"

"I have enough to coast for a while." Abby bit her lip. The idea of using up her savings didn't thrill her. "Then I'll get a job, I guess. With Greg's glowing reference."

"All I'm saying is that you should be the one to tell him."

She opened her mouth to protest and exhaled instead. Sarah had agreed to let her out of the lease. Why waste air arguing over Greg? "Fine. I promise I'll call him. Happy?"

Sarah paused. "Yes. Thank you."

Abby retreated to her room, brooding. The words spilled out too fast. She hadn't meant to promise.

Friday, March 16

The weeks leading up to moving day dragged as they vanished. As Abby tried to pack, cancel utilities, and hire movers all in the last few days, she rued the wasted time. She didn't remember moving ever being this hard, but then, Mom always helped her before.

For her part, Aunt Ruby turned out to be a generous negotiator. After she'd agreed to rent the house to Abby, she called back, apologizing that she needed to keep the upstairs back bedroom as storage but could furnish the rest in exchange.

"No one wanted to pay for a storage locker after Pearl died," she lamented. "So there it sits. But the good stuff you could use."

"It's too much." Abby had protested, but without conviction. Sarah crammed their apartment with edgy, minimalist tables, chairs, and shelves, so Abby sold Mom's furniture after the funeral. She owned a bed and a bookcase. Even the desk and swivel chair in her room were loans from Sarah. She needed the items her aunt offered.

"Hush, child. All the furniture's already in the house. I'll have Will bring it down from the upstairs. He's a good boy," she'd said, and because he would be doing so much for her, Abby resolved to let go of their rocky beginning.

Questions about the lease caught Aunt Ruby off-guard. Abby suspected the house sat vacant because her late husband had been the one to handle tenants and rental payments. She promised to put a lease together by the time Abby arrived.

Carte blanche. Exciting. Like jumping out of a plane, only without the threat of imminent death.

In their last chat before moving day, only one subject remained. Each time they talked, Abby expected Aunt Ruby to mention the ghost again, but she never did. At first she accepted the delay, thinking perhaps it would be better to discuss it in person, but she couldn't stand it. As Aunt Ruby's voice took on the wrapping-up tones of farewell, Abby cleared her throat.

"I did have one other question for you." She paced circles around her bedroom. "About the ghost."

"Oh, dear." Aunt Ruby's laugh layered over the murmuring television in the background. "I forgot I tol' you that silly story."

Abby's heart raced. "You didn't tell me the story, though. Not really. I wondered if you would."

The noise undergirding their conversation silenced. She must have muted the TV. Abby waited.

After a too-long break, she offered a too-bright response. "A prankster neighbor boy when I was a young'un. A joke. I shouldn't ever have mentioned it."

Abby stopped pacing. "That's it?"

"That's it. Little rascal, I forgot his name, used to knock on the door and run away. It took us months to catch him."

"It's a cute story. I'll write it down." And she did, in spite of her absolute certainty that Aunt Ruby was lying.

Monday, March 19

"Are you sure more of this stuff isn't yours?" Mounds of boxes surrounded Sarah—things to donate and things to sell and things to keep and things she wouldn't commit to a specific category. "I'm positive this coffee table belongs to you. Plus I saw one I wanted in the IKEA catalog."

Loose hairs tickled Abby's neck. She twisted her sagging ponytail into a bun. Two days deep and her focus ebbed away. She was sick of packing. "Nope. I remember when you bought it. And I thought that catalog was junk mail, so I tore pages out of it to wrap my coffee mugs. Hope you don't mind."

Sarah closed her eyes. "Did I tell you what my fortune cookie said, the night you got back from Georgia? 'You will lose a friend to a thousand paper cuts.' Of course it made no sense at the time."

"You're making that up. And I'm kidding. It's on the bookshelf." Cabinets, drawers, and open boxes yawned across the kitchen. Abby sorted their belongings, divided their lives—an easy job because they shared so little. She had no use for the objects piling high in Sarah's boxes, yet the empty space in her own disturbed her. A stranger could know Sarah by her garlic press, silicone bakeware, and sushi mat. Abby's microwave-safe bowls and ancient aluminum cook pot paid her few compliments.

"You don't actually eat food out of that pot, do you?" Sarah shrouded china figurines in bubble wrap and mummified them with masking tape.

"Usually I stick with convention and put it on a plate first." She wedged it into the box. "Why?"

"It'll leach metal into your food. You need to throw it out."

Abby reached into the cabinet for the cereal bowls. If half her stuff survived the haul, she'd call it a success. "It belonged to my Great-Grandma Blanchard. She used it all the time and lived to be eighty-six."

"She was probably riddled with diseases they hadn't discovered yet." Sarah winced before Abby even registered the comment. "Oh, forget I said that. I'm sorry. Delete."

"It's okay." Such a handy phrase. It let people off the hook. A quick fix. An easy answer.

"Take that orange anodized one. It doesn't match the rest. You can have it."

Abby shrugged and placed the shiny orange pot in her box, nested inside the banged up heirloom. "Thanks. Won't you have a hard time unwrapping those again under all that tape?"

"Maybe." Sarah counted the figurines and sighed out an oath before looking up again. "I talked to my brother last night. Why was he confused when I asked if he planned to help us today?"

"You move from one bad subject to another with style and grace."

Sarah's lips didn't even twitch. "You promised."

Abby opened a new bag of packing peanuts and dumped them over her dishes, assuming they would provide enough cushion and not caring either way. "I figured he'd be busy at work. Last I knew he hadn't hired my replacement yet, so . . ."

"Blah, blah, blah. You're in luck. When I realized he didn't know what I was talking about, I didn't rob you of the privilege of telling him yourself."

She focused her attention on assembling a new box, one to contain the last miscellaneous odds and ends that didn't quite fit under any other label. "Come on. I don't want to end our friendship on a sour note."

Sarah stopped short. "What, you aren't even going to keep in touch?"

The scratching of cardboard and the screech of the tape gun stilled. Abby picked her words. "I didn't mean it like that. Only that we won't see each other all the time."

"Right. Sure." Sarah returned to filling boxes. Eventually she broke the silence with a strange story about meeting a semi-famous chef at the organic grocery, but the conversation stayed stilted for the rest of the night.

Tuesday, March 20

The movers arrived early. They showed up in crisp uniforms, flashing identification and sporting clean-shaven dimpled cheeks. Abby relaxed into the certainty that she was supposed to go. It was all working out too well to doubt it. Buried in the substratum of thoughts without words, she hoped Mom still helped her along.

Sarah tried to give instructions, but the professionals made short work of loading up the truck. She switched gears to making breakfast, a spread of scrambled eggs and sausage she plated as they carried out the last pair of boxes.

"Here." Sarah shoved a tumbler of coffee at Abby. Her voice broke with uncharacteristic huskiness. "You packed yours and I know you didn't sleep well, so take this with you."

"Your favorite mug? No way."

"Consider it a bet we'll see each other again, and sooner than later. Are you sure you can't stay and eat?"

"Too many butterflies. Plus if I don't leave soon, I'll get to sit in Akron's rush hour this morning and Chattanooga's tonight." They hugged, unspoken forgiveness for petty squabbles tendering both ways. "I'll text you when I get there."

She followed the movers out of the apartment, took one last oxygen-deprived ride down the cigarette-stinking elevator, and refused to look back at the building in case Sarah stood in the window waving an awkward goodbye.

The Mustang's engine took an extra second to turn over, and in that second Abby panicked. Not car trouble. Not now. Please.

The old car whined and roared. Clearing her throat on a cold morning. Abby petted the steering wheel. "Don't quit on me today. We'll be in warmer weather soon."

The moving truck flashed its lights, and she gave a thumbs up. She pulled out of the complex parking lot and made for the highway.

She cleared Akron in plenty of time.

The throngs of headlights on the other side of the interstate jolted her more than Sarah's caffeine infusion. While everyone else fought their way into the city, Abby set her cruise control. She meant to take full advantage of the emptiness of the road, including the time to think. She could keep that promise to Sarah if she worked up a plan.

Greg should get out of work around five. By then she'd be halfway through Tennessee. It would be too late to argue about staying. The miles would speak for her resolve. She practiced aloud as she drove. "It's for the best. This is what I've decided. I called to say goodbye."

Minutes before nine, her phone shouted out the specially selected ring tone she applied to all of his numbers. "Danger, Will Robinson, danger." She groaned and checked the display. He called from the office. Rare for him. Mr. Model Employee, making personal calls on company time.

"Hello, Greg." Another mile marker disappeared into the periphery, and with it her idea that the distance would make her case. She wasn't out of Ohio yet. Not even close.

"Abby, hi. Sarah said you needed to talk to me?"

She bit her lip. Their story should have been different. "Yeah. I'm moving away. She thought you should know."

"Oh." How could anyone inject one syllable with so much disappointment? He tempted her to pity him, but Abby steeled herself. "When? I want to help."

"No. I'm literally in the car now, driving to Georgia." She clamped her mouth shut. He didn't need to know where she was going, although it hardly mattered. Sarah would divulge all details.

"Georgia?" A shuffle came over the line, followed by the unmistakable sound of Greg's office door closing. The same sound that heralded the end of her employment at the digital imaging contract firm where he still worked. "Who are you staying with?"

"No one. I found a place. Besides, I have family in the area. I'll be fine."

"Where did this come from? Your life is here in Ohio, with your friends. What about Sarah?" Abby almost hoped he would name himself as a reason to stay. A retort readied itself on her tongue, but he trailed off instead. "Do you need money?"

"I wouldn't take yours if I did." She struggled to preserve the civility a best friend's brother deserved. Like she needed to owe him any favors. "And why the renewed interest, Greg? I thought you finally moved on."

"Ah. This isn't how I wanted to tell you about this." He paused for a long moment. "I've been thinking a lot about spirituality. God. Contentment. Forgiveness."

"And by association of opposites, you thought of me?"

"I can't get any peace over where we left off. I wanted—"

"Please stop telling me what you wanted. If you haven't noticed yet, you can't always get what you want." She scrambled through the script in her head, trying to stick with what she'd planned to say. "I've made my decisions. I only called to say goodbye."

He held his tongue until Abby assumed their connection dropped. She was about to hang up when he spoke. "I called you, remember?" The line went dead.

Abby lost the movers long before the Kentucky state line. She risked the speeding ticket for the freedom of whipping down the interstate toward the southern roots she'd never before acknowledged. For better or worse, the hard conversations were behind her. She soothed herself that she was running *to*, not from. She chose this. An adventure. Only when she worked her way back around to the arguments she planned for Greg did she click on the radio and banish all thought.

CHAPTER 8

KENNESAW

Will sat on the porch steps of the house, face cupped in his hands and elbows propped on his knees. Dusk drew inky shadows under the cover of the trees along Pike's Landing Road, though the headlights of passing cars frequently cut the gloom. Main Street traffic buzzed at the corner intersection, and the clangor and screech of the trains eclipsed the anxious song of cicadas. Evening had fallen.

Finally one set of headlights stopped in front of the house, idling for a moment, then vanishing into the darkness. Will lifted his hand in greeting and rose to his feet, but Abby's eyes hadn't yet adjusted. She got out of the car without speaking to him, groaning as she stretched out besides the compact little car. He meant to call out to her, to welcome her, and yet seconds passed in silence. The resemblance struck him before, of course, but this view of her profile in the low light knotted a lonely ache deep in his gut. He indulged in the illusion for a long, guilty moment before clearing his throat to speak. "Glad you made it down safe."

Abby jumped. "Who's there? Oh, Will. I didn't see you. Tell me you haven't been waiting long."

He tossed the keys up and caught them. "I don't mind. It's peaceful out. Where's the moving truck? I'll help you unload."

"An hour or two behind me, I think. All I have with me are clothes and my laptop."

"I'll wait."

"You don't have to stay. I'm paying those movers good money. They can earn it as far as I'm concerned."

He stared hard into her face. She gave a small laugh and looked away. A joke. She was kidding. Will tried to smile. "Then let's go inside and get your lease signed. Care to do the honors?" He tossed the key ring and she grabbed it out of the air. "Good catch."

She jingled the keys. "You said before the lock sticks?"

"I'm guessing it'll limber up with use. Needs jimmying is all."

The lock resisted the key entirely at first. Abby tried forcing it, to no avail.

"Be easy," Will advised. "When it's lined up right it'll fit, but jamming it strips the lock over time. There, you see? Now the trick is to give it a jiggle in the last quarter-turn."

"Very scientific." The wry remark didn't mask her obvious pleasure when the tumblers aligned and the knob turned on the second try. "Aha. Success."

They stepped into the house. Will flicked on a light switch and almost bumped into Abby as she froze in the doorway.

Awe. Wonder. The inner space threw its arms open for her. *Come in,* it whispered. Abby hung back to see if the sighed welcome would repeat. It did not.

She found her voice. "You did all this for me?"

Will shuffled his feet. "Mrs. Watts wanted it done."

The room had been transformed. The walls shone a butter yellow that brightened the kitchen as if painted with sunlight. A long pine farm table encircled by six chairs filled the dining room. The dark cabinets remained, no longer out of place with the crown molding stained the same deep cherry color. The mixed wood styles looked charmingly mismatched, rather than simply uncoordinated. Even the ceiling was whiter than she remembered.

"How did you fix the water stains?"

"They're only covered up. I didn't replace any drywall. Not that it couldn't use patching."

She ran her hand over the tabletop. "And you carried all this from upstairs?"

The edge of his lip curled. "Your uncle helped some."

Sensing she touched a nerve, Abby switched tacks. "Thank you. I feel so incredibly welcome. It's beautiful."

"You ain't even seen the rest. Come on." His eagerness spilled over and washed up around her. She followed him into the parlor bedroom, excited in spite of her exhaustion.

The smaller room reeked of fresh paint. An antique oak-framed loveseat, upholstered with light green brocade and accented with amethyst-colored patterns, picked up the lavender shade of the walls. In the corner, a narrow oak dresser faced out at an angle. The furniture reduced the available space in the room, but her bed would just fit in the opposite corner. She drank in the cozy mental picture.

"I used purple in here on account of the sofa. Mrs. Watts said yellow wouldn't have done much for it. I don't know about decorating, but that was her mama's prize piece once upon a time."

She touched the stiff, prim cushioning. "It looks like no one has ever sat on it."

"You're pretty much right. Ain't worth much if it never gets used, though. You can't hurt it. Don't think you can't put your feet up."

Abby wasn't so sure. "How old is it?"

"Couldn't tell you. Old." He edged out of the room and waved her along. "The rest is more modern. Not by much, though."

"Show me." Will's energy gave her a boost, a temporary balm for the ever-present drag in her limbs. She followed him down the narrow hallway to a comfortable living room. A tweed couch against the wall was set off on two sides by claw-footed end tables and matching brass lamps. In the far corner, a squat brown leather chair with squared edges completed the room.

In spite of the beckoning whisper, her idea of how a haunted house should look folded in on itself. Will showed off a place that was dated and kitschy, but altogether normal. The ghost would be flattened and trapped beneath the layers of paint. She shivered. "I didn't expect any of this. It's perfect."

"Don't let looks fool you. It's far from perfect." He started cracking his knuckles but stopped when she winced. "I don't think Mrs. Watts understands how rundown it's gotten."

Abby touched the glossy wall, half-expecting to smudge paint onto her fingertips, and pretended not to notice him watching her with those same long stares as before. He didn't make any sense. All this work because of her, and yet he radiated discomfort, almost as if he hoped she might still change her mind and head back to Ohio. "What do you do besides work for my aunt?"

He avoided her eyes. "That's all, and that's plenty. She keeps me busy."

"And she pays you enough to live on?"

As soon as the words escaped her mouth, she regretted them. People back home either answered a question or told the asker to back off, but Will dangled by his good manners, helpless. "What can I say? I'm a simple man. What about you? Got a job lined up?"

"Not so far." She licked her dry lips. "But I'm not stressing. I'll find one."

"What are you lookin' for?"

Was he paying her back for prying? No. He wasn't the type. If innocent questions sounded like existential quandaries, she had herself to blame. What *was* she looking for? Something impossible? "I'm a researcher."

He raised one eyebrow. Sarah would have been jealous. "What kind of research?"

"All kinds." Billing inquiries. Old draft orders. Self-proclaimed simple men. "Mostly historical."

"You'll like Kennesaw, then. Maybe you can get hired on at the college or the museum."

"Thanks for the ideas. I haven't seen much of the town yet, but I won't want for a sense of yesterday living here. This house is a time capsule."

"Or was 'til I went and wrecked it." Nonetheless he stood even taller with his thumbs hooked through his belt loops. "But I only got finished with the first floor. You should see the upstairs room before you sign the lease, right? Come on."

"I'd be well and truly out of luck if I changed my mind now, but lead the way." She trailed behind him up the narrow staircase.

The front bedroom housed all the gloom Will had chased from the rest of the house and then some. Abby surveyed the room, sobered at its grim walls that lost what might once have been a pretty shade of blue to a dull, decaying gray. Fragile paper blinds with bamboo ribs hung at the window, the rosy orange glow of street lamps illuminating the edges. The patterns in the dust told her the furniture had come from here, where squared pockets of cleanliness interrupted the blankets of fuzz. Other pieces remained, and she could make out the shapes beneath the dingy sheets draped over them—headboards and footboards against the wall, two wing chairs in the middle of the room. The only one she couldn't identify was a tallish blocky shape in the corner.

Will leaned against the doorframe in an oddly familiar way. "This here's the time capsule, for now at least."

A train whistle blew. Were the tracks visible from the window? She crossed the room to look out, her footsteps loud and crude upon the hardwood. She tugged the cord on the blinds, but the wall mount loosened and the whole apparatus came crashing down. Abby let out a shriek and jumped back.

"You all right?"

"I'm fine." If the wall mount bashed in her head, she still would have said so. "I didn't mean to . . . sorry. I'll—"

"Leave it. It needs replaced anyhow."

She covered her face with her hands. The stale scent of the twine cord clung to her fingers. "Good times. I approve of the upstairs and you have a lease for me to sign."

"Yes'm, I do." Amused or annoyed? His tone didn't tell her. A case could be made either way.

They returned to the kitchen. The sheets lay on the counter. Were they already there when she came in, or had he produced them? She couldn't remember.

She read the sparse document, laughing to herself at how it compared with the complex apartment lease she'd broken days before. Aunt Ruby had typed up two copies of the agreement, affixing her wobbly signature to each. She required Abby to park on the street and not the grass, and she prohibited entrance to the back bedroom, leaving candles unattended, and allowing male visitors to stay overnight. Not counting ghosts, she assumed.

Even more curious was the final paragraph, set off by a line break even though it consisted of a single gangly sentence. Abby read aloud to get the sense of it. "'Rent payable by cash or check in person or by mail is due the first of the month unless it's a Sunday and then the second, and payments don't count toward any past or future debts.'" She checked

Will's face for signs of trickery. "Is she serious?"

Will looked to the ceiling, as if for strength. "There's no tellin' with her."

Abby read the lease one more time, as if she had the luxury of refusing or Will the power to alter the terms. What could she do but sign? Night had fallen, the movers would arrive any time, and it would be a long search for the next friendly face if she made an enemy of her aunt.

It wouldn't stand up in court, if it ever came down to the question, and what debts did Abby have with her? "She drives a hard bargain." Abby winked and she signed her name to each sheet. "There. A done deal."

He picked up one copy. "Keep the other. I'll take this back to Mrs. Watts." He lingered. "Guess that's everything."

Abby opened her eyes wide and leaned inward. He wasn't bad-looking, not at all. "Will?"

"Do you want to go to church with us next Sunday?" Abby took a step backward as he rushed on with his invitation. "Mrs. Watts goes to the Baptist church. The one I told you? I take her—or, she takes me since she won't give up driving, but either way, most Sundays, whenever she feels up to it. I know she'd like it, we both would, if you—"

"Oh, no. I wouldn't want to impose. You guys probably have a set routine."

"Wouldn't be any trouble to stop and pick you up on the way. Fair warning though—she drives like a fiend. We could meet you out front of the church instead if you wanted to walk there."

"Will, all this," she said, waving around, "really is enough. I've never felt more welcomed. I owe you, and I don't say that lightly."

"I'm not keepin' track."

"What I mean is, I don't want to feel like a burden."

"All the more reason to come. Jesus loves when we bring Him our burdens."

She bristled. "I'm no churchgoer, okay? It's not for me," she said, louder than she intended. "My mom gave it a try, and that was enough for our family."

"Why? What did she think?"

"I forgot to ask her before she died." Abby's stomach lurched even as the words escaped. Mom's death worked as a shield often enough, but never before had she brandished it as a weapon.

"I'm sorry." His voice hit that low tone, same as almost everyone else. The Death voice. "I'll be praying for you."

She huffed out a short breath. "Don't waste your time." Too much, but her lips wouldn't form an apology.

"I got it to waste for now." He backed toward the door. "But you've had a long day. If you need any help—"

"I won't."

"Let your aunt know," he said at the same time, and she blushed. "G'night." He let himself out. The old lock clicked behind him.

Left to her self-imposed exile, Abby still didn't feel alone. The mood hung around like a sour smoke, an extra presence gnawing at her conscience. Chasing after Will meant apologizing, and she couldn't offer a real one. Not yet. She tested the words aloud as proof. "Thanks for the invite. I'm still not accepting it, but I'm sorry for playing the pity card. Let's be friends."

She picked up the lease and studied her aunt's signature beside her own. Will might not have been the one asking. For all she knew, Aunt Ruby could have told him to extend the invitation. Did it make a difference?

No.

Cuyahoga Mission Church gave Mom a handful of new friends and a place to share updates on failed procedures and treatments. The pharmacist filled the medical prescriptions and the church filled the spiritual ones, and both came to the same results. Hadn't Abby humored her with attendance on Sundays? And uttered all-thumbs prayers for healing over and over again, without a crumb of evidence that anyone heard them? Abby's upbringing had presumed only a casual indifference to religion, and so her antagonism ran exactly as deep as the demonstrated failings of her mother's new faith. Suzanne Blanchard-Wells went hardcore for Jesus, and died anyway.

None of which was Will's fault. He trampled her bruises in trying to welcome her, and she lashed out.

She stepped out on the porch and called into the darkness. "Will?"

The night swelled with the song of crickets, and a siren wailed close by, but Will didn't answer. She couldn't make out his shape in the darkness, and then all shapes dissolved in a blinding bright white. Ghosts? Angels?

A telescopic tunnel to Paradise?

Hardly. High beams. The moving truck had arrived.

CHAPTER 9

Wednesday, March 21

The persistent chirp of her dying cell phone annoyed Abby off the couch. She rubbed her face while checking the messages. The tweed left a crisscross impression on her cheek. At a quarter of two in the morning, Sarah had texted her a string of question marks.

Cursing, she remembered her offhanded promise to check in. She tapped a short note back. "Here. Safe. Exhausted."

In seconds, Sarah's response buzzed into her hand. "ur alive!! Told Greg the ghosty got u."

That Sarah. She wouldn't quit. Abby fired back. "Come visit if you're not chicken. Don't bring Greg." The low battery indicator blinked its last-chance warning, so she found an outlet in the kitchen.

Her throat hurt. She ran water into her cupped hand to gargle and gagged on the coppery taste. Later she'd make a trip to the hardware store for a water filter. Better start a list.

Stacks of boxes lined the wall where the movers had left them, most marked but some not, hiding pieces of her life waiting to be exhumed. No coffee until she found the box labeled "Open Me First."

She passed the day emptying the cartons, but by early afternoon uneasy flutters breathed against her ribs. At first she took them for hunger pangs and paused to eat the emergency granola bar packed in a pocket of her purse, but it only turned the flutters to mild, ominous nausea. Abby braced herself against the kitchen counter and closed her eyes, but her head spun until she opened them. Paint fumes. She took a break on the porch steps. The open air helped, but not as much as she wished it would.

The boxes dwindled out of sight as the house swallowed signs of her presence. What cluttered a two-bedroom apartment failed to even stake the cavernous rooms as hers. The eager welcome feeling shifted to a sense of being overshadowed. Consumed, even.

Abby forced a short laugh. "Right. Because if a house could get hungry, what else would it eat besides Ohioans?"

By the time the honey light of afternoon streamed through the blinds, she'd finished bundling packing peanuts in garbage bags and breaking down cartons for recycling. Decision fatigue set in—Mr. Coffee to the right of the sink, extra bed linens on the top shelf of her closet, her photo albums on the living room end table, then the kitchen cupboard, then her nightstand—but movement held the dizziness and nausea at bay. She didn't know where to put Sarah's orange anodized pot, so she placed it on the cold stove top and decided not to decide. Best to save her last bit of energy for the final row of boxes. The hard ones.

They cradled the mélange of papers from Mom's house, miscellany that still wanted sorting. Old pay stubs and income tax filings, college tuition statements, Mom's diploma and professional certifications, to say nothing of all the nonsense from the hospital, funeral director, and estate attorney. Foolish to drag the assortment of files halfway across the country, but dumping them sight-unseen didn't work for her either. Ninety percent of the papers belonged nowhere but a landfill. The other ten percent were treasure. Some to unearth, the rest to bury.

No rush.

Aunt Ruby's letter to Mom had been inside Box One. So far it was the only item she had removed. The family tree, meeting Aunt Ruby, the ghost hunt—all of it helped maintain her grip on Mom, the parts of her that still existed. Shared connections, feelings, memories. And maybe her soul.

She perched on the tweed couch, its firm cushions correcting her posture like a tight-lipped matron, and tried to decide what to do with the files. Though chemotherapy robbed Mom of the strength to weed out the contents herself, she'd still made it as easy as it could ever be by boxing them up. Abby could afford to put them away.

Like a time capsule. Of course.

Not an ideal solution, not as long as the upstairs bedroom still awaited its facelift, but the idea clicked into place with a sense of poetic justice. All the unfinished business should rest together in one uneasy tomb.

She hunted around the bottom of the staircase for a light switch and, not finding one, looked for a fixture above. In the shadowy corner of the landing, the murky figure of a man stood still and silent, watching her.

She staggered backwards against the wall at the foot of the stairs. "Who—" she called, but the figure vanished when she blinked, blending into the shadows. She couldn't swear she saw anything at all.

"Come on, Abby. You can't find a ghost if you're going to jump at shadows. Either go check it out or cart yourself back to Ohio."

She hefted the nearest file box and marched to the second story, balancing it on her hip while she paused at the landing. A gnarly cobweb trailed down from the ceiling, coalescing with the shadows. "See there? Mystery solved."

One by one, she carried the boxes up to the front bedroom. When the last of the five filled the vacant corner, she circled the room, examining each draped bogey, every shape and shadow, even the feather-light dust bunnies gathered in the corners, and committing them to memory. If they shifted, she would know.

The second floor did not want to swallow her. If the room hosted any vibration or imprint, it was one of indifference. The upstairs front bedroom only echoed her own footsteps back to her, stinking of must and ennui. The room didn't want her there.

She stiffened with a cold crawl that seized her unexpectedly. A response. Where was the stimulus?

Rubbing her arms briskly, she spoke, trying to sound sure of herself. "Aunt Ruby says you're a knocker. Is that true? Knock once to say yes."

Disinterested silence.

She sauntered across the room, hands on her hips. "I guess it doesn't matter. I don't even believe you exist." She let the challenge hang in the air, but if the ghost heard, it remained unimpressed. "Look, I'm here for evidence, not to psych myself out with cobwebs and creaking stairs. If you're real, fine. Haunt me. I want to be convinced."

Maybe, but what she wanted was never a factor, was it? Her approach was all wrong. The ghost didn't need to prove itself.

The remaining furniture circled her, wearing the dirty white sheets like lame Halloween spooks. She glared back. "You won't mind if I out the imposters, will you?" She snatched the makeshift drop cloths. Swirls of dust danced through the air. She sneezed, then snapped the last sheet from the awkward mass in the corner.

Her tantrum revealed a roll-top letter desk. She ran her fingers across the smooth oak finish of the privacy shield damming up dingy papers edging out from underneath. Before Mom's cancer diagnosis, before the humiliating way she lost her job, ferreting out old documents had been one of her greatest pleasures. That tempting, seasoned shade of yellow bid Abby to pluck Aunt Ruby's letter out of the jumble of Mom's papers in the first place. The pages peeking out of the desk teased and hinted that discovery could be hers again.

Her rampage forgotten, Abby dropped the pile of sheets. "Knock once for 'keep out,'" she called. Fair warning. She grasped the desk's handles and tried to roll back the shield.

It didn't budge.

"Okay. I get it. The shield sticks, same as the lock on the front door." Shimmying it up and down won her less than an inch of play. The desk's contents probably blocked the roller apparatus in the back. "And if I tip it forward, whatever it is will shift to the front and make room for the shield to roll back like it's supposed to. Should I risk it? Why yes, I think I should."

Abby attempted to lift the back of the desk off its legs to tilt it. Too heavy. She could almost hear Will's voice taunting, "Built to last."

"All right, all right." She gathered the sheets she'd dropped on the floor and recovered the furniture, pausing once for a sneezing fit. Maybe she'd wash the sheets later. All this dust flying around couldn't be healthy. As for the ghost, whether he had taken up residence in the front bedroom or not, the head-on approach failed. She needed a strategy. "I know when I'm beat. You win this round."

She sneezed again as she descended the stairs.

CHAPTER 10

Friday, March 23

A loud knock startled Ruby clean out of a perfectly good afternoon nap. These Meals on Wheels volunteers beat on her door like she missed the Lord's Trumpet. As if they were so far behind her. Let the one with no bifocals cast the first stone—but never mind. Next time one of them tried to bust down her door, she'd complain. "Leave it on the porch," she yelled. "I ain't decent."

That sure stopped the knocker cold, but a timid voice followed. "Aunt Ruby?"

She rousted herself out of the chair and answered the door. Poor Abby stood on the porch, rubbing her knuckles. "Goodness sakes, child, come in. I figured you was my Meals on Wheels."

"I'm sorry I didn't call first. I thought you'd like some company. And actually, I have an ulterior motive." All this before she even closed the door behind her. "If it's not too much trouble, can I look through the old photos and papers again?"

Ruby blinked a few times. Direct, wasn't she? Even for a Yankee. "Will took all that back up to the attic weeks ago."

"I can climb up there and get the boxes. I don't mind."

Persistent too. "Not today. Better to live in the present, I say. It's all you ever have. But maybe another time."

Her smile took on a plastic quality. "Maybe. That'd be great."

"I'd hate to ask him to haul them boxes again so soon."

"Yeah, don't do that." Abby ran her hands over her hips as if looking for pockets her slacks didn't have. "Forget I asked."

"Stay and visit a while. Do you want some sweet tea?"

"No—I mean, yes. I'll get it though. Don't go to the trouble."

Ruby shrugged. "Might be a splash of lemonade left too."

While Abby disappeared into the kitchen, Ruby slipped away into her crowded little bedroom. No sense letting this visit go to waste. She pulled her nicest beach tote out of the closet, the vinyl one with pink and orange flowers. She liked it a bit much to give away, but when would she go to the beach again? Not in this life. She upturned it. Sand sprinkled into the carpet. Hilton Head Island, probably, or maybe Tybee.

If she'd known Abby might drop by unannounced, she would've been ready. Then again, maybe this way was better. At least the mess in her room gave her plenty of options for goodies to fill the tote. She pulled a stopped owl clock off the wall and set it on the bed while she took out an old pair of pillowcases to wrap it. A glass ring tray she bought at a yard sale a fistful of years ago. A music box with the ballerina figure missing.

What else? Abby would have that drink poured by now. Ruby took Pearl and Jim's silver-framed anniversary portrait off the dresser and slid it into the bag. She had promised it to Audrey. Abby might as well have it.

Ruby disliked candles and almost tossed in a lavender-scented one she received a few Christmases ago, but thought better of it. Why prompt the girl to burn the house down? She should have outlawed candles in the lease—or did she? Oh well. The tote was half-full. Good enough. Only one more item to add. She slid the ledger out of its hiding spot and planted it into the bag behind the frame. That nosy girl would dig right in.

When Ruby trudged back to the living room, Abby was inspecting the trinkets on top of the TV. Little porcelain pigs and painted mice circled around her and John's last portrait taken for the church directory. Upstaging them all was a Betty Boop figurine sporting her signature pout and a butterfly clip above her ear, her long black dress flaring out at the bottom with saucy red and pink hibiscus blossoms on the skirt.

"I have a present for you." She shouted it, the way her friends did when they took out their hearing aids.

Abby jumped, and for an instant Ruby worried she'd knock over

Betty. "Oh, you snuck up on me. I like your collection."

"That?" Ruby waved her free hand. "The older I get, the more junk piles up, and me with no kids to farm it out to."

She grimaced. "I have the opposite problem. I inherited all Mom's stuff, but that house is huge. I finished unpacking, but you could hardly tell anyone lives there."

"Good thing I have you a housewarming gift. No reason for a grandniece of mine to be doing without. Here." She passed the tote to Abby.

"I wasn't expecting—"

"Of course you wasn't. That's why it's a surprise. Now go sit yourself down and take a look."

Ruby took her own advice and settled into her armchair. To her credit, Abby's face remained in a pleasantly neutral position as she poked through the bag. "This clock is so interesting."

"It takes a nine-volt. I don't have an extra. Sorry."

She whipped the pillowcases, and the white-on-white monogram unfurled. Ruby swallowed hard.

Abby stared. "S?"

"Found it at a thrift store. Looks like an A to me."

"I could see that. Yeah. Right here." Abby traced the initial with her finger. As the girl laid the pillowcases aside, Ruby took off her glasses and rubbed her eyes. She hadn't been paying attention.

Though she expected the girl to fawn and fuss over the portrait, Abby studied it instead. "My grandparents?" At Ruby's nod, she touched the glass-covered faces. "Thank you."

"Don't mention it."

At last she withdrew the ledger from the tote. She fanned the pages and looked up in confusion. "What's this?"

"Mercy." She let a hand flutter at her chest as if scandalized. "How'd that get in there?" She made no move to retrieve the book.

To her dismay, Abby simply hopped up off the couch and laid it on her TV tray. On top of her Bible, no less. Ruby picked up the ledger and thumbed through it. "I've got a bad habit, you know, of sticking papers in books for safekeeping and losing them. Oh me, what did you find in there?"

"It looked like a list of accounts. Probably important stuff. But thank you for the gifts." Abby leaned over her chair and tried to hug her, though she couldn't get her arms around and the angle was bad.

"I suppose most folks your age would rather have money—"

"Not me. I love mementos. I'll always think of you whenever I see them. Besides, my mom—" Her voice caught. She paused and began again. "Money's not a concern. Not yet."

Ruby listened, but Abby clammed up on the subject. She picked up the anniversary portrait again. Pearl and Jim immortalized in the funny faded colors of the day, holding hands and poised to kiss, their white cake decked with silver bells and a big '25' before them. Ruby took the picture herself. As it happened, she took all the pictures that day, which explained why she wasn't in a one of them.

A sharp pain stabbed between her breasts, either conscience or heartburn. "Try not to think bad on her."

Abby lowered the frame, question marks in her eyes. "What do you mean?"

"For not being a grandmother to you before she died. Pearl didn't agree with Richard marryin' your mother. Wouldn't give them any help. And I reckon she was right. Look how it turned out." The clink of melting ice shifting punctuated the silence. Abby hadn't touched her drink; now she took a measured sip before speaking.

"I see. That's fine. I never missed her. And I've tried to let my mother's private life remain her own." Proud words, stiff words. As Abby wrapped the portrait with one of the pillowcases, Ruby debated whether to believe 'em.

"She always was a daddy's girl. Your granny, I mean."

Abby's eyes flashed. "Is he the ghost, then? Your father?"

"There ain't—"

"You said there was. You called it a 'real haunted house.' So which is it?"

Ruby smoothed the creases from her pink Bermuda shorts and looked down her blue-marbled legs. Like moldy cheese, gone old and funny. Lord, have mercy.

"You listen here. I loved my daddy, but he had as many faults as anyone. It so happens he didn't think much of anybody from too far north of Kentucky."

"Why not?"

Ruby met Abby's eyes. "They don't teach the Civil War in school up there in Ohio?"

"Oh. Sure, they do. But your father couldn't have been old enough—"

"He wasn't, but that don't matter. He had his reasons."

"The Civil War was a reason?" Abby's eyes flashed. "You're telling me he believed in slavery?"

"Where'd I say that? This family never owned any slaves. Suffered every bit as much as them that did, though."

"None of which was my mother's fault."

"I know that, but Pearl—" She cut herself off, remembering words she didn't want to repeat. "Eh, the point is, Pearl did what she always done and kept to Daddy's rules. And when your parents came to me and John, I did what I always done and broke 'em."

"Mom never mentioned any of this to me."

"Truth has a way of coming out after people pass on." The pain in her chest flared again.

"I don't want to know. If she didn't tell me herself . . . I need to go."

Ruby plucked the remote from her TV tray and flipped the channels. "Don't run off, child. The Weekday Picture Show comes on next. A classic film-a-day. I never miss. Stay and watch with me."

Abby hesitated, then a little pinch twitched around her eyes. "Maybe another time." She gestured at the tote bag. For the first time, Ruby noticed the washed out colors, the loose threads where the strap attached. "Thanks again."

"You're welcome. You can put your glass in the sink. I'll wash it later. And speaking of washing, you might not want to run those pillowcases through the washing machine." Ruby found the channel she wanted and laid the remote aside. "I'd be willing to bet they were embroidered by hand."

Abby fiddled around in the kitchen, probably washing her drinking glass, and let herself out with a too-cheery goodbye. What a disaster. Ruby should've waited.

For whatever reason, the classics channel was on a streak of playing Technicolor pictures around lunch time. All Ruby's favorites from the olden days were in color. Those bright, beautiful scenes broke her heart, even still.

The wheezy hum of the mail truck pulling away caught her ear. The extra large digital display on her table clock gave her five minutes, which meant she really had ten. Time enough to check the mail. Tempting as it was to let Will bring it in, she didn't like for him to see when her checks came. It left her feeling the need to explain, though he never said a word about money. He hardly said a word about anything, bless his heart.

Her house shoes wouldn't hold up against all the rain they'd had, so she changed them for Audrey's tennis shoes. That lime green color didn't much appeal to her, but oh well. They fit all right and kept her feet dry.

She stepped out and squinted. A perfect, cloudless day greeted her, not a puddle in sight. Sunny and warm. Didn't make sense. It'd been raining for the better part of a week, and cold besides. Hadn't it?

She trekked out to the mailbox, but the contents hardly proved worth the trip. She didn't need her glasses to work out what all came, either. Three bills, two advertisers, no checks.

"Ought to've come today." Had she gotten it already? She remembered opening her last one, but the time since felt fuzzy and thick. A week or a month? Or did she finally set up that direct deposit? Maybe she should call the bank. "Never mind. It'll get here when it gets here."

She sized up the return trip, still stinging with disappointment. Mercy, when did walking down her driveway and back turn into such a production? A yellow square stuck on her front door barely garnered notice. Probably some foolishness from the Meals on Wheels people.

No, it couldn't be. She recognized it from the deck of notepaper in her own kitchen. Though it'd been years since she read a page at the end of her outstretched arm without her glasses, from three feet away she could make it out. Like the paper, the handwriting was familiar.

Will—

About the other night . . . If you have time later, come by the house. Need your # too.

Abby

"Sneaky." Ruby peeled it off the door. She rubbed the adhesive residue with her thumb until it disappeared. The girl wanted to talk to Will, did she?

Once inside, she slipped off the ridiculous tennis shoes by the door, stuck Abby's note to one of the advertisers, and dropped it and the rest of the mail on the kitchen island. The opening swell of music floated in from the television. Returning to the living room, Ruby squinted at the screen and sighed at the gray blur. There went the streak. She retrieved her glasses from her tray table in time to catch the title card of the movie. *Meet John Doe.*

Humph. Even with her glasses, swashy gray films weren't much worth watching, and she didn't care for that one in particular, as a matter of fact. Funny, keen as she'd been to see it in the theater when it first released. One more reminder from that horrible, golden year. How was it that she couldn't remember the past week with any certainty, yet a seventy-year-old movie could spark flashes so real and true she'd almost swear she could touch them?

She clicked off the TV and hid the ledger in her room. Maybe she preferred the past after all. She could forget the glasses, close her weary eyes, and see it clearly, in the fullness of its color.

Friday, January 23, 1942

A gentle tapping, and boy, hadn't she been waiting for it! Ruby bounded to the door and nearly laid a kiss square on her sister's lips. "Ew, Pearl, since when do you knock?"

Pearl stepped inside with her handbag slung over her wrist, a folded newspaper under her arm, and that dopey superior expression on her face. She left the door ajar. "My key's stuck in the lock again. A better question," she teased, a sing-song in her voice, "is who you meant to point that kisser at?"

Ruby crossed her arms. "I'll kiss whoever I want. It's my birthday, in case you forgot."

Mama harrumphed from the kitchen. "As if you'd let anyone forget. Don't get too full of yourself to wash these lunch plates."

"Mama," Ruby complained. Pearl stuck out her tongue.

"That's enough, both of you."

Ruby stepped around to the other side of the dinner table, putting more distance between herself and the sink. "Pearl, you wash 'em. That can be your birthday present for me."

Her sister smirked. "Too late, Rue. This here's your gift from me." She spread out the newspaper on the table, and the headlines above the fold screamed. "BELL SELECTS MARIETTA FOR BOMBER FACTORY."

Ruby scanned the opening sentences. "Gee, thanks, but I don't think I need an airplane factory."

"The paper, silly. Everyone knows how you like to keep up with goings-on in Marietta. I'm surprised you didn't get the scoop already." So smug. "They're saying once the new plant is built, it'll bring maybe sixty thousand jobs to this county. Two-thirds women."

"What's all this ruckus?" Daddy strode into the kitchen from the back of the house, smelling of soap and rail grease. "Happy birthday, Peanut."

"Thanks, Daddy. What do you think? Hang it up on the railroad and move to Marietta?" The idea of living in the city excited Ruby worlds more than wasting her life in this hick town. The old-timers still called it "Big Shanty." How embarrassing.

He scooped up the newspaper and read the first few paragraphs of the story with a deep scowl that didn't suit him, then tossed it back down on the table with disdain. "I ain't workin' for no Buffalo man."

"Huh? Where'd you see that?"

"Says right here." He thumped a big calloused finger to the page. "That Larry Bell came from Buffalo, New York. Some nerve he's got, bringing his big plans down here."

Mama set the plates down on the table. "Gil . . . "

"As if a foreign war on two fronts wasn't enough, they want another war between the States."

"Daddy, look at all the jobs it'll bring. We're all on the same side now," Ruby protested, but her father leveled the room with his authority.

"Sure, 'til the fightin's over. They'll board up the factory and that Larry Bell'll laugh all the way to his Yankee bank." He thumped the page again. "And women don't belong workin' in a bomber plant no-how. I don't mind you girls helping out at the hospital and the telephone company, but no daughter of mine'll be workin' a factory job."

"Yes, Daddy," Pearl said. Ruby kept what she hoped was an agreeable silence. "I only brought it because there's a big to-do about it."

"They should have held off 'til after my birthday." Ruby crossed her arms. "I don't want my party ruined by a dumb ol' factory." She checked Daddy's expression. He looked pleased with her choice of words.

"What's this I hear about a party?"

"Christie!" Tensions forgotten, Ruby threw herself into the hat-rack of a man lingering at the threshold, ignoring admonishments from around the room.

He brought in the cold. A chill raced over her skin as his breath tickled her earlobe. "Happy birthday, pretty lady."

Mama cut the greeting short. "Ruby Rae, I done told you. Now you can wash dishes in front of your beau."

"On my birthday?" she whined, but Christie surprised her by joining Mama's chiding.

"I'll help if you like." A faded Irish accent gilded his words, an inheritance from his mother that came out at odd times. "I don't think you'd rather do them later."

"Why, what's later?"

"You'll see." The crinkles beside his eyes told her not to argue.

While the two of them washed and dried, Pearl set the table and Mama finished up supper preparations. Daddy sat at the head of the table, smoking and reading the rest of the report about the Bell Bomber plant.

"I tell you, Velma, this galls me to no end."

"Gil, we're fixin' to eat." Mama whisked his ashtray away.

"Carpetbaggers." He chased her across the room to stub out his cigarette. "They think we've forgotten."

He let it go long enough to ask the blessing, but the supper conversation camped on the new aircraft plant, and though Ruby wanted to hear more, she didn't like that the news came at the expense of her celebration. Especially not with Daddy treating it like Sherman's March to the Sea. After a while, she stopped trying to redirect the conversation and fell quiet, listening. Daddy dug in his heels, dead-set against the plant, and Mama predicted Marietta would run out of housing for all the employees. Christie joked that they'd have to build it out of recycled soup cans, sidestepping the need to voice an opinion on the matter. Pearl chanced to wonder aloud what the pay would be, drawing Daddy's ire again over this new Yankee invasion.

But think of all those jobs. Daddy was wrong. Larry Bell and his bomber plant would at last bring the good life to their boll weevil-eaten county. Hope, not devastation.

"One traitor did enough to wreck this family," he said. "It's only the grace of God that we got back on track." Sure as shootin', that signaled the conversation's end.

"Thanks for supper, Mrs. Hart." Christie tottered on the edge of his chair, ready to bolt. "Nobody roasts a chicken like you do."

Mama allowed him a rare smile. "Don't run off so quick. We still have cake."

"Yes'm." He looked no less primed for flight. From the corner of her eye, Ruby saw Daddy wink, but before she could comment, Pearl cut off the light switch and Mama set a single-layer chocolate birthday cake on the table before Ruby, an extravagant use of their sugar supply with rumors of rationing on the horizon. Nine candles broken into halves flickered to mark her eighteen years.

"Sing fast, before them stubby candles melt into the cake," Mama ordered. Ruby watched the red wax rolling while they sang. She blew out the candles and realized too late she'd forgotten to make a wish.

While Mama sent plates of cake around the table with military efficacy, Daddy stepped into the parlor, a room where he normally had no business, and returned with a box wrapped with newsprint.

"Aw, Daddy." Ruby reached out her hands, but he placed the box on the table, his face solemn.

"Don't shake it. Or drop it. This is from your Mama and me."

Ruby tore the paper an inch at a time, like the package contained a keg of gunpowder. She lifted the cardboard lid and her eyes bulged at the contents of the box. She wasn't far off.

Nestled among familiar rags lay an antique long-nosed revolver.

Mama hovered. "I'll need them dishtowels back."

"What is it?" Christie said, but Pearl sat back in her chair with a knowing look on her face.

"It's one of Grandfather's pistols. They gave me the other one when I turned eighteen."

"My mother gave 'em to me," Daddy corrected her, and Pearl blushed.

Ruby was afraid to touch it. "Daddy, why?"

"You two might not always have your old dad around to look out for you," he said gruffly, and Ruby looked up with alarm.

76

"You ain't—what's wrong?"

"No, no. Didn't mean to give you the wrong idea. But I'll sleep better knowing both my girls can handle a weapon."

"Thanks, Daddy. You don't have to worry so much, though. I have Christie to watch out for me."

Pearl got up from the table with her empty plate, finished with cake and festivities. "Yeah? And who's gonna look out for him?"

"The Good Lord," Christie answered. Everyone laughed except Ruby.

"I reckon that's right, son." Daddy looped his thumbs through the straps of his overalls as if noticing he carried the scent of smoke and grease in his clothes. "Whew, what a long day. And a long week. Think I'll wash up and turn in."

"This early?" Disappointment needled. The plant dominated the talk for most of her little soiree, and now it was over. Mama cleared away the dishes and the cake, and the celebration faded like so much gun smoke.

"Too much excitement for an old man." Ruby kept from rolling her eyes, although she noticed Mama didn't similarly restrain herself.

"Good night, Daddy." She gave her father a kiss on the cheek and turned to Christie to ask if he would be leaving, but he spoke first.

"Let's sit out on the porch a while, birthday girl."

"It's too cold," she said, but that crinkle about the eyes appeared again. He put his hands in his pockets. It made him look shifty and maybe he knew it because he pulled them right back out again.

"I still haven't given you your present, though."

She perked up. "Okay." He opened the door for her and she found a space on the porch steps, saving room beside her for Christie.

He closed the door behind them, pausing for a moment. "There's a key stuck in the door."

"Pearl's. I forgot to tell you not to close it. We might be locked out. I'm surprised you didn't see it when you came in."

"I did, but I forgot it in the commotion 'til I saw it again."

Ruby huffed. "What commotion? We had dinner and cake and argued about the new plant."

"Then let's not waste another word on it." Christie opened his mouth, closed it again, coughed. "Ruby, will you—take a walk with me?"

"You said you wanted to sit."

"You were right." He rubbed his arms. "It's too cold to sit."

She raised her chin. "Or, you could borrow your daddy's car and we could go take in a picture." Ruby jumped to her feet and began twisting on the stuck doorknob. "I've been wanting to see *Meet John Doe* ever since it came out, and they finally got it at the Strand Theatre. We can make the nine o'clock show if we hurry."

"I don't—"

"Please, Christie? It's not too much, is it? I'll buy my own ticket."

"No, no. I'll take you—next weekend. Let's . . . C'mon."

She fell in step behind Christie, not hiding her pout. Some birthday. Fussed at to wash dishes, outshined by a factory, and taken for a walk in the cold. "Where're we going?"

"You'll see," he said again. The usual clamor from the nearby rails rattled Ruby's teeth. The trains screamed louder in the winter without leaves on the trees to muffle the reverberations through the air. When it had passed, Christie cleared his throat. "I talked to your father. He might could get me hired on as a brakeman."

"Swell," Ruby said evenly. She didn't relish the idea of jumping into arms that smelled the way her daddy always did, but she knew better than to fuss about a good payin' job. Though she didn't know why he brought it up right then.

They walked the short stretch of dirt road, fingers loosely entwined. Christie steered them toward town, although Kennesaw shut down well before dark, even on a Friday night and especially since the specter of war came knocking.

Even so, a sliver of light slipped through the heavy blackout curtains in the meeting space above the dry goods store. "Wonder what's going on in there," she remarked.

Christie squeezed her hand. "Why don't we go see?"

Gallantly, he pounded on the wooden double doors, and at once they swung open from the inside.

"Surprise!"

The crowd of faces circled inside the general store made Ruby's heart expand, if only for a moment. Her best girlfriends from school, along with their beaus. Christie's pals from the farm where he worked. Their neighbors and friends all turned out for her.

"All right, everybody upstairs," Christie shouted over the din of laughter and clapping. "Mr. Lewis was good enough to let us use the front for the surprise, but let's clear out. The party's upstairs." Giggles and a staircase stampede accompanied the muffled licks of someone taking up a banjo. "Dancing up front and cards in the back."

He grabbed Ruby by the hand and led her up the creaky wooden stairwell. The old Masonic Hall, long infused with pipe smoke and dust mites, didn't lend itself to decorations too well. Garish red and pink paper streamers draped the doorways and windows, and Christie obviously delegated the bedsheet banner hanging at the far wall, which read "HAPPY BIRTDAY RUBBY" in bold two-foot letters.

The party burst to life like a spring-loaded snake in a trick nut can. Carefree if mostly left-footed pairs flocked to the makeshift dance floor. Card sharks congregated at two tables in the back, flicking playing cards about with showy indifference. Beside them, her girlfriends chatted at a small table in the corner set with a punch bowl and pretzels.

Finally Ruby found her tongue. "Did you set all this up?"

"Were you surprised?"

"Of course," Ruby said, though in her heart that was a lie. The lighted window on the second story tipped her off from the street, but why ruin what Christie must have worked hard to create for her? "Thank you so much."

His lean, farm-boy chest puffed out ever so slightly. "We'll see if I can keep from squashing your toes." Christie put out his hand and she took it, doing her best to look pleased.

A couple hours hence, when Ruby's feet wouldn't dance another step and her cheeks ached from smiling for all her well-wishers, the party slowly scattered. Several of their more reserved acquaintances hung in the background longer than she expected, and others shot looks of apology and question toward Christie as they came up to bid her happy birthday and good night. "Sorry we can't stay," their friends said again and again, until no one remained but a handful of chums who shooed them away, promising to clean up.

The street was much too dark and quiet after the lively ruckus, and the night air much too chilly. He clasped her left hand and rubbed it between both of his. "Wasn't that a gas?"

"The best," she lied. It wasn't bad. She wouldn't take away from him that he tried to make her happy, even if the bravura turned out smaller than she'd like.

"Sorry about the banner. But the rest went according to plan—almost."

As the turned the corner back on her road, she peeked at his face in the dimness. Impossible in that deep cold, but she would have sworn Christie was sweating. "Almost? What went wrong?"

He didn't say right away but walked her up to the front step of her parents' house. How she missed the days before Pearl Harbor and blackout regulations, when they would leave the porch light on. The half moon must've heard the rationing rumors too. It cast a stingy light that wasn't quite bright enough. "Not wrong, exactly. Only—Ruby, do you know how much I love you?"

With a coquettish head tilt and a pout, she teased him. "I think so, but why don't you tell me again?"

She expected a goodnight kiss, of course. Her due as the birthday girl. Instead, he took a deep breath and recited, his voice quavering, "'Who can find a virtuous woman? For her price is far above rubies.'" The kisser she had prepared turned into pursed lips until he pulled a shabby little box out of nowhere, opened it, and knelt down to the cold earth. "Ruby Rae Hart, will you marry me?"

Finally, something good! She snatched the box from his hands. Inside was an old-fashioned gold ring, its smallish ruby set too deep to sparkle much, though maybe she could blame that on the darkness. It held the lackluster sigh of brown and distant years, and she resisted the expression trying to form on her face. "It's . . . beautiful."

"It was my granny's." Christie looked apprehensive. "I knew you'd probably like a diamond, but with times the way they are . . . " He trailed off, making room for her reply. She took a long moment to steady her voice and hoped he couldn't see her fighting tears.

"Are you sure? I wouldn't want to take an heirloom out of your family."

His face reddened. "It'd be our family. I know it's not much . . . "

She realized what an ugly thing she'd said. Christie's mother had trouble, or so people whispered. He was the only surviving child.

Even worse, she still hadn't answered his question. Part of her, a big part, wanted to run. They loved each other all right, but love had always been easy and sweet. Romance, attention, and surprises. Its crushing power had never once occurred to her, not before that moment.

Now all the expectant stares of their friends made sense. What would they think of her if they heard she rejected him for offering her an ugly ring?

"It's perfect. Thank you. And you've known I would ever since you rescued me out of that pine tree. Marry you, that is."

Whatever hurt her initial reaction may have caused him, her response smoothed it over. He rose to his feet and wrapped those long arms around her, and she leaned into his chest, soaking up his warmth. "Say it again," he said against her ear.

"Yes, yes, yes. Forever and ever."

He teased the ring from its box and slid it onto her finger. It might not have the brilliance of a new ring, but Christie's eyes made up the difference. "Look at that, a perfect fit."

Actually, the ring was at least a full size too big. She twisted it around her finger. It would spin when she wore it and sail right off if she flung her hands around.

She clenched her jaw and swallowed hard. Didn't matter whether she liked the ring. She had Christie. Forever.

"I love you." She tasted the words. Tried them on. They fit as big and jangly as his granny's ring, and unlike a ring, words couldn't be resized. Somehow she'd have to fit them instead.

CHAPTER 11

Wednesday, March 28, 2012

Brooding on the front steps, Abby picked paint chips from the wooden porch railing. One unspoken assumption down. How many more to go? She'd expected full access to the archives of Aunt Ruby's attic. The promise of more time with those boxes influenced her decision to move quite a bit.

Even days later, the rebuff still stung. It wasn't the first time, either. Aunt Ruby had shooed her out for fast food when she asked to look at the old Bible again. When she got back, it was mysteriously misplaced. She couldn't remember why she wanted the second look. The memory breezed away from her in the tangled limbs of facts.

Mom used to praise her research skills, but Abby never knew how to take the compliments. Search engines and courthouse indexes yielded up their data to her easily, but Mom had the knack for interpreting the details and unlocking secrets with her greater wisdom. Trying to solve mysteries without her was like one-handed typing.

She arranged paint chips like pieces of a puzzle that refused to fit together. Time and weather had worn away too much of the connective bits, until every piece was an island. One stuck to her index finger, and she examined its irregular shape. "Like cloud pictures. Except I don't know if I'm looking at a horse or a unicorn." She slid the paint chips into the semblance of a unicorn. Unsatisfied, she brushed them away and dusted off her fingertips on her jeans.

Maybe it wouldn't be so bad if she had some distraction. Will must have ignored her note. Fine to joke about the forgiving Baptists up the hill, but he wouldn't forget her harsh words so easily.

Her cheeks flushed at the thought of him. She had decided a sexy little antagonism wouldn't do any harm, and now he didn't want to play. She penned the note planning to apologize, but days passed and he never came.

His loss. He was a boy working odd jobs. She couldn't let him steal her focus.

She mulled over her next steps. Tricks of the light preyed on her mind, and gut instinct could lie. For certainty, she needed a response, but her first attempt to call out the ghost failed.

In the recesses of memory, Mom's voice came unbidden. *Everyone deserves a name.*

Abby put her hand over her eyes and let the pain bubble in her chest. She could hear the gentle indignation, a conversation they had dozens of times in different ways about a problem that cropped up all over the place. Daughters disappeared into marriages and were never heard from again. Wives appeared from nowhere, their maiden names long forgotten as motherhood descended. Lost infants were remembered rarely, with tiny markers in their family's plots, most often nameless, sometimes appearing in death indexes with the initials S.B., for stillborn. Mom hated to write "Unknown" in a name blank.

She lowered her arm and retreated indoors. "All right. I guess I'm looking for a name."

Her laptop won a semi-permanent spot on the big pine table until she came up with either a desk or a reasonable substitute. She opened it and brought up her genealogy file. Scientists had the scientific method and genealogists had the standard of proof. She'd make a list of possibilities and systematically eliminate them until she knew the so-called ghost's name and story.

"I'm looking for people who have lived in the house. Which means a trip to the courthouse for the deeds and tax plats. But for now . . . " She tapped in a few keystrokes. "Google says Kennesaw's first settlers came in 1838. And they called it Big Shanty. Good to know."

Doubts plagued her as she navigated the branches. Like starting with a famous historical figure determined to find a link, her methodology amounted to working backwards from a conclusion. The odds were always against that kind of researcher. "Wish you were here, Mom. I can't do this without you."

She paused on her father's entry. Richard Wells. No middle name, at least none Mom knew of. A common enough name—at least one in every city, if the Internet could be believed. Of course, courtesy of Uncle Blake, she now knew where to look. He only stopped in for a short while during her initial visit, but he spent the bulk of their time bragging about his daughter and dropping hints about her father's whereabouts and activities. "Ever seen a *cow eat a* car?" he joked. Abby stared at him, uncomprehending, until Aunt Ruby finally explained.

"He lives in Newnan. Coweta county. Blake, has anyone ever laughed at that joke? For heaven's sake."

 Like everyone, he assumed Abby came to Georgia to confront her father, but how could she? The dates of his ancestor profile told an incomplete story at best.

Richard Wells
B. 9/17/1965
M. 1/1/1984
Dv. Before 1989
D.

One other date muddied up his story: her own birthday on March 30, 1984. Abby didn't know when her parents split or why. She only knew that in her earliest memories, he was already gone. And out of all her memories, one of the worst rose up from the moment she invoked his absence and named the void.

They never talked about him. In the day-to-day and the year-to-year, Richard Wells simply did not exist. Fifteen or sixteen and mature for her age, Abby gave Mom little need for sharp words, until the day she posed the question, a touch inflammatory and designed to provoke. "So what's the story on my dad, anyway?"

Her mother's retort still reverberated back. "I'm not discussing him with you. Don't ask again."

Stunned, Abby promised she wouldn't.

The years since had dulled but not entirely deadened the sting, even though Abby had long since diagnosed its source. She'd asked as a friend, and Mom answered as a parent. Eventually she buried her questions under respect for Mom's privacy, assuming there would be time to talk about it. Only there never was, and while those questions wouldn't or couldn't rest easy, her promise remained in effect. After all, look what happened when she tried to break it.

She gritted her teeth. No. That was Greg's broken promise, not hers. At least Aunt Ruby allowed her a peek before spurning her one request. Shame piled on top of shame.

She groaned and closed her laptop. Enough. First, to the courthouse to find out who owned the house and when. With luck, the evidence would point toward whatever misfortune rallied into a ghost story. Not that she entirely dismissed the idea that the house hosted an otherworldly being. Even now, she had the overwhelming sense that she wasn't alone.

A loud knock snapped her out of her thoughts. Startled, she jumped out of the chair and stubbed her toe on the leg of the table. "Who's there?" she called, palms sweating.

"Abby? It's me, Will."

She threw open the door and sure enough, there he was, looking tan and golden in the rising heat of morning. "Hi."

"Whew, all settled in already. Here I figured you might need help finishing up."

"Come in, come in." He made her tongue-tied. "No, I got it all done. And that wasn't why I left you the note."

"What note?" He stepped inside and Abby shut the door behind him. It took a hard shove to close all the way.

"You didn't see it? I left a sticky-note on Aunt Ruby's door. I guess that was Friday."

"I'm sorry, Abbs. I didn't get it."

She drew up her shoulders. The game was back on. "No problem. But if you didn't get it, then why are you here? Shouldn't you be mad at me?"

"I've never been much for holdin' grudges." Will stepped inside, bringing a swirl of the cool air behind him. "Nippy for March, ain't it?"

Her heart warmed. If she'd stop picking fights with him, they'd be friends soon, maybe more. "This isn't cold. There's snow on the ground in Ohio right now. Your blood is thinner than mine because you've lived here longer."

"We'll see how much you like that thick blood of yours in August," he drawled. "But I'm glad the house is working out. Did you find anything for me to add to the fix-it list?"

"Not so far. But I don't know when I've been so aggravated, trying to—" She stopped short. She still hadn't mentioned the ghost to him, and after their last little spat, hadn't planned to. With the first of the words out, she sighed. "Trying to figure out this supposed ghost story."

One corner of his mouth quirked up. "Has Mrs. Watts been tellin' tales?"

He knew. Her breath quickened. "She dropped a hint or two and left the rest up to me to figure out. I haven't gotten anywhere so far though." Abby paused, but Will didn't warm to the topic. It would be hard to get answers out of him, but harder still to bring it up again. "What's the story?"

He backed one step away, fiddling with his belt loops. "Mrs. Watts had a stroke a while back. Ever since, she's more apt to say whatever's on her mind."

She rubbed her forehead, deflated. His answer was hardly better than Mom's had been, all those years ago. "You're saying she's making it up."

He spread his hands wide, at a loss. "She'll tell you this house is haunted, but I believe the truth of the matter is that people get haunted. Not places." She crossed her arms. He sighed. "You're ill at me again."

"No, but I disagree. Tell me you've never heard a bizarre story you couldn't explain away."

"I don't pretend to understand all about souls and spirits, Abbs, but the Bible says that to be absent from the body is to be present with the Lord. That much, even a simple guy like me can grasp."

"Sure." How could she turn this around? She cleared her throat. "We're both talking about the same basic concept. Life after death. It's fair to want some evidence."

"I don't think you'll find any. That's a matter of faith."

"I'm not so sure. Family traditions usually have a nugget of truth tucked into them if you search for it. Even if there's no ghost per se, maybe I can help her with whatever's haunting her."

"Maybe, but digging up what folks have buried don't sound like help to me. That's my opinion."

Abby frowned. She couldn't agree of course. What else did she move for, if not to interrogate this house, this family, into giving up its secrets?

"It hurts me to think of whoever-it-was being forgotten."

He hesitated. "I can show you where your kin is buried, if that'll ease your mind. I clean up the grave sites twice a month, and I'm planning on going this weekend if the weather's pretty. You can come help, if you want. Saturday, in the morning before it gets too hot?" *Sadder-dee.*

"I'd love to. I've always liked cemeteries," she confessed.

"Not me. I've always hated 'em. The ones you go to see ain't really there." He looked down at his shoes. "But you don't need me to tell you. I'm sorry."

"It's fine." She turned away toward the kitchen, looking for a way to busy herself and avoid his eyes. "I'm sorry too. We ended on a bad note last time. My fault."

He followed her into the kitchen, either not taking the hint or feeling way too at home. Maybe both. He leaned against the edge of the counter next to the sink. "Abbs, you know how people pray for a miraculous recovery when someone's real sick?"

"Yup." She hoped he didn't want to keep arguing about religion. "Heard it all before, Will."

"Hear me out. How about them ancestors of yours? What if they prayed from heaven for your mom to come on up and join them?"

His words punched her in the gut. The pretty portrait of Great-Grandma Blanchard appeared in her mind's eye, but instead of the light kiss of airbrushing, flesh-toned cheeks and natural pink lips smiled back. Her eyes twinkled—green instead of the painted-on blue—before the picture dissolved.

Will still waited for a response, as if he hadn't plucked the heart from her hope and presented it to her, bloody and still beating. She managed a light snort. "That's a nice way to think of it, if you have to think of it at all. But if I was in heaven, I'd ask for a better miracle than for someone else to die."

"But it's not death. It's eternal life."

Abby pressed her lips together. She'd asked for his help, after all. He was offering the best solutions he had. It wasn't his fault he couldn't get past the small-minded ideas his church fed him. "Will, listen. How about a truce? Since I'm basically stuck with you—"

"How'd you figure that?"

"Aunt Ruby says you're handling all the house stuff, which makes you my acting landlord, doesn't it?"

He rocked back on his heels. "I s'pose you could say so."

"And I'd like it if we were friends." She took a deep breath. "I'll give up the ghost, so to speak, if you'll agree not harp on me about your religion. Deal?"

"I ain't harpin' on you. I'm—"

"Please? It's because of my mom."

He would say no, serve up a saying he heard in church, and finish her off with some Bible quotes. Maybe he'd even promise to pray for her again, and she resigned herself to letting him. He meant well—but he surprised her.

"I'll do my best not to step on your toes."

"Good enough." She flashed him a smile to seal their agreement and retreated to the refrigerator. "We've been standing here in the kitchen long enough, haven't we? Would you like a sandwich? I made iced tea. I figured if I'm going to live here, I'd better learn to like the stuff."

"Thanks, but I'd best get movin'." He edged away, restoring a more comfortable distance. "Busy day, as always. And I ain't sure I trust any tea made by a Yankee. No offense."

She held up her hands. "You caught me. It's from a powdered mix." He dipped his head in quiet amusement. Satisfied that for once they'd part as friends, she reached into the cabinet for a glass. "See you Saturday."

He didn't answer, and when she turned she saw why. He'd let himself out, closing the heavy door without making a sound.

She plunked an ice cube into her glass and stood in the kitchen, sipping her tea and replaying their conversation in her mind. Halfway through her drink, she dumped it and the rest of the pitcher down the sink. "And what about you, Will Laughlin? What is it you've got buried?"

CHAPTER 12

MARIETTA, GEORGIA
Friday, March 30

At a stop light, Abby pinched her sweaty blouse away from her torso to let her skin breathe. She couldn't believe the heat. They called this spring?

Guess I'll be squeezing the car A/C repair into my budget. Happy birthday to me.

What a boring way to splurge. Not that hard-boiling her brain like an egg all summer qualified as entertainment.

She drove the newly paved streets, glimpsing what she could of the City of Marietta's personality. The stylized façades lining the city square gave her a superficial idea of the community, as well as the money the town had to spend on itself, but orange and white construction barrels belied the faux-historic Americana charm, edging the side roads and surface streets and blocking the shoulder of the roadway. A flagman donning a florescent yellow vest waved her around a crew jackhammering the sidewalk, filling the city streets with the noise of progress.

Cobb County's seat bustled and hummed in a way Kennesaw's lolling historic section never would. She doubted she'd have picked up and moved to Georgia so easily if this place had formed her first impression, though it was hard to say why. It wasn't the streets buzzing with traffic and crawling with people that overwhelmed her. She'd lived most of her life in downtown apartments, after all, and by that account, Marietta should have stirred up a longing for home instead of anxiousness and unease.

She missed the entrance to the paid parking lot across from the Probate Court. Checking the map display on the GPS, she planned to circle the block for a second pass. As she crested the hill, relentless rows of white headstones sprawled across a vast green landscape alongside the road. A national cemetery, its perfect, uniform lines orderly and precise, its soldiers in formation, even in death. She could hardly take her eyes off it to drive.

Maybe if she had time later—but she laughed at herself and dismissed the idea. The cemetery was beautiful, but it had no part in the hunt for her silent, invisible, nameless roommate.

Though maybe not nameless for long. She wedged her way into the lot, wincing at the price on the parking pass dispenser, and tossed her ticket on the dash as she pulled into a space. The deeds would tell her when the house came into her family and who owned it before.

Abby approached her own ghostly reflection in the county courthouse's gleaming glass doors like another version of her, trapped inside. A ridiculous idea, but she couldn't shake it.

The officer at the security checkpoint waved her through the metal detector without incident, but on the other side, she froze, instantly lost. Everyone around exuded belonging and purpose. Though Abby saw no directory, they all knew exactly where to go. From the lofty skylights to the shiny marble tiles, the courthouse gleamed with precision, not a cog out of place except her.

Soon someone would ask what she was doing there and she wouldn't have an answer. She took a step backwards. Another inch would bump her up against the security guard, and he noticed.

"You're clogging up the works, ma'am." His voice was not kind, and Abby entertained the idea of making a run for the door.

Great idea. She could put this down as the birthday when she got arrested for causing a disturbance in a government building. Her grandchildren would tell their grandchildren.

Past the officer, down the corridor to the left, a sign like those she'd seen in more than a few Ohio courthouses pointed the way to the Recorder of Deeds. "Sorry, I was confused." She darted away. She'd be safe among the archived land records.

Behind the frosted glass door, a woman with spiky white hair sat behind an outdated monitor. She glanced up at Abby, a peculiar combination of makeup and interest arching her brows. "May I help you?"

The woman's accent gave Abby a picture of a poisoned peach. She coughed and attempted to meet her eyes. "I'm looking into the history of my family home."

The deed recorder's genial expression didn't even twitch. "And where're you from?"

"Cuyahoga Falls, Ohio. It's north of Akron."

"We don't have any of those records, sugar." She folded her hands. "I meant, where is the family home you're hopin' to find?"

Abby's cheeks warmed. "Oh. Kennesaw. The historic district. Pike's Landing Road."

The woman stood from her swivel chair. The nameplate on her desk called her Deidre Kemp. Her smart red separate and white pencil skirt made Abby wish she'd dressed better. "Bless your heart. Let me show you how to use the indexes."

Abby held up her hands. Finally, a sense of surety, of rightness and know-how. "No need. I've done this plenty of times."

Deidre sniffed and reseated herself behind the desk. "Suit yourself."

Abby took a moment to size up the challenge and scanned the rows of volumes. The deeds held the answers. Somewhere close, the name she sought waited for her.

The record of transfers formed links in a chain she could follow through time, maybe as far back as the first settlements. She hefted the W volume of the general index from the shelf and combed its pages until her great-aunt's name showed up in the leftmost column.

Grantee: Ruby Watts. Grantor: Gilbert Hart. Date: October 9, 1972. Deed Book 27. Page 122.

Her lip twitched. The chase was on.

She scribbled notes and swapped the volume for the H index. There would be time to poke around in the hilltop cemetery after all.

The oldest index entries were handwritten in meticulous Spencerian script. In spite of her eagerness, Abby paused to run her fingers over the dignified lines. Mom would have remarked on the diligent clerk who had penned these elaborate pages, or maybe on the century-plus between the secret being recorded and its discovery. She could almost imagine Mom there in the room with her, looking over her shoulder and cheering her on. Chill bumps rose on her arms as she found the next link.

Grantee: Gilbert Hart. Grantor: Warren Hart. Date: May 20, 1902. Deed Book 6. Page 480.

She ran her finger down the column. No line naming Warren Hart as grantee. No other Hart entries at all.

She moved on to the deed books in spite of the gnawing in her chest. No time now to admire penmanship. She skimmed the page twice, then forced herself to read it slowly. Oh no. Problem.

She had run full-on into a brick wall. The deed referenced no earlier document nor any previous owner and marked the end of a too-short chain.

Abby turned toward the deed recorder and caught her watching, amusement lurking below a look of concern. "Hit a snag, sugar?"

"Maybe a small one," Abby admitted. "I had hoped to trace the property back through the deed books a little further than 1902." She rechecked the date in hopes she'd misread it. "This deed describes the property but it doesn't reference any previous transfers."

Deidre made no move to help. "That's a shame. You hit the end of the line."

"What? That's not so long ago in the grand scheme of things. Someone had to own the land before then. The area was settled in the 1830's. I researched it."

"You didn't research enough, sugar. Ever heard of a little campaign called Sherman's March to the Sea? The courthouse and all its records were destroyed in the War of Northern Aggression."

Abby squinted her eyes shut, as if a moment of darkness could ease the blow. Destroyed. "That's terrible. How will I figure out when the house came into my family?"

"Cheer up. If the recorded chain of ownership ends in 1902, it means there weren't any deed transfers filed from 1864 until then. Whoever sold it at the turn of the century owned it going back to the Civil War." Deidre examined her nails, bright red acrylics. "Why don't you go check probate for any activity on the other side?"

She picked up a phone and punched a button without waiting for Abby's response. "Make a wish, Sylvia. I'm sending you a genie." Dropping the phone back in its cradle, she zinged out frosty instructions. "Across the hall, then the third door on the left. You can't miss it. Good luck, sugar."

"Wait," Abby protested. "Can I at least make a photocopy of this one?"

The woman pointed to a yellowed behemoth of office equipment in the corner. "One dollar per page. I hope you have quarters. We can't make change. Departmental policy." She turned to her screen, pointedly ignoring Abby as if she'd vanished altogether.

She anticipated the need for quarters, but not the temperamental beast of a copier. After six dollars and as many bad copies, she gave up. She could cobble them together into a legible whole later and call it a cheap price to escape the Recorder of Deeds.

If Sylvia in the Probate office minded Abby's intrusion, she had the good grace not to show it. "A genealogist," she said in greeting. "My condolences."

Abby bit her lip. "Why do you say that?"

"Only since this is a tough county for research, but don't let me discourage you. You'll want to use our digital index. It'll point you to the wills. Also the auxiliary papers, inventories, and letters, but most people don't care about those. Get the goods and get out, right?"

"I guess. No, I take it back. I want every scrap I can find."

"That's the spirit. Let me know if you need help. There's the copier." She dropped her voice. "Officially, we don't make change, but I keep a roll of quarters in my desk. It's my money and I can swap it with whoever I want, right?"

Abby exhaled, like a desert traveler stumbling into an oasis. "Thank you. I can't tell you what this means."

She fed surnames into the digital index, Hart and Wells and Watts, jotting down the volume and page numbers for wills and the loose papers one by one. As she finished with the indexes, she relaxed into the comfortable rhythm of carrying the probate books from the shelves to the long counter, leafing through their giant pages, transcribing their clues in her notes, and returning them to their slots. She tried not to look up too often and spoil the daydream of Mom at the other end of the counter, poring over the tomes in search of the clue that would unlock the mystery.

Most of her relatives had died intestate, without assigning their worldly possessions. Her grandparents, James and Pearl Wells, proved the important exceptions, but they still followed a predictable pattern. He left all worldly goods to his wife and she, like any good mother, told her children to share. Her grandparents' wills mentioned a property on Pike's Landing Road and another in Marietta. As best Abby could gather without returning to the deed office, her father, Uncle Blake, and their sisters liquidated the real estate and divvied up the proceeds.

That doesn't make sense. The house went to Aunt Ruby.

Abby read on. Gilbert Hart's will left his property to his two daughters. Abby compared the property descriptions, tracing an imaginary map onto the counter with her fingertips until she understood. They divided the lot. Grandma Pearl got most of the land and Aunt Ruby got the house. It made sense. Jim and Pearl Wells already had a home in Marietta.

By the end of the day, Abby's eyes were crossing and she'd found only one other probate record that specifically mentioned the house. Warren Hart named his grandson, Gilbert, as the sole beneficiary, but the will only mirrored the deed transfer. Her feet ached from standing at the counter, and her dry fingertips pulled from handling paper all day. The last record referenced in Warren Hart's index entry was a letter of guardianship. She stifled a yawn. Almost there.

She couldn't decide if the document was important. The court appointed Rose Hart custodian of Gilbert's inheritance until he reached the age of majority in 1909. On the third pass, insight broke through her fatigue.

He inherited from his grandfather. Not his father. Why?

Abby consulted her notes for Warren's son and Gilbert's father and found George Hart in the interstice. Why didn't he inherit the family home instead?

"Because he was dead." She shook her head even as her lips formed the words. She'd drawn a big question mark by George Hart's date of death.

How would Mom have approached it? She starred George Hart's name. "Died" in 1861, had a son in 1888. If he wasn't already dead, then why didn't he inherit the house from his father?

She tapped her pen on her notebook, keeping tempo with her racing thoughts. This discrepancy popped up once before. Why didn't she follow through on it?

Because Aunt Ruby distracted me, that's why.

As soon as she'd asked about George Hart, Aunt Ruby sent her out for milkshakes—and a ghost. "Disinherited?" Abby whispered. "Is that enough reason to haunt the house, whenever he died?"

"How's it going there, missy? We're closing up in fifteen minutes," Sylvia warned her.

She hoisted the giant volume to the copier. "Almost done, I think."

Abby assessed her work as she ran the photocopy. A whole day spent to circle back around to questions she should already have answered: who was George Hart, and when did he die? The cemetery trip with Will would prove interesting, at least. "Thanks again, truly."

"You're so welcome." Sylvia unlocked her desk drawer and withdrew a giant leather purse. "Did you find a missing inheritance that needs claimed?"

Abby tucked her notes into her own bag and zipped it. "Not quite. Maybe next time."

She hesitated in the hallway. They didn't split the property until the Seventies. She only had half of the trail. No need to be scared of Deidre the dragon lady. Sticks and stones. She reentered the Deed office with her head down.

"Oh, looks like you caught me." Deidre's genteel smile was undergirded with daggers. "I planned to slip out a few minutes early today."

"Two minutes," Abby said.

She checked her watch. "I'll give you eleven, sugar."

Abby quickly found the property transfer and subsequent sale for her grandmother's share of the Hart property. It looked like her father, Uncle Blake, and their two sisters sold the land after Pearl passed away. Abby made the copies without reading any deeper. If the need arose, she'd have them. She crammed the pages into her notebook, and as she left the Deeds office a second time, Deidre waited by the door with her purse and keys in one hand and the other poised over the light switch.

Abby slipped by her without a word. Behind her, the dragon lady sniffed. "Not even a thank you. That's a Yankee for you."

Abby crossed the marble floor into the lobby. Blinding afternoon sun streamed through the glass façade. A few other stragglers interrupted the stillness, but the busyness of morning had gone. On her way out, Abby spotted a framed map in gentle brown tones with blocky ornamental type across the top. She paused before it.

Cobb County, Georgia., 1860. Hmm.

Bold lettering marked such places as Fort MacDonald, Allatoona, and Kennesaw Mountain, although the town itself was missing. She sought familiar road names and saw none. No landmarks connecting with the present day appeared either, until the familiar symbol of a rail line emerged in the tangle of routes and boundaries. The Western & Atlantic rails ran north to south through the map, right past the Big Shanty depot.

Big Shanty. At once she had her bearings. Big Shanty was Old Kennesaw. The town had a different name back then, one she would have passed over if she didn't know to look.

The routes near the depot resolved as early versions of the Main Street and Cherokee Street of today. She studied the map a few minutes more, noting with satisfaction that her proximity to the rails let her find on the map the triangular lot where her house now stood. Tiny slant letters labeled the lot as railroad worker shanties.

"Ma'am, I'll need you to wrap it up." The security guard startled her. "If you don't want to be shut in for the night, that is."

"Sorry." Abby dipped her head and hurried out. Even over the din of five o'clock traffic on the street, she could hear the lock click behind her.

CHAPTER 13

That evening, her new collection of photocopies and notes papered the kitchen table. Not a wasted day. A good day. "Mom would tell me to quit moping. And she'd probably ask how badly I want this." Abby rubbed her eyes, knowing she should take the extra effort to organize, and she would—later. First she needed a break from curlicues and paper cuts.

She wandered through the house, trying to feel a presence, a cold chill, an inarticulate whisper, a sad longing that could pass for evidence of life after death. Her first attempt to invite contact failed. She liked George Hart for the ghost so far, but she had no idea what would rattle his chains, if he had them. And even if the story was a lie, who started it, and who repeated it?

Her phone buzzed with a new text, and she plucked it from her back pocket. A one-word message from Sarah appeared. "Surprise . . . "

"Surprise what?" She tapped the reply button as a loud knock— "shave and a haircut"—came from her front door. Sarah didn't wait a second for her to answer, either.

"Are you in there? And don't say you're not. Your car is here. Open up. I have to pee."

Abby hurried to the door. "Sarah?"

"Happy birthday to you. Wow. I can't believe you left our great apartment for such a dump." Sarah's round eyes took in all corners of the porch as she hoisted the strap of her travel bag over her shoulder. "If I annoyed you that much, I guarantee you could have found housing projects nicer than this right in town. No thousand-mile quest required."

Abby pulled the scrunchy out of her hair, shook out her ponytail, and tugged on her tee shirt. Sarah was dressed in black cropped pants and an off-the-shoulder white blouse, with chunky white bangles on her wrist. "What are you doing here?"

"I came to get my travel mug, of course. And it'll be a minute before I do without it again, let me tell you. I burned my hand using a flimsy paper coffee cup at the airport."

"That's what the recycled cardboard sleeves are for." Abby moved aside to let Sarah in the door.

"They were all out. No, don't mind me. I was kidding. I came because I couldn't let you have a birthday in a new town without anyone to celebrate with." She stared at the stacks of papers lining the table. Abby's screen saver came up, and without asking permission, Sarah stroked the touchpad. "Genealogy. Of course. You know you're crazy, right?"

"Thanks." Abby coughed. "Dare I ask how long you're planning on staying?"

"Two nights. You're not sick, are you? We'll make it a big birthday weekend. And if you can drive me back to the airport on Sunday, that would be fantastic. It was worth the cab fare to surprise you, but—ouch. Expensive." Sarah set her bag on the kitchen floor and looked around. "Did I mention you're crazy?"

"It's amazing compared to when I first saw it. Will did all kinds of work in here."

"If that's supposed to explain why this was a good idea . . . But let's move on. Time for you to show me what Georgia girls do for fun."

Abby smirked and held her hands out as if to display the mess on the table. "Allow me to introduce you to the wonderful world of genealogy."

"Thanks, but no." Sarah flared her nostrils slightly. "I suspected this might be the situation, so I took the time to Google some options. I'll email you the list. Although seriously, if this is all you do, you need to branch out. Expand your social circle."

"You make it sound so easy."

"And you make it sound so hard. I realize you're not going to have any actual fun without me, but you could make the effort. Take a cooking class. Join a book club. Find a church."

She put her hands on her hips. "*You're* telling me to go to church?"

"Hey, this is the Bible Belt, isn't it? I'm only suggesting nominal levels of social engagement would be healthy. At minimum, it would give you a break from the archives here. Greg's been talking about your mom's old church lately. It works for him."

"Then I'm glad I stopped going." Her straight face cracked. In spite of the sarcasm, she was glad to see her friend. "Come on. Let me show the place off. You can have your choice of my finest accommodations—my bed or one extra-supportive couch."

"Hmm, making me an offer I can refuse has never worked before, has it? All right then. Impress me. Starting with the facilities."

"Ah, yes. Right back here. In the pantry."

Abby led her through the rooms, musing how Will had done the same for her weeks earlier. She took Sarah's silence for judgment, not that she cared. In the short time since she'd moved in, she'd grown attached to the house and its quaint charm.

"The upstairs isn't ready yet," Abby said from the third step. Sarah lagged behind.

"Is that where the ghost lives?"

Abby laughed. "It sure is. Are you scared?"

The shadow of a real pout crossed Sarah's face an instant before she lifted her chin in arrogance. "Of course not. Lead the way. And I have another social suggestion for you: a rock-climbing group. You could train on your staircase."

"What do you mean? They're plain, normal steps. Must be the ghost messing with your head." It was funny, though. The steep stairs did feel less intimidating with Sarah there. At the top of the stairs, she noticed the trailing cobweb still hanging from the wall and hastily brushed it away. The threads clung to her fingers. She wiped her hand on her jeans, but the sticky tickle remained on her skin.

"I'll have use of this room as soon as Will has time to clear it out and paint. I don't know what I'll do with it. I'm thinking probably an office." She hit the light switch and watched Sarah look around. Her inscrutable gaze suggested she was percolating some biting quip. When their eyes met again, Abby had no expectation for what might come out of her mouth, and still Sarah managed to surprise her.

"Who's this Will you keep talking about? I thought the place belongs to your aunt."

"It does, but he's my de facto landlord, I guess." Abby rubbed her fingers. "He's Aunt Ruby's caretaker."

Sarah crossed her arms. "That's weird."

"He's weird," Abby admitted. "Cute, though."

"Huh." Sarah tossed her hair. "That reminds me. Greg says hi."

"I'm sure he does." Abby turned to go back downstairs, then stopped short. "Hey, I need your help."

Sarah cocked her head to the right, her way of faking a raised eyebrow. "The fact you're asking now does not fill me with warm-fuzzies."

Abby paused. Sarah's concern caught Abby unaware. She should feel either touched or angry, and she couldn't decide which.

"It's not that big a deal," she said finally. "I need your help to lift and tilt this desk."

"Why?"

"So whatever the shield is catching on will shift forward. I want to open it and see what's inside."

Sarah rolled her eyes. "Please tell me that when you lived with me, you didn't brazenly snoop through my stuff."

"Of course not." As a matter of fact, she had made a habit of checking Sarah's bank statements any time she got the chance, out of fear that she'd spend her portion of the rent on fancy cookware or new lamps, but then she switched to paperless statements and Abby had to trust her.

Sarah moved toward the desk, curious. "You do realize this is technically what Greg fired you for, right?" She tried opening the shield and hemmed when it stuck as it had for Abby. She pinched one of the loose corners of paper escaping from the desk and gave an experimental pull. The cardstock rectangle shifted loose.

"'You and a guest are invited to join us for the Twenty-Fifth Annual Southern Belle Reunion Gala, to be held at the Marietta Civic Center on Saturday, October 7, 1967,'" she read. Abby took the invitation and examined it with a pang of dissatisfaction as Sarah continued loosening documents from the jaws of the old writing desk.

"What are you doing?"

"We don't want whatever is in the back to crush the stuff we can see sticking out of it, do we?" Sarah asked, cramming her fingers under the one-inch space. "Who knows? If you're lucky, there might be photos. Oh, here's a find. 'Congratulations on your purchase of a new Sears refrigerator.' Dated 1966." Her eyes scanned the page further. "Check it out—lifetime warranty."

"Be careful," Abby said, thinking of how thoroughly she'd destroyed the paper blinds in this room. She joined Sarah, working gingerly to free eclectic little scraps of paper from the desk.

"Victory." Sarah teased out a black-and-white wallet-sized print of a young woman in a nursing uniform. "See? I was right. We could have damaged this."

"Let me see. Is it labeled on the back?"

Sarah flipped it over. "No, but hold still." She held up the photo, looking to it, at Abby, and back again. "It's your grandmother." She handed her the print.

"How can you tell?"

"Guessing, of course, but you look exactly like her."

Abby studied the tiny face. Her lips curled around some frozen word. The photographer must have caught her mid-sentence. "I wonder what she was saying."

"Maybe she asking a completely unanswerable question," Sarah suggested. "Do you want to do this or not?"

Abby set the collected pages on the floor, carefully placing her grandmother's photo on top. She and Sarah took opposite sides of the letter desk and looked into each other's eyes. In spite of her criticism and mockery, Sarah looked intrigued.

"On three," she said. Abby nodded.

"One, two, *three*."

A heft, a shuffle, and a dull thud as they let the desk hit the floor again. Without waiting, Sarah grasped the handles of the shield and lifted it easily.

"There. Easy-peasy. Okay. I'll let you collect up whatever you want in there. Meanwhile, I have a feeling you haven't eaten food that required more than boiling water since you left Ohio, so I am going to make dinner for us."

Sarah left Abby in the room. A swirl of emotions hit her, primarily jealousy that Sarah had actually been the one to open the desk, but also excitement that its secrets would be laid bare. She leafed through the jumbled assortment of papers.

Someone had stuffed them away without evident concern with

organization. The rude manner of access hadn't helped at all, of course. Some items were instantly recognizable: a pocket calendar from 1956 mingled with birthday cards and recipes written in firm, old-fashioned penmanship. A temporary driver's license issued in 1968 gave her aunt's birthday, January 23, 1924. She tucked it into her pocket to add to her family tree later.

Underneath a Marietta city directory from 1940, she discovered a tiny passbook detailing a steadily increasing bank balance. Between March 5, 1941, and January 29, 1942, Ruby Hart made not a single withdrawal, but after that all the pages were blank. Abby pulled out the drawers and checked all the letter slots, collecting an assortment of bric-a-brac—a key ring, a broken pair of glasses, a lapel pin declaring "I like Ike," which reminded her vaguely of a Pepsi logo—and set them on top of the stack of papers.

She backed away, measuring the desk's proportions with her eyes. One drawer, shallow for the depth of the desk, prompted her curiosity. She gave it a slight tug. It yielded readily and something inside it clinked. Holding her breath, she lifted out a wooden tray and discovered a false bottom and a tiny compartment with a lock no bigger than the sort that protected a diary.

"Hmm. No temptation like a secret." Abby tried to turn the lock with her pinky nail, but its tight mechanism wouldn't budge.

Replacing the drawer, she closed the desk and carried her treasures down to the dining room table, setting them in a chair as she gathered up the papers already scattered across the space. She laid out the items from the desk one by one, still thinking of the hidden compartment and too feverish with her finds to examine any of them closely.

Sarah broke through her reverie. "Abby, do you realize the only food in this house is packaged macaroni and cheese and hotdogs?"

"Not true." As soon as Abby lifted her eyes from the pastiche, they itched to return. "I have buns on the counter and two cans of chili in the cabinet right of the sink."

Sarah began putting away the pan and utensils she'd gathered. "I can't work with this."

"Whatever. Whip us up a batch of Macaroni and Cheese Chili-Dog Casserole."

Sarah made a face. "That's disgusting. Come on. We're going out."

Abby looked over the pile of discoveries waiting to be made. Will had a key—but he wouldn't walk in uninvited, would he? What about the way he'd gripped the door jamb of the upstairs bedroom, looking almost possessive? Or the too-comfortable way he leaned on her counters?

She couldn't trust him. Not yet.

"Hang on." Abby carried the pile of papers into her room. Her scattered makeup collection took up the space on top of the dresser, so she set the pages on top of her bed, and then, unsatisfied, put them underneath instead.

"What are you doing?"

"Hiding this stuff from Will."

For once, she'd actually bewildered unflappable Sarah. "Wait, does he live with you? You said he was your landlord."

"He is. Sort of. But if he drops by—"

"If you think he might bust in any time he wants, then you need to tell him off. I'll do it. What's his number?"

Abby rubbed her nose. The dust bunnies were breeding under there already. "You don't understand. I'm still finding the boundaries."

"With your *landlord?*"

"Never mind." Abby rose to her feet, dusting off her hands and knees. "There's a restaurant over near the railroad tracks. Let's go there. It's close enough that we can walk."

The setting sun glared, and Abby shielded her eyes. It helped her ignore the weird looks that Sarah made no attempt to hide. She knew her friend well enough to know that she didn't mean it when she flung out words like *crazy*. It was when she stopped questioning Abby's sanity that she doubted it.

Even worse, the lapsed conversation had fermented as they walked, and now she didn't know what to say. They waited to cross the street. "I know this is all pretty bizarre."

"I am absolutely not judging you." She jangled her bracelets. "And I won't tell Greg too many of the embarrassing parts."

Abby sighed. "Tell him any embarrassing part you want. Maybe it would help."

The crosswalk signal changed. Sarah stepped into the street. "Has he called again?"

"No. Thankfully."

"You hurt his feelings by not telling him you were moving."

"I was going to call him, honest."

"I know." Sarah brooded for a long moment. "I'm sorry if sometimes I go over the top trying to get you back together. I love you both. That makes it hard."

"You don't have to pick a side." As they walked toward the square, the sidewalk led through a small commons, white with dogwood blossoms and dotted with historic plaques. Abby didn't think much of it until they walked up to an obelisk engraved with the words "Veterans' Memorial" and she stopped short beside it.

"What's wrong now?" Sarah complained. "I'm hungry."

"Look at this. It doesn't even have any names on it." Abby walked around the four-sided monument in disbelief. "Who puts up a memorial that doesn't honor anyone?"

"It's a you-know-who-you-are honor. That way they don't have to keep updating it any time there's a new veteran. The more important question is, so what?"

Because she was dying for clues. "It's for one of my mysteries. One I haven't done much with yet, actually. I found World War Two draft orders at Aunt Ruby's house, but I can't figure out how the guy named on them is connected to her."

"Did you try Googling it?"

"Yes, I tried Googling it."

"Then I'd say you should forget it, because if Google doesn't know, there is a high probability that no one on Planet Earth cares. Are you on Planet Earth, Abby?"

"Yes. Sorry." They reached the end of the commons and Abby hit the crosswalk button. "There's the restaurant, on the other side of the street."

The prospect of a stony, silent weekend loomed as they approached and entered the restaurant. Not until the hostess seated them and the server had taken their drink orders did Sarah address Abby again. "I came up with my entry for the cooking show in the nick of time. Sarah's Shrimp Soufflé."

Abby took it for the peace offering it was. "Yeah? Tell me all about it."

The assortment of papers from the letter desk delighted Abby almost as much as it maddened her.

They returned from dinner, too late and too tipsy, singing oldies as they walked the streets home. Sarah hadn't so much claimed her bed as commandeered it, so Abby quietly retrieved the contraband files from under the bed and spread them across the living room floor. Separated into piles by category and date, the haphazard mish-mash of ephemera glimpsed only part of the odd life of Mrs. Ruby Hart Watts, with no tidbits newer than 1968 in the entire eclectic bunch. She closed up and stored the desk when she got married, Abby guessed. A large envelope full of brittle newspaper clippings full of unfamiliar names, perhaps Aunt Ruby's friends from long ago, a smattering of business cards, and other meaningless minutia she set aside to examine the more interesting finds, like the photo and the savings passbook. What happened to interrupt the steady stream of income? It recorded no closing withdrawal transaction. Could she have somehow forgotten the account?

Abby entertained a brief fantasy of turning up an abandoned fortune, the effects of compounding interest making her and the rest of Aunt Ruby's family instant millionaires. New old money. Wouldn't it be nice if the lottery of birthrights could for once work in her favor?

When she came across the party invitation Sarah had read aloud, she made a small connection. She'd heard "Southern Belle," but the invitation actually read, "Southern Bell." What a modern woman, working for the telephone company and putting her own money in the bank. No need for a man, even back then.

No whisper of a ghost, though. Abby stretched out on the couch. Aunt Ruby said the valuables were under lock and key. That might include more secrets, too.

She closed her eyes to think about it.

CHAPTER 14

Saturday, March 31

Early in the morning, Will climbed the roof of the house on Pike's Landing Road. He inspected the shingles again to give himself a reason, if not a right, to be there. A shutter on the dormer window looking out of the back bedroom threatened to come loose. One more thingamabob that needed fixed, but he hadn't brought any tools.

He ought to be more concerned with not getting caught, since he had no excuse besides the blooming dogwoods. He doubted that would carry much weight with Abby. Those weren't the branches that interested her.

They were perfect, though. The crisp breeze kept them dancing and swaying around him, easy and light. This time of year, the hot days and the cool ones mingled and swapped places. This morning leaned colder than a southern son liked his springtime, but the chill hadn't hurt the dogwoods any. The best, shortest season blanketed his town in white, an earthly cloud cover, a hint of heaven. He spent each day filling his eyes with their fragile beauty, and each night hoping for one more day.

Maybe some time he'd head north after the dogwoods greened, to go where spring sprung later and drink in a double portion of God's goodness. Wouldn't be this year or next, though.

He kept trying to pray, but a well-loved face waited for him every time he closed his eyes. She only lasted a breath before morphing, slowly, subtly, completely, into Abby's face. He couldn't get over it. "I will set no worthless thing before my eyes," he whispered, but that didn't sit well either.

If God wasn't under that girl's skin . . . but she didn't want to see Him. Maybe her hard heart would never see.

The swift, familiar sting of conviction pricked him. Her heart wasn't his to know and her eternity not his to question. Bad enough to have agreed to her bargain, and now he wanted to brush her off as beyond saving?

He already knew the Lord when tragedy struck. He'd never say it was easy, only that full dark never stole his certainty, not once from the first moment of agony or since. How was he supposed to explain hope or grace to her if her ears closed up at the first syllable of any word she deemed too religious?

He couldn't imagine the starless sky Abby faced.

She needed Jesus as much as anyone, but she didn't want to hear. She needed a chest to beat her fists against and arms to wrap around her, but she refused the One who waited to comfort her.

I could stand in the gap. The idea filled him with shame. That's not what that Scripture meant, and he knew it.

The sun gained on him, calling him a fool for squandering these hours and saving up his work for the midday heat. He stared out over the treetops a few minutes longer, reluctantly climbing down before the black shingles could burn him.

CHAPTER 15

Abby hovered in the suspended reality between sleep and waking for a while. One by one, little intruders slipped into her languid world. The scratchy fabric of the sofa. The lazy sunlight spilling through tattered mini-blinds. The sound of knocking.

She startled to full consciousness and sprang to life, swishing mouthwash and tossing her dirty hair into a ponytail before answering the door. She clutched the door jamb against the wooziness of an almost-hangover and watched Will's retreat. He carried what looked like a plastic bag full of dirt in one hand and a rake in the other.

"Will," she called. He turned toward her with eyes that shattered boundaries and toppled familiarity. Unmistakable pleasure took shape on his face. Fondness, even.

"Good morning, Abbs. You ready?"

"Right. Yes. But I have a friend over. A female friend," she hastened to add, lest he think she broke Aunt Ruby's specific stipulation. At least she had a legit reason not to invite him inside. She didn't want to lie to him any more than necessary, but he couldn't be allowed to see the sprawl of papers she left in the living room. "She popped in last night. It was a last-minute deal."

"Another time, then."

She swallowed hard. The same brush-off Aunt Ruby gave. "No, I'll leave her a note. She'll be fine until we get back."

"You should stay with your friend," he admonished gently. "The dead can wait."

"I'm the one waiting right now, while she's busy sleeping like the dead. Give me a sec." Abby dashed off a note to Sarah about needing to run a quick errand and told her to make herself at home. She threw on fresh clothes and met a patient Will on the porch.

"Sorry," she said, catching her breath. "That was more like a couple of secs."

Will did a double take, and Abby silently replayed her words. "Oh my—goodness. I didn't mean to say—"

"It's all right." *Saul-raht.* Had she considered his accent low and uneducated before? Now it sounded like peace.

She noticed him blushing, though. Maybe not perfectly peaceful.

Will crossed Main Street before following it north, the same route she and Sarah had taken the night before but on the other side of the street. Such a funny town. Across from the small manicured green where the Veterans' Memorial stood, she and Will passed by a three-story brick building that looked at least as old as her house. Its windows were dark, and if time had an odor, its musk fell heavily from the doors. She touched the padlock bolted to the second storefront with a shiver of longing.

"Where exactly is the cemetery?"

He pointed with the handle of the rake. "Up ahead, near Summers Street. The whole property used to be the Summers' farm, and their graves are the oldest ones in there." He glanced over at her. "If you care to know."

"I do. I love history."

He nodded toward the buildings on the hill behind the green. "Up there's the locomotive museum I told you about, and the depot across the street from it, right where it's always been. Of course it's been rebuilt a time or two." He gestured at the brick building as they passed. "This one here used to be a general store and a Masonic hall."

She laughed. "Love it. And oh, you'll like this. I actually found the depot on an 1860 map. These streets were laid out the same as now, and I'm ninety-nine percent sure my house was a railroad shanty where the Western & Atlantic workers stayed. Pretty interesting, huh?"

Will frowned. "The railroad probably owned the land, but the depot ain't that old, and neither is the house. Looks it, I know. The last of the railroad shanties have been gone for almost twenty years. Even those came after the Civil War." He stopped at the crosswalk and Abby hit the button. "Where'd you see that map?"

Her cheeks burned. If she didn't lose her hearing when she got old, she would pretend like Aunt Ruby did. Until then, there was no dodging his question. "At the courthouse."

Will waited until the crosswalk light changed before speaking, maybe so he could keep his eyes on the road and the cars around them instead of looking at her directly. "If you like history you might know this, but Kennesaw got hit hard during the Civil War. You can't tell by looking now, but Sherman burned this town, Abbs. Second week of November, 1864. I've heard he left a blacksmith shop and nothing else standing when he was done here. And even before that, the name 'Kennesaw' supposedly comes from the Cherokee word for a burial ground. If there was such a thing as ghosts, this town would be full of 'em."

"I didn't realize. I wasn't trying to rewrite history."

"You couldn't if you wanted to. It already happened. It don't matter if anyone remembers it or not." He paused. "Abbs, you're tryin' to find hope in the past, but the world and its lusts are passing away. Hope belongs to the future."

Oops. Touched a nerve. "A little morbid fascination with yesteryear is not that big a deal. What about your history, Will? All these times we've met now and you still haven't said a word about yourself."

"Oh, not much worth sayin'."

"Sure there is. Here's an easy one. How did you end up working for my aunt? I assume you're saving up for school."

"God put a need in front of me, and I filled it. No plans for school. No plans at all, really." *Attall.* He watched the ground. "I'm kind of between things."

"What things?" She hoped her voice sounded soft and inviting, but he wouldn't look at her.

"I don't guess I could say without breaking your rule. Again. Besides, we're here."

He strode right past a squat brick mainstay bearing a bronze nameplate engraved with the words "Kennesaw City Cemetery, Est. 1863." She hung back longer than the moment necessary to read the sign. Will might have claimed to be a simple man, but Abby had her doubts.

He led her down among the graves and she stayed two steps behind, taking in the stone-dotted landscape. The cemetery hid from the small-town business of Main Street, enclosed by a tree line that helped mute the knowledge, if not the noise, of cars and trains running beyond its edge. Will pointed with the rake. "That fenced area is where the Summers' graves are. Your family's plots are down from there, near the back."

Abby followed, stepping carefully as they left the main path to walk among the tombstones and memorials. She'd tripped over a gravestone three years ago and broken her ankle, consigning a hot, miserable summer to a walking cast for her failure to watch her steps. Everywhere she saw little evidences of memory and devotion—flower arrangements and flags, mostly. Some graves were decorated with trinkets, like one with a small collection of ceramic cats before it, and quite a few glinted with circular aluminum emblems honoring military service. They made her curious. "Hey, Will? What's in the bag?"

"Easter lily bulbs. Mrs. Watts gets one from church every year at Easter. Finally had too many of 'em in her front flowerbeds, and of all places, she wants 'em replanted here." He dropped the bag on John Watts' grave, unconcerned whether his feet crossed directly over the dead man below.

She gaped at him. "You don't think it's wrong to walk right over him?"

"I don't see how the mowers would keep to that rule," Will said. "You gonna be all right with me planting here? I won't dig but a few inches deep."

She studied the stone. John Watts passed away in 2005. How strange to see Aunt Ruby's name and birthdate engraved on the right side of the stone, with the ominous blank space for the date of her death. The stone put her five years younger than the date on the old driver's license. Hilarious. If she were having the stone cut today, would she slough off another five? "I'm fine. I guess you're right. I think it's a nice way to remember him."

He tossed her a bulb. "And I think flowers are for the living. The dead can't enjoy them."

"But you believe there's an afterlife."

"I do."

"And you don't see the contradiction in that?"

"Nope."

She played with the bulb, tossing it from one hand to the other.

"And since they're safely tucked away in heaven or wherever, you say we should forget them."

"I say the effort's better spent on live people." He hesitated. "Like your friend."

Abby held her tongue for a long moment. "I'd like to believe in . . . I don't know, maybe not the standard halos-and-pitchforks version of heaven and hell, but more of an essence. A continuation. Something . . . ongoing."

"You can't just settle in on what sounds nice, though. Wantin' to believe in something don't make it real."

"I could say the same to you," she countered. She dropped the bulb back in the bag with the rest.

"So that's why you're hounding after ghosts?"

He made it sound so stupid, saying it out loud like that. She tried to laugh it off but her throat hitched. "I guess. My mom and all. Proof by proxy."

He withdrew a garbage bag from his back pocket and handed it to Abby to unfold. "I'll rake if you'll bag up the debris."

They worked in self-conscious silence, the subject thoroughly dead when she spoke again. "Do you think I'm nuts?"

He didn't look up. "Does it make any difference?"

"Suppose it does."

He raked along the edge of the retaining walls, coaxing grass clippings and stray pine cones along the narrow strip into a pile. "I promised not to step on your toes."

"But now I'm asking you."

"Then I'll tell you. I don't think you're nuts, but you're looking in the wrong places. Here, for instance. I don't like cemeteries because they honor death when Jesus already conquered it." His voice was even, though Abby noticed how he kept at a square of earth he'd already stripped bare. "You're lookin' for an afterlife. Well, He's it."

"Okay. You believe that, but you don't have any evidence."

"His empty grave is evidence."

She saw she wouldn't dissuade him but couldn't stop herself from arguing. "Have you been there? And if it's empty, you can't prove anyone was ever in that grave. Let alone any specific person."

He stopped and leaned on the rake, watching as she crouched down,

115

stuffing the bag. "There's a Bible verse about that, you know."

She rose up and pretended to stretch, but the truth was she didn't like the feel of him towering above her. "I didn't know. Although it makes sense that there would be."

He looked up as if the words were written in the sky. "'Now faith is the substance of things hoped for, the evidence of things not seen.' What if that means faith based on proof isn't faith at all?"

Abby swallowed hard. She brought it up, and she could shut it down. She stuffed an armload of pine straw and grass clippings into the garbage bag. "Then faith sounds to me like an easy answer for a hard question. Sorry, but knowing is better than hoping."

She waited for a rebuff that didn't come, but she knew better than to suppose she had won. The conversation hung unfinished, licensed to continue in some other when and where.

Names from the charts Aunt Ruby had helped her fill in whispered out of the stones, too many to remember. Now that she knew where to go, she would have to come back to figure out who was who. The plots were home to ghost-candidates she hadn't even considered.

Will meanwhile worked quickly and without interest in the details on the headstones, stooping often to pull weeds. "I'm slowing you down," she said.

"You're not." He tied up the bag of pine needles, grass clippings, and tattered remains of silk flowers. "I only got one garden trowel, though. You could look around while I plant."

While he crouched before John Watts' tombstone with the bulbs, she wandered the squared paths between plots. George Hart's grave was conspicuously absent among her long-dead relatives. Why didn't she think to bring her phone, a pen, or any way to take notes? Instead, she circled the two plots with her head down, minding her steps and engraving names and dates in her memory, or trying to.

When at last she lifted her eyes, a name at a distance winked back at her, so fast she turned away before she realized it and had to find it again as the rest of the scene registered in her mind. Down near the tree line, four headstones bore their time of fruitless waiting. She approached for a better view, no longer taking heed of the cemetery's obstacles, and held her breath as she studied one shared gravestone of a man and his wife, two tiny matching markers, and a cylindrical stone bearing on its face the name she recognized. She'd found W. C. Sosebee.

Crouching down as she'd seen Will do, she traced the dates with her finger, 1921 to 1942. It was him. It had to be.

A cluster of grape hyacinths and ground ivy grew wild at the edge of the woods. On impulse, she plucked a weedy bouquet and divided it between the four graves. As she leaned down, an absence struck her. No adornments marked the grave, no miniature flag, no insignia, no token of his service to his country. "Who *are* you?"

She backed away from the plot and took it in as a whole. A wide stump before the graves suggested the City's efforts to keep the forest from marching forward, although little shoots of new growth poked up from the roots. The trees littered the plot with acorns and pine straw. As for the graves themselves, the shared marker most likely belonged to his parents. Joseph Sosebee lived from 1895 to 1962, and his wife Bridget was born in 1899, although the date of her death wasn't cut into the stone. Tears brimmed her eyes at the sight of two little graves, hardly better than field markers. "Infant Son – 1924," read one, and the other, "Infant Daughter – 1926."

"Everyone deserves a name," she whispered.

"Doing all right?" Will came up behind her. She blinked until her shining eyes wouldn't give her away. She couldn't tell him the truth, so she started talking, hoping a plausible story would fall out.

"Yes. I found this." She gestured at the graves. "I hate that the mother's death date isn't marked. It's kind of horrible. And you probably think I'm kooky, standing around crying at random people's graves."

"I think you're a sweet, tender-hearted girl," he corrected her. "If that ain't too strange a remark for a graveyard."

"No, it isn't. What's weird is being called 'girl' by someone so much younger than me. What are you, eighteen?"

"Twenty-one going on ninety-one, according to Mrs. Watts."

Twenty-one. Seven years wasn't a bad difference. For a second, she soaked in his words and his kindness like an invisible essence that deserved to exist and be seen.

Then the moment was over, and she relaxed into her lie. "Sometimes I look at gravestones or old houses or whatever and I see a story. This one struck me. Her children died young, she outlived her husband, and there was no one left to remember her when she died."

Will studied the plot with a stoicism that didn't suit him. "What'd I tell you about flowers?" He scooped the one off W. C. Sosebee's grave and tapped her lightly on the nose with it.

"It's just a weed. And I prefer lilies."

"Silly, you should've kept that bulb." She propped the flower up by the tombstone again, and Will tilted his face heavenward. "Come on. I'll walk you home."

He turned away and Abby followed, but not without casting a last look over her shoulder at the stones by the tree line. He could believe whatever he wanted, but he was wrong. She shivered. The grave would always win.

As they left the cemetery, she offered to carry the rake on their way back, but Will wouldn't hear it. "I do this all the time, Abbs."

She conceded, satisfied that she'd at least tried to help. "By the way, I cleaned that front bedroom out. It's ready whenever you want to come over and move the furniture."

His face clouded. "I didn't forget."

"I understand if you don't have time for it right away. I don't need that room."

"You're entitled to it, though. I'm sorry. As soon as—soon. I promise." He winced on the last word.

"No rush," Abby said, but she did feel rushed. She wanted a reason to see him again, one he couldn't refuse. Without thinking twice, she let the words fly. "Oh, I meant to tell you. I think the fridge is trying to die on me."

"I'm not surprised. What's it doin'?"

"It's making a weird knocking noise. Not all the time, though. It's intermittent."

They turned onto Pike's Landing Road and came into sight of the little house with its overgrown ivy trellises. "I can look at it now."

"No, no. My friend is still here. Maybe tomorrow? I'll be back from taking her to the airport around five-thirty tomorrow afternoon."

"All right." He nodded. "'Til then."

Once Will was gone, Abby attempted to open the front door quietly in case Sarah slept in. The sticky lock mocked her as she tried to find a noise-free jiggle that would release the catch inside.

She needn't have bothered. Sarah sat at her kitchen table, scrolling through whatever had captured her attention on her cell phone. Other than glasses in place of her contacts, Sarah looked none the worse for the wear. Her hair was wet from a shower, and an empty coffee mug sat at her elbow.

"I hid your papers again. All your piles are safely separated with paper clips. Also, what on earth type of errand could have possibly been so important on a Saturday morning?"

"I had to get my emissions done." Abby crossed her fingers. "I forgot it last week."

"I'll bet they had a hard time checking it, since you left your car here." Sarah finally looked up, studying Abby through narrowed eyes. "What's his name?"

"Whose name?" She should say W. C. Sosebee. Maybe she and Greg would have more luck Googling him. At least his parents' names would let Abby renew efforts to find the Sosebees' historical records. She'd pick up with the census after Sarah left.

Why didn't he have a service marker? And what was wrong about—

Sarah tapped her fingers on the table. "The name of whoever got you all sweaty and starry-eyed. But I get it, wanting to keep him to yourself for a minute before filling in your best, closest friend in the whole world . . . ."

"I knew you'd understand. Let me shower off the sweat and stars, and then we'll go have some fun."

"Excellent. As long as your idea of fun doesn't involve searching for dead people."

"No, no. And waste your visit? Definitely not. After all," she said, Will's smile beaming in her mind's eye, "the world and its lusts are passing away."

CHAPTER 16

Sunday, April 1

Even with the windows down and the vent on high, the midday heat turned the inside of the Mustang into an oven. The sun glinting off the back bumper of the car ahead burned Abby's retinas, but when she fell back enough to save her eyes, another car swooped into the gap. If the next road sign she saw welcomed her to hell, it wouldn't surprise her one bit.

Gridlock choked off the interstate, and she crawled back from the Hartsfield-Jackson airport. The stop-and-go traffic didn't bother her so much through the city, where the glass-paneled towers stretched into the heavens in all their stern and angular glory and the sun flared off the gilded dome of the Capitol Building. But north of the city where no particularly inviting scenery availed, Abby cursed the road beneath her tires and every other driver sharing it. Sarah's plane would make it back to Ohio before she even hit the Kennesaw city limits. After creeping a scant three miles in twenty-five minutes on I-75, she squeezed the steering wheel and practiced deep-breathing. Will would understand. There might have been a horrible accident up ahead. She should be thankful she wasn't in it herself. Calm. Peace. Zen, or whatever.

She almost had herself convinced when the bottleneck loosened up. With an eerie synchronization, the cars all around her resumed a normal speed. No hint of an accident, road construction, or debris. Not so much as an animal carcass to explain why half of the state of Georgia spent the afternoon parked on the Interstate. The traffic jam evaporated like rain on hot pavement.

Abby laid on the horn. "Are you clowns kidding me?" she screamed. "For a mess like that, someone ought to be dead!"

Another driver, a young mother by the look of her, caught Abby's eyes for a split second, then looked away and changed lanes. Caught throwing a tantrum on the highway—wow. It would take her a while to top this one.

Abby beat back her embarrassment by pretending she hadn't seen the woman's expression, and that her flaming cheeks only reflected the shimmer of heat rising up from the highway.

Either the spent charge of anger or the absence of Sarah's exuberance invited the malaise back into her body. Or maybe it never actually left. A few days of distraction couldn't cure whatever was broken inside her, no more than a change of scenery could. What a gross miscalculation she'd made. All she'd done was to become a stranger, a newcomer who didn't know to account for traffic, getting her ears bent by accented words and dialectic phrases, still learning her way around, and no better off than she had been in Ohio.

She changed lanes. That wasn't true. She was better off for knowing Will.

And for Will's sake, she drove ten miles over the speed limit the rest of the way to Kennesaw. She did it because five-thirty raced her to the house and looked like the favorite to win. She hurried with a curious regret prickling at the back of her skull, knowing that the sweetness of anticipation would soon concede to reality, that he would check the refrigerator, find it in working order, and disappear again.

When did he start to matter so much to her? Although she had enjoyed the time with Sarah, she couldn't help being the slightest bit glad to see her go. After Abby absconded with Will on Saturday morning, Sarah wouldn't leave her alone about him.

"How did you guess?" she'd finally asked, exasperated.

"I heard him knocking, so I checked through the peephole. Of course, I wasn't about to answer the door for some strange man."

"And you didn't think to wake me, I assume?"

Sarah shrugged, plainly enjoying her little game. "After you raved about how comfy your couch is? I couldn't. I figured him for a Boy Scout on a fundraising mission."

"He's too old for Boy Scouts."

"Then the fishbowl view deceived me, but he's still way too young."

"He's not that young. He's outside all of the time."

"That should make him look older, not younger. And I think Greg is much handsomer, actually."

Abby's fingernails dug into her palms. She forced her hands to unclench. "You think so? Even when we were together, he always reminded me of that guy you met at Beth's Christmas party. Remember how you gave me your phone so I could I untag all the Facebook pictures while you—"

"Don't finish that sentence," Sarah commanded. "Unlike some people, I know how to leave the past alone."

After that, Sarah hadn't breathed another word about either Will or Greg.

Blue lights flashed behind her. A mini-heart attack seized in her chest as she slowed and moved to the right, but the cop blew past her, apparently in pursuit of a hotter target.

She ought to be thankful, and truly, she was. Thankful for Will, thankful that only a handful of minutes separated them. The burden of awkwardness crumbled more each time they spoke, and under her reserve, Abby found unabashed regard for him.

Afraid to push her luck, she crept through the square at the excruciating twenty-five mile-per-hour limit. She turned down Pike's Landing Road at five-forty and almost drove up the sidewalk to avoid a wild driver barreling toward Main Street. Abby honked and the driver tooted back and waved, friendly and oblivious.

An obscene gesture drew into the muscle memory of her right hand. She stopped short of presenting it when she recognized the other driver as Aunt Ruby. She managed a wave instead, and only then she noticed Will sitting in the passenger seat.

Abby prayed for the first time in months, but the earth couldn't be bothered to open up a nice big chasm for her.

She pulled up to the house and to her surprise, Aunt Ruby's reverse lights blinked on. She zoomed backwards up the empty street, parked in front of the house, and rolled her window down. "Hey, we caught you right on time."

"Huh?" She turned off the ignition and got out of the car as Will did the same, stepping out of Aunt Ruby's maroon Sentra and swinging his door shut at the exact same instant Abby slammed hers. The tandem sounds cinched a parallel, a continuum of kindred souls that stretched across existence, and Abby was convinced beyond all rationality that she and Will came from the same place at heart, and would eventually reach the same destination.

"Hey, Abbs. Looks like we didn't miss you after all."

"Yeah, I'm sorry. I hit a ton of traffic on my way up from the airport. Um . . . " She trailed off with a question in her voice.

"Mrs. Watts decided we're going to evening service at church tonight." He cleared his throat, a not-too-subtle emphasis. "*She* wanted to ask if you'd join us."

"I can't." She gestured to her summery khaki shorts and the blowzy white linen top clinging to her. "Two hours in that clunker of mine with no A/C."

"Oh, you smell fine. Get in," Aunt Ruby called. Abby caught Will's wince and blushed.

"All my churchy clothes are long-sleeves and sweaters. I don't have any light enough for a day like today."

"If that's the only reason to stay away, then c'mon. You look . . . " She hung on his next word, but he stopped himself and chose a different tack. "Mrs. Watts is wearing blue jeans and purple flip-flops. We're like a family. Come as you are."

At this, Aunt Ruby revved the engine. "If I tol' you once, I tol' you twice, William. They're mauve."

"Aunt Ruby, give him credit. He did know to set off your antique sofa with a lavender accent wall," she half-teased. "And speaking of family, I have a new bunch of questions for you."

Abby winked at her, mostly for Will's benefit. If he could breech their agreement, so could she. She looked for his reaction, but he either ignored the wink or hadn't seen it at all.

"What's that again, child?"

"It's not important, Aunt Ruby. You guys have fun, I guess."

Will bore a slight slope in his shoulders. "Maybe next time?"

What made him so desperate to get her into church? Could they be members of a cult? She couldn't think of her aunt having any association with a cult, except possibly leading one.

"Maybe," she said, and for spite added, "No promises."

"Hey." He caught her with his low, tender voice and held her with his eyes. "I'm sorry about this."

"It's okay."

"No, it's not. I'll come back by tonight, once I see Mrs. Watts home. Eight o'clock. We'll see if we can get that fridge talkin' and then work on clearin' out the upstairs room for you."

But the chase was the fun part. She knew that well enough from Greg. She worked up a smile. "Can't. Too tired. My friend Sarah doesn't visit—she *happens*. Her idea of a birthday weekend is most people's idea of a hurricane. I think I'm going to turn in early tonight."

His hands fell to his sides. "I missed your birthday."

"Yeah, it was Friday." She shifted her weight from one foot to the other, wondering why she even mentioned it. "You didn't know."

He waved her words away, not allowing her to make excuses for him. "I'll make it up to you." He paused, the Sentra idling behind him and a battle playing out on his face. "Do you like music?"

Aunt Ruby honked her horn, making them both jump. "I ain't gonna be late on account of y'all."

He shot her an apologetic look and backed away. "We'll talk soon," he said at the same time as she nodded and answered, "Yes, I like music."

"Be good." Aunt Ruby honked again with a child's delight and peeled out with Will barely inside the car. Abby watched the brake lights illuminate at the corner. The Sentra was already halfway onto Main Street when its right turn signal began to blink. Whatever it would take to get Aunt Ruby to give up her keys, Will evidently hadn't discovered yet.

Abby gathered her purse and GPS from the car and trudged up the porch steps. She'd told Will the absolute truth about being too tired to squeeze one more exploit into the weekend, but not about going to bed early. How could she possibly sleep?

I like him. I think he likes me. He didn't quite ask her out, but this was significant progress. And when he eventually did? She giggled. She might beg for a rain-check, the longer to savor the anticipation.

The tricky lock released with only a little teasing. Maybe her fortunes were finally due for a change. That, or maybe the ghost decided to make itself useful by keeping the doorknobs rattled. "I like it, ghost." She knocked on the doorframe as she entered the house. "Nice and practical."

After the brightness outdoors, the kitchen appeared dim. The coolness inside made her suddenly aware of the filmy sheen covering her body. Ugh. And Will saw her like this. She headed straight for her room to inspect the damage.

The reflection over the dresser stilled and stared. A single item, familiar but out of place, flared to her eye like a flashpoint. A translucent orange bottle with a white cap and bluish-white label lined up neatly beside her makeup on top of the vanity. The useless pills she'd forgotten to take from her medicine cabinet back at the apartment, Sarah had so kindly returned.

The fresh imprint of Sarah's voice brought an old comment to mind as if she stood right there repeating it. *Sounds to me like somebody's off her meds.*

Her pleasure over Will's display of interest whirled away like smoke as Abby took in Sarah's scolding, complete without a word.

"I didn't ask you to come." She scooped up the pill bottle and pitched it into the trash. She snagged her phone from her back pocket, snapped a picture, and keyed a furious text to Sarah. "Thx 4 nothing. Here's how much I need you."

She sent the message and stared down on the pill bottle, almost wanting to pluck it out from its bed of used tissues and gum wrappers and throw it a second time, that memento of her last solid relationship. Without Sarah, she had no one.

"Wrong. I've got Aunt Ruby and Uncle Blake. And Will too, if I play my cards right. I'm home. I belong here." She lifted her chin and called out. "Don't I?"

If silence stood for assent, then the house heartily agreed.

CHAPTER 17

NORTH CANTON, OHIO

"Brudder!" Sarah met Greg at the gate in the Akron-Canton airport with exaggerated joy, embracing him as if it had been years and not days since they'd seen each other. "You have no idea how happy I am to be home. Seriously. Listening to those people's accents is like waking up in an episode of *Duck Dynasty*. And the pollen is absolutely unholy. I have a date with my neti-pot tonight. The sooner, the better."

"Welcome home, Sissy. How was your flight?"

Sarah backed out of the hug and glared at him. "It was a flight. You're supposed to ask me how Abby's doing."

Greg shielded his eyes from the afternoon sun pouring in the windows at the gate. "You forgot to email me the script. Sorry I don't know my lines."

"That's okay. To answer the question, not good. I'm concerned."

He walked away, trying to prompt Sarah to follow. "She's probably still adjusting."

"Oh, she's adjusting all right. That's the whole problem. In typical Abby-fashion, she's creating her own spiral of doom. And since you have a little experience with escaping the vortex—"

"Not funny."

"Do I look like I'm kidding? She's up to her eyeballs in some genealogy mystery thingy, and she took off Saturday morning with a guy. She said he's her landlord, but that can't be right. He's super-young. Like, I don't know, college-age."

Greg inhaled sharply and looked away. The airport had the scents and sights of a mall, full of enticements that weary travelers fell weak for: fried foods in the restaurants, shot glasses in the gift shops, glossy tabloids at the newsstands. "Whatever makes her happy."

Sarah's phone chimed, and she stopped in the middle of the walkway to check it. "Okay, she got my message. Huh. I expected swearing. Maybe Fratboy is good for her."

Greg resumed walking. "Too much, Sarah."

"Because you're not listening. She's on a complete vacation from reality."

He rubbed his cheek. "That's not exactly breaking news. The stated purpose of her move was a ghost hunt, correct?"

"Yeah, about that. I'm minorly freaked out."

"'April Fools'? Ha ha."

"No, listen. I did hear strange noises."

"Right."

"But most of it was normal old-house stuff. Once I could have sworn I heard someone walking across the roof. Which is weird, but not, like, ectoplasm weird. And I heard it when I first woke up, so I might have dreamed it. The main problem is Abby. She's changing."

Greg furrowed his brow. "How?"

"I promised not to embarrass her to you," she said matter-of-factly, "and in light of that, I don't know how to explain. You'd have to see her." Her eyes lit up as she heard herself. "Yes. That is an excellent idea. You need to go see her."

He turned to face her, exasperated. "And do what? I'm the last person she wants to see. No confusion on that point, yeah?"

"You're wrong. You're exactly who she needs. Look, her mom is gone and no one can change that, but if you could convince her to move back home, that would be a hint of normalcy. A reality reboot. Or at least you could stop her from drooling over random guys. She needs you."

Greg scowled instead of answering. His empty hands suddenly shamed him, and he took Sarah's carry-on. "I'll pray about it," he muttered.

Sarah heaved a sigh. "You do that. And put in a vacation request at work, in case you get an answer."

CHAPTER 18

KENNESAW

Stopping to invite Abby along put them in danger of arriving late to church. Less than a dozen times in her long life had Ruby been guilty of being tardy to church, and most of them weren't her fault. No excuse for walking in after they started. She'd sooner miss the whole service than show up late.

Will didn't care when they got there. He matched his pace to hers, and she hurried as much as her worn-out body would let her. He held one side of the big double doors leading into the sanctuary, and once she could see inside, Ruby relaxed. A healthy pre-service clamor rose up from the small crowd, not-quite-everyone in place. They made it.

Ruby slowed her pace. The back of a reddish mop hovered over the sloping shoulders of some woman taking up her usual spot in the third row, left side.

Humph. Bad enough they hauled the traditional pews out to replace them with these flexy blue chairs. Her daddy'd been on the finance committee when they bought them straight-backed wooden pews and even helped haul 'em into the sanctuary himself. He hadn't been a stern man by any means, but he had definite ideas about the correct handling of the Word of God. Ruby doubted he would have abided microphone-preaching and cushioned chairs.

Used to be when she came into the sanctuary, she could picture every detail of marching down the aisle on Daddy's arm. Him with his hair slicked down and wearing a suit coat that bunched in the shoulders, the pine boughs tied up with white ribbons clipped to the end of each row, seeing everyone she loved and who loved her standing, admiring—but year over year those memories became copies of themselves and faded into shadows.

She learned time was cruel by the details that wouldn't recede—how Pearl pointed out the small stain on the wedding dress Suzette loaned her. Or how the ceremony began ten minutes late because Christie had been in line at the Lewis building, waiting his turn to register for the draft. Why'd they have to have registrations on Valentine's Day? Uncle Sam even took his share of their wedding day. Looking back, she could only call it an omen.

No one remained who'd been present that day. Not a single one still living, besides her. Like pins fixing her life in place, they'd been pulled out one by one. Agnes meant to be there but said she had to work, a claim Ruby knew to be false. She forgave and forgot twice a year ever since.

How she missed the pretty white church as it stood back then, its high, sharp steeple patterned in the rows of narrow windows, each topped by triangular embellishing panes. That one got hit by a storm and was condemned in 1951, and its stodgy brick replacement only lasted 'til 1968. She and John could've been first to wed in the present sanctuary, but opted for City Hall and a simple ceremony followed by coffee and cookies. "We're too old for a church wedding," she'd insisted, and so kept her first wedding day hoarded. Protected. Too silly to admit, but even then she didn't want to muddle up her memories.

And now she could remember it any old way she wanted, because who'd know the difference?

Enough. Will and not Daddy escorted her into the church, and folks who bothered to notice saw a withered old woman, not a fresh-faced bride. Normally Will gave her the aisle seat, but today Sharon Petersen sat there, smearing lip balm over her mouth, oblivious to the fact she'd stolen Ruby's place.

She approached the end of the row with a loud cough, thinking Sharon would have the good sense to scoot down two seats.

"Hey, Miss Ruby," she said. "You made it right on time."

"Evenin', dear. Is anyone sittin' here?"

"You are!" She attempted to flatten herself to the chair, a resistible invitation for Ruby to climb over her to the seats she blocked.

Save me the room next to yours at the nursing home, Agnes. She navigated her rear-end past Sharon's face. An unbidden jealousy pricked her. True, Agnes had to give up her hoity-toity assisted-living apartment, but at least she didn't have to fool with the likes of well-meaning church folk or vulture relatives.

All at the expense of seeing friends, Ruby had to admit. She resolved to visit soon. After the stroke she lost the habit of going out that way, and she hadn't been to see her friend's downgraded abode. She'd soon fix that. Like it or not, she wasn't an age for putting her business off.

Which also meant she'd better figure out how to deal with Abby.

She didn't want Will to have to climb over Sharon and her both, so she moved down far enough to allow him a place to sit between the two of them. Setting her purse beside her, she tried to get comfortable. Sharon got right to work making eyes at Will, laughing too loud and puffing out her newly glossed lips too much. Ruby shot out disapproving glares, but Sharon wasn't looking at her.

He's spoken for, she wanted to tell her, but of course that wasn't true. Not anymore. Then the opening chords struck and if Ruby hated one sin more than lateness, it was chatter in church. Even during the casual evening services. No, sir.

After the worship songs, the assistant pastor led a prayer. Ruby only half-listened. Stubborn Abby, blind and deaf to obvious hints, poking her nose in all the wrong places and troubling old bones. Now with a fresh crop of questions. Mercy.

A chorus of amens went around the room, but Ruby kept her head bowed a moment or two longer. No one remembered Christie. What happened was never her fault.

Except if that Abby kept digging long enough, what might she find to suggest otherwise? The Internet didn't make much sense to Ruby, except that now the computers knew what time itself forgot. Anyone's guess what it held. What happened to pulling the girl's strings?

She raised her head, serene as the dawn. Misdirection backfired and temptation failed outright, but the one big string still dangled, waiting to be pulled. Richard.

The assistant pastor interrupted Ruby's plotting, his reedy voice booming through the obnoxious sound system. "All right, everyone take your Bible and open up to the book of Romans. Tonight we're looking at a question everyone faces sooner or later: where is God when the pain comes? Romans eight twenty-eight. Let's read."

Ruby thumbed the pages in resignation to another of the hazards of life-long church attendance. She'd taken in so many versions of this same sermon, by now she could preach it herself.

After service they paused for brief chit-chat, but Ruby didn't let their conversations linger on. They filed out of the sanctuary and into the blue dusk, and Will offered his hand. She took it, not for balance but because she enjoyed his consideration. Some might call him old-fashioned, but Ruby had lived long enough to know that manners weren't so commonplace way-back-when either.

"I always like when Pastor Jason preaches. Too bad Miss Abby wouldn't join us. I think she might could've used some of that."

"Mmm," she replied, a sound straddling the fence of agreement and indifference. She'd called out a couple of amens but mainly stayed caught up in her own head. To win Abby to her side, she needed a confrontation of sorts. Plenty of schemes and stories had occurred to her, but none that didn't risk getting caught in a lie.

Then that Sharon Petersen, ignoring the rule banning food and drink from the sanctuary, twisted the cap off a Mountain Dew and released the coiled hiss of pent-up fizz. As much as it had annoyed Ruby, that hiss inspired her. The whole situation had enough emotion bubbling through it already. All she needed was close confines and a good hard shake.

"Maybe next time. She could help you fend off Sharon Petersen."

"Hush, you." He lowered his voice. "Folks might hear."

"Let 'em." She paused, thinking of how Abby and Will murmured at each other over at the old house. Had she taken a shine to him? Or him to her?

She couldn't afford for him to spill the plan to Abby. Literally. Blessed are the peacemakers, and he'd get the tar blessed out of him if he interfered with what she had tucked up her sleeve. Poor Will. Only one way to go, but she hated it. On occasion she pitied him, but the rest of the time she stayed nothing short of glad he hung around.

She eyed him sideways as they walked to the car. "Speaking of Abby, how's she liking it here so far?"

Will rubbed his forehead. "Wish I knew what she came looking for."

"A boyfriend," Ruby guessed.

"Can't help her with that."

"Of course not. You're too busy with me. You shouldn't have to follow an old lady around all the time, a boy your age."

"Who else should I follow around?" He put those precious dimples on display, exactly the expression that made the Sharon Petersens of the world think they had a chance. "God gave me a job to do."

"But the worker's worthy of his wages, William, and I . . . " Her pride choked out the words, but it wasn't a secret how far behind she'd fallen on his pay. "You can't work for nothin'."

He opened the car door for her, squirming. She hated herself for the spot she put him in, where he wouldn't lie and couldn't tell the truth. A stiff breeze sent a flurry of cherry petals dancing across the parking lot. Spring fading already, almost as soon as it sprung. Maybe it prompted his reply. "To everything there is a season."

She climbed in the driver's seat and cranked the Sentra while he circled around to the passenger side. That Will. She couldn't let him go.

"Seasons change, though," she said when he got in the car. "I wondered if you'd mind terribly if we worked out a different arrangement for those wages."

As soon as the floodlight welcomed them back to her little house, Will bid her a good evening and disappeared off into the night.

She didn't blame him. The El Camino sat in the middle of her driveway and if she didn't have to, she wouldn't go inside either.

"Where you been?" No greeting from Blake, no attempt at civility. Ruby hung her pocketbook from the coat tree. He wouldn't find any money in her billfold to filch, not 'til her Social Security check came.

"Out with my boyfriend. You shouldn't have waited up." He snorted and turned back to the TV. Ruby went into the kitchen and groaned at the dishes stacked in the sink and the garbage piled high. "Blake, come take out this trash."

"In a minute," he called.

Shameful, letting it sit and stink until the commercials. Ruby wouldn't have it. Might as well have been a bag of rocks, but she managed to heft the trash up and drag it out to the green roller bin in back of the house, fuming all the while and grieving a little too.

Will would've done it without her asking.

CHAPTER 19

Wednesday, April 4

"Mr. Stevens, your eleven o'clock is here." An HR lackey deposited Abby at the threshold of the manager's office and then slithered back to the corporate underbelly she came from. The name plate by the door read "CLARK STEVENS."

"Come in, come in. Which one are you?" He shuffled a stack of résumés. "Abby Wells. Short for Abigail?"

"Short for nothing." Clark Stevens gave her an odd look, and Abby resolved to change her standard response. These Southerners didn't get it. "I mean, no sir. Just Abby."

"All right. Have a seat and I'll tell you about the position. We're hiring two processing specialists to take the data entry responsibilities off our account managers. You'll be responsible for scanning—good to see you have imaging experience—and correcting OCR errors before saving to the database. Of course, we're looking for someone who places the highest priority on speed and accuracy, but I'll be honest with you. We have some strong personalities around here, particularly in the sales department. Plenty of qualified candidates have applied, but we're looking for the one who truly fits with our organization." He laced his fingers together to illustrate.

"I've worked with salesmen before. I wouldn't say I'm easily intimidated."

He gave a tight smile. "Perhaps better if I say we need someone who can accept instruction from multiple sources. Tell me about yourself, Abigail."

"Abby," she reminded him. She opened her month and some nonsense spilled out about her education, integrity, and lofty standards of excellence, but halfway through her answer she could tell Stevens had already determined she wasn't the cog for his machine. The position wasn't too different from the one Greg hired her to fill, and that was the problem. In that interview, she had quickly decided she wanted him more than the job, and had peppered her answers with innuendo and double entendres.

He was supposed to call her, not hire her.

"Very good, then," Stevens said. "I've told you what the successful candidate looks like in our eyes. It's your turn. Tell me what you're looking for."

She tugged on her suit jacket. Not a question she anticipated. "I'm looking for . . . a paycheck." She laughed at her own joke. He smiled patiently. "I—I'd like an opportunity that allows me to expand my knowledge base of, um, scanning. And working with people. Strong people. With personalities, I mean."

"I see. Moving on—"

"Because I think when people pass through our lives, it changes us. You know, it makes a difference somehow. I want to leave a lasting impression."

He stared. "It's just scanning and data entry."

Abby stared out the plate-glass window behind Stevens, no longer speaking to him. "I want to know for sure if it even matters that I'm here."

"We'll call you next week with our decision." Clark Stevens showed Abby to the lobby, and they shook hands like honest people. She had planned to grab lunch in the cafe in the office park, but when she escaped the building, she fled for her car instead. There would be plenty of other choices on the way home.

So the interview flopped. It wasn't like she had her heart set on scanning. Mom used to coach her to find the upside in her disappointments. This failure was an opportunity to think bigger, to figure out what else she could do. No more applying for jobs like the one she had before. Her illustrious scanning career was over. In the long run, it was a good thing.

Maybe eventually she'd believe that.

She found a sandwich shop and called Aunt Ruby from the drive-thru queue, hoping to invite herself over. A few sideways questions might reveal more about George Hart and the divided property, but Uncle Blake picked up and she chickened out. After hanging up, she remembered the existence of caller ID and waited on pins and needles for a call back that didn't come. Not easily intimidated. Right.

She parked in front of the house. The maybe-haunted house and her only refuge. She went inside, but the sourness still clung to her. Georgia was not going according to plan.

"No. No whining. Who exactly set the expectations here?" She unwrapped the Veggie Panini and ate over the kitchen sink. As good as it looked on the menu picture, it didn't retain much appeal after the twenty-five minute drive. Too much mayonnaise, not enough onion, and stone cold to boot. "But the ghost doesn't do appearances. Fine. Maybe it's about waiting for him to move."

She chewed thoughtfully. "How does that sound, ghost? Will you show up for a stakeout? Knock once for no, and not at all for yes." She listened, heard nothing, and smiled. "Good. It's a date."

Abby choked down a quarter of the sandwich and threw the rest away. When she changed out of her interview suit, she found a gob of mayonnaise on the lapel.

Friday, April 6

It took Abby an hour to assemble the gear for her stakeout, and two days to assemble the nerve. "Pillow. Blankets. Cell phone. Thermometer. Granola bar. Bottled water. I have never been more ready to meet a ghost." Abby arranged her bedding as a pallet in the middle of the upstairs room and sprawled out, appreciating the discomfort of the floor. "Yes. Roughing it. I've been treating this like it should be easy. Probably my biggest mistake yet."

Funny that her ghost-hunting kit bore an awful resemblance to the items she carried to the hospital and then the hospice for Mom's last week. Except for the thermometer, but then, the hospital had their own.

"Okay, ghost," she whispered. "I'm where I said I'd be. It's all you now." She launched a game of Angry Birds and tried to be patient.

At first, every scrap of wind and skittering squirrel made her draw up tight to listen. Gradually, typical sounds became familiar and she no longer jumped at the scratching of tree branches or the crackly tap of pinecones hitting the roof. The frequent roar of trains passing in the night kept her awake until it didn't.

She woke with a crick in her neck, both nostrils swollen shut, and her lips badly chapped from hours of mouth-breathing. "I can be stubborn too, you know," she called out, but the stiffness between her shoulders gave her doubts. A foam pad and a bottle of Claritin would support a lot more stubbornness, and she ended up acquiring both before nightfall. She stocked up on Easter chocolates to boost morale.

By the third evening, Abby was thinking of giving up. The upper room housed a creepiness factor of ten, but it registered a zero on the paranormal activity scale. Worse, Aunt Ruby still hadn't called her. A week of radio silence followed the church invitation. If she'd known it was a test, she would have accepted it. Will made no impromptu visits either, and Aunt Ruby was still her only way to get a message to him. Not that it worked so well the first time. He must have forgotten all his promises to her, the way they stacked up unanswered.

Don't pout. Drop by her house and say hello, the soft-Mom voice nagged.

"I will. Only I'd rather be asked." She laced her fingers as Stevens had done. "You know. Fit."

She lay flat on her back, staring at the ceiling. If she kept her eyes open and focused on one spot for a long time, all sorts of illusions appeared—shapes and waves and flashing lights—and vanished when she blinked. A face of sorts, distorted and grotesque, emerged after a while, and she concentrated on it, fascinated.

A dull clunk startled her into blinking, and the face disintegrated. Bigger than a squirrel. A cat, or maybe a raccoon. For several seconds, silence reigned, then a heavy drag from the back of the house, and the unmistakable sound of footsteps above her, drawing nearer to the spot where she lay frozen. Some muted scuffles, and quiet overtook the house again.

Not a twitch, not a breath. Her heart thrummed, the only part of her with the sense to want to escape. Abby stayed rooted to the floor. No tricks for her eyes now as they darted all over the room.

The shadows remained unchanging. For some span of minutes—twenty? forty?—she kept still and silent, desiring to hear more and fearing the same. Probably less time than it seemed, but long enough for her heartbeat to regulate and her eyelids to droop. The sounds resumed, reversed. The gentle scrape, the light steps, the drag, the clunk.

He came. He left again.

She forgot to check the thermometer, but it didn't matter.

The ghost was real.

Friday, April 13

"Apple pie, apple pie." Shouldn't a bakery, even a grocery store mini-bakery, have a wider selection than bear claws and baguettes? Or one over-browned apple crumb cake versus three perfect cherry pies?

Out of the blue, Aunt Ruby restored Abby's faith with a summons to Friday night supper. After the call, she marveled in silence for a while, listening for words in the old-house creaks and moans. "I didn't know you were a messenger, ghost," she kidded, half-believing it was true. Here was her wish, spoken moments before the ghost debuted, fulfilled. If the timing didn't quite align, it was still as near to evidence as she'd come yet.

Aunt Ruby strong-armed her into promising to bring a homemade apple pie. She was so flattered and pleased to be invited, she agreed. "Easy as pie," she joked, and they both laughed. She belonged. She was home.

Abby had spent the better part of the week picturing her first *family* meal—Aunt Ruby, Uncle Blake, Will, and herself crowded around the dinner table, reaching for serving spoons and passing the butter. She continued to camp in the room upstairs, wanting to thank the ghost, but he didn't visit again.

No matter. With Uncle Blake, she planned to stick with safe topics, where he worked and how he spent the weekends. The conversation could go deeper with Will. Over dinner she might finally prod his story out of him. He wouldn't want the attention, but Aunt Ruby would tell him not to be bashful and probably fill in whatever he tried to leave out. There'd be a sober moment—on the phone her aunt made reference to getting her affairs in order—but Abby didn't expect to have much part in that conversation. Yes, she laid the evening out like a series of snapshots ready to be tucked into the pockets of an album. Memories, planned in advance.

Except they'd be eating cherry pie, not apple.

Abby stopped short on her way to the checkout, causing a traffic jam with a shopping cart trailing close behind. "Excuse me," she mumbled. She should get a glass pie plate. Five minutes in the oven would create the illusion of being fresh-baked. Sarah would be proud of her domesticity.

No, Sarah would write her own recipe for an apple-strawberry pie with lemon glaze, and if it didn't turn out, she'd blog about it. What if one of them was allergic to cherries? Should she go back for the burnt crumb cake?

As long as she was second-guessing, what if the questions she had planned backfired? She assumed small talk would ease into genuine conversation. Instead of appearing involved and engaged, what if she only reminded them all that she was an outsider?

"Stop it." She rubbed her temples. "I've never even heard of a cherry allergy."

"Yeah? Congratulations." The middle-aged man driving the cart behind her snorted and went around.

Abby bypassed the bakeware aisle, cheeks burning. Why kid herself? Aunt Ruby would know the difference between store-bought and homemade.

She refused a bag at the check-out for earth-friendliness and as a result nearly dropped the cherry pie on the pavement as she fumbled for her car keys. The lock remote quit working a couple years ago and replacements were too expensive, and now she balanced the pie in her left hand as she nudged the door open. No sudden moves.

She set the pie on the passenger seat, then thought better of it and moved it to the floorboard. She forgot the whipped cream. What time was it?

As she turned the ignition the clock lit up 4:27, but the engine sputtered, coughed, and stalled.

"No. Don't do this." She tried again. This time the Mustang whined before rolling into a quiet purr. Too quiet. The engine hummed with half its normal power. Maybe less than half.

"Why?" She expelled a feral groan and reached for her cell. No big decision about who to call. Every single soul she knew in the entire state would be at her aunt's house. Hopefully Will would answer.

"Hello?" The small, craggy voice of age broke her heart.

"Aunt Ruby, it's me. Abby. I'm at the grocery store and my car is acting up. Do you think Will—"

A muffled jumble of noise cut her off, and then a surly bark. "Yeah?"

"Uncle Blake? Hi, it's Abby. My car started, but—"

"Then what's it doin'?"

She exhaled a short breath. "Like I was saying, it's running but it doesn't sound normal."

"Where you at?"

"Publix on Highway 41. I'm around the corner from you guys." She was about to thank him for coming to her aid when he answered.

"Ain't far. You got two legs, don't you?"

"Blake, for heaven's sake," Aunt Ruby called out. "If you can't fix it then call her a tow. I'll hold supper."

A heavy sigh. "Stay there." He hung up.

She tossed the phone in her purse without looking at it. Tears brimmed; she blinked them away and new ones sprang up to replace them. "Obviously. Where could I go?"

"I've never even heard of an idle control valve." Abby followed Blake across the shop's parking lot, pie in hand. The changeable letter marquee claimed "Fast Frendly Svc," but no one in the place had moved with much urgency, and the shop owner laughed in her face when she asked if it would be ready by morning. "I hope they don't find more wrong while they're working on it."

She tried the door of Blake's El Camino and found it locked. He got in the driver side, cranked the engine, turned on the vent, and checked his mirrors before leaning over to unlock the passenger side.

"Sonny'll take care of you. I made sure his shop tech knew you were my kin."

Was that supposed to matter? What if he hadn't? The questions burned, but Abby minded her words as she buckled in. "At least my three hundred bucks goes toward a friend."

"Ain't like you're hurtin' for it." Blake backed out of the space and drove out over the "in" arrows painted on the blacktop. "What with Aunt Ruby charging you half the market value on the old place. It's worth at least double what we sold Mama's piece for. Cut you some deal, didn't she?"

"I guess. I'm sorry." The apology popped out. She didn't know why.

"Not that anyone in their right mind would pay to live there." He gunned the engine and squealed the tires pulling onto the roadway. "But don't get too comfortable."

"That definitely won't happen," she muttered.

Silence like kudzu wheedled and choked out the exchange, so Abby pretended to be fascinated by the view out her window, which for the moment mainly held a truck yard and a long row of boxy warehouses. A diesel truck ahead of them belched out a cloud of stinking black exhaust and a rush of memories with it—dirty snow and tahini and the sting of smoke in her eyes as Sarah politely kicked her out.

Blake twisted a dial, and cold recirculated air blasted through the car. "Phew, he's runnin' rich."

"What does that mean?"

He gave her the side eye. "I guess you wouldn't know. Forgot who I was talkin' to. My daughter used to spout off car specs like you wouldn't believe. Almost as good as her old man here. She could put on a donut by herself in less than twenty minutes. Changed her own oil and checked her own belts too. She definitely could've fixed that broken-down Mustang of yours."

"Aunt Ruby said I had some cousins."

"Did she? I figured she forgot about Audrey. The old house was supposed to go to her." A red light caught him, and he used it to glare full into her face. "But listen here. Don't be thinkin' you can swoop in and lay a claim. Ain't any more slices left in this pie."

"I . . . Uncle Blake, I don't want any 'slice of the pie.'"

His grip on the steering wheel relaxed visibly, but he kept up his abrasive tone. "Good, 'cause there's none for you."

The light changed. Uncle Blake flicked a switch on the radio, blasting a homemade southern rock recording before he laid on the gas pedal. The twangy licks and nasally vocals pouring through the speakers were too loud and dreadful, but Blake's music beat his conversation a thousand times over, at least.

She didn't speak until he turned down Hiram Street and slowed before Aunt Ruby's house. Her short driveway could accommodate up to four carefully parked cars, but Blake pulled into the middle, blocking Aunt Ruby's red Sentra on the right and an unfamiliar white Mitsubishi Lancer on the left. She wouldn't have guessed an import for Will, and she might've said so if she had any desire to make conversation. Instead, she took in the details of the car. Meticulously clean from the chrome rims to the gleaming spoiler. A pine-shaped air freshener hanging from the rearview mirror. A vanity plate that read, "2B RICH." And below that—

Her fingers and toes went cold and her head stayed only loosely attached to her neck. Blake cut the engine, and at the edge of her peripheral vision, she caught him sneering.

The tag on the white car said "COWETA."

CHAPTER 20

"I'm not feeling well." It wasn't even a lie. Her head pounded and her stomach did backflips. "I think I'm getting sick. Tell Aunt Ruby I'm sorry."

Instead of the scowl and sarcastic barb she expected, Blake squinted at her. "Guess your Mama didn't ever teach you there's no free rides in life."

She pressed her lips tight and dug into her purse. The smallest bill in her wallet was a ten; she folded it in half and stuck it in the dirty ashtray. "Actually, my father is the one who didn't teach me that. And you can tell him I said so."

His face twisted into a pleased smirk, as if watching her move a pawn to put her queen in check. "I might do that."

She escaped the El Camino, slammed the door harder than necessary, and stalked off. Halfway through the crosswalk over Main Street she remembered the cherry pie, but she didn't turn back.

A train at the rail crossing chugged and howled. Forget Kennesaw, her family home, her ghost story. Forget Aunt Ruby, her uncle, her father, and even—her heart squeezed—Will. She couldn't lose what she never had.

The Georgia experiment had reached the end of the line.

She trudged back to the house and sat on the front porch steps, mentally repacking the same boxes she'd already recycled. She would have to collect all new ones. Without her car parked in front, she probably looked as much like an intruder as she felt.

Sarah would act annoyed, but the gratification of being right would win her over. Resigned, Abby dialed the deleted number from memory. An Eighties-throwback assault blasted through the lines. Rickrolled by ringback. How very Sarah.

The music played long enough that when it clicked off, she expected Sarah's voice mail instead of the breathless live version she got. "Sorry, sorry." She dispensed with any greeting. "I was on an attic ladder and couldn't pick up right away. Sam and I are looking at houses."

"Oh. That's . . . " Abby crossed her fingers. " . . . wonderful. But I'm the one who should be apologizing."

"Forget it. I didn't want to upset you, but—well, I did a little. You know."

Abby's jaw tightened. The less said on the subject, the better. "How's the house hunt going?"

"We're standing in one that's fantastic. I mean, incredible. And it's a foreclosure. Bad for them, but good for us." Muffled complaints butted in, and when Sarah spoke again, an edge gilded her tone. "Except *Sam* doesn't like it because the flat screen won't fit in the *family* room except on the wall that'll catch the glare from the *window*." She dropped her voice. "I'm so aggravated at him. He doesn't even want to go to Florida with me for the taping."

"Taping?" She pictured Sarah's mummified figurines.

"Don't you ever get on Facebook anymore? I made it to the finals round for the cooking show."

"What?" Yet again Abby's tongue froze for a too-long moment as she groped for the accepted response. "Congratulations. That's awesome."

"Not quite. Prize money will be awesome. Competing on TV is merely cool. I'll call you later and give you the skinny."

"No. I'm busy tonight. In fact, I'm supposed to be at Aunt Ruby's."

"Glad that whole long-lost family bit is working out. I wouldn't have dreamed it would be going this well."

Abby coughed. "Yeah. It's great."

Sarah switched modes, from wrapping-up to interrogation. "What's wrong? Don't say nothing, either. I know you."

"N—I mean, it's not important. We'll talk. Tell Sam he'd better not miss that taping and that he doesn't need such a big TV. Good luck."

"Real quick, before you go." Sarah's voice took on hushed tones. The

Death voice. "You got some mail."

"I did? That's odd. I haven't missed any."

"Maybe because this one was already forwarded once. From your mom's old place." Abby didn't respond, and Sarah rushed on. "It's from the hospital. I didn't open it, but it looks like it could be a bill."

"Impossible. All of that's been handled."

"Hold your fire, governor, I'm just the messenger. I'll send it down. Along with a little something to cheer you up." A loud banging, perhaps a door slamming, interrupted her. "Sorry. I've gotta go. We have some crisis unfolding. Call me later this week?"

She closed her eyes. Same old Sarah, not putting her life on hold. Abby could see her standing in the middle of a bright house with an open floor plan, bossing movers to be careful with her glassy modernist possessions, relegating Sam to the family room, and refusing to help him mount the TV to the wall. Smooth, unstoppable Sarah, too busy forging ahead to be a haven for Abby's retreat.

"Yeah. Okay. Bye." She ended the call, damming up the dinner, Aunt Ruby, her father, her failures. The torrent was bound to break loose eventually, but for the moment, she had a problem with an easy answer.

The hospital had been paid in full. And she could prove it.

Mom's files waited in the front bedroom at the top of the stairs.

CHAPTER 21

Piles. Piles everywhere. Abby relegated the bedroll to the corner for a different kind of ghost hunt.

Her plan to find the paid statements quickly devolved into semi-organized stacks. Old utility bills and credit card statements. Apartment leases and the awkward legal envelope containing the closing documents for Mom's first and only house purchase. Silly mementos too—handmade birthday cards and movie ticket stubs. Abby's growth chart, carefully folded and preserved inside a manila folder. Even an entire notebook filled with early attempts at poetry written in a girlish version of Mom's penmanship. Abby ran her fingers over the lines and read the first few verses.

That's okay, Mom. Can't be good at everything.

By the third box, her rancor had tapered off. The collected memorabilia contained jagged edges, of course—the receipt slip for the flute Abby had begged for then abandoned prompted a spontaneous fit of tears—but much of it soothed, a hot water bottle against sore, tired muscles.

She'd almost forgotten what she was looking for.

Near the front of box five, among old papers she didn't recognize, a folder with a single sheet inside demanded attention. It resembled her lease—sparse type-written lines of text with signatures gracing the bottom. In fact, that resemblance stopped her cold and made her take note.

The names at the bottom mocked her; the simple phrases told secrets she didn't wish to know.

John H. Watts and Ruby Watts signed on the left side, and Richard Wells and Suzanne B. Wells on the right. Fifteen thousand dollars. Two percent interest. Whoever typed the homemade instrument hadn't bothered with the date. Only Mom noted, for posterity's sake, that she signed on February 16, 1984.

She read the page three times, trying to understand it in any sense other than the plainest one: Aunt Ruby loaned an enormous sum of money to Abby's parents six weeks before her birth.

"But they must have repaid it." Abby reopened the box containing all the canceled checks from long before the days of debit cards and imaging. "Or at least, I know Mom would have repaid her part."

Mom ordered from whichever outfit offered the best freebies, and the boxes of checks were random, haphazard, and undated. Abby opened each, stacking them by date and shuffling through the checks, searching for any made out to John or Ruby Watts and finding none.

Mom never paid back a cent on the loan.

"Of course she did." Abby argued into the emptiness. "She got a cashier's check or a money order."

Except she didn't. Abby remembered clearly, at their celebratory lunch before the closing on the house, Mom marveling and fussing over the cashier's check for the whole purchase price, securing it three times before Abby warned her to stop messing with it. "Can't take me anywhere, eh? I've never needed one of these before," Mom confessed. "I don't know how to act."

She refused the memory. "No. Mom never would have signed this. How many times did she tell me, never go into—debt. Right." She covered her eyes but the document appeared behind them, mocking her. She repackaged the miniature boxes and loose papers slowly so as not to damage them, but no longer much concerned with the bits of their unearthed history or the hospital bill she set out to find in the first place.

In her room, she opened her own files and retrieved the lease, her copy that Will left the night she moved into the house, and found the phrase that suddenly, inevitably, made perfect sense. Getting affairs in order. No unfinished business.

"'Payments don't count toward any past or future debts,'" she read aloud. "She wants to collect on Mom's half of the loan. This whole time, she's been scheming to siphon off me to pad her retirement."

Could she do that? Abby didn't know the law. What if she owed for Mom's loan? How much would the interest come to, unpaid for almost thirty years?

She slumped down hard on the bed. Whatever she had assumed family meant, it came down to faults and grudges, old hurts and unforgiven debts. She shouldn't have come.

She sneezed, once, twice, three times in a row. Karma would punish her with a summer cold or a nice pollen allergy for faking sick. Maybe she deserved it.

For the rest of the evening, she employed the Internet as legal counsel, taking what comfort she could from anonymous strangers who opined she probably wouldn't have to pay and ignoring trolls who asserted she definitely would. The sun went down, darkening the quiet house and leaving the glow of her laptop the only light and her clicking the only sign of life.

Her phone vibed against the table. She jumped. A second later, that goofy ring tone followed. "Danger, Will Robinson, danger."

Greg.

For all the spite she'd fostered for him, for all the words she had held back and the handful she hadn't on the rare occasions they'd spoken—Sarah's birthday party being the worst—in that moment, her heart leapt at his face on the caller ID screen. She exhaled to rid herself of anxiety and answered with restraint. "Hello?"

"Abby. It's me."

"Hi." She paused, trying to root a neutral greeting out of her brain. "I didn't expect to hear from you."

"I got a call for a reference last week. A guy named Clark Something."

She covered her eyes with her hand as her feelings of comfort dissipated. If the cosmos offered a way to blot this day out of the history of time, she wouldn't hesitate. "Was it before or after Wednesday?"

"Before. On Tuesday, I think. Is that good?"

She sighed. "I interviewed Wednesday. I knew he had his mind made up when I got there. Did you tell him to shred my application?"

"I told him what I tell all of them—that if I could, I'd hire you back in a minute."

"Peachy. But that isn't why you called."

He sighed. Not good. That puff of air wouldn't cushion the hammer about to fall. He sighed like that before he let her go. For an instant, she'd been confused. Why would he dump her at work? Then he passed her a separation form on company letterhead, completed except for her signature.

According to Greg, Abby broke it off. According to Abby, he should have been smart enough to know firing her included a break-up whether he wanted one or not.

"I'm sitting here, staring at my itinerary, asking myself why I let Sarah rope me into her schemes."

Her empty belly turned to stone. "What itinerary?"

"Promise you won't be mad."

She gripped the phone tightly. "No-o."

"I knew you'd say that, and just that way." He laughed humorlessly. "I called to ask if you'll have dinner with me Sunday night. Maybe at the little place by the railroad tracks? Sarah raved about it."

"Wait. No." She closed her eyes; behind them she saw Sarah, her troubled expression out of sync with her nonchalant demeanor. "You should have called before you paid for the ticket, Greg. I would have told you not to come."

"Well." He cleared his throat. "I know, but Sarah thought . . . "

"Yeah, she does that sometimes. Thinking. So annoying."

"Hey, now," Greg said, a mild warning. "She cares about you. I do too."

"You didn't buy a plane ticket out of concern for my well-being."

"No. I did it because I love you."

If he'd hoped to shock her with passion, he'd miscalculated. They'd dabbled with the L-word before he fired her, and she'd almost expected it. She smirked automatically, but of course he couldn't see her. "You've got to sell it, Greg. Make me believe you."

"I do. You know I do."

"You know my big problem with 'I love you'? The 'I' part always comes first." She rubbed her eyes. "Is the ticket refundable?"

"Of course not."

"Then, yes." She surprised herself with the snap decision, but relaxed into it. "I'll have dinner with you. But I'm not driving you to or from the airport, and you can't stay at my place. It's in my lease. No co-ed sleepovers."

"Is that all you think you mean to me?"

She bristled. If she wasn't more than a little curious what he wanted, she would have changed her mind right there. "No. That's all you were to me."

"It'll be good to see you again, Abby." His sarcasm put the cap on the day, and she found she didn't have the energy to return it.

"I . . . Until then, Greg."

She nearly dropped her phone trying to disconnect the call. She didn't need him, but if he insisted on hearing it again in person, why deny him?

That didn't mean she intended to let Sarah off the hook for her interference. Her fingers trembled as she tapped out a text.

"Did you seriously hand me off to your brother? You are the worst friend I've ever had." She fired it off, and from the response, Sarah had been waiting for it. The new message dinged back at her within seconds.

"Luv u 2, sweetie. Nice 2 hear from u today. Call/text if u need me."

Abby cradled her face in her hands. That dark old friend stole inward, curling around her heart and sapping her strength, weighting her limbs, sinking her until she became like the slab below the house or the earth below the slab. The holes she hoped to fill only widened, and everything she tried to leave in Ohio gained on her. The distance was meaningless. If she meant to discard her life, she'd have to cross a far wider gulf. Only fear of darkness on the other side kept her frozen in place.

CHAPTER 22

Ruby ached in places she didn't know she had. Her own body rebelled against her. Mercy. Had her bones joined the chorus with Blake and the rest of them, wishing she would hurry up and die?

All this set-up wasted, but no use getting mad at Abby, even if they had gone without any dessert for the evening. Best she kept away if a bug got a hold on her, although Ruby guessed the pollen or the heat had more to do with it. Thick yellow pollen clouds littered the air without a speck of rain to wash them away.

She swept all around the island in the kitchen, washed dishes and dried 'em, ground up a deodorizer in the garbage disposal, took the leftover chicken apart and portioned it, froze the bones for soup, and stored the cornbread in the breadbox under a yard of cling wrap. By morning it would be stale, although once she crumbled it up and poured buttermilk over it, she wouldn't know the difference. The collards—well, she didn't like 'em, and nobody else did either. The whole pot went straight to the trash. "Don't close your eyes," she mumbled while she wiped down the stovetop a third time. "They'll stick that way."

When her kitchen ran out of surfaces to clean, Ruby leaned on the island and brooded. The evening was a perfect disaster. On and on Blake went, flapping his yap. "She's got nothin' on Audrey," he kept saying. As much as Ruby knew she ought to pick up the gauntlet in Abby's defense, she was so tired. She let Blake carry on his arguments to no one.

Meanwhile Richard kept whitewashing history for his new little wife 'til their crowd left early. Hard enough to motivate him to come up once.

"It doesn't serve anyone's best interests to dredge up the past now," he'd said, so she tipped her hand a bit about settling old debts. Then he came all right, him and Mimi and her brood. He had the hang of being a father now. Raising another man's young'uns and never seen his own daughter. Shameful. Well, it was none of her business.

"Pearl, if you're listening," Ruby called out, "you might could scare those boys straight any time. Lord knows you didn't do it while you was alive."

Her sister's voice answered, clear and high as it'd been at twenty and sharp as if in the room with her. *Don't blame me. You're the one who missed her shot.*

"Did not," Ruby fired back, but it was true. Once Blake laid into his diatribe, he left nowhere for Ruby to interject any talk about money, and without Abby there, Ruby faced them alone, her against all of them.

No children. Two dead husbands, dozens of dead friends. No legacy, no one to remember her well. Relatives who ignored her 'til she had what they needed, and now she had nothing. Crazy, they'd say of her. Stingy, mean. And what would Abby write under Ruby's name in her history? "Eccentric old lady. Believed in ghosts." If she found out which ghost and why, Ruby's dark secret would end up recorded, footnoted for all time.

If not, she could be gone in a day, and forgotten in two.

"No." She blew her nose. "Won't none of 'em forget ol' Ruby. That much I'll make good and sure."

Blake would get all he had coming. Richard too, as far as that went. Bless her if she couldn't fry 'em both in the same pan. "I'll make the appointment Monday morning." She nodded. "Yes. All I gotta do is not die before it gets here."

"Who're you talkin' to?" Ruby jumped; for all her woolgathering, she hadn't heard the bathroom door open at last. Blake pulled up a chair, making himself at home. Same as always.

"Oh, wishin' I didn't make so much food. Be a dear and take some of it home for me, would you?"

Blake didn't take any extra prompting, but lumbered straight to the fridge. He'd take every scrap of the chicken, but if it got him to leave, so be it. Maybe he wouldn't check the breadbox. "Oh, good, there's three pieces of cornbread."

She groaned softly and rubbed her arthritic knuckles. If only he didn't give her so much reason. "Leave some for Will, you big oaf."

The crinkle of a plastic grocery sack couldn't drown out his reply. "That freeloader can starve."

She shook her head. Did he even hear himself? "Don't you forget I'm going out to see my friend at the nursing home one day this week." Ruby knew full well she hadn't mentioned her plans to him yet. She watched Blake's face, a slow sequence of dullard pantomime. Irritation appeared and bossiness followed, and for the finale, relief at an obligation deferred.

"You know you don't need to be driving. If your doctor knew you was still toolin' around—"

"Never mind, you. I'm ridin' with Edna." Ruby didn't even know anyone named Edna, but Blake didn't know that. Satisfied, he grabbed up his sack full of spoils and wrapped his lips around vague words about calling if she needed him as he hurried out the door.

With the house quiet at last, Ruby took to that worn-out Bible on the TV tray for comfort. The cracked spine flopped open to First Samuel twenty-eight; she turned to the New Testament to hunt that verse Will liked. The one he showed her so many times, you'd think he came up with it himself.

"Prefer rather to be absent from the body and to be at home with the Lord," she read, and leaned back in her chair, contemplating the words and longing for the respite of the house where Abby now slept. Maybe she read it wrong, but she didn't reckon "home" meant a far-off cloud locked away behind the Pearly Gates. Home for her had been that old house. Even after Mama died and Daddy went to live at the rest home, that old place never felt so terrible-lonely. This house she'd shared with John lost its heart the day Bradley Brothers carried him out of it. Back in the old days, she'd always liked having a ghost around as a go-between for her and heaven. On nights like this one, she missed it.

CHAPTER 23

Sunday, April 15

Abby walked to the restaurant. She could have asked Greg to pick her up, but if the evening went as she expected, she'd be walking home too. Best to manage expectations and not let him think she needed the ride.

Besides, the walk directed the jitters. No second chances. They'd had a good thing going. He was the one who ruined it.

She hated herself for missing him, even a little.

The highway crossing bells dinged and the gate arm came down, blocking traffic from the intersection for the approaching southbound train. Abby covered her ears and entered the restaurant to escape the deafening blasts of its horn.

She scanned the dining room. Greg sat in a booth at the back wall, playing with the crumpled paper from his straw. A sweaty glass of ice water puddled beside a bouquet of gladioluses lying across the table.

He killed her, looking so normal and significant all at once, like a William Carlos Williams poem. She almost bolted, but then their eyes met. A small defeat. She was committed.

He rose, scooping up the bouquet, welcoming. The flowers made her angry in ways she couldn't name. *I crossed three state lines to get away from you. Avoiding you shouldn't be this hard.*

His hair had grown since she'd last seen him, but he'd shaved off the scruff he normally favored. He wore a polo shirt she didn't recognize and chinos, wrinkled from the day's travel. Abby bypassed the hostess station and approached the table, torn between manners and fury.

"These are for you." He held out the flowers. "The Easter lilies and stargazers were sold out."

He remembered her favorites. She supposed she didn't have to make a scene.

"Thank you." She gave him a polite hug, keeping her face well out of reach of his. The familiar, tempting scent of his cologne whispered not-too-distant memories of slipping out the basement-level door of their office building to the parking deck below, where her best chance of meeting him unseen lay under the concrete and steel shadows.

She could feel his reluctance to release her as she backed out of the embrace. "You're getting some sun, living down here. Oh, and before I forget." He produced a dog-eared envelope from his back pocket. It bore a yellow forwarding label, some scribbles, and the hospital logo she'd recognize on sight for the rest of her life. "Courtesy of Sarah."

She stuffed it into her purse and put it and the flowers down as they eased into opposite sides of the booth. "I'll hand it to you, Greg. You know how to make a girl feel pursued."

"I didn't know if you'd show up."

"Then it was mildly idiotic of you to come all this way." Remembering her decision, she added, "Bless your heart."

He drew back and stared. "Listen to you. All rooted in. No different than if you were born here."

"I wouldn't say that." Not after the reunion she'd dodged. "But it's okay. It's a new beginning. You know what they say. 'You can never go home again.'"

"I don't know anyone who says that. Ohio's a big lonely state without you in it. I think you'd be welcome."

"Greg, don't."

A fresh-faced girl of twenty burst into their conversation. "Good evening, folks. My name's Jillian. What can I get y'all to drink?"

"Water," she said, thankful for any excuse to break away from Greg's intense gray eyes.

He didn't look at Jillian to answer. "Iced tea, please."

"Sweet or unsweet?"

"Ah." He rubbed his cheek as he did when frustrated or annoyed. She found the familiar gesture almost cute. "I changed my mind. I'll stick with my water."

"Unsweet." Abby took the chance to show off her acquired knowledge of Southern culture. "He wants unsweet."

"Water and tea," the girl repeated, and hurried away from the cloud of tension gathering over their table.

Abby stared at her hands. "I suppose Sarah gave you a full debriefing."

"She hit the highlights. How you haven't found a job or made any friends. How you stay holed up in your house, digging through stolen documents—"

"See? Nothing has changed." She squared her gaze with his. "Except this time, it's none of your business."

"All right, where did Sarah get it wrong? Tell me about your wonderful new life."

"I don't work for you anymore." She clutched her purse. "I don't have to explain myself to you."

"Abby." He reached for her arm and missed it, but she paused, too curious to leave. "Abby, I came a long way to ask you one question." He coughed. "What it would take to get you to come home?"

"I am home. I live in a house that's been in my family for generations, and for the first time in my life, I have more than one relative living in the same town."

"Being related to you doesn't make them family. You hardly know these people. You can't trust them—"

"I don't want to point out the obvious, Greg. Can I leave it unsaid?"

"No. Out with it."

"Fine. I trusted you, and look where that got me."

The server returned with their beverages, her cheeks flushed. Abby snuck a glimpse around the dining room. At other tables, chatter and laughter prevailed. If their quiet words didn't rise above the din, the somber mood swirling around them most certainly did.

"Do you know what you want?" Jillian asked tentatively.

It was a good question. Abby wanted to leave in a huff and to stay and spar, both at the same time and in mostly equal measures. In either case, Jillian couldn't help her. "Catfish, with extra hushpuppies."

Greg picked up the menu. "I'll have—who on earth would eat a fried pickle?"

A defensive expression appeared on the server's face. He held up his hand.

"I'm sorry. That was rude of me. I'll have the pork tenderloin. Thanks." He handed off his menu and waited for Jillian to leave again before confiding in Abby. "When I saw 'Shrimp and Grits' listed on there, I had to question Sarah's taste."

"That's what she ordered, as a matter of fact. It smelled amazing, but I haven't tried it yet myself."

"Then they haven't made a full convert of you."

"Give me time." Her words didn't sound as light as she intended them.

"I have," Greg said. "I know it's been a tough six months. I know I made it worse."

"And now you want to hit the rewind button, is that it?"

He fixed his eyes on hers. "As much as possible, yes."

Outside the restaurant, another train clamored by, its danger muted by the walls around them. Low light and a safe distance, she supposed, rendered the trains romantic. They registered only a snapshot in her world, a moment marked by a blaring horn, warning everyone out of its way. A moment significant only for the coincidence of her awareness of it. Now as the fading racket of its steady progression from terminal to terminal slowly died back, for the first time she wanted to know where those trains came from, and where they went.

"You can't, Greg." She put her hands over his, a gamble to make her point, and she watched hope light in his eyes before pulling them away again. "It already happened."

"We can change what happens next."

"I wonder." A sense of the inevitable crawled across her flesh. What force could derail catastrophe? She doubted cancer, job loss, and grudges would be persuaded. "This exact moment is all we ever have."

"Then let's not spend it bickering."

She flexed her fingers, the nerve endings alive with the echo of the brief touch of his. She didn't have to take the collision course. Not every time. "Deal."

Defeated by bread pudding. What a way to go.

Later, Abby lay on the couch with one arm over her eyes, not caring if her mascara tattooed the crook of her elbow. The darkness brought clarity. She could see in it the unassuming moment of brokenness as it looped in her mind over and over again.

Once she set down her tartness and accepted his company, the conversation had slipped on like a terry-cloth robe, well-worn and forgiving enough for the layers underneath. That was the problem. He was too easy, too comfortable. Too much like home.

Her appetite had been lousy since November. She didn't care for dessert, but Greg wanted to hear the choices. "Might as well," he'd said. "I'm on vacation."

Jillian recited a practiced litany. "We have chocolate cake drizzled with a semi-sweet raspberry sauce, New York cheesecake served with fresh sliced strawberries, mango-key lime pie, and warm banana bread pudding with a vanilla glaze."

"Bread pudding." Both Abby and Greg spoke together, and a moment of connection crackled to life. Among the might-be-love quirks they held in common, they'd first discovered a shared love for bread pudding.

"I can't." Abby groaned a little and leaned back. "I'm stuffed."

"I can, and I will," Greg replied.

An extra spoon. Afterward Abby agonized over it. If she'd thought to ask for an extra spoon, maybe it would have turned out differently. Maybe not. Maybe her train aimed for the same terminal no matter what she did.

Instead, she refolded her napkin and wished, suddenly and urgently, to be away from him before her heart could change direction, setting her up for a collision course of another kind. She could hate him when she didn't have to see him, the same way she could resist the mere mention of bread pudding much more readily than the huge, fragrant dessert Jillian set before him.

"Wow. That's a work of art." He stuck his spoon into the center and took a big mouthful. "You're missing out. This is incredible."

"Let me try a bite," she'd said impulsively.

"I don't think I can spare a whole bite," Greg teased, but he dug the spoon down into the dessert again and passed it to Abby, who took the sample without a second thought.

He hadn't exaggerated. Dense, sweet, and perfect. She closed her eyes in bliss of warm banana and vanilla. "Mmm. Lucky me. I can have this wonderfulness any time I want."

"I might have to visit again."

Abby didn't know what to say, how to tell him no without raising both their ire again. She passed the spoon back. "Thank you. It was delicious."

While he finished his dessert, it slowly dawned on her what an intimate thing she'd done. Strangers and enemies didn't eat after one another. Sharing his spoon meant accepting his mouth, close akin with consenting to his lips.

Nervous, she licked the lingering sweetness from her teeth. She saw him notice.

He paid the bill, refusing the cash she offered, and they sat a moment longer, neither sure how to close the evening. At last she stood, gathering the flowers with her. Baggage. "I should get home."

"I'll walk you to your car."

"It's in the shop," she admitted. "I . . . "

"Let me take you home, then."

"It's not far."

"Not compared to Cuyahoga Falls, especially." He bounced a key ring in his hand, but it didn't jingle. "Humor me. They gave me a Passat for my rental. Keyless ignition."

She didn't like where the evening was going and wanted to refuse him, but still she followed. What alternative did she have besides walking home in the dark, a stupid idea if she ever had one? She carried the flowers with the hand closest to him and hung her purse from the other, tucking her fingers around the shoulder strap to put them out of his reach. He led her to the car and opened the passenger side door for her.

Straight home, no joyriding. He was not invited in. This was the end.

"You aren't going to have much chance to show it off," she said as he slid in the driver's side. "I'm literally around the corner." She pointed when he pulled out of the parking lot. "That street up ahead. Second house."

"Wow. That's disappointing. I was hoping . . . "

"I don't know my way around yet," she lied. "We'd get lost in two seconds. I mean, I see it has a nav system, but . . . I'm so tired."

"Sure, me too." He put on his blinker. That was different. She didn't remember him bothering with signals much in the past.

"This one?"

"Yeah." She studied him for signs of judgment about the rough exterior, but he didn't react to it. Later, on the couch, Abby figured out that he had too much else in mind to care about her house.

"Thanks for dinner. Um, see you, I guess." She jumped out of the car and he followed, practically chasing her to the front porch.

"Abby, wait." As she dug for her house key, he grasped her arm lightly. Chills ran up to her neck and down her back. Even her skin took his side.

"I've missed you." His low, husky voice stirred the mortar around her heart. "I don't know how to tell you."

"Then don't," she said, and meant it, but he took her words the wrong way and leaned in to kiss her. Abby turned her face.

"I—I'm sorry." He looked stricken. "I didn't mean—"

"I know what you meant." Her bones jellified, and she clung to the porch rail.

He backed away slowly, hands up, fingers splayed. "I thought . . . "

"You need to go."

"Abby."

"Now."

She watched him turn away, a shadow-man backlit by the headlights. Once the car door slammed shut, she fiddled with the lock, not wanting to see him trying to catch her eye. Not wanting to read the expression on his face.

Clouds blew by the crescent moon and the darkness neared completion. The front porch light didn't work in spite of a brand new bulb. She'd have to remember to tell Will. The shadows reminded her of the night she arrived, how he had leapt out of nowhere. She hadn't wanted to show it, but he'd scared her half to death then. Now she wished he'd make a repeat performance.

No such luck.

Only after she was locked safely into the house, her purse dropped on the kitchen table and the gladioluses in the trash, as she curled into the couch's stiff embrace, did she dare to reflect on the evening. She tallied her mistakes and his, trying to lay blame. "Stupid bread pudding," she moaned.

The blue-white glow of Greg's cell phone broke ranks with the sallow lamplight bathing the drab hotel decor. Heavy rust-colored curtains drawn across the open window held in his dark mood as much as they blocked the world outside.

"How'd it go?"

He read Sarah's text without answering it and stretched out across the lumpy mattress, paging through a hotel Bible, too green in his faith to know what he sought.

Sending back a simple "Not well" would invite questions. His bossy little sister might even call for the full rundown, which Greg had no desire or energy to relay for her. "As expected" would let Sarah dream up her own version, a tempting alternative but ultimately no better. She'd base her inevitable schemes on the events in her own wild imagination.

"You made this sound like a problem I could fix," he tapped into the phone, then deleted the message without sending. Blaming Sarah didn't help matters.

His memory burned with little flashes of the day. Getting bumped from his flight and waiting for the next. Speeding up from the airport only to arrive too early, sitting alone for twenty minutes and enduring the wait staff's pitying small talk. That hug, a shade less condescending than a pat on the head. The bit with the tea. Sweet or unsweet. What a question.

And of course he had shared his dessert with her. He didn't imagine the gap closing. No. It was real.

Or maybe he'd simply forgotten why he came in the first place and tried too much, too soon, too fast.

He sighed. Going for the kiss killed the whole evening. He mistook an echo from their shared past for a shout of welcome. The old ember glowed for a bright couple of seconds before he blew it out completely.

"You're right. She's different," he finally wrote. That would have to do. He hoped Sarah would read enough into it to let him be alone with his misery.

He didn't know this Abby. Wasn't certain that he wanted to know her, in fact. Sarah gave him the idea that the old Abby waited for him to find her, to tempt her out of seclusion, to rescue her from her demons. Wrong again. The conspicuous Southern affectations baffled him. She'd helped herself to this world, all but bled desperation to fit into it.

What would it take to get you to come home? He asked her to issue the challenge, the occasion he could rise to meet, and instead she dodged.

A new text from Sarah chimed. Apparently, she understood more than he gave her credit for. "She's hurting. Don't give up. Luv u bro."

I won't give up. Not yet. But I'd sure like to know what I'm supposed to do.

A memory floated forward, picturing the day she'd discovered a nail in her tire. They'd been together maybe four months by then. He'd put the donut on her car right there in the parking garage, ruining a good shirt and igniting office gossip in the process, and hardly even caring about either.

"My hero," she'd said. Playfully, yes, but how he'd liked the sound of it.

It was a good memory, maybe even an important one, but he would need more than memories to go up against that ghost story she fixed as the cornerstone of her new life.

God, I need to show her something real. He placed the Bible back in the nightstand drawer where he'd found it, frustrated. She snooped into the sealed divorces. Worth risking her job over. Simple enough to guess whose she wanted.

For all the upheaval Abby created, he doubted her priorities had changed much. There'd be plenty of time to figure it out if she wouldn't agree to see him again. A long week lay ahead.

The lows on the weather report disgusted him. He changed into sweats too heavy for the warm night air, closed the window, and turned on the commercial grade air-conditioner. It jangled loosely. The image of spider carcasses tickling the vents blew into his mind and wouldn't leave.

He snapped off the lamp and let the phone's glow illuminate his navigation to the bed. He tossed aside the spongy pillows and lay over the thin covers, waiting to feel cold enough to want them and drinking thoughts of unsweet Abby.

CHAPTER 24

Monday, April 16

For the umpteenth time, Abby wished for a way to get in touch with Will. Not that it mattered. No way would he be available on a weekday to meander around the Civil War museum. Always running off to do Aunt Ruby's bidding, never any time for himself—or for her.

No. That wasn't fair. He must not have known about the dinner. She stepped into the lobby and finger-combed her windblown hair into presentability. He would have warned her. She knew he would've.

"Excuse me, ma'am." A woman with salt-and-pepper curls wearing a volunteer badge stopped her from passing on through to the exhibits. "Let's get you a ticket right quick. Seven dollars."

Abby blushed and fumbled her way to the bottom of her purse for the cash and ended up paying with her debit card. Maybe because of Will's uncomplicated approach to life, she had expected the self-guided tour to be free. Hadn't she learned yet that money made the world go 'round? Greg and Aunt Ruby figured it out. Even Mom warned her.

The temperature dropped a good five degrees past the threshold of the museum's lobby. Abby rubbed her bare arms, wishing for a sweater. The cold couldn't be content to stay back in Ohio, could it? Like Greg, it had followed her. Or maybe uneasy spirits were to blame for the chill. Will did say that by all rights, the whole town should be haunted.

Too bad she didn't think to ask him about the museum's must-see displays. The soldiers represented by aged trinkets sealed behind glass cases weren't real to her; they were as faceless and anonymous as her dear old dad. Through dog-eared playing cards and tin drinking cups and a travel-worn pocket Bible, they reached out of the past and begged remembrance. A waxy animatronic man in a replicated gray uniform stood by to tell her about them, but she didn't hit the button that would bring him to life.

She studied an exhibit of standard-issue military swords, and beside them, a collection of brutish mid-nineteenth century medical instruments. Abby backed away to compare the different blades in the two cases. Unlike the gleaming officers' sabers, some of the doctors' saws appeared less than entirely clean.

Hugging herself, Abby turned away, no longer preoccupied by the frigid air. Those horrors of healing disturbed her, so much more than the weapons of war. How much pain in exchange for a hope of life? How much could the physician take and still leave a stump worth saving?

Amazing that an hour before, this had seemed like a good idea.

She clenched her teeth. Like a weakling she succumbed, and now she'd pay the price. Less than a minute of wanting someone else to take charge, to shoulder the immense weight of sadness and betrayal and loss, and Greg found it. Not only that, he popped up in the middle of it, not at all the shade of the past she had hoped would come calling. A "miracle," though not one she would have requested.

And how long would he stay? The Greg she knew wouldn't have booked less than five days. Where Sarah jetted off for a weekend adventure, her brother bought travel insurance and emailed himself backup copies of his reservations. So unfair. Abby had arranged her life with as few obligations as possible, and for the first time, it was a problem. She left herself no excuse.

She could spend the whole week in the museum. A poor joke at best. Though the salt-and-pepper-haired volunteer would certainly accept her money day after day, those saws and swords would cleave off what remained of her mental health, seeing as some already assumed it dangled by a flap of skin.

As she wandered around the war exhibit, a glare of overhead light bounced off the glossy display of a photo reproduction. The obscured image caught her interest as none of the visible exhibits could. She shaded the image with her hand to view Atlanta's burned-out ruins in sepia tones. The dazzling city she'd driven through to and from the airport did not reminisce the image at all. She stared hard at the picture and the history in brief recorded on a time-line placard beside it. One word stood apart, and she touched it and read it aloud.

"Terminus." The city's first name weighted her tongue, the answer to a question she hadn't asked. For all its thriving metropolis, Atlanta too began as a railroad town. With her finger she traced the edges of twisted rails along the laminate surface of the photo. Would modern Atlanta have grown as grand if it had never burned?

She'd make sure to ask Will about it.

A boy of about ten ran past, narrowly missing her as he whooshed by. She turned in time to see his mother chasing after him.

"Ethan, look out where you're going, please." She met Abby's eyes and mimed pulling out her hair with both hands. "Homeschooling. Gotta love it."

Abby retreated half a step. "Guess he's excited for the next section."

"Not as much as he is for the General. But sorry he tried to mow you down." The woman continued around the corner. "Stop right there and do not run ahead of me again."

Abby lagged behind, not wanting to end up in a rolling dialogue with Ethan's mother for the rest of the afternoon. What had the woman meant about a general? A statue, maybe? Would that be exciting to a kid? No. Probably an actor, or another animatronic storyteller. Unless . . . weren't important people sometimes preserved?

She shivered. No. That was for heads of state and religious leaders, not generals. Especially not those on the losing side. Besides, Will hated death. He wouldn't have recommended a museum with a body on display.

Except did he say he *liked this place, or that I would?*

She couldn't remember.

Around the corner she found heavy wooden double doors, and beside them, a red LED timer counting down from 3:57. A small sign below it clarified, "Minutes Until Next Showtime." Annoyed, Abby waited out the clock until the doors swung open unaided as if by magic, accompanied by an artificial whine of creaky hinges. As she entered the small theater, she nosed around until she found the automatic door openers and a small pair of surround speakers. A touch of the theatrical for the kiddies.

The overhead lights dimmed as the projection screen lit up and a canned harmonica rasped through the sound system. She stood in the roped aisle and felt awkward, took a seat in a kid-sized chair and felt silly. At least no one watched her flounder. She had the whole theater to herself.

The short featurette dramatized a "Yankee plot" to steal a steam engine and use it to destroy supply lines between Atlanta and Nashville. The Union soldiers, Ohio infantrymen rendered as mustache-twirling caricatures with accents vaguely reminiscent of Brooklyn, saw their raid foiled by a determined conductor who spoke like landed gentry. The demarcation could not have been clearer, and the actors' exaggerated delivery chased her thoughts back to the Recorder of Deeds at the county courthouse, brushing her cheeks with veiled insults and shame. Was that how she sounded to them?

At least their film cleared up one mystery. The General was the steam engine and not a mummified officer. A small but welcome relief.

The short film painted the familiar Civil War narrative in opposite hues. Northern villains and Southern heroes offered a standing invitation to imagine history as it would have been written had the Confederacy ultimately prevailed.

Abby hurried out of the small theater area before the screen darkened, eager to fill her mind with other thoughts than to choose a side in a war that had been over for a century and a half. She moved through the few remaining exhibits, expecting to stumble through the gift shop and back into the April wind.

Instead, a giant room swallowed her, and Abby shrank at the sight of the massive red and black steam engine. A gilded number "3" decorated its front and a gold-lettered name plate its side. Before her, imposing and magnificent, stood The General. Not a replica or a tribute, but the one and same hijacked and recovered that spring day so long ago. A train whistle blasted from a hidden speaker, celebrating the crown jewel of the museum.

She walked around the black chain cordon, awed by the sheer size of the engine. From up close she understood how control of that immensity of machinery would be worth the heroics on both sides. Its dormant power whispered words indeterminate even to her, and all the position and authority of the cab beckoned to her. A place to see both the question and the answer at the same time, the pain and the salve. If for so much as one second she could take charge of that strong tower, in that moment it would bear up all her burdens.

Ethan and his mother finished their tour ahead of her. No one else crossed her path throughout all the winding displays and exhibits. Apparently the museum didn't get much traffic after lunch on a Monday, or maybe she'd picked a slow day. A perfect day.

Forgiveness is better than permission. Before she could overthink it and chicken out, she stepped over the chain.

She'd half-expected an alarm to sound, but only the serene automated train whistle accompanied the breach. No time to think. They still might catch her at any moment. She grabbed the iron pull bars and hoisted herself upward to the red box enclosing the conductor's cab.

"Hey, how come she gets to climb up there? I want a turn."

"Ethan, stay with me."

Maybe they hadn't cleared out after all. Abby froze, petrified of losing her footing before an audience.

"Miss, you need to get down from there at once." She recognized the voice of the woman who made her buy a ticket. Oh well, a middle-aged museum volunteer couldn't do much.

"Security, ma'am." Abby inched her way around to face her accusers. What was it with her and security guards? Couldn't stay out of their way.

The uniformed guard glared up at her. "I'm going to ask you to carefully step down from the steam engine. Immediately."

"I'm sorry. I only wanted—" She stopped short. She only wanted what? They wouldn't care about her explanations. She looked down from the platform and a wave of vertigo blurred the world. How did her short climb create such a long way to fall?

"Ma'am, you do not want me to come up after you," the security guard warned her. Her vision cleared enough to read the daggers in Ethan's mother's expression and the security guard's name tag—"Mike." The sick feeling remained.

New goal: get out of this without vomiting on Mike. "Right. I'm coming."

All told, Abby got off light.

"Banned for life." Testing the words aloud made them that much more real. She plunked her keys down on the kitchen counter and made for the dubious comforts of the couch. "So much for forgiveness. Beats getting arrested, I guess."

And joking beat serious consideration of what she'd done. Climbing a steam engine? What had gotten into her?

That voice not quite like the one she'd sell her soul to hear again joined in the interrogation. *What are you trying to prove?*

"Haven't you been paying attention?" she called out. "You wanted me to have faith, right, Mom? Here I am. Best seat in the house, and nothing to see."

Worthless words. Theatrics, and for no one's benefit but her own. Why pretend Mom heard? To kid one ghost about another? The roof-walker hadn't returned, and what made him any more real that the cobweb figure at the top of the stairs or the tricks of her tired eyes? Maybe she imagined them all.

Aunt Ruby believed the house was haunted, but Abby didn't. Never had, not really. Will was right. There were no ghosts, none besides the regrets and longings she brought with her.

"All right. I want answers." She jumped up from the couch. "Lay your cards on the table. It's time to play your hand. You are the single laziest ghost I ever met. Knock once to disagree, and not at all if I'm right."

Silence would have been better than the ordinary house noises: the hissing vents and the thrumming ceiling fan and the trickle of water whispering through the pipes. The plainness of the moment stole her oomph, but still she pressed.

"That's what I thought. I'm sick of trying to shake you out of the woodwork, so if you have a story, let's hear it."

That soft memory voice fluttered once again. *Everyone deserves a name.*

"Sure, Mom. I'll play." She tried a kinder inflection. "George? George Hart, are you here?"

Silence reigned. Either the ghost recognized the lie in her voice, or no ghost existed to listen. She mounted one last challenge. "Of course you aren't here. You're dead. You're dead and I'm alive."

No answer, and yet a change. The house sounds dwindled and bowed in a deep hushed stillness. An expectation.

A sour stone burned in Abby's stomach. She tried to speak but words wouldn't come, and the certainty that she was not alone wrapped around her heart.

There was a Presence. One that wouldn't be manipulated by her storms and rages nor persuaded by her demands. One that would not be shaken.

The stillness ceased without warning. The refrigerator hummed, a reminder of her lie to Will and his unfulfilled promises.

She rubbed her arms and tried to laugh at herself. A "Presence"? Whatever.

She'd almost talked herself out of her fear when she heard it. Not in the front bedroom with the desk and the files, but trapped in the locked back room, muffled and indistinct, there came a knocking.

CHAPTER 25

Ruby hated that lawyer so bad, she wished he was family so she could disinherit him.

She explained how she wanted her will set up about fifteen times before he made like he understood. He didn't fool her none. Too lazy to do the legwork. Didn't have a fill-in-the-blank cookie-cutter version of what she asked for. Once she suggested that her husband's old friends from the City Hall might recommend her an estate attorney who could write a will, he stopped fartin' around and got to business. Lucky she didn't have to drop any names, since all of them good ol' boys were dead.

Regardless, the new will was written and signed and on its way to the courthouse for filing, if that lawyer could be trusted to do that much without prodding. Finally, that whole nasty business laid to rest.

Mercy. She patted her lips though she hadn't spoken out loud. Laid to rest, humph. Death peeked around corners; it winked at her in the mirror then vanished; it hummed along with the radio and then faded away. It wheedled into her mind and her words, leaving a humid vapor around her heart and a thick fuzzy taste on her tongue.

She went straight from the lawyer's office to the nursing home where Agnes stayed. It sure wouldn't win any prize for coziness. The residential corridors sprawled out from the squat central hub. On the whole it had the look of any rundown institution, a violation or two away from being condemned.

Ruby trembled.

All the handicap spaces were taken up, so she had to park with the general population, a terrible long way to haul her tired ol' behind. It entered her mind to go on home. Agnes would like a phone call almost as much as a visitor, probably.

Quit makin' excuses, for heaven's sake. You're here already, ain'tcha?

Oh, it smelled inside! The sour odor of filth waiting to be cleaned, with sting of medicines and ointments and disinfectant, together composed the steady reek of human dignity leaching away. It stank like Death sidling up to the bedside of anyone who dared to rest their eyes.

As she entered the lobby she found a long welcome desk flanked by two orderlies in hospital-green scrubs. Lined up before them, a row of old folks in wheelchairs, gazing up at a TV fixed on a rusty steel arm in the corner. Women and men with little to tell 'em apart, most watching the program but some wearing vacant stares, drool running down the sides of toothless mouths, hanging open and ready to catch flies.

They had the TV turned up to hear from the next county. Ruby recognized the voices from one of her shows. Even got caught in the glow for a second or two. *Stay,* her awful host whispered. She'd nudged Blake and Will out of the way. It'd be tomorrow before anyone missed her.

If I went home and died, it'd be tomorrow before anyone found me.

Although by the looks of them orderlies, she could die right here and not get noticed, too. "S'cuse me," she said. The nearer of the two pried unwilling eyes off the TV screen. She sized him up. A youngish fella, all Adam's apple and elbows. "I'm here to see Agnes Clemons."

"Room number?"

Ruby dug deep for the most ladylike sass she could muster. "I don't reckon you could tell me?"

He rolled his eyes and with great effort, tapped at his keyboard. "Discharged on two-twenty-four of this year." His gaze swung wide back toward the TV, but Ruby wasn't quite ready to be dismissed.

"Goodness sakes, son, does it say where she went?"

She watched his annoyance drain as he hesitated. Never mind, she wanted to say, if only to buy one more moment of not knowing the truth. Too late though. She asked, and the answer wouldn't turn back. "Released to Bradley Brothers. I'm sorry."

Bradley Brothers. The funeral home.

She thanked him—for what, she didn't know—and walked out of

there as fast as her old legs would go. Death cackled behind her.

Her last friend from her years at Southern Bell, gone, taking her saucy tongue and independent streak with her to where her sweet-as-pie voice would be heard no more. Agnes, who declined her invitations to join their church choir 'til Ruby quit asking.

"I handled all that church business when I was a young'un," Agnes had finally told her, and Ruby let that be the end of it. Truth be told, she'd been relieved at the time. "Sharing the Good News" always felt like a byword for annoying her friends. More than once, Ruby doubted whether she had any good news to share.

Now Death laughed long and low.

As soon as she stepped through the doors, the humidity of an approaching storm fogged up her glasses, so she took them off to search the sky. Finally the rain they needed so bad, but Ruby cared only for straining her eyes with the foolish hope she'd see a figure waving from the edge of one of them heavy gray clouds. "Oh, Agnes. Why'd you have to go and die?"

Another pin loosened. For the life of her, Ruby couldn't say whether she had any left. And how much longer did she intend to leave her own business unfinished? Oh, her errands were done, such as they were, but she wasn't ready to go. Heavens no. Not yet.

CHAPTER 26

As soon as she left her house for Aunt Ruby's, the rain broke loose. Abby crossed her arms and marched through puddles. She stood at the corner of Main Street for an eternity, but the cars wouldn't slow for a pedestrian in the rain. The afternoon had turned so gray and foul, they probably didn't even see her.

It was a cold rain, a cleansing one. She breathed easier than she had in weeks as the downpour rinsed away the pollen, but the cherry blossoms and Bradford pears took a beating. Rivulets raced along the curb, draining browned, ruined petals into the sewers. She tried to swallow the disappointment rising in her throat. It couldn't always be beautiful.

The sidewalk disappeared as she turned onto Hiram Street. Her heart quickened at the thought of her father's Lancer, but now the driveway was empty. Even Aunt Ruby's Sentra was gone.

It served her right. Abby pushed stringy, soaked hair out of her face. She should've called first. She should never have come.

Lightning flashed, closely followed by a sharp report of thunder, and she gritted her teeth. Aunt Ruby's porch would give her temporary refuge, but then what? She wouldn't spend another night—scratch that, another minute—in the house until she got some answers.

The needling droplets stung her skin. Water blinded her; it trickled behind her ears and down her back, clinging and chaffing, weighting her clothes and squishing out of her shoes with every step.

At last she reached Aunt Ruby's stoop. The porch awning afforded her no protection from the hard rain splattering up from the pavement, and Abby shivered, hunched over her knees, wet and waiting, though her mind kept working the knots.

Kennesaw was a nice town, a safe town. A lot of old people kept their doors unlocked. Aunt Ruby wouldn't mind. Or at least she would understand. Abby didn't know it would rain when she left. It wasn't breaking and entering if the door was open.

She tried the knob. It was locked.

A splash of guilt, but Abby bottled it up and studied the porch. Heavy planters full of tangles of monkey grass occupied both corners, and a white wicker rocker took up the space that remained on the right. Next to a grayed and worn out welcome mat sat a small ceramic frog. She lifted it up and found the key underneath.

"Don't watch, Mom," she said, but the wet whoosh of a car turning in stayed her hand. She quickly replaced the key and the frog as Aunt Ruby parked. Half-formed excuses gathered on her tongue, but Aunt Ruby cut the engine and stayed in the car for several minutes. Waiting out the rain? No, she wasn't watching the window nor the skies. She just stared into her steering wheel for the longest time.

Abby relaxed. It wasn't her day to get caught. At least, not again.

Either her distraction passed or Aunt Ruby abandoned hope that the rain would let up. She emerged from her car, though not without a fight. She gathered a giant navy purse and poked an ASPCA "cats and dogs" umbrella up and out, fluttered it a couple of times, then gave up and tucked it under her arm. Her cane tracked for the ground, followed by one leg and the other. When at last she stood, Abby caught a glimpse of the boxy pink blazer she wore, one that should have been retired when *Who's the Boss?* went to reruns. The rain and spatter from the umbrella dotted it and for a moment before she broke free of the car and closed its door, she resembled a butterfly too weak to escape its chrysalis. Abby couldn't remember if she'd always looked so small.

"For heaven's sake, child, what's the matter with you? You're soaked to the bone." The heavy drops flattened her hair as she climbed the front steps, and Abby edged out of her way.

"I need to know whatever you can tell me about your grandfather. George Hart." The shiver in her voice ruined her bravado.

Aunt Ruby closed her eyes, moving her lips in some silent petition before responding. "Come in. You ain't still sick, are you?"

"Allergies, I think. The rain is helping."

Aunt Ruby opened the door and let herself in. "Don't stand there drippin'. Go dry off and I'll make some tea."

Minutes later, Abby emerged from the bathroom, slightly drier and no warmer. She found Aunt Ruby in the kitchen, watching a tea kettle on the stovetop. She'd taken the opportunity to change clothes herself, and now donned a green and yellow sweater with a dizzying chevron pattern.

"I didn't mean to intrude."

"Yes, you did," Aunt Ruby said. "But I'll admire your zeal, anyhow."

"I know I've worn out my welcome on the genealogy stuff, but this is different. I've been to the courthouse and the graveyard, and all I find are question marks. And now . . . "

I think I've made him angry, she meant to say, but the tea kettle whistled and Aunt Ruby turned to attend to it.

"George Hart turned his back on his family to find his own fortune." She poured water over the tea bags already resting in a pair of mugs. "He died of black diphtheria, and even that was too good for him, to hear my Daddy tell it. He left a wife and child with no choice but to crawl back to the same ones he betrayed."

"What happened?"

Aunt Ruby passed a steaming mug to Abby and took the other, dunking the teabag. "I done told you. That's the story."

"But he had to have some unfinished business, right? What has he got to be angry about?"

"Who?"

"George!" Abby's voice cracked. "George Hart."

"Who said he was angry?"

"He visited me today. At the house."

A violent tremor shook Aunt Ruby's hand, and the scalding liquid sloshed over the brim of the cup. She cried out as it shattered on the floor and splashed tea on them both.

"I'm so sorry." Abby grabbed the dish towel by the sink and fell down on her hands and knees to clean up.

Aunt Ruby stooped down. "You'd best quit mindin' other people's unfinished business and think more about your own. If you want to learn a lesson on George Hart's account, then watch out who you trust, 'cause if you throw in with the wrong side, it'll be the worst of you that gets remembered."

Abby drew in her breath at the sharp words. Places aren't haunted, Will had told her. People are. "Aunt Ruby, I don't understand."

A bright flash of pain bit her, followed by a too-late warning. "Careful you don't cut yourself."

Abby winced as she pulled a bloodied shard of glass from the heel of her hand and tried not to bleed on the towel as she mopped up the mess.

"It was my fault. I'll take care of it."

"Broom's in the closet." Aunt Ruby shuffled out of the kitchen.

When Abby dumped the dustpan full of glass into the trash, the window over the sink peered out into a gray sky and a lull in the rain. She hurried to give her aunt another apology and a hasty goodbye. Though her heart and head remained full of questions, there would be no more answers here.

CHAPTER 27

Ruby's joints ballooned. Her favorite mug sacrificed for that girl's desire to know what sort of thieves, traitors, and ne'er-do-wells she descended from. Never should've breathed a word about any ghost in the first place, but mercy, how was she supposed to guess a girl Abby's age would be so concerned with loss and loose ends?

How indeed. Safe in the middle of her own living room, Ruby quivered, her heart paddling like a cramped-up swimmer, desperate not to dip below the choppy surface. Oh, she found the perfect way around Daddy's word of law all right, never figuring it for a millstone about her neck . . . or Christie's.

Enough. She wept her share of tears for him, but he died a long time ago. So long ago, but still turning up now and then. It didn't make any sense. He was never the kind to hold a grudge.

Saturday, October 24, 1942

She had brought home the *Cobb County Times* every single week, at first leaving it on the coffee table, then in the kitchen, and even once on Christie's pillow, trying to get him to read it. Rarely he skimmed the world news as deep as page two, but she couldn't interest him in the bomber plant at all.

"Mr. Hart made real clear where he stood on that, Ruby." Behind their bedroom door, he relaxed into secondhand cotton britches and a threadbare undershirt, but she could always say for Christie that his private face wasn't too different from his public one. Whether speaking to or about him, Ruby's daddy was always and only Mr. Hart. "And as long as we're living under his roof—"

"But we don't have to. The Bell Training school is going in right by the Clay Homes." She twisted up close to him, kissed him for emphasis. "It would be so convenient, and we'd have a place of our own. For us and the baby."

His blue eyes widened. She'd gone too far. "I mean, someday. Someday soon," she said, walking her fingers across his rib cage and around to his back. Autumn's delicate chill in her fingertips raised goose bumps on him.

He furrowed his brow at her but didn't pull away. "I promised, didn't I? We'll rent us a house once we've got this war beat. What if we moved and then I got called up? You'd be alone."

"They won't draft you."

"They might. Probably will. You never know what'll happen." He touched her hair, still in its complicated updo, and gently tugged a hair pin loose. "I always think I could find the pin that lets it all down at once."

"I wouldn't use so many if one would do." She fluttered her eyelashes, trying to look like a Hollywood starlet. "But you're welcome to try."

Down below, Daddy's boisterous laughter interrupted, coming muffled through the ceiling and floor but still as unromantic as a sound could be. "Humph." She yanked out the pins herself one by one until her hair spilled free.

"Ruby." He pulled her close again. "This won't last forever."

"It's embarrassing."

Instead of agreeing, he had the audacity to wink at her. "Your parents have been married a long time. I bet they're not ashamed."

"If you loved me . . ."

"I love you." He kissed her eyelids. "Is it that hard to believe?"

"How much do you love me?" she demanded.

"More than I can say at one time. I'll have to spread it out over the next seventy years or so." His kisses grazed her cheeks, found her mouth. Those roughened hands wandered, quickening her breath until she almost forgot they were arguing. Almost.

"You still gonna kiss me like that when you're ninety-one?"

"I reckon you'll have to wait and see."

He won and she knew it. Still, she couldn't resist one more nudge. "In case I forgot to say, the Bell employment office opens up tomorrow."

And there she found the end of his patience. A fine chisel appeared along his jaw line, mirrored in the edge in his voice. "Good night, Ruby." He clicked off the lamp and they didn't speak again until morning.

Ruby finished brushing out her hair in the dark, and even though a tear or two escaped, not a single tell-tale sniffle did. She laid her wet cheek against the pillow and traced the monogram she embroidered herself, listening for his breath to deepen, sorry but unwilling to say so.

Monday, April 16, 2012

It wasn't their last conversation on the matter, but it was the one Ruby most wished she could relive. More than once she'd prayed to fly back to that October evening and not pick that fight, but of course God didn't answer those kinds of prayers—or if He did, He answered 'em fully and carried off the misery of the first spoiled chance. Ruby hated to think that maybe God had indeed bent the universe for her, and she mangled her own future regardless.

"It wasn't my fault," she whispered, but that didn't change times all done and gone. She yanked out a tissue and dabbed her eyes. Maybe she still had a few tears left to go.

CHAPTER 28

Turned his back on his family. The ones he betrayed.

Abby sat at the big pine table in clean, dry pajamas, silently working the clues of George Hart's puzzle and brainstorming for the missing pieces. Oh, the possibilities.

A latecomer to the Gold Rush. A war profiteer. A Confederate deserter. Maybe in the devastation of Atlanta, George Hart had turned tail and run, a moment's cowardice branding him even in death. *It'll be the worst of you that gets remembered.*

She massaged her brow. Less imagination and more data. Aunt Ruby's story was too vague and the facts too few, evidently a part of the family history that she thought best forgotten. She slammed the door and locked it without realizing that locked doors were Abby's favorite kind.

Her stomach rumbled, but she didn't want to stop working. She woke her phone to order a pizza. "Three missed calls?" She checked them and Greg's office picture filled her screen, the one she copied from the company intranet a year ago. The tailored suit and tie, the handsome smirk she used to relish.

"Oh, Greg." She hit the dial-back button. "I guess I wasn't clear enough last night." She intended to blast him, but as the line rang, a better idea came.

"Abby, hi. I was about to try you again. Did you get my messages?"

"I've only been home for ten minutes," she lied, a nonsense reason not to have listened to them, but he took it.

"Good. I'd rather tell you straight. I was way out of line last night. I could make excuses about how beautiful you looked in the moonlight or how much I wish the road would have been different for us, but that doesn't change what I did. I'm sorry."

Gag-worthy. "Did you practice that much?"

"All day. All true."

"Fine. I give you a four-point-eight for sentiment and a one-point-seven for originality. I'll even let you make it up to me."

"Name your price, fair maiden."

She almost smiled. "Take me to pick up my car tomorrow morning, *without* invoking any former pet names, and we'll call it even."

"What time should I be at your house?"

"Nine. No, eight-thirty. I want to be there when they open."

"Deal."

She hung up content. Maybe she could end her acquaintance with Greg gracefully yet, and send him home satisfied that they did not belong together.

In the meantime, the ghost awaited. She phoned in an order for pizza and opened her laptop to peruse the scanned pictures from her visit back in February. With luck, she'd come across the ruby slippers—the answer she didn't know she had from the start.

She paused on the one of Warren and Gilbert, an old man and a young boy sitting on a porch. Her porch. She zoomed in until the image pixilated and blurred. The railing had been replaced, but the door, window, and tin mailbox were the same. The photo had been taken in front of the house.

"And where were you, George? Dead, disowned, or holding the camera?"

The knock at the door startled her. "Whew, that was quick." She grabbed a wad of cash from her purse and threw open the door to find Will waiting outside.

"Hey, Abbs." His eyes slipped down from her face momentarily. "Did I catch you at a bad time?"

"Not at all." She blushed to the roots of her hair. The tank-style PJ top she wore wouldn't have embarrassed her in front of a random pizza guy, but she crossed her arms and sucked in her tummy for Will. Crunches. Starting tomorrow, thousands of crunches. "I wasn't expecting you."

"Sorry 'bout that. I came by because I heard what happened."

"Last week, you mean?" She waved her bandaged hand, then resumed her shielded stance. "No big deal. I went over yesterday, but after my no-show to dinner, she's extra-thrilled with me at the moment."

"Ain't your fault. I don't know why she pulled that." He shook his head. "I've never known her to have much to do with your—Richard. Never met him, myself."

Abby took her turn to give him a once-over. Time to toss a pebble and see if it made ripples. "I hoped you would be there. Not him."

"I'm not exactly family." He ran a hand through his hair. "Besides, I've been awful busy lately. And I've fallen down on the job, making promises every which-a-way. Lemme give that fridge a listen for you."

"It stopped acting up. That's why I didn't mention it again."

"Ain't that the way of it?" He shoved his hands into his pockets. "Secondly though, I believe I told you I'd make up for breakin' our last appointment. They're havin' live music at the restaurant by the railroad tracks Thursday night at seven. I thought . . . if you're free . . . "

"Wonderful. I mean, yes. I'm free as free can be." She lowered her arms and gestured for him to come in. "Where are my manners? I've got a pizza on the way."

"Can't." He backed away. *Cain't.* "I'm out of daylight to get home and I've got another early mornin' tomorrow."

"Then Thursday at seven it is." Did she catch him sneaking another downward glance? She couldn't tell. "We'll make plans for the upstairs room."

His lips turned down at the corners. "I haven't forgotten. 'Til then, Abbs." With one final inscrutable look in his eyes, he turned away and made for the street.

She went into her room and flopped down on the bed, then sat upright, hugging her knees to her chest and squealing. She had a date. A date with Will.

Maybe he'd finally judge her worthy of hearing about his mysterious family and home life. If not, then her first priority would be to win that distinction. Beyond that, she hoped to find out what he liked to do besides go to church and save Aunt Ruby from herself. How did he wind up in such an odd role instead of school or a real job?

Her imagination wandered from chatter over dinner to their

nebulous plans to fix the front bedroom. Would it take two hours to move the leftover furniture to the storage room and paint the walls? Three? Would it be enough time to establish an inside joke, or to fan the spark struggling to ignite?

And besides that, what should I wear?

She snagged a handful of tops from her closet—a classic pink button-down, a baby-blue cap-sleeved tee with a ruched bodice, and her favorite, the black wrap blouse that looked perfect with jeans and her ballet flats.

The same ballet flats that could not be found anywhere. She dug to the bottom of her closet, checked by the front and back doors, and hunted them under a pile of laundry.

Lying on her belly on the floor, she saw a thin book under her bed. She reached for it and pulled out the Marietta directory from Aunt Ruby's desk, and a long trail of dust bunnies with it.

"Huh. Misplaced during Hurricane Sarah, I guess. Better stash this with the rest before I forget." She thumbed the pages and the book fell open around a thick sheet stuck inside. When she unfolded the document, her injured hand trembled, and she had to lay it flat to read it.

It resembled the title to her car, except with twenty-five dollar denominations in the corners and a familiar portrait of George Washington on its face. She scanned deeper. It was a 1942 series E defense savings bond. Her voice quaked as she read the lynchpin phrase aloud. "The United States of America for value received promises to pay Mr. W. C. Sosebee, payable on death to Mrs. Ruby Sosebee."

Distantly, a heavy fist pounded on the door, and a booming voice calling out. "Hello? Pizza delivery!"

CHAPTER 29

Tuesday, April 17

Greg arrived five minutes early. Abby stepped out to meet him, research notebook in tow, as soon as she heard the car pull up. She still didn't want to let him inside the house.

The sun cut through the trees. It would be a beautiful day, but the morning air was crisp and the grass dewy. She was tired of being cold.

She kept her eyes down as she slid into the passenger side. "Morning."

"That's the rumor. I want to stop for coffee if it's all right with—Abby, what happened?" Greg caught her bandaged hand.

She yanked it away. "Nothing. Can we go?"

"That's a lot of gauze for nothing."

"I cut myself on a broken mug." She curled her fingers around the edge of the notebook. "It bled a lot, but it's healing."

His eyes tracked her hand as if he were trying to see through the dressing. "I know we're not . . . But you can talk to Sarah. You know that, right?"

Her sinuses hurt. She massaged the bridge of her nose, but it didn't help. "It was an accident. If we can proceed without any reference to certain medications, I'll buy your coffee."

He rolled his shoulders and put the car in drive. "Not necessary, but consider the hint taken."

Greg ordered for both of them at a drive-thru coffee house. She protested by ignoring the drink, but after a few minutes the rich scent wore her down. She sighed into the cup without meaning to and caught Greg smirking from the corner of her eye.

"Better than sweet tea, isn't it?"

"I can't think what's not better than sweet tea. Other than being in a confined space with my ex, that is."

"Yeah, I can see how Ohio was a tight squeeze."

"This might amaze you, but I like it here. I'm not moving back."

He glanced over at her. "Since 'here' happens to be a confined space with my ex, it's fair to say that I like it here, too."

She leaned back into the seat and groaned out loud. He let out a rolling laugh, and she had to bite the inside of her cheeks to keep from joining him.

The levity ended soon enough. Sonny didn't have her car ready.

Abby crossed her arms. "You said on the phone it would be waiting out front."

"A little mix-up. The manufacturer sent the wrong part. Normally I'd put a rush on it, but you're already getting the family discount." He grinned and Abby instinctively looked down. His teeth were nasty. "Give me 'til Friday or Saturday. In the meantime, you want to consider getting a transmission service. The bolts on the trans pan don't have any tool marks on them, and that tells me you've never had it done. Ticking time-bomb, is all I can say. I can do it for three-seventy-nine."

Greg hung back, keeping out of her business but not far enough. She should have made him stay in the car. "Thanks, but I'll get my boyfriend to do it."

A ridiculous bluff. He might change a tire like a champ, but in his shirt sleeves, Greg didn't look like he knew a trans pan from a frying pan.

Sonny must have heard that one before. He leaned back, straining his tee shirt taut against a massive beer belly. She didn't fool him a bit. "Suit yourself, missy. I ain't your daddy."

Abby climbed into the rental. So many unanswered questions surrounding George Hart and W. C. Sosebee, and instead fate stuck her with Greg. Again.

"Sorry about your car. We'll come back Saturday. I don't have to be at the airport until late afternoon. I'll talk to him."

"No, I can handle him. If I need to, I'll get my uncle involved. He knows him."

"You mean he came recommended? I don't know if I'd trust anyone who vouched for that guy." He cranked the car. "Where to?"

"Take me home."

"You're sure?" He looked at the heavy binder in her lap. "I have a full tank and no schedule."

She stared down at the blue cover of her notebook. "I was planning to go to the Central Library to do research."

"About your ghost?"

"Don't make fun of me, Greg."

"I'm not," he said. "I'm interested. The story must have originated somehow."

"Yeah, but I don't know how. Aunt Ruby won't say. She acts like she's sorry she mentioned it."

"Maybe that's a clue. Maybe it's not a flattering story for her."

Abby pouted. "I don't see what part she plays. It's a Civil War ghost."

"You'll figure it out." He backed out of the parking space and threw the car into drive. "Lead the way."

MARIETTA

As a passenger, Abby paid closer attention to the county seat's charms than she had while driving to the courthouse. Maybe future archeologists would see what she saw now: a transition between two layers of civilization. Old converted residences mingled with the square modern hospital complex. A grand marble-faced church reflected blinding sunlight while the nearby shops extended neon invitations to all. As they approached the downtown area, she took the opportunity of a stop light to admire the Strand Theatre's tottering balance between historical preservation and the business of the hour.

The hillside cemetery across the street from the library caught her eye again with its rows of white markers, but she resisted the familiar pull. In the expansive landscape of marble stones, she'd wander without knowing what she sought like a ghost herself, walking fruitlessly until forever collapsed in on itself. She'd come back, maybe. Without Greg.

"And there went the turn. Sorry I missed it." He ignored the GPS and drove up to Fairground Street, claiming a shorter route that turned into a maze of one-way streets and then broad highway congestion. All told, Greg drove around another ten minutes before he was able to retrace the original route. Ten more minutes she had to spend with him than were strictly necessary. He probably did it on purpose.

It was, however, a gorgeous library.

They entered through the security detectors that kept the books from walking off and passed the technology center beside the circulation desk. Blue-pallored faces frowned into each computer screen. A giggling passel of kids lurked among the rows of bookshelves behind them, entertained by story hour.

Abby turned her attention to the sign for "The Georgia Room," as she'd seen on the library's website. Off to the left, past a wide curving display of new releases, heavy double doors guarded the library's historical archives.

The temperature dropped at least ten degrees beyond the doors, as if The Georgia Room were populated with old ghosts instead of reference collections. Silent researchers sat one to a table, copying from books into notepads or keying into laptops. The reverent air made Abby feel as though she'd entered a church. *The only church where I belong, at least.* Will wouldn't approve.

"This must be heaven for you." Abby hadn't realized Greg followed her into the library's alcove. His remark mirrored her thoughts a little too well, but a loud "Shh" rising up from the stacks saved her from having to respond.

"I'll go find a magazine rack," he whispered. "Have fun."

He sauntered off. She didn't like it. He was getting comfortable, enjoying her dependence. She'd half-expected him to lean down with a perfunctory little kiss, the everyday sort reserved for the goodbyes and hellos that didn't mean much.

A library assistant at the front desk had her head bowed deep in calculus homework, so Abby walked around to examine the room's offerings instead of asking for help. She wandered through the shelves and stacks, getting a feel for the layout and the types of titles included, and brooding over the questions before diving into their answers. In spite of her limited time, Abby wanted to luxuriate in the gallery of knowledge.

The reference section situated in the middle of the room encased rows of fat volumes. Among them she found a set of oversized red books. *Index to Cobb County Cemeteries.*

A good place to start. She took the first book in the series off the shelf to study its organization, then traded it for volume ten of the twenty. *M for middle. The middle of Marietta.*

Pages and pages of names passed before her eyes, a directory of the dead. She didn't search long before finding the Marietta National Cemetery lists, transcribed for posterity. She checked her own surname first, though if Aunt Ruby could be believed then none of her dead would be there. No heroes, not in this family, but Abby did recognize one name. A chill ran over her skin as she read the entry.

Wells, Audrey. LCpl; 8th ESB. Marines. Mustered in 22 Sep 2008; Mustered out 4 Aug 2011. B. 10 Sep 1990 D. 4 Aug 2011. Section W590.

Audrey. Her heart softened as the loss of a cousin she never knew jabbed her. If Uncle Blake was difficult or coarse, she could blame his pain. That much, she understood. Once Greg left, she'd make that trip to the cemetery to pay her respects.

She turned to the S section and found not a single Sosebee. No surprise there. She looked for Harts and one name stood out, as if it had waited a long time for release from its prison of paper and ink.

Hart, George. PVT; 1st Battalion of Ga. Infantry. Mustered in 31 Oct 1864; Mustered out 19 July 1865. B. 1845 D. 1895. Section H102.

A veteran at twenty, dead at fifty. Was this George Hart a match?

Abby rifled through her notebook. When she found the page she'd copied from Aunt Ruby's family Bible, she recognized first the big question mark next to George Hart's dates. She traced her finger down the index page again and compared the two Georges.

The birth year matched. The death year didn't.

The cemetery date allowed for a son in 1888, at least, but if George was alive until then, why did the family Bible list his death on January 19, 1861?

Abby tapped her pencil absently. Aunt Ruby said her father kept up with their lineage. Who would have handed it down to him? Probably the same person who bequeathed him the family home, the grandfather, Warren Hart. Strange. George's branch broken off the tree, but his son grafted back in.

Abby jotted down the entry from the cemetery transcription and sidled up to an open computer terminal. She clicked away from the library home page and over to Google to establish context. She typed in her query in simple terms: "January 19, 1861. Today in history."

"Georgia secedes from Union," claimed the first headline in the pool of results. Abby scrolled to find the same detailed in different words all the way down the page. She added George Hart's name to the string and came up blank.

If anyone on Planet Earth cares . . . She keyed in a search for his military unit and tapped the enter key. Almost at once, George Hart's story took a turn.

The First Battalion of Georgia served toward the end of the war. Federal forces mustered the battalion in Marietta on October 31, 1864, and their orders took them northwest to Dalton to guard the Western & Atlantic rails.

Abby sketched a map in her notebook. Wouldn't those men have been more useful further south, fighting Sherman's forces while they burned their way through Georgia? She didn't understand until she read the entire piece again. The critical words jumped out.

Federal forces.

George Hart served in a Union regiment.

The second week of November, 1864. Abby's stomach sank as the pieces came together. George Hart's father helped settle Big Shanty, and yet he kept a rear guard for the man who destroyed his town.

Aunt Ruby had told her version of the tale. George "turned his back on his family to find his fortune." Abby doubted a soldier's pay amounted to much of a fortune, but the story told was the one repeated.

More likely, he chose conviction over family, and the resulting grudge rippled forward through time until even Mom and Abby herself were caught in its tide. Her parents got no support from family when they got married. Whatever happened between them shaped her entire life. And *this* was the reason why?

"George Hart, a hero betrayed—" Abby wrote, but the pencil snapped in her hand. She got up from the terminal and clutched her notebook to her chest, breathing deeply for calm as she circled the Georgia Room's other offerings. One mystery down. One mystery left.

Toward the back of the secluded archive, rows of tiny drawers housed the microfiche reels. She studied the labels. *Macon Telegraph, 1920-1957. Pickens County Progress, 1902-1979. Forsyth County News, 1923-1944.* And inventoried among the rest, *Cobb County Times, 1940-1945.*

W. C. Sosebee, you're mine. Abby paused briefly before the drawer, as if it contained sacred scrolls instead of yesterday's news.

"Do you need any help?" The library assistant broke into her reverie. An older gentleman had taken her place at the desk. He must have busted up her homework party.

She plucked a boxed reel out of the drawer. The library assistant jutted out her lip as Abby helped herself.

"No, thanks." She loaded the reel into the microfiche machine as the girl watched. "I've got it."

And she did. The machine was similar to ones she'd used before, and she acclimated to the sensitivity of the zoom and focus dials as she scanned seventy-year-old headlines for items of interest. She scrolled through the reel slowly, not knowing which articles mattered, but paused over the first mention of the Bell Bomber plant.

Like the employee handbook at Aunt Ruby's. That's where the draft orders were. Where I fell down the rabbit hole.

She read every article headed with a mention of the plant, noting important details and paying for copies of the longer, more detailed pieces. The airplane manufacturer would bring thousands of jobs to the area, and unmistakable breathless thrill came through the words and years. Cobb County men registered for the draft on February 14, 1942, and she printed that article as well, but a small item tucked into page five of the next week's edition nearly zipped by unnoticed.

"'Hart, Sosebee Wed.' Score." She ignored a shushing from some other patron of the Georgia Room. She zoomed on the small item and printed another page with a swipe of her credit card.

The former Miss Ruby Rae Hart and Mr. W. C. Sosebee were wed in a very pretty Valentine's Day ceremony. The bride wore a white chiffon gown with a fingertip veil and carried a bouquet of wintersweet and pine boughs. Her maid of honor, Miss Pearl Hart, donned a smart yellow frock with matching hat. The single ring ceremony was performed by Pastor Fred McCollum at the Kennesaw Baptist Church. The couple will reside with the bride's parents on Rocky Street.

"Rocky Street." Abby read it again. "Not Pike's Landing." She snapped her lips shut before she could receive a rebuke.

Aunt Ruby said she lived in the house until the Sixties, which left two options. Either she lied, or she told the truth.

It was a puzzle, and she'd been collecting pieces all this time and still hadn't glimpsed the picture. She spread the heavy notebook across her lap, balancing the pockets that threatened to spill out with notes and photocopies. Her fingers skipped across the pages, groping for a missed clue to tell her about Rocky Street, the first hint discovered and the first she disregarded. Mom would've done better.

One of the land records sliced a nice paper cut into a knuckle on her injured hand. She stuck her finger in her mouth to curb the sting. The pages reminded her of the dragon lady at the courthouse. If they weren't the most likely place to find an address, she'd have been tempted to ignore them.

"Ma'am? Are you going to be long on the microfiche machine? I—"

"Yes," Abby hissed. "I will. I have this whole reel yet to go."

The man's caterpillar eyebrows shot halfway up his shiny bald head. "Huh. Kindly let me know when you're done?"

The land records were a puzzle themselves. She never did get around to assembling one whole copy from the multiples of partials. Pages drifted from her lap as she attempted to lay out the deeds, wills, and transfer records in some semblance of order, but she wouldn't let the man hurry her along as the Recorder of Deeds had. The vital clue wouldn't be obvious. It would only be found by searching for it.

She forced herself to slow down enough to recognize the truth or lie buried in dry legalese. Gilbert Hart once owned the entire lot on the corner of Pike's Landing and Main, the whole property existing as one big tract before he divided it between his two daughters. The 1902 deed relied on the surveyor's boundaries and Aunt Ruby's deed used the present street address, but the land transfer of Pearl's parcel specified that the property was part of the lot formerly described as 27 Rocky Street.

Aunt Ruby didn't lie. Mr. W. C. Sosebee and his bride lived in the house when his draft orders came. Exhaling a small victory sigh, she turned her attention back to the viewer. As she watched the weeks of 1942 slide across the screen and his window of life dwindled, Abby grew anxious over the inevitable mention of Sosebee's death. She'd already found him in the cemetery. She knew how this story ended.

Nervous that she had missed it, Abby backed up the viewer each time her tired eyes blurred. Vague headlines nagged, and she skimmed many of the stories. What if his death was obscured with a poor headline or buried under inches of copy?

Abby paused on a curious December headline. *Southern Bell Executives Host Gala.* The article gushed over a Christmas party for employees of the telephone company. Aunt Ruby might have attended— unless she quit her job when she got married. The bank passbook entries ended, but maybe she got a new one under her married name.

Almost certainly, though, W. C. Sosebee wouldn't have attended the gala with his wife. She hadn't found his obituary yet, which probably meant she already missed it.

What if they didn't run it in this paper? No one said the *Cobb County Times* was the only paper covering the area, and not every family placed obituaries. They could have chosen any newspaper or none at all. She considered giving up when a headline in smallish bold type rolled across the viewer. *W. C. Sosebee Buried Today.*

Abby's hand flew over her mouth, covering a small shriek. Somewhere in the room, another annoyed "Shh" barely registered. The short obituary would have left her longing for more details on any ordinary genealogy quest, but in this case, the details were more than enough.

William Christopher Sosebee, 21, died last Thursday at the Bell Bomber plant after falling between two railcars. Mr. Sosebee has been an employee of the Western & Atlantic Railroad since January of this year. He is survived by Mrs. Ruby Sosebee his wife, parents Joseph and Bridget Sosebee, and an uncle Thomas Laughlin of Acworth. Burial was today in the Kennesaw City Cemetery.

She read the small item three times, printed it, and then shut down the microfiche machine. She didn't remove the reel nor get up from the chair.

William.

Laughlin.

It made such sense—his claims to be a simple man, the way he turned up out of nowhere at convenient times. Twenty-one going on ninety-one. Of course.

She frowned as she remembered him carrying the bulbs and rake to the cemetery. But some ghosts could move objects, couldn't they? If he could knock on doors and walk on the roof, then why not?

No. She shook her head. He was solid. He was real. Wasn't he? He looked normal . . .

Don't let looks fool you. Didn't he warn her himself?

She tried to remember if she'd ever touched him. Had they shaken hands over the lease or brushed arms accidentally on the way to the cemetery?

Of course not. After nursing a crush on him for weeks, the smallest touch would have burned on her skin. Even at the cemetery he tapped her nose with the flower.

The proof she'd asked for dodged and flitted, breaking her heart all over again. What was she hoping for? That Will was alive and Mom was dust? Or that they both continued in some formless, untouchable state?

Would she be seated alone tomorrow night?

Abby glanced around the room. A handful of researchers tapped at their laptops and intently traced lines of reference texts. A quiet little afternoon at the library continued on around her, oblivious to the crushing stone in her chest.

Back to flipping notebook pages, and a quiet panic rose before she found the draft orders on the third pass. "December 31, 1942." She breathed out the lowest whisper, slow and deliberate, for confirmation that she could still breathe. The key detail she'd missed that day in the graveyard jumped out at her. W. C. Sosebee's tombstone showed only the year of his death, but any date in 1942 would have caused him to miss that appointment. "You never reported for duty that day, did you, Will? Because you were already gone."

A feeling of vertigo came over her, slight compared to the stunt on the train, but disconcerting nonetheless. She closed her eyes. All the moments with Will, the words exchanged and those unspoken swirled in her head until the sensation passed. No wonder Aunt Ruby wanted her to back off. But what kept Will tied to the house? Why did he stay?

She clicked the microfiche machine back on. The railroad supervisor or the building contractor would have followed up on that horrible accident with an investigation, an inquest, a reprimand. There had to have been some kind of justice.

Abby took her time through the remaining weeks of 1942, reading each headline slowly for hints or clues. The December 31 edition ran an article announcing "Seventy-one Cobb draftees inducted this morning," and her stomach turned to lead. Will should have been one of them. The names were not listed, but she felt certain of it. The news of his death hadn't made it through official channels in time. The paperwork crossed and they drafted a dead man, and Aunt Ruby, widowed at eighteen, received his draft orders in the mail.

Then she did find mention of the accident, but not in the way she had expected.

Only Two Lives Lost Constructing Bell Plant

Abby read the article once with confusion and again with horror. The men listed had died tragically, but neither of them was Will. Only in the final paragraph did she understand.

In December W. C. Sosebee of Kennesaw was killed accidentally, but this fatality was not counted in the official total because he was a railroad employee at the time of his death.

Her eyes burned. It counted to Aunt Ruby. The slim volume of W. C. Sosebee's story had closed, but the epilogue was still being written.

Oh, Will. Chill bumps rose on her arms. No wonder he couldn't move on. He hadn't received justice. Not at all.

There was more to know, but nothing the newspaper could tell her. Abby removed the reel and switched off the machine again, leaving the small box in the return tray. Before she was halfway to the door, the bald man hurried over to take her spot.

Greg must have been listening for her, because he racked a car magazine and crossed the lobby to meet her as soon as she emerged from the Georgia Room.

"Any good finds?"

"No," Abby choked. "I mean, yes, finds. Not good ones."

"Have you been crying? For pity's sake, it's supposed to be a hobby."

"No. Some woman in there drenched herself with perfume. I'm fine."

"Tell me." Someone at the circulation desk coughed politely and Abby gritted her teeth. She'd gotten herself banned from the museum fair and square, but she wouldn't let Greg cost her privileges here.

"There's nothing to tell. I want to go home."

Greg rubbed his cheek and they walked out of the library, each passing through separate side-by-side security detectors. Outside, the bright sun made her squint, but she hugged the binder to her chest and walked fast to keep ahead of him.

Heat waves shimmered off the car. Greg started it with the remote as he approached. "If I lived here, I'd buy one of these. No waiting for the A/C to get cold."

She frowned. The last thing she needed was him to move south. "No way. Not worth the price tag."

"I bet you'll change your mind in the summer. Here, I mean. The weather will be perfect back home." They got in the car and he turned to her, their tiff in the lobby dismissed. "Are you hungry?"

"Greg, I appreciate this. Truly. As long as you understand that you aren't winning me over. If this is a strategy, it's not working."

"I don't have ulterior motives, Abby. I told you exactly why—"

"And I'm trying to respect you enough to be honest. Will you let me?" She took a deep breath. "I'm saying that there won't be any repayment. Not in the short term, not in the long term."

"You're killing me here, you know," he said. She snapped her attention to him, startled, but he kept his eyes on the rearview mirror and backed out. "Love isn't a transaction. Or I don't know, maybe for some people it is. But I love you even if you tell me to leave and never come back."

"You'll get over me."

"If I have to," he agreed.

A long silence stretched between them. If she died today, Greg would be her unfinished business. What if she were already dead and didn't know? The two of them would circle steps in eternal dance, endless and powerless to change their fate.

But Sarah did say she didn't have to go through this alone.

Chills rippled over her bare arms. "Greg? How about a second chance?"

"I'm listening."

She gave her best smile. *Sell it, Abby. Make him believe.* "Meet me Thursday at that same restaurant by the railroad tracks. Dinner and clean slate. What do you think?"

He frowned. "I'd like to see you tomorrow."

"I'm busy tomorrow," she lied. "Take it or leave it."

He smiled faintly. "Thursday, then. What time?"

"Six-thirty. I hear there's supposed to be live music."

CHAPTER 30

KENNESAW

What would it take to set Will free? The million dollar question. One Abby dwelt on to avoid the longings of her heart, sealed behind an invisible, firmly-fixed boundary. Keeping after the story helped evade the question of whether the sum total of her experiences, from her father's absence to Mom's cancer to her affection for Will, might all fit together, a massive joke that the universe played to teach her better than to want what she could never have.

To her surprise, Greg left her in peace without trying to invite himself in again. She'd be safely alone, as alone as she ever was in a haunted house. The mystery all but solved, she put away her notebooks and only needed to return the directory to the desk upstairs where it belonged. She no longer had to wonder when the ghost would reveal himself—he already had, and regularly, since before she'd even moved in. Never intruding, though. Hadn't Ruby claimed he was a knocker? A gentleman.

"I'm at least half-crazy." Abby replaced the drop cloth covering the old letter desk. "But do me a favor and don't tell Sarah I admitted it."

When she turned to descend the stairs, the ambient light from the shadeless window in the front bedroom caught a hint of metal at the top of the doorframe to the locked back room, the one Aunt Ruby used for storage. The room that wasn't included in her lease.

No guilt tugged at her this time. After all, she was entitled to an upstairs room. He should have cleared one or the other of them for her already. Now that she knew his secret, there should be no more cause for delay.

Abby tested the doorknob. It wiggled but wouldn't turn, as she had expected. "Locked. And you said you didn't have the key because it's right here. Clever, Will. Clever." She reached up to the top of the doorframe, her fingers brushing the matted dust in pursuit of the metallic glint. The object slid, flashed, and dinged brightly against the floor.

She stooped with a momentary panic, but the curious little key had landed at her feet. No thicker than a dime, it obviously wouldn't match this door.

"You fit a different kind of lock." She held the key up before her eyes. "A tiny one."

She palmed the key, intending to take it downstairs and put it in the kitchen drawer where she kept her copy of the lease and her paid utility bills.

Then the dots connected. She turned on her heel and nearly lost her footing on the top step.

The desk had a lock. Not on the shield, but inside the secret drawer.

She hurried back into the room and jerked the drop cloth, ignoring the slight sound of ripping, and tugged the drawer loose from the false bottom. Inside was the closed compartment, the same as she left it, guarding its minute secret.

Abby fitted the key into the lock. It released with a satisfying little click. She opened the lid, but the contents confused her all the more.

"Another key? Seriously?"

She took it out of the shallow wooden box and examined it. Tarnished brass, but with sharp-edged teeth. Seldom used, then.

Without hesitation, she stepped out into the hall and tried the key in the back bedroom door. The knob twisted under her hand.

She sucked in her breath and choked it back out. Thick dust and the distinct smell of mildew clouded the room. Dust caked every surface. It even clung to the walls, bespeckling them in weird dark clusters. A surgical mask would have been a good idea, and an oxygen tank a better one.

Boxes stacked shoulder-high lined one whole wall. The ones on the bottom were sunken, in danger of collapsing under the weight and years. A closet door stood open where two century-old dresses hung, limp rags in human forms, their dull colors tired of being, and a haphazard pile of garments draped a coat tree in the corner. Abby wasn't sure, but one of them looked a lot like a Confederate soldier's jacket.

The room held other oddities—a curio cabinet full of sad clown figures, a huge cherry wardrobe, and loose shelves that probably once belonged in the erstwhile pantry. None of these items interested her, for in the middle of it all, with a foot of space around it on every side as an invisible sign of reverence, stood an antique bassinet.

She stared at it for a long while, finding her courage before stepping close to the ancient cradle and peering inside.

It was empty. Thankfully, wonderfully empty.

A wedding gift from hopeful parents, she guessed, meant to encourage the newlyweds to provide a grandbaby. "Gilbert and Velma wouldn't have wanted a crying baby in the house, but your parents? They would have been anxious about carrying on the family name. Maybe they gave you the same bassinet you slept in." She swallowed hard. "And your brother and sister. And instead you died, and Aunt Ruby put it up here where she wouldn't have to look at it."

Pure speculation, but heartfelt and honest, like Mom would have done.

The thick, rank air stuck in her lungs. *I have to get out of here. Immediately.*

For once, Abby saw no need to dig any deeper. She backed out of the room, locking it from the inside as it had been and replacing both keys where she found them. She sneezed three times. The third one hurt and left her covered in goose bumps.

"Bless me," she said aloud. At that moment, she felt in dire need of a good blessing.

CHAPTER 31

Thursday, April 19

Ruby wiped sweat from her forehead. Should've worn her gardening hat.

Used to be that a glorious oak tree shaded the Sosebee plot. Glorious till the day Ruby realized that the tree's roots spread out same as its branches did. Beneath the ground they would claw and pry at the burial vaults, his and his family's, until it found a crack or erosion. With persistence and time, they'd overtake his remains, and her old love would go up into the tree. The last place he'd ever want to be.

And once the roots had done their work, the city felled the tree. It didn't change the twisting and winding fingers below the surface, but at least she didn't have to think of them as much. They left the stump, though, and Ruby made sure not to trip on it as she stood back to admire her handiwork, such as it was.

It wouldn't take.

The lilies Will planted on John's grave poked out of the ground, plucky and fresh, but still weeks away from budding. The stalk she'd brought from the florist tottered, its artificially matured blooms making it top-heavy, and the clay soil supporting it too loosely packed. It'd wither and die, probably, and it wouldn't come back next year.

"I tried, Christie." She spoke at his tombstone. "Lord knows I tried."

"Miss Ruby?" She flinched, and the speaker raised her hands, abashed. "Didn't mean to sneak up on you."

"Sharon?" Mercy. Of all people, Sharon Petersen would be the one to intrude. All dressed up, more than usual, but she wouldn't turn any heads today, not with her makeup smeared and her frizzy auburn curls undone by the humidity. "Goodness sakes, child, what're you doing here?"

A tear slicked a track down her face. "My stepdad. Mom needed a few more minutes, and I saw you down here." She wiped her cheek and nodded down at the grave. "An old friend, I take it?"

"You might say that." Ruby clacked her dentures. Not this whelp of a girl. Not here, not now. What business did a church chair thief and failed flirt have—

"I've never lost anybody close before." She sniffled wetly. "I know he's with the Lord, but I sure hope it gets easier."

"Eh." She hesitated before patting Sharon's back. "Folks are all different. Some say it does and some say it don't."

"What do you say?"

Ruby stared down at the Easter lily. It leaned to the left, not moving, not doing anything but invisibly dying. "The first time him and me met, I was five years old and stuck in the top of a pine. I climbed up so high I was afraid to get down. Then Christie happened along. He was taking a cheese sandwich to his daddy for lunch, as I recall. He heard me carrying on and climbed up after me."

"He helped you down?"

"No," Ruby said. "Not exactly. I shimmied right down the other side of the tree. I wasn't afraid with him there."

"That's a sweet story, Miss Ruby."

"That ain't the end of it. Once I made it to the ground, he made a mistake and looked down. Got dizzy, lost his footing. Fell right out of that tree. I'll never forget the sound of him hitting the ground, not if I live to be a hundred and ten."

"Oh." She looked down at the grave, but Ruby continued her story.

"I got scared and ran away, but he was all right. Banged up and bruised, of course. The mockingbirds made off with his daddy's sandwich. He went home to get another and his mama made him pick his own switch." She swallowed hard. "He joked about it after we got married. Told me it was the only time a tree got the better of him twice in one day."

Sharon smiled faintly. "Funny."

"I always imagined his spirit stayed on. Not because he blamed me," she added. "But it made it easier to think he stayed right close."

"But that wasn't real."

"He's with the Lord too," Ruby snapped. "The way people talk, you'd think heaven was three counties away. I remembered him how I wanted to. And when I'm gone, no one else will."

Sharon kept the peace for a blessed moment. "How do you want to be remembered, Miss Ruby?"

Her heart flip-flopped while she gathered up her trowel and watering can and gave the lily stalk a last look. A stiff wind would blow it down. "As someone who never got her husband a whuppin'."

"But if y'all got married later then obviously he didn't hold it against you."

"He didn't have to. When he fell . . . " She faltered. Even now, she couldn't bring herself to tell his secret. "I didn't know the real damage done 'til it was too late to ever say sorry." She directed her words at the gravestone, even knowing that if her words made it through the clay and casket, they'd still never penetrate the barrier between her living lips and Christie's dead ears.

And that Sharon Petersen, who wouldn't know the last word on a subject if it walloped her upside the head, piped up one more time. "That sounds like a terrible burden to carry around, Miss Ruby, if you don't mind my saying so."

CHAPTER 32

"Breathe, Abby." As she transferred the contents of one purse to another, a powder compact slipped off the edge of her bed and landed on the hardwood. "Oops. Seven years bad dates. Except I've already paid into that account." She snatched up the compact and opened it over her cupped hand, prepared to catch stray shards of the broken mirror, but found the glass and the powder intact.

She checked the time. Greg would have been waiting at least five minutes, probably debating whether to get a table or stand in the lobby. What if he got the point before she and Will arrived?

"If so, then it's for the better. No messy confrontation. No accusations and name-calling." She rifled through the selection of tops strewn across the room. "And if I miss it that much, I can always call him up later and fight over the phone."

She opted for the black blouse, noting with dismay that it hung and billowed more than she remembered. Her curves had ceded to the collar bones and ribs jutting out and trying to escape.

Her cosmetics collection was equally lacking. Why didn't she have any sexy make-up? Her color palette included peachy browns and practical nudes, without a smidgen of red lipstick or a nub of black eyeliner.

She made do, painting the best come-to-bed eyes she could manage. She brushed and smudged and blended until a type of powdery beauty appeared in the mirror. All that remained was to find her ballerina flats, wipe down the sink so Will wouldn't see her mess, put on earrings, and find a magazine to read at the table so she could look casual about her waiting when he arrived.

She was still searching for her shoes when Will's now-familiar knocking came. "Two seconds," she called, racing around the house, removing embarrassments before she let him in. While she bordered on panic, a breezy thread of sweetness floated through the door, the sound of Will whistling to amuse himself while he waited.

As she opened the door and faced him, she sucked in her breath. She had it all wrong. The clothes, the makeup—they couldn't transform a simple evening into what she wanted.

Will stood on the porch, looking much as he always did. A white tee shirt stretched across his wiry frame, jeans with wear in the knees, and the air of a man who has put in a full day's work. He showed no sign of any special preparation for their evening. What had she expected? Flowers and a polo shirt? That was Greg's routine, not Will's.

Flowers are for the living.

"Wow. You look nice," he said, his tone cautious.

"Thank you." Heat rose in her cheeks. "Let me find my shoes and we'll go." Her ugly, naked toenails caught her attention. She should have painted them.

Will took several seconds to answer while his eyes turned her inside out. "You feelin' all right? You sound stopped up."

"I'm fine. Allergies." She escaped to her bedroom, closing the door as quietly as she could for privacy to resume her search, but the flats would not be found. She didn't remember seeing them since Sarah's visit, and she dashed off a hurried text. "Do you have my ballet flats?"

She continued looking, but the reply came in less than thirty seconds. "Yes. Oops."

Steeling her jaw, she resolved for plan B. "Okay. Forget comfort. Go for impact." At the edge of the pile of shoes, a barely worn pair of silver stilettos caught her eye. Purchased for a party two years ago, abandoned since, and so expensive . . .

Slipping them on, she remembered instantly why she hadn't worn them again. The work of staying upright placed weird stress on her knees.

She wobbled her way back into the kitchen. "Sorry about that. Ready."

"Whew! So tall. Are you sure about those?"

No, she wasn't. Did he ask out of concern, or to rebuke her for trying too hard? She laughed off his question, batting it away with one of her own. "Did the fridge make any noise for you?"

"No." He frowned. "It seems all right."

"Maybe I was wrong," she said, because with Will here, meeting her eyes, focusing his care and concern and energies on her and her little problems, she only wanted to be wrong about him. She winged a semi-serious prayer skyward, in case anyone could hear. *Please let him be real.* "Maybe the ghost made it act up."

He cleared his throat. "Let's go."

They stepped outside and she fumbled her keys in locking the deadbolt. Could she relax for one minute? Forget Greg, forget ghosts, and be happy in the moment?

Impossible. She wanted to ask, and at the same time didn't, whether he called this a date or a debt. He'd try to spare her feelings if the answer wasn't one she would like, but his eyes would tell the truth, and that might be more than she could bear.

Without her car, their only choice was to walk. By the Veterans' Memorial, the ache in her knees shot like needles into her hips, and when they crossed the threshold into the tiny restaurant, Abby fought wincing with every step. The powerful air conditioner in the lobby raised goose bumps on her arms.

"Table for two," Will told the hostess. Across the room, she saw Greg, sitting in the same booth where she'd met him days earlier, his face blank with disinterest at a television screen over the bar. She tracked his gaze. Baseball. The Atlanta Braves against the New York Mets. Neither a team he cared about. She wondered if he'd picked one or the other to root for.

Her heart pounded out the alarm. How would Will react when he understood that she used him? And why didn't she think of that sooner? If Greg approached them—

"Can we sit outside?" Abby blurted.

"Normally yes," the hostess apologized. "But a private party reserved the patio tonight. Follow me, please."

Even though she tried not to look at Greg, their eyes bumped. She saw the flash of recognition first and the assessment right behind it, and she watched as he withered in his seat. He sipped his tea, and when he set his glass down on the table, his downcast eyes didn't search for hers again.

Good.

The hostess led them to a table decorated with a small vase of Peruvian lilies and located uncomfortably close to Greg's. He must have been caught sizing up his competition, because Will dipped his head in a polite nod. His courteous ways ran so deep, he honored his enemy without knowing it.

Greg would overhear their conversations, if he stayed long. Abby swallowed hard. All right then. She'd make it count.

"Are you okay, Abbs?"

"Sure. Why?" she chirped.

"Your face." Will gestured at his own. "You're awful splotchy, like you're havin' a reaction."

Wonderful. She pressed her clammy fingers to her cheeks. "It's hot in here." A ridiculous claim. The fine hairs on her neck tickled under the deep freeze of air-conditioning. "I'm sure once I have a cold drink I'll be fine."

"Show's supposed to start in a few minutes." Will glanced at his invisible watch, a gesture Abby found so endearing and cute, she couldn't help but smile.

"Thanks for this."

"I promised, didn't I?" *Dit'ny?*

"You did. But you know no one ever means what they say. In my experience, most people don't bother keeping their word."

"I'm no better, Abbs. Trust me."

She leaned in, wanting to hear more, but Jillian the server wedged herself past a busboy to greet them.

"Good evening, folks. Can I take your drink order?" A note of recognition crossed Jillian's face. She jerked her head in Greg's direction, a question or a warning, and Abby bit her lip, as if to agree. *Yes. Awkward.*

"Pinot grigio," she said.

Will held up his hand. "Nothin' for me."

"I'll be right back." Jillian hurried away to the next table.

"You're not drinking?" Her stomach churned. If she'd surprised him with her obvious expectations for tonight, then he might not be prepared to pay.

"I'm not thirsty." He winked. "Came for the company."

She dipped her head and lowered her lashes to hide tears. And if her suspicions were true? Then he hadn't paid for a drink in seventy years.

No need to start tonight.

The lights dimmed and the bright ringing of an acoustic guitar warming to the crowd dominated the small restaurant.

From the corner of her eye, she saw Greg signing a credit slip and tucking his card back into his wallet. He rose to leave, and as he walked behind her, Abby leaned toward Will. "You're always looking out for me. I can't tell you how much I appreciate it."

Folksy opening chords jangled forth from a lone performer, a skinny boy with hair in his eyes, saving Will from the "aw shucks" reply Abby knew he would have made.

Jillian brought her wine and a complimentary water for Will. The drink had an acidic bite, but Abby downed a few nervous sips and the sting faded. Though Greg had left, her brain conjured two trains approaching the depot, destined to collide. How well she could picture it. Lights flashing. Signals dinging. Horns blowing, warning her to clear the track.

Stop it. Greg is gone. She inhaled the wine's weak bouquet in slow, deep breaths. *Collision course averted.*

The young musician quaked with shyness through his first song. A high-schooler, maybe. Abby let his ballads wash over her, even thinking she might look him up later. If he had any recordings, she could relive this night in melody as often as she dared. The best part was the volume, and the atmosphere, and the way the sound pounded with her heart and vibrated the air in her lungs.

Too soon, her last sip of her wine sat alone in the bottom of the glass and she swirled it, not wanting to ask for another yet. Will hadn't touched his water. A rivulet of condensation trickled down the side of the glass, like the sweat that rolled down his face when she greeted him at her door. That was Will—full and untouched.

Maybe untouchable.

Abby flagged the server with a slight wave. She took the last sip and gestured to the glass. Jillian nodded and whisked it away.

"I'll pay for my drinks," she said, once Jillian moved out of earshot. "I insist."

He shrugged. "I know better than to argue with an independent woman."

The remark practically begged her to ask questions, but her thick tongue refused. Was Ruby the independent woman he meant? How had he learned not to argue with her? When she kept her job with the telephone company?

Her hands needed an anchor. She shouldn't have surrendered the empty glass. And another mistake: in her haste to get ready, she never stopped by her jewelry box. No necklace or earrings to entertain her nervous fingers. No sanctuary at all but the glossy tabletop, so she tapped it lightly in time with the music and watched Will's hands, calloused and still and folded. What did he hold in those loose fingers that made the lacking so appealing?

The time slipped by. She wanted to talk but didn't know if she should, or even what to say. She swallowed the lump in her throat. "He could play forever."

Will shook his head. "Pretty sure he's close to the end of his set."

"Oh. Too bad." She cursed herself. Idle words broke the spell. "I didn't think it would be over so soon."

"They usually have two performers. Another one will go after him, probably."

"So you're a regular here?"

His hand twitched. Abby barely caught it. "Used to come more often than I do now."

Abby fixed her attention on the balladeer as he sang about love and death and desire, and imagined Will singing certain lines for her. She could pretend. Date or not, they came together, would leave together. It wasn't wrong.

Will stayed wrapped up in the music, and Abby couldn't focus anywhere but on him. He was unburdened and light, remarkable for his ordinariness. She plotted her move, how to touch the plane where his thoughts came from and taste the peace he carried on his lips.

Among the crowd all focused to the boy with his guitar, her world shifted sideways as she felt Will's eyes on her. She easily read the questions in his face. *Okay? Having fun?*

She offered him a sweet smile that she hoped he could read as well. *Yes. Yes. All the yeses there are.* She sensed an understanding passing between them, a knowledge organic and beautiful and somehow impermanent. She slid an open hand across the table.

And just like Greg, he saw what she did, knew what she meant, and hesitantly withdrew his hands to his lap.

She shrank. Wrong, of course, but about what? Did it matter whether he hid a ghostly form that couldn't grasp her hand or if he simply didn't want her touch? Either alternative worked out the same. Emptiness and wanting.

The final strains of song reached out into the room and were enveloped by eager hands applauding. Whistles and catcalls rippled through the dining room, a racket that couldn't drown out their silence. It eclipsed the profound silence in the house, at the grave, in the news clippings. This silence rang deeper than plain emptiness. The space between her and Will wasn't empty; it was full of death. A death louder than life.

She wouldn't lift her eyes to see pity or rejection reflected back. Jillian arrived with her drink as the coppery peals of guitar strings and a smattering of encouraging hoots called attention to the front. An unexpected familiar face dismissed the shaggy-haired balladeer.

Uncle Blake. This evening kept getting better and better.

He played a couple of chords, frowned, and stopped to fiddle with the tuning keys. She glanced at Will, who still kept his eyes down. Any distraction to dim the glare of embarrassment would do. She faked a smile. "Look, it's my uncle. We should go say hello before his set."

He finally raised his face, turned first to the front and then at her. She found none of the judgment or disdain she expected. Only nervousness. "Do you care if we don't?"

Her smile melted away. "No, I guess not. What's wrong?"

"Him and me don't always get along." The firm set of Will's jaw told her that he wouldn't say more.

"Do you want to go?" She held her breath.

His lips parted. Closed again. Trembled. He nodded.

"Okay. I'll pay and we're out of here." She waved again. This time Jillian missed her, but Blake's eyes narrowed in their direction. "Sorry, Will. I think he saw us."

"S'okay," Will said, but the hesitation creeping at the edge of his voice suggested otherwise.

Abby was ready with her debit card as soon as Jillian made another pass, but while she waited for her to run it, Blake leaned toward the sound tech for a moment and placed his guitar on the stand. A microphone voice boomed close behind. "Five minute intermission, folks. The bar's open."

Blake sauntered up to their table. "Ain't this cozy," he spat. "Guess workin' for Ruby came with benefits after all."

Will stood and backed away from the table. "This isn't what it looks like."

Abby's breath caught in her throat. *Isn't it, Will?*

"Don't lie to me, boy. You left her little love note behind when you was goin' through Ruby's mail."

"I didn't—"

"You oughta go ahead and move in together. I think I might enjoy throwin' you both out when the old bag kicks the bucket."

Will's shoulders squared. "You don't talk about her like that."

Blake balled fists at his sides. "Or you'll do what?" He flicked a glare at Abby. "We're done here. You ain't worth my time, and y'all deserve each other. Word of advice, boy. Keep an eye on your billfold. You know what happened to Richard."

He returned to the stage and picked up his guitar like nothing happened. Will strode out the front door of the restaurant, leaving Abby alone.

Jillian hung back for a moment before she stepped up to the table again. "Here you go. Come back and see us." She handed Abby the pay folder with her card inside. In a lower voice, she added, "I'd pick the other guy if I were you. This one seems like trouble."

Abby dipped her head and blushed. "Thanks." She retrieved her card and chased after Will.

When she stepped out into muggy air, she didn't see him right away and couldn't call out for him over the roar from the approaching train. She stood below the elevated embankment, watching the railcars go by with her hands muffling her ears. As the horns subsided and the steady clacking of the caboose faded, she dropped her hands. Tires screeched and a couple of cars honked at each other, but they avoided a dust-up.

Will's voice came out of the shadows. "I always have liked trains."

Her scalp prickled at the remark. Did he remember that day? A sudden loss of balance, a short drop between the threshold of life and death? Had it been quick? Painful?

She shoved away the macabre thoughts. "Tell me I didn't get you fired."

He shook his head. "If he could get rid of me, I'd have been gone a long time ago. Come on, I'll walk you home."

Her ankle wobbled over a piece of loose gravel on the pavement. "You were right about these shoes. They're going in the trash. My toes are tingling. Doesn't that mean nerve damage?"

"I don't rightly know," he said as she kicked off the annoying heels, narrowly maintaining her balance in the process. "But you'll be worse off walking around barefoot. There could be broken glass."

"I'll take my chances." They crossed the parking lot and headed for the house. By the rosy orange glow of the street lamps, he looked otherworldly. Then again, she probably did too. The cover of darkness made an appealing place to try him, that she might lay her doubts and fears aside. "Will, can I ask you one question?"

He pressed the button at the crosswalk. "Sure, Abbs. Ask away."

The hated nickname sapped her nerve. She changed tacks at the last second. "Could you please not call me 'Abbs'?"

"Oh. Sure. I'm sorry. I didn't know it bothered you."

"Yeah." She gave a nervous little laugh. "Every time you do, it makes me self-conscious about my pouchy tummy—"

"Ab—Abby, you don't have a—"

"Yes, I do." She tugged her blouse halfway up to prove it. Two glasses of wine and she was babbling about nerve damage and practically stripping in public. Mom would have been so proud.

The light changed, but Will didn't move. He stared at her with a strange look on his face. "I didn't know you had a belly ring."

She lowered her shirt and a universal truth washed over her: no one ever dies when they most wish they could. "Congrats. Now you do."

"Abby, Abby." He finally stepped into the street as she limped and lagged behind. "What am I going to do with you?"

Whatever you want. "Tell me the truth." The alcohol had her feeling lightheaded, and she wasn't sure what might pop out of her mouth next.

He gave a sidelong look, one eyebrow arched, as they reached the curb. "The truth? I've never lied to you. Not once."

They passed under pink blossoms fouling the air with the lurid sweetness of the flowers falling to decay. "But you've omitted a bunch. Haven't you?"

"Did you enjoy the show? What we saw of it, I mean?"

"That wasn't especially smooth, Will."

He stopped walking and looked at her. The shadow of the Veterans' Memorial hid his face, but his voice sounded sad. "If we're gonna salvage any part of this evening, talkin' about me ain't how to do it."

"Fine. It will be an awful memory tomorrow, at least." She wiggled her toes against the pavement. "But yes, I liked the music. A lot."

He turned away again, walking faster. "Good. Then we're square on one count, at least."

"When Blake said you should watch your billfold around me—"

"He was bein' hateful. I wish you wouldn't dwell on it."

"But it surprised me." She sniffled. "When he saw us—"

"I reckon there's plenty that would surprise you about me. We hardly know each other at all," he pointed out. "I could tell one fact right now that'd make you wish you never met me."

"Please don't. I'm glad I met you." Abby struggled to keep pace with him.

"You have skeletons in your closet too, I bet, but it ain't my job to pry 'em loose."

He walked ahead, creating distance as they rounded the second street corner. If she let him out of sight, would he vanish completely? He'd done it before.

"I have a tattoo," she lied, and in spite of himself, he slowed to look at her.

"Do you?"

"Yes. But I can't show it to you." He didn't respond, and the silence turned awkward as they approached the house. "Will?"

He covered his eyes. "I don't need to see your tattoo. I believe you."

"You shouldn't. I was kidding," she said. "But I'm ready to ask my question now."

"All right." He lowered his hand. "But after a build-up like that, I don't promise you an answer."

She sat down on the rickety porch steps. "Remember when you told me you didn't have the key to the back bedroom?"

He stood a couple yards off from her, hands in his pockets and edging the stepping stone walkway. "When I first showed you the house."

"Yeah. I found it."

"Why were you lookin' for it?"

"I wasn't," she said, defensive. "A piece of metal caught the light, and it turned out to be the key." She fidgeted. That version was almost true. Close enough.

He didn't speak for a moment, and the shadows kept both of them from reading faces. "How'd you know what it opened unless you tried it in the door?"

She looked at her feet. "Maybe I occasionally have trouble minding my own business. It's one of those skeletons you mentioned."

"Huntin' ghosts again."

"I heard footsteps on the roof. Footsteps and knocking."

"I can explain the footsteps. And you said the fridge—"

"I lied about the fridge. I'm telling the truth about this." She stood up and held out her hand to him. "If I told you I was scared, would you come inside?"

He hesitated. "I shouldn't."

She dropped her arm to her side, stung. "Why not? Because of Blake?"

"Because I'm still your stand-in landlord."

"So? I dated my boss once. Nobody got hurt." That lie blared so loud in Abby's head, Will certainly must have heard it.

"That's not the only reason." He held her gaze for several seconds. She loved and hated the way he made her feel so thoroughly seen. "But if you're so scared, come on. I'll show you somethin'."

CHAPTER 33

When she finally climbed into the Sentra, Ruby pulled a crumpled tissue out of the center console. Allergy season couldn't end soon enough. Especially since she was mainly allergic to Sharon.

Ruby silently chided herself. Did mean old ladies turn up their noses at her the day they buried Christie? For heaven's sake.

She backed out onto Main Street, and in her rearview mirror, a Silverado's grill came up on her too fast. Ruby hit the gas pedal and jerked forward, narrowly outrunning him. A flush of adrenaline left her jumpy. A short way home, then rest.

She coasted up to the red light in the square. That sure looked like Will silhouetted in the creeping dusk in front of the restaurant, but if he was hungry, he could've let himself in and ate at her house—

Then Abby slipped out behind him. Ruby craned her neck to see more, but a flash of headlights and an angry honk called her down. She honked back.

Her heart galloped. Where'd that other car come from? So far she'd been lucky, but two close calls in a half-mile stretch? She never planned to learn to drive in the first place, not 'til after Christie died. Since the stroke her license was no good, but if she left herself at Blake's mercy, she'd never get out of the house at all.

Was that reason enough to want another death on her record?

Her heart thumped out irregular beats, nervous and sick, and she had no relief in making her turn onto Hiram Street either. No rest for the wicked. She laid her hand on her chest.

Thursday, December 10, 1942

Their bedroom got tighter in the mornings while they dressed and groomed and got in each other's way. "I'm going to the beauty parlor after work," Ruby said. "But I'll ride over to the Golf Club with Agnes and meet you. Now the party's at seven so get there fifteen minutes beforehand. I think you should wear Daddy's suit coat. The collar's worn out on yours and I don't have time to turn it for you."

"Here's an idea." He met her eyes in the reflection of the mirror, not face to face. "What about instead we go for a fancy dinner and a show?"

"Oh, no." She pinched hairpins from her china box and reserved two at the corner of her mouth while securing a roll of curls with a third. "Don't be tryin' to wiggle out of it. You've known about this for a solid month."

"You have too, but you didn't find time to turn that collar."

She rolled her eyes. "If you're set on wearing your own, I'll see if Mama'll do it."

He drew his cap from of the deep pockets of his blue coveralls and completed his W&A railroad uniform. "I don't care if I never wear a suit coat again, Ruby. If you're so keen on rubbing elbows with a bunch of fat cats this evening, I don't see what you need me there for."

Might as well play her hand, Ruby figured. "Because Mr. Rutherford will be there, and he's your ticket with the higher-ups at the Bell plant." She jabbed a stray lock with the last of her hairpins. "He could get you a foreman job with a snap of his fingers."

She lifted her chin, but Christie didn't argue back. Those blue eyes searched hers as if he didn't know her. "Guess you schemed it all out, then."

Ruby patted her hair. "You have your marching orders, soldier."

He grimaced at her. "Don't kid about that. It won't seem funny when I get called up."

"*If*, you mean. And that's all the more reason for you to go along with it. Once you're buildin' planes instead of mindin' trains, you'll have work vital to the war effort. You'll get a deferment for sure."

"Is that how it works?" he drawled, and leaned in for a quick kiss. "I'd better go."

"Don't be ill." She slithered into his arms. "Think how much happier we'll be. Remember what Daddy told you? 'Happy wife, happy life.'"

"I do all I know to make you happy."

She kissed his jaw and whispered in his ear. "Then promise me you'll be there tonight."

He squeezed her tight and drew back. "I promise."

Seven o'clock, eight o'clock. She didn't doubt him, not at first.

Ruby saved Christie a seat next to her at the dinner. The folded linen napkin standing tall on his place setting drew attention 'til she finally flattened it against the plate.

The band kicked up, and Ruby turned down a half-dozen guys wanting to spin her around the room. Her tongue wore out its excuses. She told one, "I'm saving this dance," and another, "My card's full," then endured dirty looks from both of them from the sidelines. Too bad Christie didn't give her a proper diamond to flash around to prove she was married. Wouldn't she like it if he walked in to see her dancing with some other fella? It'd serve him right. He promised.

"When's your beau supposed to get here?" Mr. Rutherford didn't bother with asking but simply grabbed her about the waist and flung her around sideways. His breath stank of whiskey.

Ruby tried to free herself. "He's my husband, and he should've been here already."

"Let's hope he doesn't dally all night. Or rather, let's." He winked at her.

"Excuse me." She squirmed away from him. Anyone else, she would've slapped.

She tried to get to Agnes, but she was busy batting her eyes at some sheik she found at the bar. Ruby ducked into the ladies' room, reapplied her lipstick, and made small talk with those who stumbled into the facilities.

"This is dandy," she said once she was alone. "I can't hide in here all night. I'll never know when he gets here." The certainty struck her soul. *He's not coming*, it whispered, but Ruby brushed it off and marched back out to the party.

In her absence, Mr. Rutherford found a brassy blonde to occupy his attentions. Ruby's stomach turned as she watched them slip into the back hallway.

"Agnes," she hissed, and shook her friend's arm. "Christie's still not here."

She stuck out her lip. "You don't want to go already, do you?"

"Don't leave, doll." Agnes' gentleman friend grasped her by the wrist. "You owe me a dance."

"I'm not. Give me a minute." Agnes turned back to Ruby with pleading eyes.

"I'll call a cab. If you see him—"

Agnes narrowed her eyes. "He'll wish he'd shipped out to war already."

Even while she waited for the cab, Ruby couldn't help craning her neck, looking for Christie to arrive. When the taxi slowed in front of the Golf Club, glistening black under the dim twinkle of street lights, Ruby almost let him pass rather than give up on the evening. With a sigh, she flagged him. The driver rolled down the window, but shadows hid his face.

"You the skirt who called?" A gruff geezer voice did the asking.

She nodded. "Take me as far as Kennesaw?"

"Which way?"

She stifled a sigh. "Big Shanty?"

"Sure, of course. Anywhere you want to go, sweetheart." Ruby rolled her eyes and climbed in. The driver hummed a Sinatra tune while the darkened city of Marietta shrank then disappeared altogether.

Ruby pouted. He broke his word. Embarrassed her. Stranded her in a sea of single fellas. She was gonna kill him.

The driver took an unfamiliar route, and she was about to ask how much farther when he spoke up. "How's a pretty dame like you end up all alone on a Friday night?"

She missed the hungry note in his tone, though it was plain enough all the millions of times it ran through her memory afterwards. "Bad luck. Stood up."

"Aww. That ain't right. Maybe we oughta take a detour. Just you and me, princess."

"I . . . I'd rather not. My folks are expecting me back."

He leered at her in the rearview mirror and flashed a tarry, ugly set of teeth. "I guess they were too tired to come pick you up themselves. It's awful late, ain't it? Too late. I bet no one would miss you too much 'til morning."

Her palms sweated. Mama and Daddy gave her that gun on account of creeps like this one, and where was it? At home in the dresser drawer, right where she put it the day she got it. She swallowed hard and mustered all the authority she could. "You need to take me straight home, mister."

He chuckled. "You got moxie. I like that."

A split-second burst of whiteness lit up the windshield and the driver swerved. Brush and gravel scraped and clinked the underbelly of the car. "Did you see that? A man in the middle of the road!"

Ruby kept quiet, trying to sort out what she saw. A figure—maybe a man—illuminated with the headlamps and as quickly dissolved into darkness. No thud of striking a solid object, nor any jolt.

"I saw that police car go by, if that's what you mean. Guess it's not so lonesome out here as all that." She held her breath for his reply, but he didn't make one.

After that the ol' coot straightened up and drove her home. He never meant any of it. Got his jollies out of scaring the daylights out of ladies, she convinced herself, though it was no small relief to pay him and send him away, grubby teeth and all.

Back to matters at hand. Christie missed his big chance to seal their future in Marietta, not to mention the best party they were apt to be invited to 'til next year, and the way the newspapers screamed about the war, he could be shipped out by then. Worse than all of that, he lied straight to her face when he promised to show. She stomped up the front porch steps, ready to light into him as he wouldn't like to forget.

Instead, Mama opened the door and grabbed hold, hugging her so tight she could barely breathe. "Oh, baby. We didn't know where to find you."

The two of them stumbled into the house. "Mama, I was at the company party. I'm fine. I'm all right."

"No." Her voice was raw. "Christie."

"What about Christie?" she asked, but Mama couldn't force out any more words. "What happened? Where is he?"

"An accident at the Bell plant's train yard. Lost his balance and fell between two cars." Daddy sat at the table with a lit cigarette between his fingers and his jaw set, but it quivered when he spoke again. "He's gone, Peanut. It happened this morning, but no one could reach you."

Ruby's blood froze. This morning? While she worked and primped and carried on. While she waited and fumed and stormed off. While she quaked under the cab driver's thumb.

Her husband had been dead for most of the day.

Her shoulders heaved. "I need to see him."

"You don't," Mama said, finding her voice. "You need to remember him as he was and thank the Lord for takin' him home. Seein' him now don't change it."

Mama's words brought the news to Ruby's heart and gut. Her best friend, lookout, hero, and lover.

Gone.

The funeral and burial were horrible in ways Ruby expected. The helpless condolences. The offish stares, as though calamity might rub off. Mrs. Sosebee caught her hand and begged her to say there'd be a baby.

Afterwards though, once all the casserole pans went back to their rightful owners and people felt comfortable to laugh around her again, the pain twisted in ways she didn't know existed. The lonesome cold of evenings and silent shuffle of mornings. Going through his belongings and finding her Christmas present, seashell hairclips from Tybee Island. The singular horror of receiving his draft orders. Walking past their tree every morning on her way to the train. The lowest branch now hung far above her head. Ruby stretched her fingertips toward it, but without him to boost her up, she couldn't reach.

He didn't need Mr. Rutherford after all. Christie found his own way into a job at Bell, though in the heap of confusion with the W&A people and the folks at the plant, it took some doing to learn how. Daddy nosed around until he got the final word.

"The plant was the job site, but he stayed on the railroad's payroll. No one said for certain, but the assignment put him on the short list for a slot at Bell's rail yard. I'd be glad to know how he managed it, though." Daddy rolled smokes, one after the next, but didn't light one. "The foreman couldn't tell me how it happened."

"Gil, please." They huddled around the table except for Mama, who grieved as she did all else, on her feet.

Ruby's eyes glazed over. She didn't care how it happened. The picture in her mind already firmed up—Christie, too near the edge, being brave but getting dizzy, holding out his arms for balance, disappearing between the cars. She had turned the collar on his suit coat and took it to the funeral home, only to be delicately informed that it wouldn't be needed. Her imagination plagued her day and night over what that meant, but she wouldn't ask.

"I didn't like his looks. Shifty. Tried to tell me Christie put in for the assignment, but I know I told y'all—"

"You said no daughter of yours would work a factory job." Ruby looked to Pearl for confirmation, but her sister kept her eyes down.

"So I did." Daddy lit one of the cigarettes. "But if he wasn't happy with his spot with the W&A, I wish he would've told me so instead of going behind my back."

Her sister chimed in. "Maybe he wanted to keep it a surprise for Ruby. You wanted to live in the city, and with Christmas comin' up—"

"It's not my fault," Ruby snapped.

Pearl gave her a curious look. "I didn't say it was."

"Never mind," Mama said. "He never stopped looking out for our Ruby and he loved the Lord, and that's what matters."

He never stopped. Ruby wiped her eyes. That was worth clinging to.

Daddy sipped coffee and Pearl chitchatted about some gossip she heard at work. Ruby let her mind wander, inevitably circling 'round the last moments before she knew, marred as they were with anger and terror, until—

A glimmer lit in her soul. The flash of bright light. The man in the road. She hadn't seen him, but he saved her.

Christie promised he would be there that night. In the instant she needed him most, he was.

She clapped her hand down on the table. "I need to learn to drive."

Her family stared. "How's that?" Daddy asked.

She swallowed hard. "The taxi driver who brought me home that night was a lout, and I need to learn to take care of myself." It wasn't so fearsome a prospect if Christie still watched over her. And his protection surely meant he didn't blame her, didn't it?

"All right, then." Daddy set his cigarette at the edge of the ashtray. "That's my girl. I'll teach you."

Thursday, April 19, 2012

"A terrible burden," Ruby agreed, now a couple of miles and more than an hour removed from her chat with Sharon Petersen. Her elderly behind rested on the stone garden bench in the flowerbeds, which had spouted a nice crop of weeds without Will tending them. "I made him scared of heights when we were youngsters, and I made him put in for that job with all my nagging." Mercy. Her heart, still fired up over the near-miss at the intersection, pressed like a weight on her chest. "But I done said I was sorry."

She faltered. Her soul churned to say the words out loud. "Lord Jesus. All these years lookin' for him instead of You. That was the worst of it. More than all the rest, I'm sorry for that."

Peace draped over Ruby like cool linens. She sat a long while in the bliss of it, not minding so much the off-kilter patter behind her breast. She watched the fading pinks and purples over distant treetops, watched as blooms and stars bled out their glory. Her breath hitched; her fingers and toes were cold. Maybe Ruby herself was the last pin to be pulled. All these years of Jesus filling His heaven with everyone she loved, and here at the last, He ended up the only one she wanted to see. She could see Him too, brightening the dim of evening 'til absolute light captivated her, consuming all else with its fire, even when she closed her eyes.

CHAPTER 34

Abby watched Will lift the latticework leaning against the eaves of the back porch and carefully reverse it so the beams of its frame faced outward. "Put your right hand here." He pointed to a vertical support. "And your left foot here in the joint."

She didn't move. "This rickety piece of junk won't hold me up."

"It will, as long as you distribute the weight right. Keep to the beams. You can't put any weight on the slats, but the two-by-fours are sturdy enough."

"I'll fall."

"You won't," he said, and she frowned. She wanted him to promise to catch her.

The flashy silver heels dangled from her curled fingers. She held them up, her last-ditch protest. "I can't climb up there barefoot."

"You're welcome to put 'em back on if you think they'll help." Any other time she would have enjoyed the smile in his voice.

"Sure, laugh it up. You haven't told me why you want me to climb the lattice."

"'Cause we don't have a ladder, so this is the easiest way up on the roof."

"That doesn't tell me what you could possibly need to show me up there."

"Abby." He spoke her name so deliberately. She should have told him sooner that she didn't like the nickname. "The footsteps you heard? That was me. I'm sorry I scared you, but I wouldn't tell you to do this if I hadn't done it a hundred times myself. Do you trust me?"

She took a deep breath and positioned her hand against the frame. "If I die—"

"Then you'll either climb higher than the roof or fall farther than the ground. Ready?"

"No." She put her foot into place, hesitated, and pulled herself up.

"Great. Right foot—yep, there you go. You've almost got it." She doubted that, but better to hurry upward than to freeze and wait for the beams to crack under her weight. "You're there. Pull yourself up."

And so she made it to the rooftop and looked out over the neighborhood in amazement. She barely blinked before Will joined her.

"See? Easy. Be real careful and find you a good place to sit."

The pitch wasn't too steep, but Abby felt far out of her element. The gritty, warm shingles bit into the sore bottoms of her feet. "I can't believe we're up here. Why did I listen to you? How are we going to get down?"

"Anyone ever mention you fuss too much?" He stepped around easily, holding his arms out at his sides for balance. "Now sit tight while I show you."

He'll fall. Abby's heart went into her throat. *He's reliving what happened on the train. In a second, he'll fall—*

He walked up beside the dormer off the back of the house and crouched down. "Listen." He grabbed a loose board at the gable and gave it several hard pulls. "That sound like your knocker?"

"Yeah." Her eyes filled. "Great. I guess it was wind, then."

He retreated from the dormer and perched besides her. "Feel better?"

"I feel ridiculous."

"Don't. Abby, you ain't the only one who ever wanted answers about the afterlife. Most people make up their minds what to believe, one way or the other. Since Jesus has been there and back, I made up my mind to believe the Bible."

She nodded toward the gable. "How did you know about that?"

"I noticed it a couple weeks ago." He picked up a stray pinecone and plucked nodes off it one by one. "Don't be mad. This is my favorite place. I come up here to think and pray and remember."

"Why?" Abby's feet throbbed in time with the rhythmic buzzing of cicadas. "What's special about it up here?"

He studied the shingles. "Memories. Promises. The view."

"When you said you've done this a hundred times . . . " She trailed off, letting her question float unasked in the night air.

Will didn't meet her eyes. "Not that many times. I exaggerated."

"You bring girls up here, don't you?"

"One girl." He winced. "Two, now. Maybe I haven't been completely honest with you, after all."

Her temples throbbed along with her feet. He was gathering his confession and she wasn't ready. She told him even before they climbed up—

"You remind me of her."

The words wouldn't assemble into sense. "That's it?"

"That's a lot." He wouldn't look at her. "How'd you like for me to hang around, always seeing her instead of you? Or calling you the wrong name? Or doing for you what I promised to her?"

"Oh. Yeah, when you put it that way." She scooted toward the lattice, hoping she could get down unaided by Will or gravity. "On that incredibly awkward note, I'm going to bed. I was going to ask you to join me, but I'd hate to offend you or your ex-girlfriend, so if you'll excuse me—"

"You wanna take that tone?" He tossed what remained of the pinecone down to the backyard. "You keep askin' questions, wantin' your ears tickled with some spook. All I got is a story about a fella who lost his girl."

Her cheeks burned. "I'm sorry."

"I am, too. I thought I could do this. You look like her." His gaze turned inward. "But you're not her."

Abby stared at the black tree-lined horizon pointing upward to the distant stars. "I didn't mean to ruin our evening."

"You didn't, Abby. I did. I was selfish. It ain't fair to you."

"But we can be friends, right?"

Will's face was sadder than she'd ever seen it. "No, I don't think we can."

Friday, April 20

She didn't wash her feet until morning.

They throbbed and burned with every step. Daylight revealed her own nasty footprints tracked from the door to her room. Blood outlined the nail beds around her toes, and the bottoms were stained orangey-brown with dirt and grit. It hurt to stand still. It hurt to move. It hurt to be alive.

She made coffee and ran a shallow bath to soak her feet. The mysticism of household chatter vanished. The Presence left her alone without the twinge of being watched.

"That's one point in the 'Will is W. C.' column." She spoke aloud, hoping for a reaction—wind-blown shutters or a flicker in the electricity, but nothing happened at all. *Attall*, she thought, imagining how Will would slur the words in his easy drawl.

"He never touched me. Not once. Not even to help me up or down from the roof. That's two. And three, he didn't drink. He never drinks, not even water. Four, he's way too comfortable in my house, and five, I remind him of somebody. I wonder who." Her voice broke. "You still love my aunt, don't you Will?"

She swished her feet around in the water and sipped coffee, watching clouds of dirt swirl beneath the surface of the water. A sinus headache hardened like cement behind her face.

"Knock once if I'm wrong, and not at all if I have you all figured out, William Christopher Sosebee."

The words barely cleared her lips before deep pounding echoed through the house. Startled, she hurried to dry her feet and hobbled to the front door. "Will—"

It wasn't Will, though, but Greg standing at her doorstep. "Hi, Abby."

Only after the door swung open did she stop to think how she must look—smeared makeup under her eyes, bed head, and wearing the same clothes from the night before.

"Greg, what are you doing here?" He couldn't be expecting much. He hadn't taken the time to shave, and he wore jeans and a Cuyahoga Community Bank tee shirt he knew she hated. A lifetime ago she had nagged him to give it away. He looked run-down and road-weary, a lackluster version of the Greg who'd been worth breaking rules for. The Greg who broke some rules, but not others, for her.

He gaped at the sight of her. "I hope I'm not interrupting. Actually, I take that back. I hope I am."

"That's none of your business. Although since I already told you about my lease, I suppose you're grabbing digs where you can. So once again, from the top. What do you want?"

His eyes flashed. "I came to concede defeat. The best man wins. Since you went out of your way to make sure I heard how well he takes care of you—"

"Jealousy doesn't become you, Greg."

"And cruelty doesn't do much for you. Do you even know what you're doing? He barely looks old enough to vote."

Abby closed her eyes briefly. "He's older than he looks."

"What then? A college sophomore?"

"Stop it. He's been through more than you could imagine."

"And yet, he's still willing to try his luck with you."

She narrowed her eyes. At last, the gloves came off. "You said I could lean on you. You promised. And the one time I needed you on my side, good or bad, right or wrong, you abandoned me."

"You took original state records home with you. Do you know what happens to government contractors who get caught in a security breach? You're lucky we kept it out of the news."

"You're lucky, you mean. Then it would have been your head to roll."

"What should I have done instead?"

She crossed her arms. "I don't think it would have mattered. You needed a reason to get rid of me to stay in good with your boss."

"Chuck said as long as we kept the personal and professional separate—"

"And you believed him?"

"Yeah. I did."

She sighed. They would argue in circles for hours if she didn't put a stop to it. "Why did you come here?"

"I told you . . . ."

"No. I mean, why did you take off work, book a hotel, and fly down here when you knew how I felt about us? And don't say it's because Sarah told you to, because I don't buy that."

"My conscience wouldn't leave me alone about you, Abby. Does it sound too crazy to say God sent me? Because God sent me." He reached out a hand and took hers. The suddenness of the touch and his familiar warmth and strength brought on a momentary paralysis. "He loves you, Abby. And so do I. How many times do I have to say it? If I could have handled work any differently, I would have. And for the record, I knew I'd lose you for it. I'm not quite that stupid."

His gray eyes pleaded, but she wrested her hand loose from his. "Evidently you are. I don't remember asking for a visit, whether you thought I needed one or not. You didn't come here for God. You came for you."

He stuffed his hands into his pockets. "And like I said, I give up. I'm going to try to catch an early flight home, and I won't bother you again."

She rolled her eyes. "Did God tell you to do that, too?"

He grimaced, like her question caused actual pain. "You weren't like this before, you know. You've changed."

She inhaled. "Smell that? The air is officially clear. I hope you said what you came to say."

The defensiveness drained from his tone, replaced with ordinary sadness. "And I hope you find what you're looking for."

"Goodbye, Greg."

Maybe he didn't like the finality of his promise, or maybe the word stuck in his throat, but in either case, Greg simply turned and walked away. Gusting breezes sent flurries of white petals swirling around him.

God loves you. And so do I. At least he figured out a way to put the "I" last. Two points for grammar gymnastics. She closed the door before he reached his rental car, but she couldn't get the vile fish smell of faltering Bradford pears out of her nose.

CHAPTER 35

"What I'm looking for." Abby circled the kitchen, tracing her finger against the cheerful yellow walls. "I think I can say with confidence that it's not here."

She dug her lease out of the drawer. Not a word on how to break their agreement, or how long it would be in effect for that matter. That funny line about past and future debts made Abby mad all over again.

Where would she go? Arizona. Massachusetts. Didn't matter. She picked up her phone and dialed Aunt Ruby's number. She'd pay her for one extra month. More than that, no way.

"Come on," she murmured into the phone. Aunt Ruby's line rang four times before a robotic answering machine picked up. She ended the call without leaving a message and checked the clock. "Weird. I thought she never missed her film-a-day."

Abby grabbed an armful of clean clothes from her room and headed for the shower. Aunt Ruby probably wasn't missing her show. More likely she turned up the TV and ignored the phone.

Hopes and humiliations rinsed away and Abby's resolve grew. Talk to Aunt Ruby now. Buy boxes this afternoon. Pack them tonight. Maybe even rent a truck and be somewhere new by dawn tomorrow. She could have her car shipped—

My car. Right. Silly daydreams. It would take more than a day to escape.

"All the more reason to get moving." She shut off the water, toweled off and dressed, then tried Aunt Ruby's number again.

Still no answer. Impatient, she hung up without leaving a message.

"I'll walk over. Check in. Say hello." Her head and sore feet alike protested. "Because that worked so well last time."

Abby dialed once more, with the same results. "Please record after the tone," the machine urged, and this time, she did.

"Aunt Ruby, it's Abby. I wanted to ask if you're up for going out today. My car should be ready and I need a ride. We could make a day of it. Call me."

Checkboxes lined up in her mind, roughing out a plan for her new life. Finding a place. Setting up utilities, learning her way around. An earnest job hunt, unless she wanted to burn through the rest of what Mom bequeathed her. How hard would it be to change her name from Wells to Blanchard? She'd give the past a good hard scrub. Another new life, the same as the one she was already living in all the ways that mattered.

"No. One important difference. No one to worry about but me. But until then . . ."

She slid on a pair of sandals. The ground-in dirt still stained her feet. With a small sigh, she grabbed her keys and left, wincing under the weight of her own footsteps.

Abby found her in the front yard.

"Aunt Ruby?" She ran across the driveway to the flowerbeds where her aunt lay crumpled and gray. "Aunt Ruby, wake up!"

Abby reached out to shake her aunt's arm, but recoiled at the wrongness of her flesh, cold and lightly damp with the dew of morning. Without thinking, she wiped her hand on her pant leg.

"No," Abby moaned. She withdrew her cell and dialed.

"Nine-one-one, what is your emergency?"

"My aunt. She's—unresponsive."

"What is your location?"

Abby gave the address and her name, and listened as the dispatcher asked her to check for breathing and pulse. Her hands shook and she nearly dropped the phone. "Ma'am? I think it's too late for all that."

"Why do you think that, Abby? What do you see?"

A keening pain in her chest, winding small through the chambers of her heart, coursed through her veins, constricting her lungs and hollowing out her stomach. "She's not right. Stiff, I mean. I think she's in rigor mortis already. She's elderly. Did I tell you that? I can't—"

"I see. Abby, I want you to remain calm and leave the scene to preserve the area. I'll send an ambulance."

"You mean, leave her lying in the dirt?"

"I understand your concern, but the EMT will be able to assess the circumstances. Have you touched or moved anything?"

Her skin crawled. "I touched her arm. I didn't move her though."

"That's fine, Abby. I'll send someone out right away."

She retreated toward the house. Discovering a body—how many years would that take off her own life? As awful as it was to hold Mom's hand through the moment of death, they anticipated it for months before. Abby never considered that a blessing. Not until now.

She almost tripped over the front porch steps. How far did the dispatcher want her to go? Shouldn't she call Blake? And—regardless of last night—Will?

The ceramic frog remained in its place on the stoop. She lifted it up, retrieved the key underneath, and let herself inside.

The house smelled of strong coffee. Had it always? The blinds in the living room were drawn, leaving only the ambient light and the flickering television to combat the dimness.

She hung back at the threshold. "Don't be shy, Abby," she told herself. "If you ever had a decent reason to poke around, this is it. She'd either have a phone with speed dial or a list of numbers. The list could be anywhere. Find the phone."

It wasn't on the base. Abby nosed around, feeling more like an intruder every minute, until she found the cordless peeking out from the plushy cushions of the blue couch. She plucked it out and found it dead.
Dead.

She shoved the word away. Focus. Phone numbers.

In the kitchen, she found the source of the aroma. The coffeemaker held a full pot. On the base, a red dot indicator shone next to the word AUTO. Abby put her hand up to the carafe and found it cold.

An old-fashioned corded phone hung mounted on a thin strip of wall abutting the entryway to the dining room. "All right. If she has a list of numbers, it'll be somewhere close."

She searched the island drawers and found them filled with flowery notepads and pens, twist-ties and rubber bands, spare batteries and light bulbs. She seized upon a tiny pocket address book but found it blank.

The ambulance would be here any moment, and maybe police too. Did she want to explain rifling through Aunt Ruby's drawers when they arrived?

She threw open the pantry. Finally. Taped inside, a yellowed piece of notebook paper held a quick reference of phone numbers and birthdays, covered with strikeovers and stratified updates.

Mama, Daddy, Pearl, John (work), Jim, Blake, Karen, Linda, Richard, Suzanne, Audrey, Abby

Abby flinched at the sight of Mom's name and her own. The phone number beneath the strikeover was long out of date, but both of their birthdays were correct.

She left off Will's name. "What does that mean? As if I don't know," she whispered. She grabbed the handset and started to dial Blake's number. The multiple cross-outs and revisions all but guaranteed the number would be current.

She touched her father's name lightly and replaced the handset. September seventeenth. Richard either changed his number less than Blake did, or Aunt Ruby saw no need to bother with updates.

"I guess we'll find out." She held her breath as she dialed.

A click of connection. A loud sigh. A male voice. "What do you want?"

She almost hung up. "This is Abby Wells, calling for Richard."

The man on the other end pulled in a breath. Over the line, it sounded like hissing. "Is this another trick?"

Abby's heart pounded. He didn't have much of an accent, not compared to Aunt Ruby and Blake and Will. Did he unlearn it somehow?

Of a lifetime of imagined conversations, none of them came. She wished to rebottle this genie and go back to the moment before last, when her father was only a name and a shadow.

"I—I found your number in Aunt Ruby's kitchen. She's not waking up. An ambulance is on the way. I assumed—"

"Of course, of course. Thank you for calling, Abby. Wow, it's great to finally talk to you. You know, I planned to come by the old house after you missed the big family dinner, but Blake said you were sick. Figured you wouldn't want to have a reunion if you weren't feeling up to par."

"Did you hear me? Aunt Ruby is—"

"I'm sorry. I got so excited to hear your voice finally. Just stay calm. I know it's a shock, but it's not unexpected, after all."

Abby scrambled for words. "I should call Blake."

"You're upset, hon. I'll call him. Tell you what. You're at the house?"

Abby nodded, berated herself, and answered. "Yeah. I let myself in."

"That's good. Sit tight and I'll be there—actually, I have to take my stepson to a baseball practice. The coach won't let him play in the game if he misses. Afterwards, I'll come right up. Around four o'clock."

"Right."

"Can't tell you how long I've waited for this. How's your mother, by the way?"

"She's fine," Abby uttered. "The EMT's are here. I have to go."

"Then I'll see you after a while. Take care." He hung up.

She placed the handset back on its cradle. Her hand trembled as she used her cell to snap a photo of the list in the cabinet. She checked the image. Blurry, but legible.

With a final survey to make certain she left the kitchen as she found it, Abby let herself out. The sun had burned off the coolness of morning. Aunt Ruby lay as she had before, but now bumblebees danced in the broken daffodils around her.

My father's coming later. Blake will be here soon. Aunt Ruby's gone. And Will is—

She froze. What if she was right about him? If Aunt Ruby was his unfinished business, what would tie him to the earth?

She walked at first, then broke into an awkward, stumbling run, trying to keep the sandals from flying off her feet. If the officer arrived, she'd be stuck here for hours, alone and outnumbered at the same time. Fire shot up through her feet and calves. The days ahead made no promises.

CHAPTER 36

Greg closed his suitcase. The latch caught the hem of his favorite collared shirt for a lopsided seal. He didn't care enough to free it. After this streak of failures, he would only succeed in breaking the latch.

Once he paid the hotel cancellation penalty and ticket change fees, it cost him more to leave early than it would to stay one more day. No point dwelling on the extra money. The trip had been a waste, and the sooner he could leave Georgia to its muggy days, pollen clouds, and obscene dedication to sweet tea, the better.

He rubbed a magnet picked up at an airport gift shop across the key card for his room to erase his stored credit information. He'd wipe Abby from his life in the same way if he could and miss all this—

The cheeky way she interviewed. How he'd known he was in trouble from the first. Sneaking around the office, wrapped in the best kind of secret. Coming to her rescue in the parking garage and sparking rumor-mill buzz at work. In spite of the final outcome, he still prized the moment love stretched beyond overpriced cut flowers and into the realm of tire-changing.

If he never loved her, he wouldn't have attended her mother's funeral. Wouldn't have wandered back to that same church when he reached the dry hollow at the bottom of his own soul. Wouldn't have found Christ reaching like an olive branch in place of the angry God he expected.

The magnet slipped from his hands. In his distraction he gouged the key card beyond further use.

He left it on the dresser. Almost always, difficult jobs broke down into simple parts. In this case, leaving the room, taking the elevator, crossing the lobby. Once he made it to the car, the rest would be easy.

Except this wasn't completing a difficult job. It was abandoning one.

Greg trudged to the elevator, dragging his luggage along behind. As the doors enclosed him, his phone rang. A tinkling wind chime ring he hadn't expected to ever hear again.

He fumbled the phone trying to answer in time. "Abby?" Only a dead void came through the line.

He tried her back, but the call didn't connect. His shoulders sagged again. Butt-dialed. Sadly fitting.

The elevator released him, and he watched the signal bars on the screen illuminate. Amazingly, miraculously, the chimes sang to him again.

"Hi." Her voice sounded small. "Are you still in town?"

"For the moment. I'm checking out of the motel. What's wrong?"

She didn't answer immediately. The urge to repeat the question tugged, but the small still voice inside counseled patience. Abby came to him this time. She would speak when ready, and a long moment later, she did. "Aunt Ruby passed away last night. I need a friendly face."

"I'll be right there." Scarred, but not useless. She needed him. Finally, he knew what he was supposed to do.

"Not now," she said. "I mean at the funeral."

Chapter 37

Monday, April 23

Knots of snakes writhed in Abby's belly as she auditioned clothes for the service. She had only one outfit chosen specifically for a funeral, and it could stay in the back of the closet until she died herself. Besides, she couldn't remember having it dry-cleaned.

Couldn't she have asked Will where he lived or learned the name of one or two of his friends at some point during the two months she'd known him? Did it have to come down to a funeral she'd skip otherwise?

Resigned, she put on her multi-purpose little black dress. It hung like a canvas bag draped over a hook. She stretched her arms out to her sides. Dowel rods. When did her face become narrow, her collar bones prominent? If possible, she had lost more weight since Thursday. She swapped out the dress for a pair of black Dockers and studied herself from all angles. How had she missed the sagging in the rear?

It's good that I don't get out much. I look terrible.

Digging deeper in the closet, she found a dark purple party dress she'd worn to a wedding soon after she graduated college. It hadn't fit in a couple of years, and though she told herself it had been too expensive to give away and too much trouble to consign, the truth was much simpler. Pure vanity kept the dress in her wardrobe, and now, without Sarah around to force-feed her all the time . . .

She held it up before the mirror. Its neckline was modest, the hemline decent. Certainly not her first pick for a funeral, but not too inappropriate either.

"This *is* Aunt Ruby we're talking about." She wiggled into the dress. It hugged the few curves she had remaining. "She would rather have been celebrated than mourned."

Flowers are for the living. Will's words came back to her, plumbing a poisoned well of hope and self-pity. She gave her hips an experimental twist. The skirt flared out and fell back, whispering against her knees. With a little cardigan to cover her shoulders, the dress was good enough. She wouldn't mind being seen like this, and Will would be at the funeral. Unless—unless.

Will loved Aunt Ruby, that much she knew for sure. If he was real, he would come and honor her memory. And if he was the ghost, he wouldn't. The funeral wasn't the ideal test, but Abby stopped expecting ideal some time ago.

She dabbed on a little powder and stepped into her shoes. Will's campaign to get her in a church succeeded after all. There the case would be decided. Either way, she'd have her proof.

Satisfied with her appearance, she checked the clock again and grabbed her purse. Dishes piled high in the sink, and she didn't want Greg to see the blackened gladiolus stems sticking out of the overfull garbage can.

I don't care what he thinks. Oh, but she did, and there wasn't time to clean up. Greg would have met her at the church if she'd suggested it, but she hadn't.

At risk of looking eager to see him, she slipped outside to wait on the porch. Behind the trees on the opposite side of the street, railcars clacked out a raucous hymn. She could still hear it fading as Greg's rental car rounded the corner onto her street, but his engine drowned out the sound as he parked in front of the house. Abby approached the passenger side, her mind absent but for the small part waiting for the lock to pop.

Greg switched off the ignition and climbed out. He bounced the key fob awkwardly and put it in his pocket. "Since the church is so close, maybe we could walk. Burn off some jitters."

"Oh." She'd done it again, fallen easily into old patterns. He was such a weasel. She almost refused, but then considered the idea. Her feet had mostly recovered from the Thursday before. She wasn't sure her black pumps were up to the job, but the pain of a blister wasn't too high a price for the right to blame him for it. "If you want."

"All I want is to do what you need me to do. Since I'm here."

She shrugged and turned away from him, following the sidewalk to the corner. "I don't remember that suit."

He flipped the tie between his fingers. "I bought it yesterday. I didn't pack for a funeral."

"I should have thought of that. It's nice. I hope it wasn't very expensive."

"Not as bad as rebooking the motel room I'd just cancelled." He kicked a pebble. "Abby, we're way past small talk. You need to know I meant it when I said that I hope you find what you're looking for."

"Huh." She tottered along the curb, hoping to make him nervous. "Had me fooled."

"No, listen. I've had a lot of free time this week," he said pointedly. "I wanted to help."

"The only ones who could help me find what I need are dead."

A shadow crossed his face. "What about your boyfriend?"

Abby concentrated on the cement. "We're not . . . he's . . . I don't know. I thought . . . "

"Abby, stop. I'm sorry. What I'm trying to say is that I have something for you." He glanced back at the car. "And I think it'll help."

He wouldn't quit, would he? She set her jaw as they crossed from the sidewalk to the church parking lot. "Let's get through this first."

CHAPTER 38

Abby crossed the threshold of the Baptist church as Greg held the heavy wooden doors open for her. Momentary déjà vu softened her knees. She sucked in a breath through her mouth, drying her itchy throat and making it sore. She hadn't set foot in a church since—

"Okay?" Greg whispered. A ridiculous question she wouldn't grace with an answer. They passed through the foyer into the sanctuary. At the front of the church, somber arrangements encircled a red cedar casket.

A small group of middle-aged women turned and stared. One leaned to another. Abby couldn't make out the comment, but she could guess.

Whatever. She didn't expect anyone here to know her. Why should she care if these people judged her by who her daddy was?

A man beat a path to them from the church foyer, and his cologne went before him, expanding his presence. He wore a faded gray suit and a wide, welcoming smile. Abby returned it reflexively, but recoiled when she placed the familiar nose, jaw line, and eyes as the ones she saw in the mirror every day. Greg tensed beside her.

"Abigail? You have to be. Let me look at you." Her father nodded approvingly. Perhaps because he saw himself stamped in her features?

"Actually, my proper name is Abby." She stuck out her hand. "You must be Richard."

He took it and pulled her into a hug. "'Richard?' Tell you what, kiddo. It's not too early to start calling me Dad."

"Or too late, apparently," Greg muttered, but if Abby's father heard the pointed remark, he ignored it. She shot the briefest of glares at him.

"Looks like your mother did a fantastic job raising you," her father said. Stars appeared at the periphery and Abby reminded herself to breathe. The bogey of her childhood and the specter of her DNA stood before her, full of compliments and camaraderie.

She swallowed hard. "This is Greg. My best friend's brother."

Of all the ways she might have described him—ex-boyfriend, former boss, potential stalker—she'd chosen the one that implied a valid reason for him to be at her side, as if to explain him or protect him. The two men shook hands, sizing each other up, neither looking impressed. They exchanged hollow pleasantries, and Abby resisted an urge to call them both out for lying in a church.

The gray moans of an organ filled the sanctuary, and Richard shifted his feet and turned toward the front, casually positioning himself between Abby and Greg. "Better get ourselves seated." He shot an apologetic look over his shoulder. "Hey, buddy, we'll catch up to you afterwards. We reserved the first row for family only."

Greg watched Abby for cues. She pretended not to see and followed Richard to the front.

Her father had dropped his voice to a low, confidential tone. "Nice kid, but you can do better. I wish I knew at your age that you can never be too choosy when it comes to love."

A nice two-cents' worth coming from him of all people, but she let it go. "Greg's not—"

"Of course he is, hon." He wrapped her shoulders with a thick arm that she found shockingly easy to trust. "Otherwise he wouldn't be here."

She couldn't argue with that.

Richard broke the side-embrace first. He went up to Aunt Ruby's casket and stared down into her face, holding a silent conversation with her while Abby sat. She wished for a seat in the last row instead, with a sea of blue chair backs to separate her from mortality or eternity. Whichever.

Besides, Will wouldn't have a place on the front row, and from here she'd never see him come in.

A tap on the arm startled her, but it was only Greg taking the seat directly behind hers. He winked and patted her shoulder.

Abby took little reassurance from him. What could he do but distract her? Already the chess pieces moved around the board madcap, without taking turns. All's fair in love and war, but who decided which this was?

Her father seated himself next to her and leaned close. His breath smelled like cinnamon gum. "We decided against a family processional. She wasn't much for pomp and circumstance."

"Where's Uncle Blake?" Abby asked, but then the organ music changed to a faintly familiar melody, an old hymn sung often in Mom's church.

"We'll talk later." A few others took places on either side of Abby and her father, and she tried to covertly watch these so-called family members. Without Blake there, she recognized none of them.

They stood, they sang, they bowed for a word of prayer that turned into many words. Abby took the opportunity to extract a tissue from her purse. The funeral conjured up images of Mom's memorial service, and renegade tears kept escaping, turning her congestion to sniffles.

"Are you all right?" Greg whispered at the back of her neck. With a slight turn of her head and a single nod, she silenced him as a white-haired man with bright blue eyes took the podium.

His generic summary of Aunt Ruby's life did little to draw out the wild card Abby had only glimpsed. Either he didn't know her well or didn't like her, but his sweeping sentiments applied to everyone and no one. "Ruby Rae Watts built an unbelievable legacy in her eighty-eight years," he declared. "She'll be long in our memories."

Throughout the eulogy, Abby fought the urge to twist her neck around to find Will among the congregation. Greg, her father, and the eulogist splintered her focus, but she couldn't forget why she subjected herself to this torment in the first place. She came from Ohio to Georgia for one reason only. Proof.

And if the moment slipped by, there'd be no second chance.

She could sneak off to the ladies' room and from there circle around to the back of the sanctuary. If she managed that undetected, she could stand watch from the better vantage point of the doors. She tried to work out what excuse she'd give Greg for disappearing.

Ah. She could deal with him later. She listened to herself, the sniffling breaths and the blood thrumming against her eardrums, and visualized how she would stand and hurry to the exit left of the altar, all her collected poise carrying her without one ounce of shame in front of these strangers who came to honor a woman she'd hardly been allowed to know. Once she proved to herself that Will had abandoned the earth, no longer bound to it by love, she could go free too.

Now, Abby thought, but the eulogist changed his tone and launched into another prayer. She froze with brief indecision. She'd missed the window . . . or had she? As the man prayed aloud, she whipped around, surveying the field of bowed gray heads, looking for a particular sandy blond one and not finding it.

Will hadn't come. There it was, her proof by proxy.

The torrent in her ears abated slowly. What had she expected? Singing angels, a stairway of light? Maybe a vapor in the shape of her mother to wave from the corner of the sanctuary and then gently vanish? Definitely not the sense of draining purpose deflating her. She sold her heart, cheap, and this hollow prize did not satisfy.

The rustle of shifting in her chair apparently disturbed Greg, and he lifted his head quickly, those gray eyes firing unspoken questions. She mouthed one word, the only answer she had for him. *No.*

"Amen." The white-haired man finished praying, and the organist picked up right on cue. A general murmur rose up in the sanctuary. Mourners gathered their purses and programs and memorial cards, and though the general mood was somber, bright voices and even laughter intersected it. Even those on the front row—her family—stood and shuffled around.

"That's it?" Abby directed her comment to no one, and no one answered.

"I've always liked that one of her and Mama." One of the women mingling near the front spoke up to a projection screen behind the stage. Abby turned. Someone put on a slide show of old family photos. The image of Ruby and Pearl was familiar from her weekend of sorting through the boxes of memorabilia. Of the two of them, she herself looked more like her grandmother than her aunt, which didn't make sense, because Will said—

"Lookie here. The prodigal returns." A stick-thin woman from the front pew approached. Abby wasn't sure whether the comment was meant for her or her father. "Oh, Richard, she's yours all right. I'm Karen," the woman said, as if that explained her boldness. "Can you believe how much she looks like Audrey? And Mama, of course."

"Two branches from the same tree," her father agreed. "And don't let

Blake hear you mention it."

"Of course not. Oh, make sure to get a picture, Richard. You and your *daughter.*" Abby stared at the woman. Cheek implants? Maybe. Even at rest, her face was somehow bubbly.

"A picture, great idea." He freed a cell phone from his belt clip. "Let's go ahead and do that."

Karen rolled her eyes. "Not in the sanctuary, goof. Aren't y'all coming to lunch? Linda's skipping the burial to make sure they have the party room at the Mexican place in Acworth—"

"I'm more in the mood for a country-fried steak and a long-overdue father-daughter date." He winked. "How about by that window there?" He passed his phone to Karen and herded Abby. For the second time, his strong arm went around her. She found it less of a comfort this time.

Karen pointed the camera. "Funeral's over, you two. Where are those gorgeous Wells' smiles?"

Her father turned on the charm. Abby made an attempt. "One-two-three, cheese!" Karen snapped the picture and then examined it before passing the phone back. "There. Beautiful. Good genes in this family."

She gestured up at the screen, where the slide show continued. A tattered shot of a toddler in a cornfield flashed away, followed by a washed-out color photo of Ruby holding a bouquet in one and the arm of a handsome man with curly salt-and-pepper hair in the other.

"Uncle John," her father explained. "What a character he was. I remember one time . . . " He trailed off as the next picture appeared on the screen, and Abby followed his gaze.

A young, slender version of Aunt Ruby stood there in her flowing white dress, lock-armed with a gangly groom, both wearing loopy grins.

"Who picked that one? No one wants to remember first marriages." Abby barely heard him, too distracted by the photograph to bother getting offended. A second later another replaced it, but not before the image upended her world yet again.

Other than his height, the man in the photograph bore no resemblance to Will Laughlin at all.

Attall.

"Nice little intermission, I guess," her father said. "Once everyone clears out, they'll load her up for the burial."

Abby ignored him and ran from the sanctuary.

CHAPTER 39

Greg chased her out the side door of the church to the walkway beside the sanctuary. "Are you all right? What happened?"

"I—" She stuttered and turned away. A patch of Easter lily crowns poked up from a flowerbed by the sidewalk. Will did say Aunt Ruby's overabundance of bulbs came from here. He would have given her one.

Greg still awaited a response. She scrounged for an excuse. "I needed some air."

"Plenty of air in the Buckeye State. Less humidity, too." He watched her eyes, so she steadied them on his pupils.

"Look. You can go. I'm sorry I dragged you here. And thank you for coming. I'll send you some money for your extra expenses."

"I don't want your money. Besides, like I was trying to tell you earlier, I have something to show you."

Her father saw them through the glass doors. He pushed his way out of the church and into their conversation. "Hey, hon. There you are." How easily she could imagine Mom falling for that smile. "Do you need a ride to the cemetery?" His eye contact and body language directed the invitation to her alone.

"She's with me," Greg said flatly.

Abby hesitated. "We walked. Guess we weren't thinking about the burial afterward."

Greg shot her a glare and stalked off without another word. There he went, abandoning her. She shoved down the pang caused by his retreat. He wouldn't change a thing, not even if he could.

"All right." Richard led her toward his car. "Finally we can talk. And we've got a lot to talk about."

She offered a weak laugh. Richard. Her father. She didn't know which way to think of him. "Twenty-eight years' worth and counting."

"Oh, definitely. Starting from the beginning. Blake filled me in about your mother. You could have told me, you know."

"I—I'm sorry. I didn't know what to say."

He held up his hands. "I get it. I do. And for the record, I loved Suzanne. Broke my heart but good when she cleaned out the savings and took you with her."

"Wait," Abby protested. She tried to find a way to frame her words without accusation, and gave up to simply state them. "You never got in touch. Not once."

"She left and I couldn't find you. Not for years, at least. And at a certain point, a man's got to face facts and move on. I had to work on forgiving myself. For not being enough for her. And you."

The sparkle left his eyes; the corners of his mouth drooped. She wanted to believe him, and would have, except for a faded line in a letter she hadn't written or received, but neither had she forgotten.

No one's heard a thing from Richard in some time.

"That doesn't seem quite—"

Her father interjected a hard bark of a laugh and cut her off. "I don't blame you if the truth is hard to believe. You've only heard one side. Completely deprived of your own right to judge for yourself." He opened the passenger door for her, and a childhood's worth of guard went up, warning her not to get into a car with a stranger. She squelched it and climbed in.

He took the driver's side. "The point is, I'd like it if we had an understanding."

"What do you want me to understand?" She meant to challenge him, but the question came out squeaky and nervous.

"I went to the courthouse early this morning. I've got a friend who helps me out with legal difficulties now and then. It turns out there's a problem with the will. Probate won't be pretty. When is it ever, right?"

"Wait. Back up. What's wrong with the will?"

"I can't get over that accent. You sound just like your mother." He started the car. "I haven't seen the official copy. The old bird liked to keep everybody guessing. Looks like she aimed to continue that from the Great Beyond. But I need you to know that we're on the same team. Got it?"

"Uncle Blake wasn't at the funeral." Abby clamped her wrist, but she hadn't worn her watch. "Whose team is he on?"

"Ours," he assured her. "Blake's not big on death. Can you blame him? Honestly, I wouldn't have come myself if I had a better chance to catch up to you."

Abby chewed on that. As they passed Pike's Landing Road, she craned her neck toward the house. Greg hadn't made it back to the Passat yet. When he did, he would leave. She'd probably never see him again. Couldn't he have put up even a little fight? "Then who's on the other team?"

Her father flashed a megawatt grin. His teeth gleamed, too white. In her mind's eye, an image of his skeleton flared, brief and terrible. In a thousand years, when only his bones remained, those teeth would look precisely the same.

"There's a lot of details to it, hon. The short version is, that kid who used to date Audrey convinced Ruby to redo her will last week. A little too convenient, eh? He got himself named executor, and now, big surprise, the spare key to the house is missing. All our family treasures are going to wind up on eBay. Blake thinks we should contest the will, and I agree."

A buzzing sensation began at the base of her skull. "Who are you talking about? A kid who used to date—"

"That yard boy she kept around. O'Laughlin, I think."

Her fingers went cold. "And you think he stole the key?"

He cast a side glance her way. "If not him, who?"

She shrugged, but heat crept into her cheeks. "I know him a little. He's not a bad guy."

He drove with a loose grip on the steering wheel. "Yeah, Blake knows him too. He's a thief and a con. Even if she actually wanted him as her executor—which is ridiculous by itself—he's not entitled to one solitary item from that house, including the key. Blake wants him arrested."

Abby hugged herself. "What else?"

He shook his head. "Too many moving parts to get into right this second. After the burial we'll go to lunch. My treat." He coasted over Main Street. The Lewis building in the square reminded her of Will's little lesson, and her ears burned to think of how he wouldn't let her put a different face on the past.

Will. Will, the kid who used to date Audrey.

What would he say, if he knew the absurd theory she'd hatched? She didn't want to think of him, the awful patience he'd shown her, his natural kindness that she'd lathered up into affection.

A train clattered over the tracks parallel to the road. Abby turned away. She still pictured him in the gory accident. No. Some other man died that day, unknown to her and separated by a gulf of time. As if that made it any better.

Her stomach danced as her father slowed to turn at the narrow driveway leading into the cemetery.

"Wow." Abby's father parked outside the cemetery gate and spent a moment staring out over the landscape. "A bunch of folks died since the last time I was here."

"The plot is down that way." Abby pointed toward the back corner where she'd spent a morning with Will manicuring the graves.

Her father gave her a side-eye. She shrugged and got out of the Lancer. Maybe she'd explain over lunch. Maybe not. He led the way, cutting across the grass instead of keeping to the blacktop-paved walkway. Abby kept her eyes down and walked on her toes to keep her heels from sinking in the sodden ground.

Crunching gravel behind them caught her ear. A blue sedan followed by a red pickup pulled into the cemetery drive and parked by the Lancer. The funeral crowd was arriving.

The orange upturned clay of the gravesite swallowed up the lilies. In place of the ground where she'd hesitated to step before, now the burial vault awaited. Abby couldn't take her eyes off the gray cement maw, couldn't stop listening to its soundless cry.

"It's a debt we all pay eventually." The trace of levity in his tone annoyed Abby, as if he admired owing a debt more than paying one.

Greg came up behind them. Abby recognized his gait even before he called her name. She wouldn't have guessed she knew him so well, or that her gut response before her head interfered would be an urge to kiss those beautiful feet crunching through the grass.

"Abby." He touched her arm, and her relief evaporated. "Can I talk to you for a minute?"

CHAPTER 40

Abby mouthed excuses, ducked her head, and led Greg several feet away. "Why are you here?" she hissed.

"You asked me to come."

"And then I asked you to leave. I can handle this without you."

"Why? Because you've got him?" He paid no attention to his volume. She shushed him, and he rolled his eyes. "Fine. Hear me out, and I'll go."

"Promise?"

"Cross my heart."

"And hope to die?" Abby shot at him.

"That's a story for another time." He took a deep breath. "I found your parents' divorce record. Did you know the first filing was dated two days before you were born?"

Abby's eyes widened involuntarily. Recovering, she crossed her arms. "Fascinating. Why were you looking for it?" She bit her lip at Will's words coming from her own mouth.

"Because *you* were looking for it, and don't say you weren't. I know you."

Her temper flared. "And I guess you didn't get fired for snooping either, did you?"

"No, I didn't. Mainly because the divorce wasn't filed in Ohio. I found it here in Georgia. Right here in Cobb County."

Unbelievable, undeniable. The obvious fell into place. Abby scowled at him. "Why are you telling me this now?"

"Because you stood me up Thursday night. I was going to tell you then."

"Then you should have waited. We're at my aunt's burial, if you didn't notice."

"Waited until when? That guy—he's schmoozing you, Abby."

"'That guy' is my father. I think I deserve—"

"You deserve better," Greg interrupted. "Better than whatever he's going to spring on you. If he hasn't already."

Abby snuck a glimpse over her shoulder and caught Richard laughing, ensconced in conversation with an older man. A breeze flitted through the green dogwood branches, making them shake with laughter too, but Abby wondered if the glint of his teeth wasn't meant, again, for her.

Greg touched her arm. "I'll leave the copy in that tin mailbox by your door. You'll have to go to the courthouse to read the whole decree. If that doesn't show you what you need to see, I won't change your mind no matter what I say."

"Tell me what it says."

"The fact it was filed here says it all, if you ask me, but you need to read it. After you get through this." He glanced at her father again. "Don't sign anything he puts in front of you until you do."

He kissed his index finger, touched it to her cheek, and turned away.

"Don't go yet." Weak, weak. "I—I might need a ride later."

"All right."

She dared a peek. His gray eyes, darkened with the influence of the suit and his slate-colored tie, revealed only confusion. No triumph, no gloating. He edged toward the back of the crowd of mourners without another word.

There weren't many to mingle with. Though the church had been almost full, not even a quarter of those had followed Aunt Ruby to the cemetery. *Long in our memories, 'til lunch.*

"All sorted out with your friend?" Her father wasted not a moment and didn't allow space for a reply. "I hope they don't drag this out. I hate cemeteries."

The remark chaffed, but Abby let it pass. Greg found one record and thought he had her father pegged. She wanted, badly, for him to be wrong.

A shuffle of assembly brushed and murmured through the crowd as the hearse arrived and the pallbearers gathered behind it. Will's absence haunted her. Where was he? And why did Aunt Ruby leave his name off her list of phone numbers?

The pallbearers proceeded with the casket, positioning it on the lowering apparatus and lining up to the side. Abby tried to listen as the graveside remarks commenced. Her gaze flicked involuntarily down to the back corner of the cemetery. She squinted her eyes, seeing and not believing.

Over W. C. Sosebee's grave, a single Easter lily stalk grew, its white trumpets bursting forth a silent song. Once she noticed it, she could hardly look away. She stole glimpses at the surrounding plots, but saw no others like it.

Lilies spread. That's why Aunt Ruby had extra bulbs in the first place. The one by itself was new. Somebody put it there.

One of the pallbearers crouched beside the gravesite to turn a small crank, and Aunt Ruby's coffin disappeared below the surface. A few flowers tossed, a final prayer uttered, and that was it. The services ended and the clot of people dispersed. Greg hung back, waiting for a signal, but Abby had none to give him.

"She lived a good long life," her father said. "And she's in a better place."

Empty words. "I miss her."

He gave her an odd look. "I didn't think you knew her all that well. But of course, we'll all miss her." He beckoned. "Come on. Don't know about you, but I'm hungry."

"I'll catch up to you." A twinge of guilt and disappointment pinged. She hadn't made up her mind about him yet, no matter what Greg had found. "I need to run to the house."

"I'll take you." A note of impatience wormed into his voice. "Let's go."

She raised her hands and gambled. "No, no. Greg's leaving. Let me see him off and pick up my car. I'll meet you."

As she thought he would, her father jumped on the prospect of getting rid of Greg. "Smart like your old man. The little place by the railroad tracks in fifteen minutes. You know where?"

"Yup." Abby winked with confidence she didn't feel. "I do."

CHAPTER 41

"I would have stuck it in my pocket." Abby upended her laundry hamper, and intimates splayed across her bedroom floor as Greg looked on from the doorway. "Absent-mindedly. Not meaning to. I'm a snoop but not so much a thief. At least I've got that going for me, right?"

"Explain again what key you're talking about?"

She emptied the drawers of folded pairs of jeans and threw them on the bed. "I knew where Aunt Ruby hid the spare key."

"And?"

"And the day I found her I used it to let myself in, but I forgot to put it back when I left. They think Will stole it."

"Abby, let them sort it out themselves. You don't need them. Forget the key. They'll change the locks and you can move past them. All of them."

She paused her search to throw him an irritated look. "I thought you chose the moral high road."

Greg crossed his arms. "Fine. You show up with the supposedly stolen key and all is forgiven, right? No one will accuse you, the outsider. That would make too much sense."

"Good idea. I should let Will take the blame. After all, he can't fire me—"

"Right." Greg sighed. "Any idea where it could be? I'll help you look."

She rubbed her temples. "I did laundry yesterday."

The hint of a smirk teased around his lips. "You missed some."

"Thanks for noticing. Go check the washer and dryer—in the closet next to the bathroom. I'll go through my pockets."

"I'll take out the trash for you while I'm at it." She stared at him. "No offense, Abby, but it's ripe. If you can't smell it, you need to see a doctor for that congestion."

"Thanks for noticing that, too," she mumbled, only after his back was turned.

She checked her jeans' pockets, first the clean pairs and then, doubting her memory, the dirty ones too. They all finished in a pile in the middle of her floor as the minutes ticked away. Her father would expect her shortly.

She was on her second pass when Greg called out. "Hey. I found it in the drum of the washing machine."

"Good." She snatched it from his hand, ignoring the minute brush of fingers. "Let's go."

Greg slowed before the house without turning into the drive. "You're positive we're not interrupting a burglary?"

Aunt Ruby's front door stood open, and the bed of the El Camino was packed tight with the TV, a pair of end tables, and boxes. "That's my uncle's car."

"I'm not sure that answers the question." Greg parked, blocking in the El Camino. Blake appeared in the doorway, carrying a dresser drawer. Unless he put it in the passenger seat, Abby didn't see how he planned to fit it in the car. He scowled when he saw them.

"Where's Richard? He said y'all weren't comin' 'til late afternoon." He noticed Greg. "And who're you?"

"Uncle Blake, this is Greg, my—Greg. Listen. I have the spare key. Will didn't take it. See?" She held it out, but he laughed at her.

"Keep it. A little souvenir for ya. I busted out a window and changed the locks this morning." He set the drawer down on top of one of the boxes in the back of the car and adjusted his baseball cap. "And you expect me to believe he didn't give it to you when he knew he was caught? I didn't fall off the turnip truck yesterday."

"Okay." Greg grabbed her hand. "You did your part. We tried. Let's get out of here."

"You get around, don't you?" He guffawed, baring teeth as prominent as his brother's. Good genes. "Reminds me of your mama."

Greg stepped forward. "Apologize to her."

Blake spat on the ground. "Roll up the sleeves on that suit coat and make me, boy."

"Greg, stop." She pushed past him. "Uncle Blake, we didn't come to make trouble. I don't know what you have against Will, but—"

"Shut up." Blake reached into the loose drawer in front of him and pulled out a gun. "Don't defend him to me. My daughter's dead because of that lyin' white trash leech."

Greg slowly shifted his position, trying to block Abby from Blake, but she zeroed in on the gun from behind him. She studied it, every detail. Long black nose. Worn wooden hand grip. Nicked and ancient.

"I bet he thinks he's real smart. I don't know how he found you, but I know this: there ain't a judge in this county who'll believe that will is legit."

"I don't know what you mean." Maybe if she kept him talking, he would explain.

He waved the gun, shooing the two of them toward the Passat. "Then let me make it real clear. In the *real* will, she left everything to Audrey. Audrey's dead, I'm her next of kin, and y'all can get off my property."

Greg moved forward, shielding her body with his. "Get in the car, Abby."

She took a deep breath and brushed by him. "It must seem like I'm trying to replace her. I'm not."

"Abby," Greg said. She ignored him.

"No one could ever replace her. I know that and I never even met her. I'd trade all the inheritances in the world to have met her."

Blake snorted. "You're as full of lies as that dirtbag Will. Maybe it was you that roped him into the scheme."

"I don't blame you. I'd be suspicious too. We all know what happened with my parents." A gamble, but it found its mark. Blake smirked.

You look like her. She risked a step closer. "She's haunting you, isn't she? That's how it is when someone goes too young, too soon. She's always on your mind. Peeking over your shoulder. Whispering things she might have said if only she were here."

"Didn't I tell you to shut up?"

"I'll bet you can hear her right now." *But you're not her.* And how could she ever hope to sound like her? She softened her voice to a whisper, and her words quaked. "She'd say, 'Put that gun away, Daddy.'"

His arm lagged and Abby lunged. She charged straight for her uncle, grabbed the gun by the barrel, and yanked it out of his hand.

"What—" he managed as Greg rushed him. Abby skittered out of the way while the two tussled. The older man put up a confused, flailing defense, and Greg drove him to the ground handily.

"But again, I'm not Audrey. And *I* say, don't ever talk about my mother again." Abby maintained a tight grip on the barrel, but her legs turned to jelly. "Don't let him loose, Greg. I'm calling the police."

"Thank you for coming so quickly," Abby said. With Blake locked away in the backseat of Officer Witter's cruiser, maybe her anxious heart would finally settle down.

"I didn't have far to come. That there," he said, pointing down the street, "is the police department. Mr. Watts used to walk to work when he was a councilman. He was good friends with my dad back in the Eighties."

Abby thought it would be unwise to mention that she'd never known her great-uncle. "He was smart to choose a home right in town."

Officer Witter examined the gun once again, this time in appreciation rather than cool appraisal. "A Remington 1858. That's some antique. Who does it belong to?"

"We don't know yet," Abby said. "If it's not mentioned in the will, then I guess whoever wants it."

"I know a couple collectors who'd pay a mint for it, even without the trigger spring. If you found the missing piece . . . " He whistled. "Of course, then you'd need to register it."

She heard another car turn down Hiram Street. A white Lancer with a now-familiar face at the wheel. Her heart went into her throat. She'd forgotten him at the restaurant. How long? Thirty minutes? Forty-five?

She watched as he passed, the cruiser's blue lights flashing in his sunglasses. The coward never even turned his head to the commotion on Aunt Ruby's front lawn.

Officer Witter followed her gaze, but lookie-loos were a daily fact of life for him, and he ignored her father. "I do have to confiscate the weapon as evidence. When you get all the details sorted out, have the owner contact me and I'll make certain you get it back."

"Thank you, sir." Greg rubbed his shoulder, the one he used to subdue Blake.

"Thanks for your card. I shouldn't need more than the statement you gave, but I'll be in touch if that changes." He tipped his hat and got in the cruiser.

As the car drove away with a single whoop of the siren, Abby turned back to Greg. His brow crumpled. She was too exhausted to ask why.

"Want to go pick up your car?"

"Nah. It'll wait."

"Okay." They climbed into the Passat and made the short trip back to the house in silence. Abby half-expected her father, waiting to ambush them, but the house on Pike's Landing Road stood as gray and lonely as ever.

Greg parked on the street, unfastened his seatbelt, and turned to face her. "When did you become the Lunatic Whisperer? I can't believe I took you into that situation."

She leaned back. The buttery leather seats cosseted her legs and arms and neck, and she closed her eyes. "You didn't know."

"If that gun had been live . . . " He trailed off. "Abby, what on earth was that?"

"A leap of faith."

"I saw the leap. Missed the faith though."

She laughed, but with a bitter edge. "Ah. What do I know about faith? Greg, the truth is, I found that gun in Aunt Ruby's house months ago. I wondered if it was real and even touched it, but I sure didn't know to look for a trigger spring." She rubbed her arms. Greg had the A/C set to frostbite. "But I knew there was a good chance a gun that old wouldn't fire."

"You took a ridiculous risk."

"Probably. I wouldn't have done it if I had much worth living for."

He took a long time to answer. "Faith is worth living for."

"Maybe for some." She struggled with the words to choose. The desire to hurt him kept pushing its way into her thoughts. "Greg, would you like to know my main problem with the whole religion-spiel my Mom bought into? All the easy answers. 'Pray this prayer and you'll have eternal life.' And when that didn't work, 'She's in a better place.' Or how about my favorite, 'You'll see her again someday.'"

"I know."

"No, you don't. Listen, my heart . . . " She paused and thumped her chest. " . . . is broken. Do you hear me? There's no bandage, no glue, no bottle of little blue pills, and no prayer that can fix this."

"There haven't been any easy answers for me. Abby, loving you when you loved me back was easy. Loving you for Jesus is the hardest thing I've ever done."

Her heart squeezed, its resistant tumblers unwilling to turn. "What made you . . . ?" She waved her hand in a circle, looking for the word she meant.

He loosened his tie. "You."

"Be serious."

"I am. I'll spare you the details of how I tried to fill the hole you left, but—"

"No," she said, mimicking him. "Out with it."

He sighed. "Booze, mostly. Working crazy hours to put off hiring someone for your spot."

"That's not a big deal."

He stared down at the steering wheel. "And a couple of one-night stands."

"Oh." The confession forced her to take a pulse on her heart for him. She couldn't pretend it didn't hurt to hear it.

"I hated it. All of it. There wasn't a good reason to continue. So I decided . . . " He shaped his fingers as a gun, pointed to his temple, and cocked his thumb.

Abby closed her eyes and turned her face. "Greg. "

"I wasn't going to tell you that, but you went there first."

She studied him, wondering if he was even the same man she'd been busy hating all these months. "Please tell me you didn't try to kill yourself."

"Sarah caught me. She passed me on the road during rush hour. You were out of town, so she decided to swing by my apartment. Two minutes later would have been too late."

"She stopped you."

"She told me I was a coward and to do it in front of her if I really wanted to die." Her eyes widened as Greg went on. "I didn't stop thinking about it. But I remembered the speaker at your mom's service. Not specifically, just that he talked a lot about hope. That's all I could remember. If I hadn't been to her funeral, I wouldn't have known where to start looking. Maybe I wouldn't have tried." He rubbed his brow. "More than you wanted to know?"

Her eyes burned. "I asked."

"I'm glad you did." She didn't answer, and he sighed. "You're sure you're up to a messy probate?"

She bit her lip. "No, not sure at all. Actually, I take it back. Will's in charge. He'll keep it under control."

Greg apparently disagreed. "I can stay another day to help get the ball rolling."

"You have to work. You've used up all your favors with Chuck."

"He'll survive."

"I will too, Greg. Go home. I'll be fine."

He opened the center console and withdrew a folded sheet of paper. "Maybe you don't need this anymore. But at least you'll have it if you do."

"At least," she echoed. Greg would leave. She would stay. This was the ending she wanted. Wasn't it? The solemn note in the lengthening pause bred doubts.

Maybe he heard it too. "If you feel like reading him the riot act after you see the actual divorce decree, call me first." The whisper of a smile touched his lips. "I can take it."

"I promise." Still more than she wanted to owe him. Less than it would take to ever repay him. "Thank you."

And since she knew he wouldn't, Abby leaned across the console to meet his lips for a soft and sullen goodbye kiss.

CHAPTER 42

Wednesday, April 25

Two days after the funeral, Abby was celebrating a completed batch of job applications with a turkey sandwich and a Diet Coke when someone knocked at the door.

"Coming," she shouted, then bit her tongue. What if her father had come back, or Blake wanted to make trouble? "Who's there?"

"It's me. Will."

Surprised, she swung the door open for him.

"Hey there. Can I come in?"

"Of course." She moved out of his way and sat back down at the table. "I didn't expect to see you. You weren't at the funeral."

"I wanted to be, but I had to work. New job. Between that and handling Mrs. Watts' estate, I ain't had time to blink. I'm sorry I didn't call first, though. I've been so long without a phone, I didn't even think of it." He lifted the thick packet in his hands. "But I brought you a present."

Abby gave a good-natured groan. "A present, huh? Looks more like official business to me. I bet it'll take days to even read it, let alone comprehend what it says." She pushed out one of the dining room chairs with her foot, and he sat.

"I never knew Mrs. Watts to have that sort of patience. I think you'll be surprised. Want the abridged version?"

She gestured at her computer. "Definitely. I've been reading job descriptions all day and I can hardly see straight."

"Richard and Blake both owed her a pile of money and she wants them to pay it to you."

"You're kidding." She reached for the envelope and tore it open. "All this to say that?"

She should have known better. Aunt Ruby liked her legal affairs short and to the point. Only a single legal-sized sheet comprised the will itself. Abby skimmed the document to find the paragraph she wanted and read it aloud.

"Whereas my nephews Blake Wells and Richard Wells owe my estate significant sums, I hereby assign their debts as follows: the unpaid balance of the loan shown in Exhibit A, payable by Mr. Richard Wells, and the accumulated debt totaled in Exhibit B, payable by Mr. Blake Wells, both amounts owing to Miss Abby Wells. The sums will be considered individually discharged upon delivery of proof of payment or expressed written loan forgiveness to the Cobb County Recorder of Wills."

"Nice that she left it open for you to mend fences if you decide to. I wouldn't get too excited about the money," Will cautioned her, but Abby shrugged.

"My father never sent me so much as a birthday card. I know what to expect from him. And after getting Blake arrested—"

"What? When'd that happen?" She recapped the scene at Aunt Ruby's house for him. She expected Will to defend himself over the accusation that he somehow caused Audrey's death, but he only shook his head. "I might be overmesteppin' here, but as a guy, I can tell you that fella from Ohio must be crazy in love with you."

"I know." She rubbed her face and perused the bulky attachments, an excuse to let the prickle of tears recede unseen. Abby recognized at once the copy of the loan her parents signed, but the pages of photocopied ledger entries took a minute. "Aunt Ruby tried to show me this ledger. Whew. No wonder Blake doesn't like me."

Will sobered. "He don't like you because you favor Audrey."

The moment quieted itself, a one-time invitation. She took it. "What happened to her?"

"She was killed by an IED in Afghanistan." Will stared at the floor for a long moment, then raised his eyes to meet hers. "We had our plan all worked out. Audrey was taking online classes in the service, and she sent most of her pay to take care of Mrs. Watts. She paid me out of that, and I used it for school back here." His Adam's apple bobbed. "She wasn't even in a combat zone. Just one of those things, they said."

Abby swallowed hard. Blake mislaid blame on Will, but she followed his logic. "My uncle said Audrey was supposed to get this house."

Will nodded. "Mrs. Watts promised it to her. We were gonna fix it up. Patched the roof ourselves, her and me."

"I'm sorry, Will." This time, the Death voice came from her own lips. How was it that those words she hated were the best she had? He would claim to be okay, and they would both know it was a social lie—

He didn't, though. Instead he closed his eyes and nodded again. "Me too."

They sat together in silence like that for a while, but there was an unfamiliar fullness, too. Abby got the sense that Will might have been praying. Her words left him wanting, but maybe they were supposed to. Maybe inadequate condolences were meant to kindle a desire for greater comfort.

At last, he cleared his throat and attempted a smile. "You won't guess what else. She left you the house on Hiram Street. The house and everything in it."

"What?" Will's face held no hint of kidding around. "She didn't even like me."

"That so?" The twinkle she knew sparked in his eyes. "Then she didn't like me either, because this one's mine. After probate's settled, that is. But you don't need to feel rushed about moving. There's plenty of time."

"What about the room upstairs?"

He reddened. "Broke my promise to you, didn't I? I'm sorry. That was supposed to be our room, mine and Audrey's, and I—"

"Will, forget it. I understand. I actually meant the other one. The storage room."

"Oh." He dipped his head. "Your granny's stuff. I can haul it over to the other house for you. Probably should handle all the junk at once."

"Do you need any help?" She shuddered. Ghost or not, the heaviness in that room and the foreboding that chased her out before still lingered. A shiver of relief rippled down her arms when Will refused.

"Nah. I'll use the Sentra to haul loads over to the other house and sort 'em there. Shouldn't take but an hour. I'm off work tomorrow."

Abby tripled his estimate. "You still have your key?" He started to hand it over, but she shook her head. "No, keep it. I just meant that I have errands to run tomorrow. If it's all right with you, I'll leave you to it."

Will shrugged. "Fine by me."

"Wait. You're driving the Sentra." Not a question. Will raised an eyebrow as she rushed on. "By any chance can you take me to pick up my car?"

Thursday, April 26

She planned to leave the house early the next morning but kept dragging her feet. Over a third cup of coffee, she read the record certification Greg brought to her for the hundredth time. It verified the existence of a decree, filed in Cobb County, that could only be found by a person looking for it.

She folded the page. Her father showed himself firsthand, how he was and who he was. Another trip to the courthouse was wholly unnecessary. Really, what more did she need to know?

As the time before Will's arrival ticked down, though, curiosity won out. As always.

"Ugh." She downed the last of her coffee and grabbed her keys. "Unless I'd rather help clear out the room, I'd better get going."

No trouble at the courthouse this time. A kindly older officer waved her through security without a problem, and she didn't have to go anywhere near the Recorder of Deeds. The dragon lady wouldn't get a pass at her today.

The Clerk of the Superior Court barely glanced at her two forms of identification, and he lingered over Mom's death certificate only long enough to collect the names. "The fee is ten dollars. You said 1984, did you?" He helped her locate the decree and left her in peace to read it.

The truth spilled in the coldest possible terms. Richard had filed for a no-fault divorce days before Abby's birth. Belatedly, Suzanne objected. He responded with a flurry of filings and she, out the money Richard had taken and caring for a newborn seven hundred miles away, gave up. It happened right around the time she visited Aunt Ruby all those years ago. He forced her to crawl back to the ones he betrayed. And that was what happened between Abby's parents.

Such a quiet little answer to that bruise of a question.

She read it over and over, almost wishing for a touch of ambiguity to soften the truth. Without a doubt, Richard Wells bailed on his wife and baby.

She thanked the clerk and left without asking for a photocopy. After Greg returned home, her need for tangible proof had dimmed. She hurried out of the courthouse, intent on having a good cry in the semi-privacy of the Mustang, but the urge passed before she reached the car.

Instead, Abby opened the picture she'd snapped of the phone list. She hadn't saved her father's number to her contacts. With a swipe and a tap it could be gone. The words of Aunt Ruby's letter returned to her. *No one's heard a thing from Richard in some time.*

Her finger hovered over the delete button when she remembered Will's observation as well. *Open for you to mend fences . . .*

"If I decide to." She hit cancel and saved the number instead. A fullness spread from the center of her chest. Somewhere, Mom was smiling.

True to his word, Will had finished and gone by the time she returned. She climbed the stairs, wanting to see the room cleared of its secrets and shadows, but Will surprised her by leaving it locked.

She came back down and noticed the note on the kitchen table. Was it there when she arrived?

"Yes," she said aloud. "It was." She picked it up and read Will's chicken scratch.

Abby,
The storage room is full of black mold. You should see a Dr. ASAP.
Your friend,
Will

From that moment on, she treated the house as Will's. Out of respect, she cleaned more often, hanging up her clothes and keeping her papers from multiplying across the kitchen table. She stepped lighter, took care not to swat the light switches or slam the cabinet doors. And she collected moving boxes.

Saturday, May 12

Greg probably thought she forgot her promise.

The email she wrote to him sat in her drafts folder for over a week. It took that long to gear up her courage to send it, and then she deleted it instead. She couldn't help reading over her own shoulder from a nosy onlooker's stance, a generation or two hence. Names and dates were worth recording, but in her heart she knew that moments deserved to happen out loud.

"Good news and bad news." Sarah called every third day if Abby didn't. "Which do you want first?"

"Bad."

"I have to tell the good first for it to work chronologically. The choice was a personality test. You didn't pass, by the way."

"Right. Thank you."

"You're welcome. Okay. Good news: I won a spot on the cooking show."

"Are you serious? Congratula—"

"Bad news: they cancelled it in pre-production."

"Oh. But winning still makes a great line on your résumé, right?"

"Definitely. The producer helped me get a column on the network's website. In the meantime, I'm launching my own YouTube channel. 'Mixing up a Miracle' is going to happen. I can taste it."

Abby had to laugh. When life handed Sarah lemons, she served up a lemon torte.

She stood at a drugstore photo kiosk, listening through a headset as she squared the anniversary photo of her grandparents for scanning. She planned to keep the original and send copies to her father, aunts, and uncle as an olive branch. "Overall, the good news wins."

"Oh, there's more bad: Sam's impossible. I can't even handle him."

"I take it the house hunt isn't going well?"

"He will not compromise. The square footage, the number of bathrooms, brick versus siding. Exhausting. I decided I shouldn't contract a mortgage or a marriage with someone I can't take for more than two hours at a stretch."

"I agree."

"Which means I'm in the market for a roommate. When are you moving back home?"

"Who said I was?"

"Look, I've tried to be patient." Sarah raised her voice. "But I've reached the end, okay? Either you come back or I'm coming to get you. You can't live in that Petri dish of a house. I do vaguely recall predicting an infestation of some kind. Do you even understand how lucky you are? Black mold can seriously kill you. Greg told me about a guy he knew—"

"How is Greg?" Abby asked, a fail-safe redirection.

Sarah puffed out a theatrical sigh. "He's happy. Or happy-ish. Even though he has no reason to be."

"Don't start," Abby warned her.

"I'm not. I'm curious. And jealous. He's different, and I want to know what that's about."

"You know, he stepped out to protect me when my uncle pulled the gun on us."

"Ugh, you told me. I don't even want to think about it. But back to Sam. I'm breaking up with him tonight. Or this weekend. In the near future. Hint, hint."

Abby laughed. "All right, stop. I can't pretend any longer. I got a job offer."

Sarah groaned. "Great. You've been a free agent for how long now? And the instant I'm ready to beg, you have to root yourself in down there. Perfect. Congrats, I guess. What's the job?"

"An assistant curator. At a museum. In Akron." She tried to wait stoically for the news to sink in, but she giggled before Sarah responded.

"Seriously? When did you interview? Oh, I can't believe—you snuck into town and didn't tell me? When were you planning the big reveal?" She paused for breath. "And a *museum*? Seriously? With *your* history?"

Her scan finished. She tapped the color correction tool, then decided she preferred its vintage look. "Calm down. You didn't miss me. We did all the interviewing by webcam. As far as my history, I took a risk and confessed the whole banned-for-life business when I answered the question about my weaknesses. I spun it as taking the pursuit of knowledge too far. They loved my 'natural curiosity and adventurous spirit,' they said. And it's not official until I accept the written offer. They extended the verbal but I'm waiting for the email. It's supposed to come next week. I planned to wait until it was signed and sealed, but I'm moving back either way, and I thought that might cheer you up. I'm requesting Tahini Tilapia for my welcome-home party."

"Hey, you'll be amazed. I perfected it. But more importantly, does Greg know you're coming home?"

Did Greg know? Probably. They had a single perfunctory conversation about the reference he gave to the museum people, but he didn't ask her any questions. Wasn't he the first to remind her that her real roots were in Ohio? The branches of her tree spread as far as Georgia, but she couldn't live cut off from her roots. Nevertheless, she extracted a reluctant promise from Sarah not to tell Greg her plans.

"Okay," Sarah said. "But if you bungle around like you did when you left, I might—accidentally, of course—spill like a cheap decanter."

Abby considered herself warned.

CHAPTER 43

Wednesday, May 23

"Stop making it complicated and call him." Sarah placed a mug of chai tea into Abby's hands. "Or go over to his apartment this weekend. I'll whip up a bread pudding for you to take. Except he'll probably assume that I made it. Although, that's not necessarily a negative. Then you don't look desperate. You'd be doing me a favor; one thing would lead to another, and then—"

"That's not exactly the message I want to send." Abby sipped her tea, a hot, sweet-and-spicy combination Sarah was testing on her. "But this is right close to perfect."

"'Right close?' That sounds like a Southernism." Sarah curled up on her new chaise, holding her own mug close to her face to inhale its steam. "Granted, I wouldn't take my romantic advice right now either. You should have seen the relief on Sam's face when I dropped the hammer. That old line that you can pick your friends but you can't pick your family? It's a lie. You can totally pick your family. But enough about him. Past is past."

Past is past. She lingered on those words, hoping, even as Sarah brainstormed the romance she felt was bound to flower again.

Abby wasn't so sure, even though Greg camped in her thoughts daily. In defiance of the stains on their history, his "happy-ish" state bothered her conscience. The evidence of it turned up before her again and again. It mirrored Will's easy countenance through dark days. She recognized it from Mom's inexplicable bravery as she stared down terminal cancer. The word Sarah meant, she knew, was peaceful.

Sunday, June 3

Perhaps as a reaction to Sarah's elaborate presentation on how she could help set up an "accidental" moonlit stroll, Abby picked the least romantic place she could think of to bump into Greg. On a drizzly Sunday after her first week in the new job, Abby slid into the back-row pew at Mom's old church, a lesson learned from Aunt Ruby's funeral.

She expected memories to haunt her and had even tucked a packet of tissues into her purse, but without a casket and mounds of funeral flowers, the sanctuary held more welcome than she remembered. Perching on the edge of her seat, she scanned the crowd.

A few people greeted her. Pleased and surprised to be recognized, she chatted in the pre-service bustle, but when the opening notes played and Mom's friends took their seats, Abby wished she'd kept her eyes on the crowd. The sanctuary had filled up, and she hadn't been watching the doors . . . .

"May I join you?" Standing beside the pew, with a sober countenance and a pinch around his gray eyes, was Greg.

"Sure, sit." She paused, choosing her words. "I hoped I'd see you."

He took the place beside her, leaving a comfortable buffer and facing the front. "I heard a rumor about bread pudding. I was disappointed it turned out not to be true."

Her jaw dropped briefly. "Like a cheap decanter." Greg attempted to hide his amusement, but Abby frowned openly, afraid of losing her nerve. What happened to the words she practiced? She opened her mouth, unsure what would pop out. "Listen. I tried to tell myself I didn't owe you."

"You didn't. You don't."

"I do. I owe you an apology for trying to use you."

His brow crinkled. "I don't know what you mean."

A light panic sent a flush to her cheeks. She might better have sent the email. If she couldn't manage to explain before the service, she'd have to sit next to him for an hour and a half with the unspoken words hanging from her tongue. "I assumed I'd get away with borrowing those documents. Mom had just died, and we were together. I figured if you loved me, you'd cover for me. And when you didn't, I blamed you."

Greg rubbed his cheek. "Abby, you mean the world to me, then and now, but what you did was wrong."

"I know." She lowered her eyes, but that felt counterfeit and cowardly, so she leveled her gaze with his instead. "I'm trying to say I'm sorry."

Maybe the same urgency to heal old wounds burned in his heart too, because he took her hand without hesitating. "I forgive you," he said. "And for what it's worth, I'm sorry too. I should have been honest with Chuck and asked for a department transfer when we started dating, but I was afraid."

"Afraid?"

Greg nodded. "That he'd say no, or that I'd end up demoted. The whole situation came out of that bad decision."

"Oh." All the built-up nerves and arguments-on-reserve dissipated, so she squeezed his hand before withdrawing hers. "Um, thanks."

He chuckled and combed his fingers through his hair. "Did your uncle make bail?"

"Yes. And I got my gun back. I donated it to the Civil War museum in memory of Aunt Ruby."

"That surprises me. Family heirloom, wasn't it?"

"But with bad memories attached." She swallowed hard. "My father hasn't stayed in touch."

He cleared his throat. "Sarah told me about your friend Will. How is he?"

She loved him a little for asking. "He's sad. But he says that sad is okay for now."

"He'll be fine when the right girl comes along. I'm glad she wasn't you, though."

She almost protested, but that pinch around his eyes reappeared, and it stopped her. He knew as well as anyone that his words fell short. Besides, thinking of Will stung more than she wanted Greg to know. "It never would have worked." She took a deep breath. "I belong here."

"Here, meaning in Ohio?"

"Here, meaning in this church, on this pew, with you in Ohio. I think."

"You think?" If he was trying for a casual tone, he missed. "What would make you sure?"

"I don't know. Maybe the leap of faith comes first." The pre-service music swelled to a crescendo, raising goose bumps, and Abby rubbed her arms as robed parishioners filed into position in the choir loft. "But if I had to point to the first clue, I'd say my mom planted the seed. She figured something out before she died. I want to see if I can find it, too."

THE END

DISCUSSION GUIDE

1. Ruby claims the valuables from her sister's home are under lock and key, but Abby is able to figure out how to access the room and finds it full of black mold. Scripture warns against storing treasures on earth, where rust (or in this case, black mold) destroys and thieves (or Abby) break in and steal. Discuss your understanding of treasure in heaven. How is it collected? What is its value?

2. Both Abby and Ruby interpret signals from the physical world (footsteps on the roof, a flash of light) to create belief systems that support what they wish to believe. Have you ever thought an event was a sign, only to become less certain later? Discuss the dangers of incorrectly correlating events in this present life to the spiritual world.

3. Abby's mother insists that "Everyone deserves a name." What does this mean to you? Do you agree or disagree?

4. Although her life has been unfruitful in some ways, Ruby's concern for her legacy has become an idol to her. It is common to desire admiration, but Jesus Himself warned against loving the approval of others (Luke 20:46-47). What are some practical ways to build a legacy while maintaining humility?

5. Abby's passion for genealogy leads her to dark places. Scripture

admonishes us to consider our ways (Haggai 1:5). Under what circumstances might some of your hobbies, interests, or passions lead you astray?

6. Greg goes to considerable trouble and expense to convince Abby to come home. Would you call his trip a success or failure? Why?

7. The story includes a number of doors and locks. The Bible mentions more than once knocking at a door in reference to a relationship with Christ: "Behold, I stand at the door and knock; if anyone hears My voice and opens the door, I will come in to him and will dine with him, and he with Me" (Revelation 3:20), and, "Ask, and it will be given to you; seek, and you will find; knock, and it will be opened to you" (Matthew 7:7; Luke 11:9). Which side of the door are you on right now? Who is knocking? How do you know?

8. Ruby believes that the dead live on in memory; Will tells Abby that their efforts are better spent on the living. To what extent, if at all, is memory of past generations a responsibility?

9. At the locomotive museum, Abby muses whether Atlanta would have grown as great if it had never burned. Heartbreak often becomes the channel of God's blessing. Have you experienced this in your own life? How does this reflect God's redemptive power?

10. A grudge spanning generations of Abby's family bears an impact on her present life. Scripture warns believers not to bite and devour one another, that we would not be consumed by one another (Galatians 5:15). How might Abby's life have been different had her grandmother chosen to break ranks with her own father's prejudice for Northerners?

11. Ruby attempts to cover up parts of history; Abby seeks to record it faithfully but often longs for the ability to change the past. In the end, Ruby surrenders the burden that hampered her relationship with Christ, and Abby is on a trajectory to begin her walk with Him. Discuss how the pain each of them experiences might be considered to "work together for good for those who love God, to those who are called according to

His purpose" (Romans 8:28).

12. Although Abby is desperately curious about her father, she feels burdened to respect her mother's privacy in order to keep her promise. Her lack of information leaves her ill-equipped when she does meet him. Do promises made to the dead remain binding? Are there appropriate times to break them?

13. Abby's relationship with her father is in an ambiguous state at the end of the story. Do you believe she will make amends with him in the future? Imagine the content of their next conversation.

14. By the end of the story, Abby recognizes that faith in Christ may not improve the external circumstances of the believers she has known, but each experiences the peace that surpasses all comprehension (Philippians 4:7), and that peace constitutes the proof she has sought throughout. Discuss your experience (as a spectator or a recipient) of supernatural peace.

15. Although W. C. "Christie" Sosebee's eternity was secure in Christ, what would you consider his fatal flaw? Discuss how such flaws damage one's testimony or relationship with God.

16. Greg struggles to show love to Abby when she is neither receptive to that love nor particularly lovable. Discuss how expressions of romantic love (*eros*) might mirror expressions of God's love (*agape*). Conversely, how are they different?

17. Abby takes no comfort in trite condolences and sees them as "easy answers." Do you empathize with her, or does even an inadequate effort to comfort those who mourn have value? Discuss a time you've experienced when words fell short.

AUTHOR'S NOTE

To me, novel research is a bit like a scale. I sprinkle ideas on the one side and facts on the other, back and forth, and hopefully the two sides more or less balance in the end. Please allow me to confess where I weighted the scales a little.

The first episode of *Duck Dynasty* aired March 21, 2012, only a week and half before Sarah's casual reference. However, she likes to be on the leading edge of culture, and I'm sure she would have caught the pilot episode.

I took a bit of license with real places for the sake of the story, including wedging fictional streets into the perfectly real town of Kennesaw. The Cobb County courthouse in particular may seem less like itself and more like an amalgamation of courthouses and annexes where I have conducted my own genealogical hunts.

Train enthusiasts will catch me on this one: the Nashville, Chattanooga & St. Louis Railway company leased the Western & Atlantic in 1890. In 1942, it would have been known as the NC&StL rather than the W&A Railroad. However, this historical detail did not fit into the story, and for simplicity's sake, I omitted it.

Most important to include is this: when I went searching for a plausible death for W. C. Sosebee at the site of the Bell Aircraft plant, I found more than I wanted to know. The accident described in this novel did claim the life of NC&StL employee Reece Woodrow Neal in December of 1942. Some months later, an article ran in the local newspaper boasting that "only" two deaths went on the plant's construction record. Mr. Neal, as a railroad employee, was not counted. Including this incident in the story has been my way of correcting that count.

ACKNOWLEDGEMENTS

Of the countless research avenues that helped me to create this story, Images of America: *Kennesaw* by Joe Bozeman, Robert Jones, and Sallie Loy (Arcadia Publishing, 2006) proved invaluable for seeding my imagination with pictures of how historical Kennesaw would have looked. My gratitude goes to the authors and contributors.

So many people supported me during the writing of this book, all in their unique ways. The friends who offered encouragement, counsel, sounding boards, and prayers along the way are too many to list, but consider this a group hug to my P31 ladies, my KFBC family, ACFW North Georgia (WORD), and the New Life Writers. In particular, Heather Day Gilbert, Gina Conroy, Sherri Wilson Johnson, Jennifer McBay Barry, Mandy Aguilar, Tiffany Nichols, Ieva Pugžlytė, Cara Slifka, Jo Ann Benefield, JoAnn Nolley, Lauren Childers, Deanna Davis, Christy Gill, and Sylvia Childers all deserve mention. You have my lasting gratitude.

Thank you to the Elk Lake Publishing team, Fred St. Laurent and Kathi Macias, for bringing this novel to fruition.

To my parents, John and Lisa Heineman, thank you for teaching me to dream. To Valerie Heineman, Jenny Greenwood, and Isy Foster, thanks for being the greatest sisters ever. Extra special thanks to Jenny for lending your crazy talent to the artwork for this book.

To my wonderful husband, Michael: for your unwavering support, for your thoughtful and hilarious critiques of early drafts, for your sense of humor about mealtimes, working hours, and the definition of "research," and for being the best Chief of Street Cred a girl could ever ask for, thank you. I love you.

To Jesus, my Lord and Redeemer, Savior and Friend, this work is for You. Thank You for taking me on this grand journey.

Made in the USA
San Bernardino, CA
26 August 2016